BATTLEFIELD!

Christopher heard the unmistakable shouts of the Saxons mingle with the hammering of hooves. He wished he did not understand what they said, for their total confidence and sheer might was intimidating. And the group was smart. Tactical. They were not the arguing cavalry of Garrett's army, but a smooth, lubricated team of mounted killers whose speed, flexibility, and split-second reactions were a gloomy surprise to every Celt who witnessed them. They were wolves. And their bellies were empty.

Arthur *sringed!* Excalibur from its sheath, raising the sword in one hand while holding his reins and escutcheon in the other. The king slammed down the visor on his helm, and Christopher did the same on his salet. Both were as ready as they would be for the onslaught. . . .

BOOKS BY PETER TELEP

SQUIRE

SQUIRE'S BLOOD

SQUIRE'S HONOR *

* coming soon

Published by HarperPaperbacks

SQUIRE'S BLOOD

BOOK TWO OF THE
SQUIRE TRILOGY

PETER TELEP

HarperPrism
An Imprint of HarperPaperbacks

HarperPaperbacks *A Division of* HarperCollins*Publishers*
10 East 53rd Street, New York, N.Y. 10022

Copyright © 1995 by Peter Telep
All rights reserved. No part of this book may be used or reproduced in any manner whatsoever without written permission of the publisher, except in the case of brief quotations embodied in critical articles and reviews. For information address HarperCollins*Publishers*,
10 East 53rd Street, New York, N.Y. 10022.

Cover illustration by Tim White

First printing: September 1995

Printed in the United States of America

HarperPrism is an imprint of HarperPaperbacks. HarperPaperbacks, HarperPrism, and colophon are trademarks of HarperCollins*Publishers*.

❖ 10 9 8 7 6 5 4 3 2 1

SQUIRE'S BLOOD
is for Robert Drake

ACKNOWLEDGMENTS

Squire's Blood was written with the help of:

Robert Drake—my agent, sidekick, shrink, and first reader.

Christopher Schelling—my editor, sympathetic ear, and faith keeper.

Joan Vander Putten—my friend, fellow brainstormer, and adviser.

David Hamilton—my sometimes partner, all times friend.

William Shakespeare's *Henry V*, act 4, scene 3, provided the inspiration for parts one and two of this novel, and as such deserves to be acknowledged.

AUTHOR'S NOTE

The Arthurian legend contains many anachronisms and contradictions that are maddening to writers who wish to be technically and historically accurate. While the military strategy, accoutrements, and politics were carefully researched, some were borrowed from other time periods for dramatic effect. Indeed, the description of King Arthur as "a knight in shining armor" is a misnomer. In the sixth century, the time Arthur supposedly lived, he would have worn leather plates. Yet if one settles a suit of fourteenth-century armor on the son of Pendragon, he is restored to his venerable image. That aside, lean back, quibble if you must, but most of all, I hope you enjoy this second volume in the Squire Trilogy.

Peter Telep

PROLOGUE

Christopher of Shores fell on his rump before the Saxon, his broadsword wrenched from his grip by a mighty horizontal swipe from the ax-wielding soldier. The young squire watched as the Saxon, his face streaked with blood, narrowed his eyes and hoisted his weapon over his shoulder.

For a second, Christopher saw the outline of the Saxon against the dull iron sky above the Mendip Hills, saw that the barbarian wasn't much older than his own fifteen years. He wished the Saxon were a lot older, his reflexes slower. But most of all, he longed at the moment to be back at the stable in Shores, to have a warm, sweet loaf of bread to his lips, and have his ears filled with the amusing tales of old Orvin.

Christopher cocked his head and reached futilely for his broadsword; the weapon lay just over an arm's length away. Every sinew in his arm tensed, and in his mind's eye Christopher saw his arm extend to the sword and his gloved fingers clench around the bejeweled hilt. With his other hand he urged his armored body toward the sword, but on the periphery he caught a flash of metal he knew was the Saxon's battle-ax cleaving the air. Immediately, he abandoned the idea of his weapon and thrust his body forward with both hands. The armor weighed him down so much that he moved dooming inches instead of hopeful yards. He looked back at the Saxon with eyes owning deep terror.

Strangely, as the Saxon's ax dropped, his body followed it. He collapsed onto his stomach, and his head bounced once off the frozen winter ground. An arrow broke the flat wool landscape of the Saxon's back; the shaft's blue feather fletching marked it as Celt.

Some twenty yards away, on a hillock that put him six feet above Christopher, Doyle lowered his longbow. With casual grace, he reached down and unfastened a leather flagon from his belt, pulled out the hemp stoppering it, then chugged down half of the flagon's contents. The clatter of hooves behind him caused Doyle to choke and expel some ale. He hustled down the slope while refastening his flagon.

At once Christopher was ashamed for needing help and thankful for the presence of his blood brother. But Doyle belonged with the rest of the archers in the Vaward Battle group led by Sir Lancelot. What was he doing here?

"One of the king's squires alone? Why aren't you at Arthur's side?" Doyle asked, his eyes never leaving the slopes around them. The battle roared just over the eastern rise, and threatened to move closer.

Christopher pushed himself to a sitting position, tried to rock his body forward to stand, but found it impossible.

"Get up," Doyle said curtly.

Christopher reached out a gauntleted hand. "Help."

Doyle's gaze lowered to Christopher's. He frowned. "The archers in my group still think you're mad to have turned down knighthood, but looking at you now, I can see why you wish to remain a squire." Doyle took Christopher's hand and pulled him up.

Christopher's armor rustled loudly and slid out of place. He adjusted the metal fauld digging into his waist, then the couters covering his elbows. "Every squire has his misfortunes."

"Misfortunes—"

"—put you on your shield, I know," Christopher finished. "Why aren't you with the rest of the Vaward?"

"Answer my question first," Doyle said.

"We were surrounded by a Saxon cavalry and I was separated from Arthur. Someone dismounted me, and this man"—Christopher pointed to the dead Saxon—"pursued me here."

"He chased you?"

"He would not engage anyone else."

"Maybe he knew you," Doyle said. Then, much darker, "You did spend a year with them."

"Not *them*. I served a *Celt* who led Saxons. Besides, I don't think Garrett's army still exists. At least not intact. Most of them probably went home across the narrow sea."

"Maybe some stayed. Maybe he was one of them," Doyle argued. "Maybe he holds some anger for you. Who knows?"

Christopher moved to the dead Saxon, bent down, rolled the body onto its side, then stared into the enemy soldier's face. He shook his head. "I'm sure I've never seen this man before."

"Look," Doyle said, pointing to a small leather change pouch which had detached itself from the dead Saxon's belt. Doyle hunkered down, picked up the pouch, opened it, then dumped its contents into his hands: a half dozen shillings. "This is a lot of money for a Saxon to be carrying around. Especially when he has no use for it." Doyle untied the man's leather gambeson and checked the shirt below. Then the silvery neck ring around the man's throat caught his eyes. "He's wearing a torc."

"So he's carrying our money and wearing our jewelry. He stole it. He likes it," Christopher suggested.

"Maybe," Doyle said, then stood. "Or maybe he's not who we think. Perhaps he really *is* a Celt."

Christopher was about to snicker at Doyle, but the five mounted Saxons, who rose over the patchy brown hogback one hundred yards to the north, made him change his mind.

PART ONE

AT SWORD'S POINT

1

Christopher picked up his broadsword, then darted for the dead Saxon's battle-ax. He fetched the ax, then resumed a position next to Doyle. Was he ready? He made a split-second inspection of himself, noticed his throat was dry and tight, and his hands, though weighted down with the weapons, shook. Time would never diminish these discomforts; they were as much a part of the battlefield as blood.

Doyle went reflexively into his quiver, withdrew an arrow, and nocked it deftly into his longbow. If he, too, was afraid, he concealed the emotion with the discipline of an abbot.

The two friends stood and faced the horsemen galloping toward them. The Saxons probably thought they looked pathetic, an easy kill, Christopher thought.

Doyle sighted the lead Saxon and let his arrow fly.

But he had adjusted the arc wrong and the arrow fell short of its target.

Even more pathetic.

"How did you miss?" Christopher asked.

"Shut up!"

Christopher visualized a battle plan in his head. He decided which Saxon he would take first, then calculated where the others would wind up once he made his move.

Doyle nocked another arrow and pulled back ninety pounds of draw. "Now," he whispered to himself. The arrow pierced the air, made a gentle arc, then came down where Doyle wanted it: in the lead Saxon's neck. The man fell right, and the reins of his charging rounsey slipped from his grip. Startled and unguided, the animal bucked and cut right, crashed into the Saxon horseman next to it. As the Saxon with the arrow in his neck careened onto the hard earth, he was followed by the other Saxon horseman, who slammed to the slope still astride his mount. The third Saxon, who was behind the first two, was not able to steer his rounsey clear of the fallen men and downed horse. Both rider and animal wailed as they made impact with their comrades.

Doyle winked at Christopher. The odds were even. The last two Saxons reined around the pileup and forged toward them.

Christopher reversed the weapons in his hands, put the broadsword in his left and the battle-ax in his right. He prepared to throw the ax, taking aim at one of the Saxons. "I have the right one!" he announced to Doyle.

From the corner of his eye, Christopher could see Doyle doing something, but he wasn't sure what. "Are you ready?"

Doyle's reply was a low grumble.

He fired a glance at Doyle. The archer was on his knees before the dead Saxon, trying to pull the arrow from the corpse's back. Doyle's empty quiver bobbed at his side.

Christopher felt the panic shudder up to his lips. "They're not going to wait for you."

Doyle looked up, his face creased with exertion. He groaned as he heaved, then fell back onto the short grass with the freed arrow in his grip.

Christopher returned his gaze to the Saxon on the

right, drew in a deep breath, then let the battle-ax fly. The enemy soldier attempted to rein his rounsey away. The blade end of the ax found a new home in the horse's neck. Christopher grimaced as the rounsey shrieked, then fell, throwing the Saxon. He heard the *fwit!* of Doyle's longbow, saw the remaining Saxon horseman clutch an arrow stuck in his leathered breast, then fall back off his ride.

The Saxon whose horse Christopher had struck got to his feet and unsheathed the spatha strapped to his belt. The man's beard stuck out in three distinct directions, inverted spikes that gave him a fierce, crazed look. His belly protruded from below his too-small gambeson, and his arms seemed to contain more fat than muscle. In either case, they were large. "Fight me, boy!" the man yelled in Saxon. He waved Christopher on with his sword.

"Throw your weapon down, otherwise my friend will put an arrow in your belly." Somewhere behind him, Christopher heard Doyle struggle to withdraw another arrow from another grounded horseman. "Don't make a liar of me, Doyle," he said over his shoulder.

"What are you talking about?" Doyle asked.

Instead of trying to translate for his friend, Christopher directed his attention to the Saxon. He noticed the man's surprise over hearing the Saxon language come out of a Celt. "You speak words I understand. How?"

"I once served a man who led Saxons. His name was Garrett."

"You must be Kenneth, his second-in-command," the Saxon guessed. "But why do you fight with Celts?"

Doyle arrived at Christopher's side with a bloody

arrow nocked in his longbow. "Let's finish up and move on." Doyle drew back his bowstring.

Christopher reached out, seized the arrow. "No."

Resignedly, Doyle lowered his longbow as Christopher released his grip. "Why let him go? So he can join another army and fight us again?"

"Run!" Christopher shouted to the Saxon.

"What are you saying?" Doyle asked.

The Saxon's actions answered Doyle's question. The soldier turned and bolted toward the summit of the nearest mound. Doyle raised his bow and fired his arrow. The iron barb found the soft flesh of the Saxon's thigh beneath his breeches. The man wailed as honed metal penetrated his leg.

Christopher glared at Doyle.

Doyle returned a smirk. "Now at least he'll be our prisoner."

"I told you no!" Christopher felt a heat flush his cheeks.

"You might be squire of the body, but you don't have any say about what I, an archer, do."

"I asked you not to do it as a friend," Christopher said.

"You had no trouble killing Mallory at the tournament. And now you have no stomach for war? I worry about you, Christopher."

"You don't know what I think," Christopher shot back.

"Then tell me."

Beyond the injured Saxon, a blue banner, depicting the Virgin Mary in white, rose above the highest slope. The king's mounted party of five appeared under the banner and descended the slope toward Doyle and Christopher. A hornsman, banner bearer, and Leslie and Teague, the junior squires, all accompanied the bronze-armored Arthur. After a moment, he came to a halt in front of the young men.

Arthur twisted off his dragon-shaped helm, handed it to Leslie, then dismounted. On the ground, he drew Excalibur from its steel sheath at his side, turned, then marched toward the fallen Saxon. The invader stood and hobbled away from Arthur. The king ran up behind the Saxon, grabbed the injured man by his shoulder, and yanked him around. As Christopher flinched, Arthur gutted the man's heart with a swift, life-taking lunge. The king withdrew the crimson blade and handed it to Teague, who waited behind him with a rag. Arthur doffed the gauntlets from his hands and tucked them under an arm. He walked up to Christopher and stood a long moment, eyeing him stoically. Then he smacked Christopher across the face.

Though his cheek stung, Christopher was thankful Arthur had removed his gloves. He kept his gaze focused on the poleyns shielding the king's knees.

"My senior squire, squire of the body of all of England, leaves me alone on the battlefield." The king shook his head in disappointment.

"I beg your forgiveness, lord."

Christopher knew there would be a lot of explaining. He hoped he could make Arthur understand that. He worried more about what Doyle would say. Why had his friend left the Vaward Battle group and become a rogue on the field?

Arthur turned his gaze on Doyle. "And what are you doing here, archer? Don't you belong in the Vaward?"

Christopher glanced over his shoulder. Doyle's gaze was lowered in shame, his lips fastened tightly. Christopher returned his attention to Arthur, saw the king nod to himself, as if he had already considered their fate and now agreed with his own decision. It was the most fearsome nod Christopher had ever seen.

2

Orvin was not keen on visiting the castle of Shores. As he walked down the winding dirt road that would take him from the village to the fortress, he felt a many-fingered chill ripple across his shoulders. He pulled his woolen cloak higher about his neck and mumbled, "You don't like me, do you?"

Winter did not answer.

As he continued down the hard path, swearing as the wind picked up, he began a debate in his mind: was the warm, tasty comfort of a dozen loaves from the kitchen of the castle worth the memories he would have to endure while walking the stones of the bailey his son had once ruled? The castle of Shores had once been *his* family's castle. His father had taken the Roman ruins, built a home, and had been its first lord. Orvin had become its second lord, and then his dear and only son Hasdale had become its third—and last. Every time he visited the castle after his son's death, the act brought him suffering. Christopher had been right about him. He hid in the stable, a recluse, running from a past he hated. How much can a man bear? He had endured the loss of his baby grandson, then his son, and finally his daughter-in-law. Sweet Fiona had not been able to bury the pain of losing her child and husband, and had taken her own life. Orvin had thought of traveling her path, but had discovered how weak he really was. But Christopher's return from the battle against Garrett's army assuaged his torment. He could see his son in the boy, could find an ember of happiness in an otherwise bleak, dark world. It was the boy who gave him the desire to go on. Christopher's training was as beneficial to the old knight as it was to the squire.

The path was deserted, for the cold kept the inhabitants of the village huddled around their fires. Seeing how alone he was, a dark image took possession of Orvin's mind. He lay on the ground with a broken back. The wind laughed as the cold knifed him. He called out again and again, but not a soul was around to help. He saw the skin of his face fade to ash. The water in his eyes froze. Suddenly his eyeballs shattered with a sound that rocked him back to reality. He blinked, then repressed the ugly thought. *I risk my physical and mental health for a dozen loaves of bread. I must be going mad. . . .*

When Orvin came upon the castle, he deliberately did not look at it; he stared only at the path ahead. He sensed the blue-faced sentries watching him from their posts high in the battlements of the gatehouse. The portcullis was already raised, and Orvin passed under the spiked grating. He came into the outer bailey, and again did not look around. He knew where the kitchen was and proceeded toward the building, paying the bundled-up herald no heed.

"Sir Orvin, would you like—" the herald cut himself off, insulted by the old man's brusque behavior.

With his breath steaming and his heart pounding, Orvin fought the desire to run the last few yards to the kitchen. *It might kill me,* he thought. He made it to the door, unlatched it, then rushed inside. He raked his long, white hair out of his eyes, closed the door behind him, then breathed in the warmth and smells of the place. The meat, vegetables, and bread all mixed into an odor that, for a moment, made Orvin light-headed. Food was indeed a gift from God, and the old epicurean desired to feast every day as if it were Christmas. Suddenly it was worth the nightmarish journey, worth the bitterness the castle brought, to be in the kitchen. He moved to his old friend the baker. The man was at his station in the back of the kitchen, preparing another dozen loaves to be slid into the oven.

As Orvin neared the baker, the rotund man turned and his eyes lit. "Ha! Ha! Ha! Sir Orvin, you've finally given in!" His voice was thick, resounding like thunder as he wiped his hands on his apron. "One of my loaves could bribe the devil into Christianity!"

Orvin grimaced as the fat man took him roughly in his arms and hugged the wind out of him.

In front of them, one of the cooks mumbled something about the baker's statement being blasphemous, but Orvin could not discern most of the words. He was still recovering from the baker's deadly affection.

"A dozen for me, Aidan."

"Let's not rush into business. Stay a while and warm up. How many moons has it been since you've stolen a loaf from me?"

"The loaves, Aidan. And I'll be on my way." Orvin had battled the weather and memories, and he would not stay longer than he had to.

The playful light in the baker's eyes faded, and the man's voice grew serious as he put an arm around Orvin's shoulders. "This is still your home. You belong here. Not out there. I've talked to Lord Woodward about you, and he says he would be honored to put you up in the keep, in your old chamber. He says he would be honored more than you know."

But Orvin knew that to come back and live in the castle as though nothing had happened—or to forget about what had happened—was wrong. If he came back, he would be accepting all of the death and getting on with his life. That's what you were supposed to do. But it was too hard. He could not fight the voice inside him that said, *You died when your son died. Your family is gone. What are you doing still alive?*

"Tell Lord Woodward that I appreciate his offer, but cannot accept. I enjoy the stable, and the hostlers are quite friendly and helpful."

Aidan shook his head, his three chins wagging. "Changing *your* mind, I know, is about as easy as pulling a sword from a stone."

"Ah, yes," Orvin said. "Only the king could do it."

Aidan turned to one of the two sweat-faced boys sliding warm loaves out of the brick oven with their long-handled peels. "Thirteen loaves for Sir Orvin, wrapped and ready for travel." The boy nodded. Aidan looked back to Orvin. "Now tell me one thing while you wait. Have you seen anything in the sky about me? What does the welkin say about my future?"

Orvin rubbed his tired eyes, pursed his lips, then stared through the baker, as if trying to recall the information. It was all an act. The skies had never revealed anything to him about Aidan, but Orvin marveled at the baker's faith in him. While most doubted Orvin's necromantic abilities, Aidan had always believed. And Orvin had to keep that faith alive. After he reasoned he had stared long enough, Orvin returned his gaze to Aidan. "You will bake many more loaves."

"Come, Orvin, don't jest! I want to know."

Orvin wanted to tell Aidan something, but he didn't want it to be an outright lie. "Hard times will come and go, but you and your family will survive them. When all appears hopeless, do not give up. And always, always, have faith in the king."

"That's all?" Aidan asked.

Aidan's helper handed Orvin a linen bundle that contained the loaves. Orvin dug in his change pouch and produced two deniers, which he handed to Aidan.

The baker pushed the money back to Orvin. "I'm no shopkeeper."

"Your count will come up short. It'll come out of your earnings. Here." Orvin forced the money into Aidan's hand.

Aidan smiled. "Don't wait so long to see me again."

Orvin nodded, then started toward the exit, threading his way through the worktables and a pair of pages running with faggots for the fires. As he unbolted the door, someone on the other side pushed it in with great force. Orvin plunged toward the cold stone. First his rump hit, then his back, then the back of his head. Each impact reverberated through his fragile bones. His bundle rolled across the floor and opened, scattering the warm loaves.

Orvin lifted his head slightly, and though his vision was blurry, he saw a young woman with long red locks. She turned quickly to bolt the door behind her but stopped as she saw what she had done. Her mouth fell open. "Oh, no. Oh, I'm sorry!" She stepped toward the fallen Orvin as a gust of wind blew the door completely open.

"Shut that door!" one of the cooks shouted.

Torn between the decision to help Orvin and shut

the door, the woman stopped, turned to the door, then back to him. Finally, she opted to close the door. That done, she rushed to his side.

Her graceful fingers stroked the back of his head as she helped him sit up. His cloak had bunched up and shielded his head from being cut by the stone, but he would have a nice bump, he knew. Her touch eased the pain. Orvin looked into her eyes and recognized the woman: she was Marigween, daughter of the late Lord Devin, an orphan who lived at the castle and was betrothed to Lord Woodward by his victory in arms. But she had denied Woodward the marriage. Orvin had heard how Woodward continuously sought Marigween while she dodged his advances. She guarded her love—and Orvin knew for whom.

"Oh, if I had to pick someone to knock over, it would not have been you, Sir Orvin," she said.

"Picking someone to knock over is always a hard decision," Orvin noted, rousing a smile from her. Being close to Marigween, Orvin could see why Christopher was taken by the woman. Her beauty was unmatched, even by Christopher's current love, Brenna. Marigween made Orvin feel sad about his old age. She reminded him of his own wife, Donella. To kiss Marigween now would be something—something Lord Woodward would behead him for, most assuredly. His lust for Marigween would remain in its prison.

"Here," she said, "let me help you up." She took his hand and pulled him to his feet. Vertebrae cracked in Orvin's back, and his entire rump was filled with an intense stinging sensation. But Orvin found it easy to ignore the discomforts.

Aidan came over to see what the commotion was about, and he noticed Orvin's loaves splayed over the floor. He cocked his head toward his helpers. "Boys, come over here and clean up this mess. Then prepare Sir Orvin some new loaves." The baker stepped between Orvin and Marigween, then proceeded to rub Orvin's shoulders. "I've seen people fall before, but that . . . you really went down."

Orvin shrugged, upset that Aidan had come between himself and the sweet, clean-smelling Marigween.

"What can I do to make this up to you?" Marigween asked.

Orvin shouldered his way out of Aidan's grip and circled around so that he could once again be close to her. Aidan must have known what Orvin was up to, for behind Marigween's back he shook his head and shamed Orvin with his fingers, then started for his bench.

"I'm in one piece. You owe me nothing." Orvin wanted to open his mouth and smile, but knew she'd find his crooked, yellowing teeth displeasing. It was uncomfortable to grin with his mouth closed, but he made the effort.

She yielded her own lovely grin. "I insist. What is it I could get for you, or something I could do for you within my means that would make you happy?"

There was one thing that Orvin wanted, but only now admitted to himself. Company. People other than the dusty hostlers who'd run out of stories moons ago and become boring. If she would just talk with him occasionally, he knew it would warm his days. She, like Christopher, made him feel young again. But how to tell her without it coming out wrong?

"There has to be something," she urged.

Orvin swallowed. "I do have the need for company now and again. Now don't get me wrong, please, my lady, I—"

She put a slender finger to his lips. "I know where you live, and whenever you wish I will come by."

Then she suddenly glowed with an idea. "I could fetch you your supplies. You wouldn't have to venture out in the cold."

"That's too nice of you," Orvin said. "I fear I shall owe you something in return."

"You will," she said, then she came much closer to him; so close, in fact, that Orvin blushed, an old knight feeling like a young squire under her spell. "I want you to tell me about Christopher. I want to know more about him. I know you trained him."

"It seems we each have something of value to offer to the other." Orvin took her hand in his own, covering it with the other. "Lady Marigween, I look forward to bartering with you."

3

Seaver led Cuthbert and Ware stealthily through the thin forest that lay below the castle of Shores. The dwarf-sized Saxon scout leader and his comrades were virtually unaffected by the cold. They wore hoods of link-mail, over which were hoods of wool, with only the eyes cut out so that they would not be identified.

As Seaver rounded tree trunks, his gaze flicking left and right, he let his mind go to the sights and sounds, filtering out his own thoughts and discomforts and dreams. The wind howled a dire tune. Overhead, branches like thin gray bones rattled and scraped into each other. Fallen and decaying leaves swirled and fluttered past him. A twig snapped loudly. He cocked his head, saw that Cuthbert had taken a wrong step. All three men dropped to their haunches. Seaver grabbed Cuthbert by his neck, shook him violently, then let him go. For a moment, Seaver considered knifing the man—but that was anger influencing his thinking and not common sense. Yes, he had trained Cuthbert for many moons, and yes, he ought to know better, ought to be more careful, but no man deserved to die over snapping a twig. Yet Seaver's leader, Kenric, would probably have killed Cuthbert. You didn't blink wrong around Kenric.

Voices. Two of them. Celts. Sentries on patrol. One, fifty yards to the south. The other, twenty to the east. They were armed with shortbows—very effective in the wood. Seaver wished they carried crossbows, for in the moments it would take a sentry to windlass his weapon, Seaver and his men would be gone like startled leverets. But an angry Celt with a shortbow could do great damage to his party, firing faster and much more accurately than any crossbowman.

Seaver kept his men inert, his senses keen on every movement of the sentries. Once the two Celts had moved to the flanks behind them, Seaver waved Cuthbert and Ware on toward the jagged limestone ramparts which lay beyond the forest.

Now, as he moved, he let his thoughts prevail once more. He considered the plan Kenric had devised, played it over again. He wondered how the other Saxon armies were doing on the Mendip Hills. It was truly a great moment for their people. For the first time since landing on these shores the separate Saxon armies were united and organized. Inspired by Garrett's dream to rule the castle of Shores, Kenric had reorganized Garrett's old army, making it the central core of three other armies that also occupied the Mendips. While the others lured the Celt armies into the hills, the castles of Shores and Rain were to be sieged, overthrown, and occupied. With two strongholds, the Saxons could finish the remaining Celts in South Cadbury, striking and retreating to the fortresses at their leisure. Seaver, a little man scorned most of his life, was now one of the most important players in a game that meant life or death for his people. If the scorners could see him now . . .

As they cleared the wood, he and his men surveyed the steep hill before them; it was freckled with elbows of limestone that jutted out as far as a yard in some places. In summer, the stones would have worked to their advantage in ascending the rampart, but now they were glossed with ice. ·

The sky was overcast, washing from the metallic gray of twilight into the deeper coal of night. Earlier, Seaver thought they might have to pause before climbing; it would be foolhardy to move about the castle in daylight. But as it was, shadows drew steadily, and he decided that by the time they clambered to the top, the vespers horn within the castle would sound, and night would cloak them.

The boots Seaver had taken from a dead Celt boy gave the scout good traction as he mounted the rampart. Cuthbert and Ware followed in his steps, trusting the ledges and ditches he chose on his way up the cliff.

Seaver tested his grip on an ice-covered stone, felt that his glove would stick. He pushed off the stone and took another precarious step up. Four more steps followed, with Seaver finding good purchase in the corners where rock met earth. Behind him, Cuthbert used the same shiny stone to pull himself up. As the scout stepped then pushed off with his hand, the hand slipped and Cuthbert collapsed onto his chest.

He slid down the side of the rampart, pulling small rocks and bits of ice with him.

Ware snatched Cuthbert by the back of his hood and stopped his descent. A moment of silence passed between all as they listened. Had the Celts above heard the fall? The air whistled around them. They heard no indication of an alarm.

Once Cuthbert had checked himself for injuries, had decided he was all right, then had shifted back to his feet, Seaver resumed leading the scouts up the rampart, this time exercising more caution. The rest of the climb was pleasantly and thankfully uneventful.

From a position just below the top of the rampart, Seaver and his men took in the view of the castle's moat, berm, and west curtain wall.

Seaver had come to the fortress twice before, the second time discovering the castle's defenses had been increased. Now, sizing it up for a third time, he saw that it appeared relatively unchanged from his last visit.

Four towers broke the wall into three sections, and behind the wall-walks of those sections, Seaver counted a dozen men. Each tower had four loopholes, and Seaver guessed there was an archer behind each who waited to shoot his arrow through the hole in the stone. Sixteen archers in the towers and a dozen men on each wall-walk. Nearly sixscore men were the castle's perimeter defense. Seaver smiled inwardly. The last time he had been to the stronghold the number had been over tenscore. Seaver knew the missing Celts were up on the Mendip Hills being slaughtered by his cohorts. If Kenric was right, there would be no spare men for the garrison to call upon. The castle lay with open arms, practically defenseless. As Seaver thought about telling Kenric of the great news, thrills fluttered through him. But he had to control his emotions and concentrate on the task at hand. The vespers horn tolled the hour.

They would break from the cover of the rampart now and find a position from which to observe the gatehouse, for the only way they would be able to estimate how many men operated inside the bailey and how many more were in the keep was to view the comings and goings of patrols and supply carts through the gatehouse. A simple fact was clear: the more men inside, the more food and other supplies they needed. Seaver had been able to come up with fairly accurate troop counts based on the amount of supplies going in.

There was a better way to get the exact number of men, but only a fool or a madman would try to sneak in and out of the castle of Shores. Only a fool, a madman, or Kenneth, a man who had once been Garrett's second-in-command. Seaver deeply missed him. Kenneth would have been a great leader of Saxons. He had been a perfect spy; he had been more aggressive than Garrett and smarter than Kenric. But there was no way to bring Kenneth back from the underworld, and there had been no way to prevent Garrett from killing him. Seaver sighed away the past.

The temperature had dropped significantly, and Seaver's joints felt stiff. His muscles were cramped from lying in the same position too long. He silently indicated to his men that they would sprint toward a thin stand of oaks and gorse shrubs marking the start of a dirt path that snaked away from the castle. It would be good to run. He was sure his men felt the same.

Seaver, Cuthbert, and Ware sprang from their observation point. Their dark garb reflected no light to the eyes of the sentries in the towers and wall-

walks. They made it to the cover of the oaks and
dodged behind them.

Peering from behind a trunk, Seaver observed a
figure materializing from the gloom. It was an old
man who carried a bundle. The man muttered to
himself as his white hair danced in the night wind.

Seaver heard a rustling in the gorse behind him,
then felt a hand on his shoulder. He cocked his head
and saw that Ware had an anlace in his grip; the small
blade gleamed for a moment as it caught a bit of
torchlight emanating from the castle. Seaver pointed
to the old man, then to his own eye, then to Ware's
blade: if he sees us, then you kill him. The scout nodded.

They watched the ancient Celt continue down the
path. And then he stopped. The old man lifted his
head and eyed his surroundings, as if he sensed their
presence.

Seaver clenched his fists. He released a quick
glance to Ware. The scout was ready for a leap-and-
roll attack on the ancient Celt.

But then, as abruptly as the old man had stopped,
he resumed his pace and the conversation he was
having with himself. He vanished at the point where
the path met the shadows.

Their tension unwinding, Seaver and his men scattered into the wood, each finding ideal observation
points. They settled down to meals of salted beef,
cold but once-boiled carrots, and weak cider.

They would move again before dawn.

4 A blazing pyre gifted the Mendip Hills with warmth and saffron light. Scores of Saxon bodies were heaped onto the flames in a grim spectacle by their Celt slayers. Ashes and embers wheeled toward a vault of black clouds. The fire hissed and spat and crackled, spewing forth a terrible stench that drove those near it to tie rags over their teary-eyed faces.

Outside King Arthur's tent, Christopher and Leslie coughed and watched the cremations continue, thankfully far enough away that the odor, while making them choke a bit, did not overcome them. They overheard Doyle being questioned by Arthur inside the shelter. Repeatedly, the king asked Doyle why he had left his position, and repeatedly Doyle gave no excuse. As the king raised his voice in agitation, so did Doyle—much to Christopher's and Leslie's shock. Finally, Doyle elbowed his way out of the tent, unfastened and took a long pull on his flagon, then marched away toward the Vaward camp in the south. Christopher called after his friend, but the archer strode away.

Leslie scratched behind one of his too-big ears. "The fire. It's almost . . . beautiful . . . in an ugly way."

Leslie was a smart boy, despite the great error he had made of mistaking Mallory for the duke of Somerset at last summer's tournament.

His gaze not leaving the flames, Christopher replied, "It's all right to talk about him. Even though he embarrasses me, Doyle is still my friend."

"I do not wish to pry," Leslie said. "There are too many other things to talk about. Like this fire. Do you see it as I do?"

"Fires are enchanting," Christopher opined, "but when they rise from the corpses of warriors, well, that makes them ugly."

Leslie tipped his head in agreement.

"You know, we could share the land with the Saxons."

"Pardon?"

Christopher turned to Leslie, needing to face the squire. "They've used up their own land. They're dying. They simply want to live."

"But this is our land and they want to take it," Leslie said.

"True. But isn't there enough for everyone?"

"Maybe not. Besides, it's not as if they *asked* if they could come here. They invaded!"

"What if we gave them some land? Establish a Saxon enclave. Show them how to farm our way. I wager it would work. Maybe the war would come to an end."

"Indeed it would," a familiar voice chipped in.

Christopher craned his head and saw Arthur, out of armor, walking toward them. Christopher could not feel more awkward. His last words hung in the air like a challenge—and the last person he wanted to combat was Arthur. He did not believe in the killing, but he knew very well who his ruler was and the respect he owed him.

The king chewed on a partridge leg and spoke between bites. "Yes, the war would be over by the morrow and the Saxons would rule this land."

Christopher swallowed his opinions and his ideas in one large, hard, bitter gulp. He lowered his head, as he was wont to do in the king's presence.

"I have some strappings to mend," Leslie said, then turned to Arthur. "By your leave?"

Arthur nodded, and as Leslie beat a hasty retreat from the philosophical battlefield, Christopher held his crumbling ground. "Seen enough death, have you, Christopher?" the king asked.

"I beg your—"

"Enough seeking my forgiveness. You have been doing that all day. Be more like your friend Doyle and stand up to me!" Arthur took another bite of meat, then spoke with his mouth full. "And look at me when you talk!"

Christopher lifted his gaze to the king. "In answer to your question, lord, yes."

"Do you believe that any man in this army *likes* to kill?"

"Some, I believe, enjoy it."

"No!" Arthur shouted, then dropped his partridge leg the ground. "They like victory. And they like peace. They know what they have to do to obtain those goals. Do you?"

"My liege, I will never disobey your orders. My loyalty is true, be assured of that. But I wonder, how many more Saxons will land on our shores? How much longer will the war—the killing—go on? I can't help but see them as men. Dying men."

"I know why," Arthur said.

The king knew of his past service to the Saxons under Garrett. Arthur could find out anything he wanted to know about anyone. It was safe to assume that Arthur knew it all. Better to say nothing now than sink deeper into the implication that he had once been a traitor. No one would ever understand that he had been loyal only to Garrett, a Celt. They would see him as a squire to Saxons—a traitor.

"You even learned their tongue," Arthur added.

"Merlin tells me I will need you to converse with them."

Though he had never met the king's necromancer, had never seen the man's magic firsthand, Christopher immediately believed in the wizard's prophecy. It *felt* like the truth. "That horseman you killed earlier? I spoke to him."

"And what did he tell you? That his people come in peace?"

At the moment, Christopher hated being honest. "He wanted me to fight him."

Arthur shook his head, then neared Christopher and slid his arm around the squire's shoulders. "You cannot change what will be, Christopher. Even with the help of a druid. There are some things that God has chosen." Arthur took in a deep breath, then let it out slowly. "This war will end soon. But there will be a lot more bloodshed. There is no other way."

There has to be, Christopher thought. *It is not what* will *be, but what* can *be.*

Arthur shivered. "Let's go inside. You haven't eaten." The king led him back toward the tent. "Oh, yes," Arthur added, "your friend Doyle may be a rogue, but he has keen eyes."

"What do you mean?"

"The Saxon that pursued you was a Celt. He was one of the wagon drivers in the rear guard. His brothers are being questioned now by Lancelot."

Christopher was nonplussed. "Why would—"

"Someone paid him to kill you. Any honorable man would have made a challenge. But this . . . it leaves me at a loss."

"I think I know who it was," Christopher said.

"There are many men who will attempt to undermine us, Christopher. Men like our old enemy Mallory, who will want to see all of us dead. Remember, you are not of noble blood—yet you are my squire. Your actions proved you worthy. But there are many who disagree. Now tell me. Who is this criminal?"

"I cannot accuse anyone until I am sure."

"You honor the code too well. If you are wise, you will not attack the enemy. Lay a trap for him." Arthur patted Christopher on the back several times, as if instilling the words into him through the action.

Christopher had to talk to Doyle. Immediately. "By your leave?"

"Where are you going? There is meat for you inside."

"Please, lord," Christopher begged, "by your leave?"

Arthur sighed, pointed an index finger at Christopher, and then his eyes filled with a warning.

Christopher took the sigh as a resigned yes, heeded the warning indicated by the index finger and the eyes, then gave the king no chance to speak. He sprinted toward the dusty gray tents that housed the Vaward Battle group on the southernmost slope.

Had he looked over his shoulder, he would have seen Arthur's stern expression soften into a smile over the abruptness of youth, then fade into a look of deep concern.

5   From the window alcove of her chamber,
Brenna searched the sky over Uryens's castle for the
moon, but she could not find it. The wind caught the
raven maid's shift and blew it gently against her as
she squinted, stood on her toes, but once again saw
only the indifferent clouds that darkened and ruled
the heavens over Gore.

"Who are you looking for?"

Mavis was sprawled across Brenna's trestle bed,
using a bunch of her long, golden hair like a paint-
brush to idly stroke her cheek.

Not turning from the window, Brenna replied,
"Just looking for the moon."

Mavis stood up, brushed off her bright green livery, and smoothed the wrinkles from her apron. "You
are coming this eve, aren't you?"

"He likes to look at the moon," Brenna said. "He
always did when I was with him. I'll bet he's looking
for it now—just like me."

"Christopher is probably eating cold pork inside a
drafty tent. He's not out looking for the moon,"
Mavis reasoned.

For a moment, Brenna thought she caught sight of
the white orb as it tried to break through the sky's
steely curtain. She stiffened and fixed her gaze on the
flash she thought she had seen. She waited. Looked.
Nothing.

"You haven't changed yet. Come on! We still need
to go down to my chamber and pick something out for
me." Brenna heard Mavis's footsteps behind her, then
felt her friend's hand touch her elbow. "If you please."

"I cannot believe how much it hurts already. My
mother tells me that Christopher and I will be married,

and how much she and my father approve of him. But I don't even know if he'll return to ask me."

"You went after him from the start. You found out he was a squire. You knew how it was going to be. Maybe you should have remained with—"

"Don't even say his name." Brenna turned from the window. "I think of it as something foul. A curse." Slowly, Brenna stepped down from the alcove.

"Then again," Mavis said, "you would have the same problem with him as you do with Christopher."

"I told him that I knew what to expect, that I knew how to wait, and that this time I really would. And I told him I knew how to love."

"Loving is easy," Mavis said. "But I know you. You will not wait for him."

"I will."

Mavis shook her head, then smiled knowingly. "You will not."

"Will too."

"Do not lie to yourself," Mavis said.

Brenna sighed. Was Mavis right? She had been very sure the first time Christopher had gone. She had told herself that if he didn't come back, she would kill herself. But then *he* had come along. All it had taken was one varlet and she had been immediately under his spell. The spell Christopher had cast over her had been too easily broken. Her love should have been made of iron—not cobwebs. What was it made of now? She could not lie to herself and say it was iron, but certainly it was stronger than cobwebs. Some kind of wood? She sighed again. Did she really know how to wait? Could she keep her eyes off the garrison men, fend off their advances, and lead a life of chastity until Christopher's eventual return? How proud a moment that would be! Her future husband

in the service of the king! She could be the wife of
the king's squire.

But what if she waited for another dozen, even a
score of moons, and he did not return? She would
have remained chaste and unmarried for nothing.
What if he did return and had lost his feelings for
her? What if he was maimed on the battlefield? Then
she would be a nursemaid as well as a chambermaid.
As before, the dark side of the future seemed closer
and more real than the bright side.

*I have to give him a chance. I have to give us a
chance. I must!*

Mavis dug around inside Brenna's livery trunk at
the foot of her bed, pausing several times to brush
her long locks out of her way. "If you're not going to
find something for yourself, then I will."

"I am not going."

Mavis turned her gaze up from the trunk. "Wynne
will be expecting us at the table. And she has invited
those three sentrics. Do you know what you are
going to make that third man feel like?"

"I care not what *he* feels like." The very act of dining with another man seemed a betrayal to Brenna. If
she went, she might as well cut her love strings to
Christopher.

"It is a meal—not a marriage, Brenna. I cannot
think of anything more rude than you failing to take
your place at our table. You are coming." Mavis
resumed her rummaging through Brenna's clothes.

Brenna wandered back to the alcove and shivered
as the wind slid its icy fingers around her neck.
"Perhaps you're right."

She did not try to justify the dinner to herself. She
wanted to feel the guilt of going, to experience it fully
and remember it always. Brenna knew that when she

stopped feeling guilty, she stopped loving him. The
pain was good; it meant she cared. Now if she could
only turn wood into iron. . . .

6 "Spare me, dear Lancelot. I tell you we do not
know who paid him!"

King Arthur's champion had one of his gauntleted
hands wrapped around the stout wagon driver's stub-
bly throat. Beads of sweat cascaded off the balding,
frightened man's pate.

"You lie!" Lancelot spat, "you lecherous, plotting,
blubbery piece of molding pork!"

Christopher watched with chilling awe as Lancelot
pulled the man off his knees and, adding his other
hand to the driver's throat, lifted him in the air. The
man howled; for a moment Christopher thought it
was the wind outside, then he realized he heard both.
Foamy saliva rimmed the wagon driver's lips as he
mouthed the word "please" again and again.

The wagon driver's brother, an equally fat man
with equally thinning hair, fell to his knees before
Lancelot and wrapped his arms around the knight's
armored leg. "I have already lost one brother this
day. Spare me my other." The driver noticed
Christopher, and slowly his face waxed over with
dark recognition. "It was you, squire. Christopher of
Shores. *You* killed my brother!" The driver bounded
from Lancelot's heels and, with his hands set like a
vulture's claws, dived onto Christopher.

Thick, stubby fingers tore past the collar of his
gambeson and sought the soft skin of his throat.

There was movement all around him: the shuffling of
feet; the clanking of armor; a low, heavy *thud!* as
something heavy hit the ground; a shout: "Guard!";
and the heaving growl of the driver on top of him as
the drooling scavenger tried to tear out his larynx. If
the driver's fingers didn't kill him, his breath would.

Christopher balled his hand and punched. He
made contact with the driver's head, then heard the
man moan in protest. Then the fleshy vise on his
neck was stripped away as the looming forms of
Lancelot and a guard wrenched the driver off of him.
Christopher sat up, pulled the collar of his gambeson
away from his throat, then breathed deeply. He
rubbed his Adam's apple and swallowed painfully.
For a brief instant his mind swept him back to the
night Kenneth had tried to murder him, choking him
with one hand while tensing to dagger him with the
other. Now, as then, there was intervention that
saved his life.

He was becoming convinced that if he died, it
would be by choking.

Lancelot pummeled the attacking driver's face
until the man was red and swollen. The knight
dropped the man like refuse next to his brother.

The brother spoke: "How can you blame him?" He
pointed a finger at Christopher. "He . . . he did it."
The man's voice was fissured with sorrow and his
breath staggered. He began to sob in his hands.

Lancelot hunkered down in front of Christopher and
offered his hand. "I never knew you could look so blue."

"People have a habit of wanting to choke me,
which is to say I have been this blue before."

Lancelot smiled a missing-toothed smile, the only
flaw among gleaming, flaxen hairs and chiseled facial
features. He pulled Christopher to his feet, then

regarded the wagon drivers while directing the words to the squire. "I'm afraid I'll kill them before we discover anything more."

"If you'll permit me, Sir Lancelot. I believe I know who paid their brother. But there is only one person who can help me discover the truth: my friend Doyle."

Lancelot's expression grew uneasy. "Why him?"

Christopher lowered his voice to conspiratorial depths. "The king told me to lay a trap for my enemy—and Doyle is the only one besides myself who knows who the enemy is. I want to keep it that way. It is fair for all concerned. I need Doyle's help."

"He may not be of much help to you now." Lancelot started out of the tent. "But I'll take you to him."

Doyle was stripped down to a pair of thin breeches. His back lay bare to the frigid breath of night. His hands were bound with leather laces and strapped onto the saddle of the brown courser before which he stood. In the light of a pair of ground-mounted pole torches, a long line of archers and varlets took turns lashing Doyle's back with a cat-o'-nine-tails. Doyle's skin was already a recklessly drawn grid of bloody lines as Lancelot and Christopher arrived.

Two older men, their surcoats marking them as sergeants, stood on either side of Doyle, whispering sweet death threats in the young archer's ears. As Lancelot charged the scene, Christopher studied the line of boys and men waiting to inflict punishment on his friend.

And there he was. Exactly where Christopher expected to find him.

The boy with the pudding basin haircut.

The in-love-with-himself arrow-shooter.

There could not be much more distance between Christopher and Innis. In the beginning, Christopher, though jealous, had tried, had honestly tried, to accept and like the varlet. He had returned from his first battle and had accepted the fact that Brenna was his—but it had been Innis who could not stand his presence, swiping him left and right with spiked innuendos. And then he had put his hand to Brenna, which had been his undoing.

Inside Christopher, two armored notions fought with heavy broadswords. He wanted to run up to Innis and twist his head off, but then he thought it might be better to act calm, bide time, exercise the patience of a skilled hunter laying his trap.

The desire to behead Innis struck a heavy, offensive blow against logic, and Christopher ran up to Innis as the varlet was about to receive the cat-o'-nine-tails. With teeth clenched and a face of fire, Christopher tore the whip from Innis's grip.

Innis, recognizing who had taken the whip from him, twisted his expression into a vaunting, sardonic grin. "I guess there's no need, really, for my powerful strokes on your friend, squire. I see my brothers-in-arms have already done enough work for their country."

Christopher reared back with the whip.

Innis held his ground unflinchingly; his conceit was maddening.

But then Christopher realized violence was what the varlet wanted. Christopher would be disciplined for striking an unarmed man for no apparent reason. Besides that, his action would illustrate that Innis was much more in control of himself than Christopher.

Logic moved in with a powerful riposte, and Christopher lowered the whip. He needed a cutting retort, but he knew Innis was the better wordsmith. While Christopher had spent the first thirteen years of his life as a saddler's son, Innis had gone to school at the Queen's Camel Abbey and had been taught by the brightest monks there. Though his father was only an armorer, Innis had somehow been maneuvered into classes with the scions of noble and wealthy families. It was the pattern of Innis's life: getting things he did not deserve—a noble education; Brenna; revenge on Doyle. At least the varlet had lost Brenna.

Someone took the whip from Christopher's hand. Lancelot had come between him and Innis. In the background, Christopher observed with relief that the sergeants were untying Doyle. He stood a moment longer, flashed Innis the blackest look he could muster, then marched off to meet with Doyle.

Christopher could not hear the conversation that began between Lancelot and Innis, but he was sure that Innis would say something to ignite Lancelot's anger. Christopher would wager his broadsword on that.

The sergeants left Doyle weltering in his own blood, not offering to help him back to his tent. Doyle pressed his head onto the courser's saddle. His whole body was surely wreathed in pain. Christopher sensed that Doyle didn't want to move, for if he did, it would cause him more agony.

Christopher moved in next to his friend, slid his head near the archer's. "Doyle, let me help you. What can I do? Does it hurt if you move? Can I get you back to your tent? How about some hot linens? We can wipe down your back."

Doyle was dour. Stiff. A bleeding statue.

As Christopher turned to fetch the linens, he barely avoided two other archers who, as if having heard him, stepped forward with steaming linens in their hands.

"I'm Phelan," the tall one with the soot-colored hair said. "And this is Neil."

Though he had to be only a year or so older than Christopher, Neil sported a thick, brown beard and a forest of like-colored curls on his head. While Phelan's appearance had a birdlike quality to it, his large nose, very much like a beak, descending his face, Neil's looks had Saxon scrawled all over them. Immediately, Christopher dubbed them "the bird and the barbarian."

"It's good to know I'm not his only friend," Christopher said. "I am—"

"Christopher of Shores," Neil answered. "It is an honor to meet you, though our friend's punishment brings us together."

Arthur was wrong. Not every young man in the army was jealous of Christopher. That is, if Neil was being truthful.

The two archers applied their linens to Doyle's back. Doyle gasped and winced, and Christopher felt himself doing the same. Once Doyle's back was relatively clean, Phelan and Neil slid their heads under Doyle's arms and proceeded to carry the archer back to his tent. Christopher walked behind the group as Lancelot joined him.

"I've been told that he was once the good example," Lancelot began.

"I haven't been wanting to admit it to myself," Christopher said softly for Doyle's sake, "but I believe my friend has a point to prove on this campaign."

"And what is that?"

"That he is a man. He once ran from the battle-field, and now not only must he stay, but he must be the war's biggest hero."

"If he lets his heart rule his mind, then his anger,

his vengeance, will kill him. Heart and mind must be balanced."

"Sir Orvin uttered those same words. It seems so long ago."

"Your friend is not unlike the king," Lancelot observed. "When I first met Arthur, he wanted to kill me so much that he lost the power of reason. It is hard, I suspect. I have felt that madness fill my mind. It seems impossible to empty."

Inside his tent, Doyle was set down on three layers of woolen blankets. He lay on his stomach, burying his face in his hands. The bird and the barbarian asked him questions about the pain, how they could help, and if there was anything Doyle wanted. The slashed archer made no reply.

"I'll fetch Hallam to have a look at him," Lancelot said, then turned and slipped through the tent flaps.

Christopher sat down next to Doyle. "If you would not take offense, I must speak with him alone," he told the archers.

Phelan and Neil understood and quietly left the tent. Christopher could hear them voice their concerns to each other outside as he palmed himself closer to Doyle.

"I was right, wasn't I," Doyle said affirmatively, his voice half-muffled by the blankets in front of his face.

"Right about what?"

Doyle lifted his head and turned to face Christopher, grimacing as he did so. "You know."

"Are you referring to the Saxon who chased me?"

Doyle let out a short, stifled groan, then said, "The Celt."

"Yes, the Celt. With nearly one thousand men in this army, how am I supposed to remember the face of every wagon driver?"

"You're not. And that's what Innis rolled his dice on."

Christopher bent closer to Doyle. "So you think it was Innis who hired the driver?"

"No, I think that wagon driver simply wanted you dead. Perhaps he did not fancy your surcoat, or was jealous of your handsome face. What do you think? Of course it was Innis. He's wanted you since the day we teamed up on him. It comes as no surprise. Unfortunately, I made his revenge on me far too easy. I embarrassed myself." Doyle tossed a longing glance at his flagon, which sat in one corner of the tent near his bow. "Could you get me a drink?"

Christopher stood and retrieved the flagon, unstoppered it, and handed it to Doyle; the archer drank the ale in a loud series of gulps, then handed the flagon back to Christopher, who set it down on the blankets behind him.

Christopher rubbed his hands together, the friction building up a small but comforting amount of warmth. "We need a plan to solve our problem, but before we consider that, I want to talk to you. And I want you to be honest with me."

Doyle rested his chin on his arm and stared ahead into nothingness. "Don't bother asking. You already heard what I told the king."

"I'm not going to ask you about anything," Christopher said. "I already know why you deserted the other archers and went on your own campaign today. And I know you will do it again. You have to kill a lot of them, don't you?"

"I thought you weren't going to ask me anything."

"You have to kill a lot them because you owe it to

the others, the others that died the first time we were here and you ran. But killing more now will never bring them back. And what you did back then was not wrong—I told you that. It was smart. In the face of defeat, save your own life. What's wrong with that?"

Doyle's hands tightened into fists, and he remained silent.

"You might not be answering any of my questions, but that is because you have no answers for yourself. Don't you understand? The angry heroes will be cremated. The ones with humility, with the common sense you exercised when you ran, those are the survivors. Those are the heroes. There is nothing to prove, Doyle. Nothing."

"Let me know when you're done," Doyle said, "because when you are, I need another drink."

7 The armies of Arthur, Uryens, Leondegrance, Nolan, and Woodward each struck decisive first victories against the Saxons on the Mendip Hills. The invaders were coerced onto the higher slopes, where the air was thinner and colder, the ground harder and more rocky. Many of the senior and junior squires in Christopher's company opined that the war was over. The Saxons had fled and the spoils and glory now belonged to the Celts. But Christopher knew nothing was over until every living Saxon was dead or off the land. Arthur had made that plain to him. And thus they rode higher into the Mendip Hills, stalking the enemy with a vengeance that reminded Christopher of Lord Hasdale's quest to kill Garrett. And with that last battle, Hasdale had ended or changed the lives of

everyone in Shores, finally paying the ultimate price himself. In an icy way, Arthur's quest, though noble in its intentions, seemed no different.

As he sat on his chestnut brown courser, feeling the easy rhythms of the horse as it cantered upward, a vision from black sleep stole its way into Christopher's mind. Arthur told him there was no other way to end the invasion, and then hordes of burning Saxons rose from their pyres and leapt on the king, carving him up with their halberds and daggers and spathas, and scorching him with flames they controlled like whips. Warning horns blared in Christopher. Questions flew like quicklimed spears and bull's-eyed blazing holes in his confidence.

Do we ride toward death?

He would die for king and country—his duty. One could say one died while fighting gloriously with King Arthur against the invaders. One would be revered and remembered. Or one could say one died for vengeance, for selfishness, for greed. But the whole point was moot. One wouldn't be saying anything after the fact.

He had to stop worrying about the greater problem of the Saxons and more about his smaller, more easily solvable problems. He forced away the vision of Arthur's demise, then turned his thoughts to Doyle.

Christopher longed to walk with his injured friend, instead of riding in the Main Battle. He had not reached Doyle last night, but would die before he stopped trying.

Doyle's group of archers led the Vaward Battle; they would be the very first ones to encounter the enemy. Doyle had been thrilled when he had learned of his placement in Arthur's army. Christopher remembered that the night before they had left

Uryens's castle he and Doyle drank—what the next day seemed like a firkin of ale—to celebrate the news. And to drown their anxieties.

But as he looked back on it, Christopher saw they had nothing to be afraid of. The campaign had begun far more routinely than expected.

The first group of Saxons they had encountered had been small, tenscore of men. Doyle's group had knocked out more than half of them before the Main Battle even got near the action. But Doyle had not been able to down a single Saxon; his shots had fallen short or had hit invaders who were already dead. Christopher remembered how much this had troubled his friend. Doyle's solo, hit-and-run mission the previous day was his reply to the chiding of his fellow archers. Christopher wished Doyle's wounds would have convinced him it wasn't worth it, but Doyle shared at least one trait with Orvin's old mule, Cara.

Yes, he had to stop Doyle from throwing his life away senselessly. He loved his friend and needed him more than ever. Christopher knew that when it came to laying traps, Doyle was the expert. It was a talent he shared with his late brother, Baines. Christopher's memories of Baines were barely hued, mostly gray, but every time he saw Doyle flash his sly smile, Christopher saw Baines. It was good to have the broadsword Baines had given him at his side, for Christopher knew if his capacity to see Baines in his mind's eye faded completely, the hard metal and bejeweled hilt of the sword never would. If only a little more of Baines's expertise had infected him in his youth, he might have been able to devise something on his own.

Laying a trap. There was another man Christopher had served, though unwillingly, who had also been an adept hunter of animal and man. He had been a true devil in the flesh, a rogue Celt who would have known how to handle Innis. Sir Mallory—the "Sir" only a title, Mallory had been no gentleman—had known how to deal with his enemies.

Then again, Mallory would have confronted and killed Innis, disregarding repercussions, witnesses, and the king. Mallory would have cut out Innis's heart and fed it to the varlet in his last seconds before death. Or something equally heinous.

The plan had to fall somewhere in the middle; not be too extreme, but clever enough to convict Innis. Christopher would be the bait, no matter what the plan, and that didn't make him feel any better. He'd much rather be facing only the Saxons. At least with them, it was only about war.

Innis's first attempt on Christopher's life had nearly been successful, and Christopher suspected the varlet would get even better at it. Innis would not stop until Christopher was dead. In a sense, Innis was like Arthur chasing the Saxons. In both cases, obsession blinded the men.

And a blind man is vulnerable.

Leslie's constant sniffling irritated Christopher. He lost his thoughts to the sound and turned to the mounted squire next to him. "Blow your nose and be done with it!"

Arthur spied the rear from his place ahead of them, then returned his gaze to the hillocks ahead.

Leslie leaned over his mount, pressed his finger to one nostril, then cleared the other onto the ground. He repeated the process as Christopher eyed the big-eared squire with disdain.

"Oh, that is better," Leslie said, trying out his newly cleared nose. "I can almost smell the sun."

"My liege," Christopher shouted to the king. "I

think we have a troubadour in our midst—a man who claims he can smell the sun."

"Ask him, my senior squire, what does it smell like?"

Christopher enjoyed the good-natured banter. His weary emotions and fatigue-riddled mind needed a repose. He regarded Leslie. "So then, our sovereign asks . . . "

"It is hard to put into words," Leslie said in a singsong way, "but it is as a thousandscore of blooming irises all bowing in the wind. And I smell now a beautiful lady coming out of the sun and drifting down to bless us all, and to love us all. Maybe she is the Lady of the Lake's sister?"

The banner bearer, quiet as a mute and twice Christopher's age, turned to him and winked. Christopher raised his eyebrows in agreement. They all could use a blessing and some love. Christopher wondered how Leslie was able to *smell* the fact that the lady would love and bless them. He allowed himself a grin, but it did not last long.

After a long day on the heels of the retreating Saxons, the horn to stop resounded, and the tents were pitched. Cookfires sparked to life under a ragged blanket of clouds. What shards of sunlight remained soon shied away beneath the western slopes.

Christopher, Leslie, and Teague cleaned Arthur's weapons and armor. They wiped down their own gear, and then Christopher inspected the job the groom had done cleaning and feeding the horses. With that done, he and the others were relieved for the evening.

While Arthur prepared for a meeting with his battle lords, Christopher donned a comfortable pair of breeches and soft linen shirt. He slid off his heavy riding boots and exchanged them for a pair of sandals. Though it was too cold for the open shoes, his toes were sore from a day in the boots. With the king's permission, he borrowed one of Arthur's heavy woolen tabards and wrapped the cloak around himself. He ventured outside, taking a path that would lead him to Doyle's shelter.

Ahead, Lancelot hurried toward Arthur's tent, clutching his own tabard as the wind whipped the garment off his back. "Going to see your friend?" Lancelot asked Christopher as they passed.

"Yes." Then Christopher stopped and turned around. "Lancelot?"

Arthur's champion paused, craned his head, then lifted his brow.

"He did not break formation today, I pray?" Christopher asked.

Lancelot shook his head no, then waved good-bye, obviously too frozen to continue the conversation.

Christopher weaved his way through the tents, noting that most cookfires were unattended. The men who had built the hearths had stayed outside only long enough to cook their meat. He saw one group of infantrymen who had started a fire inside their tent and had cut a smoke hole in the ceiling of the shelter. They would be hating that hole on the next rainy day, for a patch would surely leak; but for the moment, they were the warmest soldiers on the slope.

Once locating the red banner inscribed with a white courser that flew from Lancelot's tent top, it was easy to find Doyle's quarters, which were pitched beside the champion's shelter. Christopher parted the tent flaps and stepped inside.

Phelan and Neil sat on a woolskin blanket and were

inspecting arrows from a small stack that lay between them. A pair of sheep-tallow candles set in the ground at the right and left rear of the tent threw up dim, eerie light. Behind the archers, Doyle lay on his side across his own blanket, staring blankly at one of the candles. He held his flagon in one hand, resting it against his bare chest. He smiled at the sight of Christopher.

"Aren't you cold?" Christopher asked.

"And a good evening to you, squire of the body." His words were meant to be distinct, separate, but Doyle had managed to turn them into a serpent of syllables. He had a blanket of ale keeping him warm; that was apparent. He sat up, his face creasing with pain as his wounded back stretched. The ale hadn't numbed everything yet.

Christopher shuffled past the archers and found a spot on Doyle's blanket. He sloughed off his tabard and cringed as he took in the view of Doyle's back. He had never seen anyone whipped so badly. Christopher couldn't be sure, but if this had happened to him, he too might drink nightly, for the discomfort and dishonor would imprison the act of sleep. He couldn't hold Doyle's affection for the flagon against him. His friend suffered in body and spirit. But Christopher was present to discuss a plan, and unfortunately Doyle was in no condition to do so.

That fact was, however, contrary to Doyle's belief. "I have put the first steps of our plan into action," the archer said.

"We'll talk when you feel better, and we're alone," Christopher said softly.

"We can go," the bird said.

"Yes, we're almost done here," the barbarian added.

"No, no. You stay. Besides, this is not a night to travel. Even between tents."

"There's a dice match in Sawyer's tent. A challenge as it were. And my humble companion and I are going to return with our pouches full of deniers!" explained the jaunty bird.

Christopher nodded. "Then may the blessings of St. George be with you this evening."

"Did you hear that?" the bird asked the barbarian rhetorically. "He's called upon St. George to help us. How can we lose with him on our side?"

"Let no man champion us." The barbarian directed his request to the heavens beyond the tent top.

"Amen," the bird said.

The barbarian scratched his temple. "Is it not blasphemy to bless players in a dice game?" he asked all present.

They exchanged uncertain looks, then nearly in unison, shook their heads no, it couldn't be. It had better not be.

The two archers divided and quivered the arrows, donned their hooded tunics, then bid Christopher and Doyle a good evening.

"Don't forget to wager my shilling!" Doyle shouted to Neil.

The hairy young man nodded, then disappeared through the tent flaps to catch up with Phelan, who had already stepped outside.

Christopher stood, then tied the tent flaps behind the archers. He shivered as a breath of winter slipped under his shirt and chilled him. With new ice clogging his veins, he returned to his seat. "Now what's this you were saying about putting our plan into action? We haven't even talked about a plan."

"We have a plan," Doyle confirmed.

"We do?"

"Indeed."

"Splendid," Christopher said, his voice honed with agitation. "Tell me. Is there any chance I might be able to—KNOW WHAT IT IS?"

Doyle scowled. "I'm right here," was what he wanted to say, but it came out, "I'mrighher."

Christopher took several deep breaths to calm himself. He was cold, not exactly comfortable on the coarse blanket which barely shielded the hard dirt below, and his patience, though heretofore eternal, had suddenly become mortal and had died. He pondered what means of torture he would use on Doyle to get the information out of him, but the already-present horror of his friend's back was enough to make him feel guilty about even thinking of such a thing. Once he had his anger in check, and after promising himself he would not shout again, he asked, "How are we going to catch the varlet of our eye?"

Doyle smiled his Baines-like smile, the one that always made Christopher feel confident and nervous all at the same time. "I spoke to Lancelot, who spoke to my sergeant. I had Innis's position moved; he has the pleasure of serving me. Now he's close. And I can watch him."

For a human ale barrel, Doyle's last was conveyed with surprising clarity. He knew the weight of his words, and forced himself to articulate them correctly.

"Excellent," Christopher agreed. "Now what else do we do?"

"You do nothing. Sleep close to Leslie and that other squire, what is his name?"

"Beague? Or League? Teague?" Christopher would never remember.

"Yes, him. I shall take care of the rest."

"What are you going to do?"

Silence passed between them. Christopher broke it, repeating, "Doyle, what are you—"

"I heard you. It is better I work alone. Now on to other things. Like ladies. Like Brenna. Don't you miss her? You haven't once mentioned her since we've been up here."

"Don't try to escape this," Christopher warned. "I have to know."

"Actually, I don't know what I'm going to do yet. But when I figure it out, I probably won't tell you. So you already know what you need to know." Then, as abrupt as a startled boar, Doyle leapt back onto his other conversational path. "She has wonderful eyes. You *must* miss her."

Though Doyle's insistence on changing the subject once again tried Christopher's patience, he found himself wanting to talk about Brenna, realizing with Doyle's aid that he had been fixed only on the battle, and then the murder attempt by Innis's hired man. Brenna had been locked away in the deepest cell of his mind.

But the battle and the murder attempt weren't the only reasons he had repressed his thoughts of her, and now, as he released her in his mind, the sky blackened into the scorched, guilty steel of God's hammer; it fell and crushed him.

"What is it?" Doyle asked. "You look about to cry."

"She does have wonderful eyes." Christopher focused on the radiating image of Brenna, an innocent angel who floated and pirouetted in his head.

"She'll wait for you this time, Christopher. Even when she courted Innis, I could tell that she still loved you. You could see it in those eyes."

The longer her image stayed with him, the more it hurt. He needed to say something. He needed to tell

Doyle; maybe his friend would be able to justify it. But how? He had done something so unbefitting a squire of the body, so unlike a gentlemen, that perhaps Doyle could not help him. Yet he had to confess his sin, and if there was no abbot available, then Doyle would have to do.

"I have dishonored myself," Christopher began.

"Many times," Doyle interjected matter-of-factly. "Four moons of frolicking to be exact. Oh, what base, vile, happy people you and Marigween were!"

Christopher was dumbfounded. "You knew?"

Doyle flicked Christopher a look that read: do you take me for a fool?

"The example I set," Christopher moaned ruefully, "the king makes me squire of the body, and I court two women at the same time. But I couldn't—" Christopher gasped. "I couldn't stay away from her. I can feel my face nuzzled in her neck right now. And when I think of what I've done to Brenna . . . at the time, I was so enchanted with Marigween, I thought of nothing but her. Even when Brenna visited the castle, I don't know, it was as if that was a separate life, that Marigween and I lived somewhere else. And I caused Brenna no pain and could love her just as well."

"I admire you," Doyle said. He pushed himself into a sitting position and faced Christopher, his eyes reflecting his sincerity. "You are a good person because you feel bad about what you have done. You want to repent your sin. But you were able to win the love of not one, but two *visions*, ladies I could only have up here." Doyle tapped his temple.

"When we return, I must make a decision."

"Yes. Don't make the decision now, for we may not return. A dead man has no problem with ladies, eh?"

Christopher returned a wan grin. "The logic of ale—eh?"

Doyle proffered his flagon; Christopher took it and downed several gulps. He lowered the flagon, then stood. "There is a friend of mine who manages one of our supply carts. I fixed and adjusted a saddle of his once; March and Torrey's poor work, of course. This supply man owes me a favor. A favor of ale, I think, this evening." Christopher winked.

Doyle returned the wink as Christopher donned his cloak, then he left the tent to fetch the ale.

8   Christopher and Doyle spent several hours drinking and talking of the battlefield, the conversation keeping Christopher's mind off of Brenna, Marigween, and Innis. When the ale was gone and the bird and barbarian returned from their blessed though unsuccessful dice game, Christopher left the tent feeling fifty pounds lighter, bound for the comfort of five layers of wool inside the king's tent.

He had shambled only one hundred yards when he felt hands pull him backward and boots slam into his heels. The ground came up and smote him rudely across the shoulders and back. Fortunately, the castle of Shores's best brew absorbed the impact; there was only a thick vibration through his body that echoed twice and was gone. He lay there, his breath steaming, his eyes performing feats of wizardry. The sky spun and collided with the ground. The clouds rolled by, huge white breakers in a blue-black tempest. He closed his eyes, reopened them, and found the sky slowing to a halt. When he tried to pull himself up, he discovered he was trapped. He forced a glance over his head. A boy he recognized as a varlet in the Vaward Battle pinned Christopher's arms down from the rear.

A shadow cast by a nearby cookfire stretched over Christopher. He adjusted his gaze and saw Innis towering over him. The varlet stared down with a grin that begged to be smacked off.

Had he been sober, it would have been a terrifying moment; but as it was Christopher felt irritated. His mind worked very simply at the moment, telling him that he would have to wait before being able to slip comfortably under his blankets and fall asleep. He didn't want to wait, he wanted to go right to bed, and why were these people stopping him? Oh, yes, they wanted to kill him. But it was Innis, a fool who would spend half the night delivering his harangue before putting Christopher to rest.

He blinked, trying to focus on Innis, but his eyes had reverted to casting spells, and he found it even harder to see anything clearly. He spoke to the blur above him. "If it is a fray you want, why not wait until the morrow?"

The mass of fluctuating flesh that was Innis answered, "You smell. And we do not honor the requests of filthy, stinking bailey sweepers."

"Have you no honor as a gentleman? It is plain to see that I am in no condition to fight, and wish only to sleep now, dear St. George. But I forget, you are no gentleman. You are a foul wretch whose heart would make a splendid sheath for my blade." Christopher amazed himself with his words. The ale had fostered a whole new boldness in him.

Innis knelt, pinning Christopher's legs under his knees. As Innis got closer, Christopher was better able to see the varlet—not that he appreciated the view. "I *will* kill you."

"No, you won't. You're an ass who hires others to do your obscene work. You haven't the stomach nor the courage to risk your freedom—and perhaps your life—to kill me."

Innis reached back and withdrew his anlace. Christopher was able to admire the workmanship of the dagger a moment before the varlet put it under his neck. It was characteristic of Innis to carry a bejeweled quiver and an expensive anlace meant for show onto the battlefield. It was a very nice blade indeed, the blade that would kill Christopher.

"What if someone comes?" Innis's friend warned.

The varlet's gaze investigated the tents around them, then lowered to Christopher. "They're all asleep."

"As I should be!" Christopher shouted, startling Innis and the other varlet. It was odd, how his desire for sleep so outweighed his fear.

"The watchman could've heard him!"

Christopher could not see Innis's accomplice, but he suspected the boy's complexion had faded several shades.

"Stop worrying!" Innis stage-whispered. "He didn't."

"You there!"

Christopher felt the heaviness come off his arms, and suddenly he was lifted haphazardly to his feet.

Innis and his friend steadied Christopher as Innis spoke immediately to the dirty-faced watchman before them. "I'm afraid our friend has been a little too generous with himself this evening, sir. He fell and could not get up. As luck would have it, we happened upon him."

The watchman was a tired, doleful man on the unforgiving side of forty, a farmer ordered into service and grieving every moment of it. The lack of intonation in his voice confirmed that truth. "I do not care what you do, what your problems are, what this boy was doing down there, or anything else. What I do care about is noise being made on my watch. Go back to your tents."

"Watchman, I am Christopher of Shores, the king's senior squire—and these dolts assailed me." Christopher tugged his arms free of the varlets' grasp, then stepped back, lost his balance but did not fall. Like a tightrope walker, he raised his arms and recovered.

"I don't want to know that," the watchman said. "I want you to go back to your tents. The more noise you make, the less I can hear the Saxons. Is that what you want?"

"Are you listening to me?" Christopher asked. "I could report you to the king."

Disgusted, the watchman threw his hands up in the air, snorted, then turned and walked back toward a pair of nearby tents. He repeated, "Go back to your tents." Then added, "And if you want to report me, do so. Maybe the gallows tree is the only way out of this for me."

Christopher frowned, shook his head, then regarded Innis, fixing him with a steely look. "Another failed attempt. You could have done it. But you hesitated. There may be hope for you after all."

"I meant what I said," Innis countered through gritted teeth. "I'm going to kill you."

"Isn't there something else to occupy your time?"

Innis decided he would argue no further, and in a huff, whisked off with his plebe in tight tow.

Christopher groped for his balance as he watched them leave. He resumed his trek toward Arthur's tent. Less than a score of steps later, he fell down on

his side, then rolled over onto his back. He laughed
at himself as his eyes took in the shifting image of the
waning gibbous moon. He saw a female silhouette
against the white-and-black orb. He stopped laughing. It was Brenna. The shape of the head. The long
hair. He had made no mistake. He blinked, and then
it was only the dark stains of the moon, the all too
familiar patterns. Christopher sat up, stood, pitched
back and forth until he had relative stability, then
staggered forward. His eyes welled with tears and his
lower lip trembled. When he drank, he would feel
high spirits or sorrow, and anything would uncork
one or the other. He discovered happiness in the simplest things, pain in the most innocent, unassuming
places. The moon reminded him of Brenna, of the
many nights they had stared at it together; but
Brenna reminded him of Marigween. He shuffled
along feeling guilty and in love with Brenna and lust-
ing for Marigween and maybe loving her too. His
emotions were in conflict; they made him pity himself
and curse the life he had chosen.

9

Orvin wondered what Marigween would think
of his morning stew. He sat on his stool outside the
stable and stirred the brew with a wooden ladle. The
fresh faggots he'd added to the fire below the hanging
cauldron brought the goulash to a steaming bubble as
the horn of tierce echoed the breakfast call from the
distant fortress. He fancied himself a good cook, but
Orvin and Christopher had had many a debate regarding the notion. Though Christopher thought that most

of Orvin's dishes tasted good, they never smelled edible. And a good cook's cooking ought to smell like something, Christopher had argued.

Facing him, in his loft above the stable, Marigween set down the bread, ale, and pork he had requested. She descended the ladder and came from the shadows into the pure, clean light of day. It was the deepest azure sky above Shores in nearly a moon. The clouds extended their limbs somewhere else, and the temperature was mild compared to most winter days.

As Marigween approached, Orvin reminded himself of Christopher's description of the stew, that it smelled like boiling shoe leather. The closer Marigween got, the more her expression confirmed that sentiment.

"I know, it smells bad, but here"—Orvin lifted a ladleful of broth out of the cauldron—"try some. You will be surprised."

Marigween's delicate face knotted. She shivered as she took the ladle from Orvin. She closed her eyes and quickly sampled the stew. Her eyes opened and her lips curled into a grin of approval. "You're right." She returned the utensil to Orvin and eyed the cauldron with curiosity. "How can it taste so good when—"

"It smells this bad, I know. Christopher asked me that."

"He did?" Marigween's eyes were lit by more than the sun.

"Indeed."

"We even think alike," she observed.

"I found the same was true of my wife and me," Orvin said, floating along on happy memories of himself and Donella residing in the castle, him training young Hasdale to fence. "Sometimes there would be no words between us. We would just *know* what the other thought. That happens after you live with someone for a long time."

"I would like to discover that," she said, turning as a stiff breeze caught her long, red kirtle and lifted it off her shift. She forced her kirtle down, then lowered her hood and let the current blow through her red locks.

Orvin, as he had before and always would, found it easy to melt into her beauty. But he had forgotten to fetch Marigween a stool, and the bowls and spoons. He rose, then realized he needed help. Marigween saw his need and hurriedly took his hand.

"I forgot a few things inside," he said.

"I'll go," she insisted. "The bowls and spoons, yes?"

"And a stool for yourself," Orvin added.

"I cannot sit on your lap?" she asked daringly, then walked toward the stable.

Orvin was speechless. His face grew warm. He sat there, wondering if she meant what she had said. No, no, no, she had only flirted with him, but her frankness had left him stunned . . . and entranced. She returned with the stool, bowls, and spoons, sat down, then took Orvin's ladle out of the old man's hand.

"Not too much for me," Orvin said. "My stomach is soft enough already."

She smiled. "Come now, Orvin, you cannot hide your passion for food from me. You fight winter wind for your precious loaves." She filled his bowl and handed it to him. "There."

Orvin concentrated on chewing quietly as he watched Marigween fill her own bowl to nearly overflowing. "I'm glad the scent has not curbed your appetite."

"Oh, no. I could eat all day."

When they had finished their meal, Orvin pointed to

an old flax-beating bench he had converted into a sitting place. The bench sat under the edge of a knot of large oaks on the far side of the dirt path. They crossed to the seat and took the weight off their feet. Orvin could not remember feeling more content, or in better company. Behind them, they heard an old sawyer from the sawmill chopping down a tree to soak for hardening over the winter, the rhythm of his ax a soft, distant heartbeat. Within the stable, the hostlers fed the rounseys; the horses neighed softly as they received their dried hay. Overhead, the pipits sang a sweet, tranquil song that Orvin often listened to for hours.

"You have kept your end of the bargain," he began. "And so now, you want to hear about Christopher."

Marigween adjusted herself on the bench so that she faced Orvin. "How did you meet him?"

In his mind's eye, Orvin watched two of Hasdale's horsemen ride into the castle's outer bailey. A young, injured boy sat behind one of the cavalry men. "It was very sad, that day. We had been attacked by the Saxons."

"If you don't want to go on . . . "

"I will," Orvin said. "But I wonder, why is it you need to know so much about him?" Orvin tested her. How much would she tell him? How deeply did she feel?

"I won't hide my feelings from you," she confessed. "And I don't think I have. It's easy to say I love him because I do."

Orvin smiled over her innocence. "I knew you remained uncourted for him, but love? How can you love someone you barely know?"

Marigween rose, turned around before Orvin, and lifted her kirtle.

"What are you doing?" Orvin asked, terrified that

someone might see her. After her comment about sitting on his lap, he did not know what to expect.

Holding the hem of her kirtle up to her breasts, she smoothed the fine linen fabric of her shift over her belly.

Though she was only a few moons along, the circular motion Marigween made with her hand indicated to Orvin the shocking news: she knew Christopher a lot better than he had thought. A whole lot better.

"Oh dear St. George," Orvin muttered.

"Only my chambermaids know," Marigween said, "and they have sworn to secrecy."

"And you are telling me this child is Christopher's?"

She nodded.

Orvin bolted to his feet. It hurt to stand so quickly, but his stiff spine was days away from his mind. "Then all of this, what is this for? For you to come and make a confession to me? I'm not an abbot! Sweet Marigween, don't you realize what you've done? You've committed a great sin!"

Marigween dropped her kirtle—and her smile. "I know that. And it makes me feel terrible. But I'm going to have a child. I cannot change that."

The stupidity of youth left Orvin baffled. "What does Christopher think about your . . . condition?"

"He doesn't know," Marigween said.

"So he may return to find he has a child. What a cruel thing to do to a young man. And you, if word of this gets out, I think Lord Woodward will personally order your burning."

"I thought you would be happy with this news. I wanted to come to you for so long; it was fate we ran into each other in the kitchen. And seeing you made me realize that I should tell you."

"My knowing doesn't matter," Orvin said, his hands trembling. "You and Christopher have made a grave mistake in the name of lust!"

"No. It was love," Marigween snapped. "And you make it sound as if it were all my fault."

"Do you know of Christopher's other love, Brenna?" Orvin hated hurting Christopher, but the boy had already fallen down the well of sin. Perhaps he shouldn't have mentioned Brenna, but he had to prove to Marigween that she had mislayed her senses, involving herself so completely with a boy as fickle and quixotic as Christopher.

"He never spoke of her—but I knew. And I did not care."

"So you lured him away," Orvin accused.

"He came willingly," she shot back. Marigween's eyes ringed with tears, and she broke into a sob as she returned to her seat.

Her crying breached Orvin's wall of logic: it made him feel miserable for the way he had spoken to her. He could not place blame, or accuse one or the other of being a fool. Both had made the mistake. The problem was before them, and Orvin sensed that she did not know what to do. She must have come to him for guidance, and what had he just offered her? Reproof. Orvin realized the tables had been turned and he was the fool.

The old fool gently placed his hand on Marigween's shoulder, but she recoiled from his touch. "I . . . I am sorry." He reached out farther, and again placed his hand on her; this time she did not flinch. "I fear for you now. What are you going to do?"

Marigween raised her head and looked at him. Her eyes were red, the lids swollen, her lids swollen, her lips rolled in tightly. She shook her head as a fit of sobbing seized her once more. Orvin took her in his arms. Marigween pressed her head against his shoulder and continued to cry.

He was right. She did not know what to do. And at the moment, he felt the same.

10 The Quantock Hills lay in a fury southwest

of their brothers, the Mendip Hills. They scowled at the Bristol channel to the north and were paid homage by the timid rivers Yeo and Parrett to the south and east, respectively. The Quantock Hills were not gracious to company, Seaver knew, but that had not stopped Kenric from choosing them as a camp. The Quantocks could not be more remote and foreboding, but they easily cloaked the twentyscore men of Kenric's army within one of their wooded valleys. There were no Celt armies scouring these slopes for Saxon invaders; the nearest breathing Englishman was nearly ten days' ride to the south, and five to the east.

Seaver, Cuthbert, and Ware rode up the rude slopes, the wind an icy Celtic curse grappling their shoulders. The ground was hard, and Seaver knew his rounsey's legs were tiring under the shock, but he would not have to drive the horse much farther.

A thin mantle of snow, melted away to reveal brown patches of dirt here and there, painted a bleak, listless picture around them. The forest had gone to the world of specters, the leafless, snow-covered limbs of the oaks and beech trees resembling bones instead of wood. Save for the wind and the clumping

of their horses, the slope was silent. No chirps from
sparrows or cries from crows or meadow pipits met
their expectant ears. The birds were tucked inside
their nests, smart enough to recognize a dark-spirited
day when they saw one.

As they neared the crest of the slope, four watch-
men wrapped in heavy woolskins, their longbows
nocked with arrows and drawn back, appeared from
the wood and alarmed them.

Seaver ripped off his hood, and recognizing one of
the the men, called out to him. "Farman! We return!"

"Seaver!" Farman called back, then turned to his
comrade. "Sound the horn of their return."

They continued on past the watchman to the crest of
the slope, then paused to look down on the valley that
had become their home. The forest below was dense,
and in a few of the clearings they made out a spatter-
ing of tent tops, though the actual number of shelters
far exceeded that visible. Many cookfires were surely
lit, but the strong wind swept clear the betraying
smoke trails. Seaver's people were there, deep below
the ivory boughs of a protective, winter mother. They
descended the slope as the watchman's horn
announced them.

Once in the valley, they dismounted and were
treated to large portions of sweet leveret, boiled potatoes, and tankards of spiced, hot wine. The provisions had been pillaged, of course, from one of the
many ports that dappled the coastline of the Bristol
channel. With their bellies full and their hearts
warmed-over from being home, the scouts retired to
their tents for a late afternoon nap.

Some hours later, Seaver was awakened by Manton,
Kenric's second-in-command. The reserved man tugged
absently on his thin gray beard as he told Seaver it was

time to make his report to Kenric. Seaver donned his
padded tunic and topped it with a heavy woolskin cloak,
thankful he was able to be warmed by the garment.
Woolskin was far too light-colored for him to have worn
during his journey to Shores, and they had no dye to
remedy the problem. As he left his tent, Seaver made a
mental note, adding dye to the list of things he wanted
from the castle and its accompanying village.

Kenric's tent was lavish by Saxon standards. Four
pole torches impaled the ground at each of the shelter's
exterior four corners, creating more than enough light
to make Seaver's approach under the purpling sky of
twilight. The heavy leather that made up the tent was
double-layered, an expensive extravagance that afforded
Kenric a draftless sleep. Seaver admired the tent a
moment before entering, ran a finger along the outer
flap, then ducked inside.

His leader sat behind a small Celt table once used
for playing that odd, and most curious game they
called chess. The tall, broad-shouldered man picked
dirt from under his nails with an anlace, and he did
not look up as he motioned silently for Seaver to take
the empty stool opposite him. Seaver complied and
sat waiting as Kenric finished cleaning his pinky nail.
Seaver let his gaze play over the interior of the tent:
the many skins that warmed its floors; the plundered
traveling trunk that lay open boasting an assortment
of small arms within its walls; the many pieces of
looted armor that Kenric liked to wear into battle;
and, most particularly, the young nymph who lay
nude, tied, and gagged on the triple layer of wool
blankets that was Kenric's bed. The Celt girl looked
at Seaver with eyes dull from pain. It appeared she
had long ago given up and was resigned to her fate.
Seaver knew Kenric would not kill her; Kenric would

slay his best fighter before murdering a beautiful woman. If his master had a weakness, Seaver knew what it was. The affliction was common.

"I *should* be anxious to hear what you have to tell me. I *should* be excited, thrilled, or worried. Why is it I feel completely at peace now, Seaver?"

The little man hated when his master asked cryptic questions, for he could never supply the right answers—but was expected to. "You already know what I'm going to tell you."

"No. The spirits came to me in my sleep last night. One of them was my father." Kenric stood; he was a head taller than most of his men, but to a short man like Seaver, he seemed gargantuan. He raked fingers through his short, curly, ink black hair, cut for him by his personal groom, then clapped his hands together. "My father told me we would grasp victory, that the Celt's time was over here. I could almost feel him stroke my hair." Again, Kenric ran his hand through his hair, then added, "I have never felt more calm in my entire life."

Seaver nodded. His own specters came to him as often, but they brought warnings and frightful images of death. Kenric was twice blessed; once with kind specters, and second with ones he knew. Seaver wished he had known his own father, but not even an apparition of the man had been revealed to him. Then again, maybe it was better that the man had died before Seaver was born. He might have discovered that his father was a lout who could never live up to Seaver's expectations. The imaginary image he had created of the man was best. Father was tall. He was strong. Kenric paled in comparison to him.

"I'm ready to hear your report," Kenric said.

Wrenched from his introspection, Seaver took a

deep breath and began, though he would not have to say much. "You were right, lord."

There was no reaction from Kenric; he kept his joy in check. His eyes narrowed with further thought. "Numbers."

"One hundred and twenty men on the perimeter. I believe another one hundred within the keep."

"Elevenscore. What about the peasant levy?"

"The villages they call Shores and Falls are occupied by women and children and the few who were too old to fight. We saw no others. Even their great marketplace in Falls was barren. It was as if we had already attacked."

Kenric moved around the table, then hunkered before Seaver, their gazes aligned. "Do you understand what this means?"

"The castle of Shores will be ours. And if Durwin's scouts find the castle of Rain as vulnerable, it too will be ours."

"No," Kenric said, lowering his voice to a faint whisper, "it means you and I will live forever in both worlds."

The excitement had finally roped around Kenric's soul. His soft tones carried with them the grandeur of the future, the promise that they would become immortal. It made Seaver feel very big, as if he could reach up, grab a cloud, and nibble on it like a sweet pasty. As he walked the land, his footprints would fill with rain and become lakes, and the mountains would be his pillows at night.

Kenric gestured to the nymph behind them. "Take her as a gift of thanks. And as an apology. Now I believe what Kenneth told me so long ago. You are the best scout our people will ever have."

His spirit set aloft by the wind of Kenric's words, Seaver regarded the Celt woman. Though comely by his standards, she did not excite him. Her height, though average, somehow stripped away her beauty and left him bored, uninterested. But he would not insult Kenric, nor dampen his own joy. He would take her, give her as a gift to Ware for a job well-done. Cuthbert, on the other hand, was an oaf. It would be many more missions before that young scout received a gift from him.

Seaver bowed in respect before his master. "Thank you, lord."

11

For four moons Christopher rode at Arthur's side as they played a cat-and-mouse game with the Saxons on the Mendip Hills. Arthur's plan was to drive the invaders over the Mendips to the Bristol channel, where on its shores he would finish them. Christopher was concerned that the farther they pursued the five hundred fleeing Saxons, the more separated they became from the other armies. Nolan and Woodward were far to the west near Brent Knoll, Uryens and Leondegrance at least three days' ride to the east. He voiced his fear, but it fell on deaf ears. Arthur lectured Christopher on his experience, on the fact that they outnumbered the Saxons two to one, that if they didn't make an ultimate show of force, the problem would never end. And, of course, Arthur's solution was the only way.

Doyle kept Innis in check. The varlet did not make a single attempt against Christopher. It seemed Innis's temper had cooled, and Christopher urged Doyle to let the problem fade away, but Doyle took

great pleasure in his verbal torture of the varlet, and
after a while it seemed that Innis and Doyle had
become the true enemies, Christopher drifting to the
periphery. But Christopher never lost sight of the fact
that Innis had promised to kill him. He had learned
moons ago to become a light sleeper, and every crack
of flame, gust of wind, footstep of watchman alerted
him in the wee hours.

It was Easter day on the Mendip Hills, a day of
rest, meditation, and, in the evening, a celebration of
the Resurrection of Christ. There would be no Easter
matin service because of the absence of clergy, but
Arthur asked the army to fill their hearts and heads
with the memories of past services, and even sang
part of an Easter trope he had memorized. The song
brought to life a vivid picture of Christopher's old
chapel back in Shores. As he listened, he remembered his mother and father. They had taken him
many times to the chapel, and he had always sneaked
outside to marvel at the carvings of beasts on the
building's outer walls. It had been a place full of
happy memories, but then was eternally blighted by
his discovery of their bodies there. Though
Christopher shed no tears, his soul mourned.

Arthur modestly avoided speaking of another fact:
it was also the day he had become king sixteen years
ago. Lancelot chipped in that reminder, and a cheer
erupted from everyone. With raised tankards, the
army toasted its king.

There was a third reason to celebrate, but
Christopher would not reveal it to anyone. On Easter
day, Christ had risen from the dead, Arthur had
pulled Excalibur from the stone, and Christopher of
Shores had been born. He felt insignificant compared
to the competition, and in past years had told only a

select few that Easter was his birthday. Of every man on the Mendip Hills, only one other knew.

"Happy birthday," Doyle said as he joined Christopher and Leslie around their afternoon cookfire. "I've been thinking of something to give you all morning. I didn't bring much with me up here. I'll get you a present when we return."

Leslie pitched Christopher a curious stare. "You never mentioned it was—"

"I'm sorry," Doyle said. "I forgot you don't like—"

"It's not that I don't like to talk about it," Christopher explained. "It is as I said, not important. Christ rose from the dead this day. Arthur became king."

"And the great squire Christopher of Shores was born!" Leslie stood and brought the tankard he nursed up in a toast.

Doyle rose, his gaze darting for a tankard he could lift. Christopher frowned and handed Doyle his own. As the junior squire and archer toasted him, Christopher lowered his head. It was absurd to feel ashamed on one's birthday, but he could not escape the significance of the other events.

"What's this?"

Christopher looked up and saw Arthur, who was shirtless and beaming as he stepped over to them from the tent.

Doyle found his seat and returned the tankard to Christopher, knowing better than to explain what they were doing to the king.

Leslie was another story. "My liege, Christopher surprises us all. He tells us that this very day is his birthday."

As Arthur's brow rose, two mounted scouts galloped toward him from the south, dodging cookfires and tent poles, leaving a steady stream of scrambling, swearing soldiers in their muddy wake.

Shading the sun from his eyes, Christopher stood and strained for a better look. It was not long before the scouts reined to a thundering halt near Arthur.

One of the men vaulted off his black rounsey and tore off his leather hood. "My lord," the scout began, out of breath, "I bring the worst news possible."

Another pair of mounted scouts descended from the north and reined in their steeds.

"Tell me."

The sound of screaming men pervaded Christopher's ears. He cocked his head to the west, saw three more mounted scouts charging through the campsites of infantrymen on a desperate ride toward the king.

"Another Saxon army numbering as many as ten-score men lies less than a day's ride behind us!" the first scout cried.

Arthur turned to the scouts who had arrived from the north, his face gripped with tension. "Do you confirm this?"

One of the northern scouts replied, "No. But we come to report that the invaders we've been driving toward the channel are not fleeing but have turned back and are marching toward us!"

Christopher could only stand in choked horror as the edifice of power Arthur had built crumbled around the man.

Arthur pivoted to the scouts from the west as they arrived and doffed their headgear.

"My sovereign lord. We count nearly two hundred invaders a half day's ride away. They must've hidden in one of the valleys and been waiting for us. They are moving."

"Have Nolan and Woodward's scouts spotted them?"

"I do not know, lord."

At the sound of more horses, Arthur turned again, this time facing the east.

It had become of circle of frightened, mounted men, with the king spinning helplessly in the middle. A scout from the east shouted, "We spied on a new army, my lord. They seem to have appeared from nowhere!"

"How many?" Arthur demanded.

"We believe five- or sixscore of men!"

Christopher plotted the parlous news in his head. They were one thousand men, about to be attacked by five hundred in the north, another two hundred in the south, and approximately another two hundred in the east, and the same number in the west. The Saxons' battle plan was perfection through simplicity. And the question burned like bile: How had the eastern and western Saxon armies slipped by them? Or was one of the scouts right—that they had always been there?

Arthur bit down on a knuckle as he thought. Christopher, Leslie, and Doyle all shared apprehensive looks. Doyle suddenly fled the group, breaking into a sprint for the Vaward camp.

"You men from the west and the east," Arthur said, his voice cracking, "you will try to slip past the invaders and enlist the aid of our brothers beyond them. Go now!"

The scouts wheeled their horses around and heeled off.

"Now you," Arthur said to the remaining men, "you will divide and scout all directions. Report as many times as you can to our battle lords. God be with you."

As the scouts separated and hurried away, Arthur pounded his fist into his palm. He jerked himself around, hunting for answers on the ground, the tents, the cookfire, the sky. His army lay as bare as his back, and Christopher could find no words to allay the king's agony. In fact, he shuddered with confirmation. He had been on a campaign sprung of vengeance before. The first time he had been too naive to recognize the portents; but during the past moons he had seen death coming, had admonished his sovereign, and now stood on his birthday, satisfied and doomed because he was right.

PART TWO

THE FALL OF SHORES

1   The castle of Shores stood in green-and-gray innocence above the horizon as Kenric's army dispersed and initiated the first step of their attack.

Seaver led a group of twoscore men through the farmland that lay between the thick wood in the distance and the River Cam. They stomped, cut, tore, and smashed the young vegetables and fruit that would have been the summer's harvest. Torches were dropped in the dryer fields, decimating the wheat. Fruit trees were hacked apart, and the plow-pulling oxen were killed and left to rot.

It was a far more organized attack than any Seaver had witnessed. His former leader Garrett had been one for storming the curtain walls of the castle and ignoring the village and its surrounding land altogether. And when that had failed, he had concentrated on the village. Presently, Kenric's plan incorporated both. The attack was slow, but systematic—a war of attrition.

With the fields destroyed, Seaver's group moved on to the farmhouse and set its straw-thatched roof ablaze. Any of the already-smoked meat, milk, butter, and cream stored there was plundered and added to the Saxon's already abundant supplies. The chickens, pigs, and sheep penned around the farmhouse were slaughtered, and the drinking well was filled with dung. Hay carts were dismantled, churns cracked open, and any other working instruments they could find were destroyed. Seaver even caught one man smashing a bench.

The farmer's wife and her two children were unfortunately at home, and they were mercilessly axed and left to burn with their house.

Seaver's group left an afternoon's worth of bloody eradication behind them. They advanced into the burgeoning darkness of the wood. Beyond was the practice field, and to the south, the village of Shores.

2 Orvin had felt ill all morning. He'd gone down from the loft to take a bit of pottage Marigween had prepared for him, but after filling his belly, a vise of pain had squeezed his innards. He lay in his narrow bed, occasionally staring out the window, where presently he spied a thick pillar of smoke dividing the western sky.

"Marigween!" he shouted.

"Yes? Are you all right?"

"Come up here! Quickly!"

"Not so quickly," she said.

Marigween had found it increasingly difficult to ascend the ladder into the loft, for with the passing of every moon, her baby had grown. Though he was no midwife, Orvin estimated she was about two moons away from delivery.

He waited a brief, but impatient moment before she appeared on the top of the ladder. "Look," he said, pointing at the smoke.

Wincing, she moved to the window and lowered

her head to peer out. "It looks as if they're burning their fields."

"With a little help from the Saxons," Orvin said.

She regarded him, looking baffled. "Saxons? How? Arthur hunts them on the Mendips."

"Why didn't I heed the warning?" Orvin asked himself aloud.

"What warning?"

"I saw it. Or rather felt it. In my stomach this morning. There had been nothing in the skies yesterday. I had searched them. Why? Why does the omen come so late?"

Marigween frowned. "I have never believed in your omens and never will. It is not the Saxons. The farmers are up to something; I don't know what."

Orvin gave her a fateful stare. "I've been able to hide you here from Lord Woodward, but I cannot hide you from the Saxons."

Marigween's chin lifted in defiance. "I cannot listen anymore. You do not feel well. Your illness attacks your mind, and your eyes." She started for the ladder.

Orvin sat up and threw off his wool blanket. A score of invisible arrows penetrated his belly. He pushed his body right and set his frail feet on the wooden floor. Timbers and bones creaked as he stood. His ankles received his stomach, or at least it felt that way.

"What are you doing?" she asked, about to descend.

"We cannot stay here."

The approaching rumble of a large, unseen number of horses shifted Marigween's attention to the road below.

Three of the hostlers who tended the rounseys and coursers ran from their duties in the stalls and vanished beyond the main stable door.

Orvin grabbed Marigween's wrist as an agonizing cry from the road met their ears. More cries joined in, a shrill harmony of hostlers losing their lives. It was obvious what was going on outside, but to Orvin's amazement, Marigween still wanted to descend the ladder.

"No," he ordered curtly, strengthening his grip on her.

"What's happening?" she cried.

"Shush."

Orvin pulled Marigween away from the edge of the loft. He retrieved the broadsword that he kept standing in the corner near his bed, then pulled the blade from its leather sheath. The weapon was caked with dust. He should have stayed in practice, should have exercised his muscles. Once a great knight, he knew his appearance and his skills were now weathered. He prayed they would not be spotted.

Sword in hand, Orvin led Marigween to the opposite corner of the loft, where they hid behind one of two tall piles of dried hay stored there.

A pregnant young woman and a wrinkled old man. That's what they were. Orvin sighed through a shiver as he helped Marigween sit down, then lowered his own brittle frame.

They heard the horses bucking and neighing in their stalls, then the high-pitched wails as each was put to death. Tears stained Marigween's cheeks as she listened to the mounts being butchered. Orvin had grown quite fond of two of the animals and grimaced as he imagined them being killed.

Finally, there was stillness. Moments beat. The air hinted of a new smell; Orvin inhaled deeply through his nose. He knew the difference between burning faggots and burning timbers. The stables were on fire. Marigween's face registered the new alarm, and she tried to push herself up, bracing her back along the side wall of the loft. Orvin stood, set his sword down, then took her hands. Feeling his arms vibrate under the strain but ignoring it, Orvin got Marigween to her feet. They had to move.

The old knight bent down to fetch his sword, and as he did, he heard the sound of someone ascending the ladder. He scooped up the blade and moved to peer from behind the hay.

The invader was young, with only the trace of a beard, and hair that was straighter than usual for a Saxon. His only weapon was a dagger sheathed and bound on his leather belt. He cocked his head, saw Orvin's bed, the clothes trunk footing it, and the scrolls lying alongside. The Saxon wandered over.

Orvin was eager to make the Saxon's curiosity fatal, but how many more lay below? A cry from the man would bring his brothers, and that would surely be the end of himself and Marigween. Perhaps it was better not to force a confrontation, but to wait until the Saxons were satisfied with their destruction and had moved on—hopefully before the flames or the smoke or both overcame Marigween and himself.

Orvin's muscles tightened as he watched the Saxon rummage through his trunk, study then discard his scrolls, rise and take another look around.

Then Orvin saw it: his sheath, carelessly left on his bed. He hoped fervently the invader would leave before noticing it. But the barbarian's eyes came to rest on the leather sword cover. The man picked it up, then realized that someone might be present— and armed. In one precise motion, the Saxon turned toward the piles of hay while drawing his dagger.

The hilt of Orvin's broadsword was slippery with

sweat. He could not get a good grip on the weapon. The Saxon stepped closer. Orvin's heart staggered and tried to convince his body to recoil. His arms quivered, and a steady hot pain wrestled with his lower back.

For a second he looked at Marigween. She cowered in an attempt to dissolve through the wall behind her. He could hear her short, uncontrolled gasps, sounds that only swelled his terror.

The Saxon was also afraid. His body was bent in an attack stance, his steps slow and apprehensive, his gaze repeatedly sweeping the room.

Orvin had to make a decision. If he leapt out, he would own the element of surprise, but he had already considered the problems of engaging the man. It was too risky. They had to go unnoticed.

He skulked back and joined Marigween at the wall. The Saxon chose to probe the hay pile on his left, and as he did, Orvin and Marigween took cover behind the right pile, but this exposed themselves to the stable below. Any Saxon who entered the building would see them.

The soldier continued his investigation, stepping completely around the left pile. They heard the floor timbers betray his advance. Orvin ventured a furtive glance beyond their pile to see how close the barbarian was—

—and found himself staring directly into the Saxon's eyes. The two men were no more than a dagger's length apart. Both gasped.

Orvin thrust his broadsword forward, but the Saxon gripped the blade with his bare hand and pulled it past him with Orvin still on it.

A stinging pain sent Orvin's hand to his shoulder. The Saxon had swiped him with his dagger. Orvin's palm came up bloody, but the cut, though long, was not deep. He spun and faced the invader.

The Saxon grinned as he wiped the sweat off his forehead with his arm. Orvin knew the man found it amusing to take on one so old and frail. Orvin gambled that experience in this case would overcome strength— though the odds of the game were steeply against him.

The lessons of combat Orvin had taught Christopher would be practiced now. It was time for the teacher to demonstrate his own skills. To act and not think, to rely on all the senses and not only the eyes, to become as fluid and easy as a gentle stream. He remembered when Christopher had fought Dallas. It had been broadsword against dagger—as it presently was—and Dallas had thrown the dagger. He would be wary of a similar maneuver from the Saxon.

Though the old knight had a greater reach with his broadsword, the Saxon boldly feinted right, then dodged left, trying to get in close to stab him. Orvin parried the Saxon's blade with his own. The edge of his dusty broadsword slid down the dagger, jumped over the small blade's hilt guard, and bit the invader's fingers. The Saxon wailed and swore.

Orvin flipped a look to the stable below and saw no other Saxons. What he did see was the eastern wall of the stable above its two-yard stone base being devoured by flames. Smoke rose to the ceiling and floated toward the loft.

Pulsing visibly with vengeance, the Saxon stormed toward Orvin. The old man tried to flee the advance but was too slow. The invader collided with him and both plunged toward the floor. Orvin felt the broadsword slip from his grip as he hit the timbers. His vision cleared in time to see the Saxon rear back his arm and, with the dagger sticking from the bottom of his fist, he was prepared to slam it home into Orvin's heart. Orvin raised both hands and they connected with the Saxon's wrist, locking around it. He fought with every shred of strength he could muster from his ancient frame, but the blade fell steadily closer toward his chest.

He heard the shuffle of footsteps, then saw Marigween come up behind the soldier. In a flash, she slid her arm under his neck and yanked his head back.

The Saxon withdrew the weight from Orvin's hands, tore his dagger arm free. He reached back with the blade and slashed Marigween across her cheek. The young woman fell backward, and as the invader turned to see whom he had injured, Orvin rolled his body left and threw the Saxon. In the seconds of freedom the maneuver bought him, he crawled away and searched for his broadsword. Orvin hurt in places he had never hurt before, and his body wept, begged him to stop, but his mind overrode everything. There. There it was. He came up with the blade.

Marigween lay on her side, blood seeping below the palm she pressed to her cheek. She whimpered like a whipped dog and was oblivious of the Saxon creeping toward her.

Curtains of smoke obscured and choked the air, and Orvin struggled for breath. If he and Marigween didn't leave soon, the Saxon wouldn't matter. Sudden panic caused sudden action. He rushed behind the advancing Saxon, and, as the man cocked his head, Orvin sank his broadsword squarely into the Saxon's left shoulder. The blade tip sought and found the man's heart. The barbarian hit the floor, exhaled his last breath, and voided himself. The fire did little to weaken the stench.

Marigween's whimpering was cut off by her coughing. Orvin shuddered as he came upon her, not realizing she had bled so much. The right side of her beige kirtle was soaked down to her waist, the blood on her neck and hand still wet and shiny. She shrieked as he grabbed her free hand and lifted her to her feet. Orvin assumed the pain originated from her cheek, but she bent over, clutching her swollen stomach.

No. Orvin didn't want to believe it. They were in the loft of a blazing stable, having just killed a Saxon, and Marigween, slashed and covered with blood, was going into labor. No, it was not labor, only those normal pains women sometimes get during their final stages of pregnancy.

"Orvin! It hurts! I think it's the baby!"

Maybe these were not the normal pains.

In all his years, Orvin had never been more challenged. If only the challenge had come when he was younger. . . . He would face any fighting man in exchange for a way out of the moment. And yet there wasn't time for self-pity. He had to get her down that ladder. And it seemed impossible.

Orvin's eyes burned as he went to the edge of the loft and checked the ladder; it was still in place, but the bottom two rungs had caught fire. There was no reason to ask Marigween if she could make it. She had to. Or die.

He went back to her side and led her to the edge. She remained hunched over, able to withstand the pain that way. Orvin pivoted and, facing her, lowered himself three rungs down. Coughing and spitting, he turned her around and guided her left foot onto the first rung, then her right foot. They continued the painfully slow process until, four rungs from the bottom, Orvin leapt off. He hit the stable floor, steadied himself, then tore his linen shirt savagely from his back. He beat out the flames on the bottom of the ladder. But the wood had become blackened and weak. Suddenly, it collapsed.

With a hard jerk the ladder slipped straight down, the third rung hitting the stable floor almost instantaneously. Marigween lost her grip on impact and slid over the last five rungs. As her feet hit the dirt and hay she fell backward, but Orvin was there to break her fall. Unfortunately, no one was there to break his. The old man landed on his rump, his body pillowing Marigween's.

Cut, bruised, filthy, and gagging, Orvin dug himself out from under Marigween, stood, then gently lifted her. They shambled outside and were barely beyond the stable before both let themselves fall to the ground, the cleaner, fresher air a shock to their lungs. Orvin's eyes were too sore to look around. He didn't care if the other Saxons were waiting for them. Death would only ease the tremendous pain. He listened to Marigween's bawling. Her baby would come now.

3

A lone Saxon messenger rode from the north toward the Vaward Battle of Arthur's army. He was met by the multiple, wide-eyed stares of Lancelot's archers, cavalry, and infantry as he arrowed his way toward the Rearward Battle, and the king.

Christopher was as amazed as everyone else. The messengers presence was highly irregular. Saxons *never* sent messengers. What was the point when no Celt could understand them? No Celt, except Christopher.

With the blue-and-white banner of the Virgin Mary whipping proudly in the wind to his right, Arthur sat erect on his courser, his eyes neither angry nor benign. He studied the messenger, and then looked askance at Christopher. "If you're ever a king, you too should have a druid."

Indeed, Christopher would have to converse with the man, fulfilling Merlin's prophecy. But by sending a messenger, the Saxons had already communicated something: they knew Christopher was among Arthur's ranks. Doyle's theory held. Some of Garrett's army still existed.

The messenger was clad in an assortment of confiscated Celt garb. The leather gambeson covering his arms and chest was of a design worn mainly by Celt hostlers, allowing them more arm movement. Likewise, his breeches were obviously of Celt fashion, dyed bright blue and extending too far: well past the Saxon's calves. The messenger's mount was a common brown rounsey, but the horse's bit, bridle, and saddle were unmistakably crafted by the hands of Celts. Christopher admired the workmanship of the saddle, for it had been a long time since he had seen one whose construction rivaled his own work. These Saxons plundered only the best, it appeared.

Four of Arthur's cavalrymen surrounded the Saxon as he reined his steed to a stop. The messenger was a brave man. Christopher eyed the over two hundred men in the Rearward Battle, and beyond, let his gaze pan the over five hundred souls in the Vaward Battle and three hundred more in the Main. So thoroughly encompassed was the Saxon messenger by his enemy that he could not be more vulnerable, and more alone.

"King Arthur," the messenger said in the Celt tongue, "I bring a message to you from Lord Wyman, who serves Lord Kenric, leader of the Saxon tribes here on this land."

Christopher and Arthur both shared the same look of absolute astonishment. Christopher sensed that Arthur wanted an answer, but all he could do was shrug. The man knew their language—and that refuted Merlin's prophecy. It also might mean that the barbarians did not know of Christopher's presence in the army. All of it was, however, mere speculation. They needed to get answers from the messenger himself.

"You speak our tongue. How?" Arthur demanded.

The messenger palmed his ruddy, fair hair out of his eyes, then answered: "I was taught by a man named Wilbur. And he was taught by a man you might know. A Celt you—and we—called Garrett."

Arthur could have looked at Christopher, signaling to the Saxon the fact that the name meant a lot to them, especially to Christopher, but instead he wisely remained inert.

Christopher studied the messenger to see if the man recognized him, if the Saxon knew all too well what he was doing. But like Arthur's, the man's face was unreadable steel.

"You mention two lords, Wyman and Kenric, and I must admit you catch me off guard with your wish to deliver a message. Am I about to kill a horde of Saxons or Celts? It seems your methods are ours."

"We are not the same barbarians who first landed on these shores. We have learned your ways, have adopted your methods of fighting, and divided our armies as you do. Lord Garrett was not the first Celt to join us, and I know he will not be the last. There is a tempest coming, King Arthur, and there are many who will be wise enough to flee it. Those who do not will surely drown in their own blood."

Arthur's face stiffened with the threat. "What man

is it that sends so boastful a messenger into the den of his enemy? How can you—an invader on *my* land—sit there so callously and not be afraid? I tell you indeed, there is a tempest coming—a storm of thunder and lightning such as your horde has never seen!"

Christopher disliked the times when Arthur's temper flared, but at the moment he found the muscles in his own jaw tightening. He wanted, like Arthur, to return to the Saxons a dead messenger—the first of many who would be killed. The Saxon had managed in only a few breaths of air to gut Christopher's idealistic solution to the war. Christopher knew he was right, that bloodshed was not the answer, but when the enemy came and spat in your face, then you had no other choice but to raise your sword. Yes, the Saxons were men. Men as proud and determined and mean-spirited as themselves.

The messenger retorted, "I make no threats, King Arthur. I only report to you the certain future. Your army is surrounded. You accuse me of being boastful, but what man looks into the eyes of death and refuses to see? I think you know the answer."

Arthur could not stifle the ire in his voice, nor keep from baring his teeth. "Give me your message and deliver it quickly—for your life depends on its expediency!"

"Lord Kenric makes a generous offer, one no Saxon has ever made nor will make again. Lay down your arms. Realize defeat. Every man will be spared. No blood will stain these green hills."

Christopher didn't know why, but some urgent desire found its way to his lips. He barged in, shouting, "He lies! My lord, after we surrender they will line us up for the slaughter!"

He knew the offer was a lie. He couldn't explain it.

He just *knew*. Like the feelings he had had about selecting weapons, about sensing things to come—like the Saxons surrounding them. He hoped he wasn't becoming some old prophet like Orvin, or some mystical, mysterious man like Merlin, but he could never ignore the feelings. He would be damned if he did.

"Believe what you will," the messenger said evenly. "But account for this fact: we have not attacked you—as any Saxon army would have already. We give you the chance to save your lives. If we wanted war as surely as you say, then how do you explain my presence?"

"What you want," Arthur said, "is this land for yourselves. Perhaps it's true that you tire of bloodshed. We can agree on that. But you will take the land, and *that* is something we will not let you do."

"Our plight is well-known. Nearly half of our population has fallen ill, and another quarter has already died. Our land has become foul. We have no other choice but to seek refuge. And we are not alone, Arthur. The Picts come from the north, the Scots from the west, the Angles and Jutes with us from the east and south, and the Danes, well, they prepare to surround this entire land. You will be fighting for the rest of your life. All because you will not let others simply live."

And that had always been the argument that made Christopher feel guilty. The Saxons were a people who were dying. As brothers in the family of mankind, the Celts should, by all the God-given laws ruling the realm, offer succor to them, and any other ailing peoples. But what Celt would be willing to share his land? And if the Saxons were given an enclave, they might eventually become dissatisfied with it and want to expand their territory. And then there would be, in effect, a civil war between the once-peaceful Celts and Saxons. Better to keep a sea between peoples, a boundary of water. But the Saxons had proven their seamanship and their desire to expand by landing on the shores of Britain. After seeing so much blood, Christopher reasoned that sharing the land with them might work, despite Arthur's fears over further expansion and civil wars. But something in the messenger's tone, and the feeling Christopher got, made him realize that these Saxons were not just looking for a new land. They were also looking to rid that land of any opposition.

"You are not gentle men," Arthur gritted out. "You are not kind men. You did not come and ask for our counsel and our aid. You came with swords, and with daggers, and with an ardor for violence. And you tell me you have no choice but to take our land. Then I say to you, we have no choice but to stop you."

"I say once more, oh great King Arthur, whom I do admire, consider our offer. Send a messenger north before day's end with your answer." The Saxon gathered his reins, about to leave.

"Your admiration insults me, and if I could I would drain it back out of my ears. Stop, and hear now my answer. Bid Lord Wyman or Lord Kenric or whoever it is you serve my anger, and voice to them with *fear* that Arthur and his noble army shall not stop until every Saxon who draws Celt air into his barbarous lungs is run through. And bid also to them the knowledge *I* have of *your* people; that for every Celt you murder, his soul shall come in the night and plague your dreams with madness. For even in death, we will be victorious. Begone. And savor my mercy for your soul."

The messenger should have been politic and closed his mouth, but he added, "My admiration is true."

"BEGONE! BEGONE! BE . . . GONE!" Arthur sighed through a guttural hiss; his face boiled with fury.

Christopher watched the messenger breach the circle of cavalrymen guarding him and quirt his mount into a gallop toward the northern rise.

Arthur summoned an immediate meeting of his battle lords, and within the passing of a quarter hour, he stood in the middle of Sirs Lancelot, Gawain, Carney, Gauter, Ector, Bryan, Richard, Bors, Cardew, Allan, Kay, and Michael. The sun would be on the horizon by the time the nearest Saxons reached them. They had a few precious hours to plan a defense.

Christopher, Leslie, and Teague stood beside their mounts, twenty yards away. Christopher could not hear the king's words clearly, but he could see the desperation in his sovereign's eyes, the heat of frustration blushing his cheeks. If he were closer, he knew he would also see the vein that always throbbed in Arthur's temple when the king was provoked.

"I suspect we will be falling back to the rear guard," Leslie moaned.

"You and Beague—"

"Teague," the young boy said.

"I apologize," Christopher said. "You and Teague are junior squires," he reminded.

"How am I supposed to gain knighthood when I cannot even engage in the battle?"

Christopher mustered the slightest of wistful grins. He knew exactly how Leslie felt. He remembered being relegated to the rear guard when Hasdale's army mounted the attack on Garrett. And he also remembered how the other junior squires had worked out a plan under the leadership of Kier. They never told Christopher until the last second that when the attack began, they were going to join it— against their lord's wishes.

What foolish boys we were. Had I known what I was going to see, I don't think I would have joined them. But I had been frustrated and excited, as they are now.

"We are as able-bodied as any in the army," Teague puffed, looking as innocent and vulnerable as a puppy.

"Honor and glory are forgotten when one is staring at the entrails of a man. Do you know what they look like, the pale white tubes that inhabit a man's belly?"

Despite the fact that Christopher knew he would never get through to the boys, he felt it his duty at least to try.

Both boys shook their heads, then Leslie said, "I have heard of the horrors from you and others, Christopher. I am not afraid."

"And I, too, am ready," Teague said.

Christopher's conscience was at peace; he had tried. But he could try some more. "Are you ready to watch him die?" he asked Teague, while tipping his head at Leslie.

"I do not wish to. But if it happens, I will have no choice."

"But will you be ready?"

Teague paled. "I don't know."

"Why punish yourselves?" Christopher asked them. "I suspect you will have many more opportunities to fight, to see death, and perhaps to die yourselves. One missed chance is not a curse, but a gift. It's God's mercy that you are in the rear guard."

"It is a curse," Leslie sighed.

"The curse is the fact that you may very well cross

swords with the Saxons." Christopher's tone grew more disconsolate as he revealed the truth to the boys. "If I know Arthur, the rear guard will be our division in the south. This will be a four-sided battle, and for that we need four armies."

The youths' eyes shone with the idea that they would be the southern heroes of the war. They would ride in like balls of bristling silver energy and roll over the Saxon butchers. Or, as Christopher saw it, flail for a few fleeting moments before they were hacked to the ground.

The meeting of the battle lords was over, and the squires watched as each knight mounted his courser and started off toward his position. Arthur waved them over, and Christopher escorted his mount with the others toward the king. As expected, Arthur dismissed Leslie and Teague, ordering them to the Rearward Battle. The boys feigned their disappointment and obeyed, ebullience and anticipation lightening their steps.

As Arthur was about to open his mouth and say something to Christopher, his attention was drawn in another direction, to the clatter of approaching hooves.

A scout from the north reported in: "My lord. The Saxons who were marching toward us have stopped."

"Has their messenger returned to them?"

"Yes, my lord. And it was only a moment after, and then horns blew. The cavalry halted. Then the rest."

Arthur nodded. "Keep watching. Let me know when they advance again."

"Yes, lord." The scout booted his mount and was gone in a flurry of hooves.

"You were going to speak, my lord?" Christopher asked.

"There is no way of knowing if the scouts I sent to draw our other armies will succeed. If they do not, we are evenly numbered, but our position is grave. I've divided us to match their numbers, but the rear guard will have to be used in the south. You must speak to the boys."

"My lord. Leslie and League, I mean Teague, feel they can meet the challenge. As for the others, I will try to inspire them."

Arthur spun around, looked up to the gossamer clouds that spanned the sky. His lips pursed and his eyes flooded with tears. "Surrounded. Having to use boys to fight a man's war. Merlin, why did I leave you behind?" Arthur fell to his knees and Christopher rushed to brace his lord. The king covered his watery eyes with a palm. "Oh, dear, sweet, merciful God. Instill some bravery in my battle lords. Why do they doubt me? Why does fear strike down my men like a plague?"

Christopher stood holding one of Arthur's arms. It was a tremendous burden his liege shouldered, and finally it had brought Arthur to his knees. The line of archers ten abreast that stood closest to Arthur and Christopher bowed their heads, hating to see their king on his knees and not wanting to embarrass Arthur with stares. They were a loyal bunch, once full of respect for Arthur; but as Christopher eyed them, he wondered if they gazed at the earth not because they didn't want to embarrass Arthur, but because they were ashamed of him.

"My lord," Christopher said, lowering to his haunches to be next to the king. "You spoke with mighty words to that Saxon messenger. Words that inspired even me, the peacedreamer. The Saxons are fighters, and we will have to fight them. I may hate it, but listening to you made me realize that. Talk to this army. Make them all realize the importance and the honor of this battle."

"More words will not change our fate," Arthur said woefully.

"Inspiration in the hearts of our fighters will make death come gentler, and cleanse them of their fears. I will always remember something Sir Orvin told me: 'Never be afraid of the truth—even in the face of the king.' Those words gave me the courage to tell you that I wished to remain a squire, a true servant to you. But now, the truth is we are surrounded, we may not get aid from our brothers in the east and west, and the dream of one land, one king, may end here. We must face that. It is our challenge. We must not be afraid. The men need to hear these things."

Arthur swallowed, rubbed his eyes with the heels of his hands, and then motioned that he wanted to stand. Christopher helped Arthur up and adjusted the king's armor for him. "All right," Arthur said. "Find me a place from which to speak to them."

4   The inhabitants of the castle of Shores were in a frenzy. All around Christopher's home, the Saxon siege was a dark, vicious, colossal beast squalling with life.

On the west curtain wall, a line of three mangonels fired heavy stone missiles at the barrier, while two ballistas launched their flaming, oversize bolts over the wall into the outer bailey. This twin barrage inspired great terror in those serfs still outside and not hidden inside the castle's keep. The great arm of

a trebuchet joined the mangonels and ballistas, fling-
ing up stones under the pressure of its counterweight.

The east curtain wall fell prey to fivescore Saxons
clutching their scaling ladders. The invaders fought
the mire and muck of the moat and made it onto the
berm, then slapped their wooden steps onto the
stone. As each wave of Saxons approached, a hail of
arrows fell on them from the castle's watchtower sentries, and from the determined crossbowmen tucked
behind the loopholes built into the wall. But for the
defenders, there were too many Saxons. They would
never kill them all. The inevitable filled the hearts of
many.

The defenders manning the gatehouse on the
southern main entrance to the castle could not get
the main drawbridge up in time. The Saxons forced it
down with the weight of their bodies as they rolled a
battering ram onto the wooden pathway. The ram
tha-wocked! against the portcullis of the gatehouse,
its four shoulder-high wooden wheels rolling forward
and back. The sentries on the wall above dumped
large stones onto the ram and its operators, but the
Saxons were protected by an armored roof built over
the the gate-smashing device. The invaders worked
diligently and finally broke through the oak grating.
The sentries in the gatehouse were rewarded with
bloody necklaces for their valiant fighting, and the
drawbridge connecting the house to the main curtain
wall and the second portcullis was lowered. Sixscore
Saxons charged like boars over the bridge, the battering ram spearheading the column. Chills rippled their
backs, and the deep-throated hue and cry of battle
burst from their lips. There was no force alive that
could stop them.

The four chutelike machicolations which rested on

the parapets of the north curtain wall enabled the sentries to drop their black, tarry, burning-hot pitch, their stones, and pour their blazing liquid Greek fire on the Saxons while providing cover behind which to retreat. But the small, wooden, walltop huts were no match for the quicklimed arrows which needled their surfaces and set them ablaze. Though their losses were great, many Saxons managed to clamber up the wall and engage in brutal hand-to-hand combat with the Celts on the wall-walk. Friends, acquaintances, all brothers-in-arms of Christopher's, fought to their last, half-stifled breaths.

Encompassing the castle, the Saxon archers fired from behind their movable wooden mantlets; the screens provided the perfect safe haven for nocking arrows and windlassing crossbows. Iron-tipped rain from the skies of Hell fell into both inner and outer baileys of the fortress. The whistle of so many arrows was a noise never before heard by any Celt residing in Shores, but it was a sound they would never forget. If they survived. Doyle's name was muttered among a few of the younger archers; if only *he* were present to help.

The attack would have been complete if the Saxons had had a siege tower, with a roof covered in leather hides. They could have wheeled the immense wooden building up to the moat and fired arrows down into the baileys, easily picking off the castle's defenders. But Kenric did not have the resources to build such a tower, barely mustering enough to construct the missile-throwing machines. It didn't matter, though, as the Saxons on every side of the castle soon penetrated its defenses.

Seaver and Ware were among the first Saxons to make it onto the north wall-walk. They feinted, parried, riposted, and flailed their way through the Celts there, leaving behind them the bodies of four young men swimming in blood pools. They entered the watchtower, where they were accosted by a crossbowman, whose loaded weapon delivered a cogent argument to freeze. But the bowman was alone, and while Seaver charged the Celt, Ware daggered him from behind. The Celt's bow went off, and the bolt hit Seaver in the shoulder. The shot did not penetrate skin, only the leather of his gambeson. It was only after the crossbowman fell to the ground that Seaver even noticed the bolt protruding from his shoulder. He pulled the shaft out and backhanded the sweat from his forehead. For a second he imagined what the bolt would have felt like had he not been wearing his gambeson. A tremor of phantom pain spiraled outward from a point above his collarbone. He rubbed his shoulder and shivered.

The Saxon scouts double-timed down the watchtower's spiral staircase and emerged into the outer bailey.

A countless number of arrows impaled the dusty ground of the courtyard and also struck many of the pigs, sheep, chickens, and geese trapped in their pens. Slaughtering day had come early for the animals.

The thatched roofs of the two supply buildings, kitchen, stable, and armory were being eaten by flames.

The horses in the stable wailed and tried to knee their way out of their stalls. The hostlers who could have freed the coursers and rounseys had already sought sanctuary in the keep.

Two boys ran from the kitchen, bundles of loaves weighing down their arms. A longbowed arrow struck one lad in the back. A hundred-pound stone fired by a mangonel landed squarely on the other boy's head.

Exploding from the kitchen door, the baker Aidan hustled to the first boy and kneeled beside the youth. The fat man's lamenting was heard on the other side of the curtain walls. A quicklimed arrow silenced him and set his clothes on fire. His huge body would burn until nightfall.

A horse-drawn cart appeared from behind the supply buildings. The cart was driven by two young squires, while four others sat among the grain and flour sacks in the back. Arrows impaled the sacks and opened holes from which fell the precious supplies. One squire tried to turn a sack around to save it, but an arrow gored him in the neck.

With a double *thud!* the cart hit the keep's lowered drawbridge, and, even before traversing it, the platform began to rise, winches and chains clanking.

The cart reined to a dusty halt at the forebuilding on the right side of the keep, and the squires leapt from the flatbed and formed a dire delivery line up the stairway. They hauled their fallen comrade inside, then proceeded to unload the grain, their gazes flicking to the sky for arrows.

It was clear the inhabitants of the keep would hold out for as long as possible, and the Saxon scouts could only guess how well supplied they were.

Seaver turned to Ware, able to ask a question he'd been too busy voice earlier. "Did you see him?"

"Not before we started up the ladders," Ware replied.

Seaver shook his head and frowned. He had left Cuthbert and two others the duty of burning down the village stable. The others had returned, but there was still no sign of Cuthbert.

"A simple job and even *that* he has trouble with."

Seaver shook his head in disgust once more, and then puffed, "Let's go."

The garrison men who occupied the wall-walks of the keep tracked Seaver and Ware and alerted the archers. From the crossed-slit loopholes of the keep came a flurry of arrows. The two short men dodged for cover behind a small hut near a shallow pond in the eastern corner of the bailey. The hut reeked of the leatherdressers' trade, but that certainly did not stop the scouts from utilizing its protection.

"We two are no match for the others inside the keep," Ware said.

"Within the forebuilding there are murder holes in the floor and ceiling, so that is not the way in," Seaver said.

"How can you even ponder going in there ourselves?" Ware asked incredulously. "Half their garrison lies waiting. They are still formidable foes. We have to swim another moat, and I still stink from the first one. This bailey is empty. Kenric would want us to strike in great numbers from *this* position. We should report back to him."

But Seaver wanted to assail the keep. If he and Ware were able to open up the castle's most defensive tower, then surely Kenric's words would come true: they would live forever—*he* would live forever in this world and the after. He could taste the glory of that, and reason was distant, trivial, a mere obstacle. "No," he told Ware. "They will marvel at us when we stand victorious up there"—he pointed to the keep's parapets—"and wave to them."

"When *you* wave to them," Ware said, and then bolted from the cover of the hut and scurried toward the watchtower.

Seaver was about to go after him, but held himself

back. Could he do it alone? Was reason that far
away? He sat on his haunches and considered his
next move. He knew one thing he would do when the
siege was over. He would have Ware executed for
desertion. Then again, maybe Ware was right. Maybe
they should report back to Kenric and not try to do it
all alone. But then they'd lose most of the glory. But
they also might die. Why was he doubting himself
now? Ware was probably on his way to Kenric's side.
The scout would cry: "Seaver has gone mad and
wants to storm the keep on his own!" Seaver had to
stop Ware before he did that. The scout leader darted
from behind the wooden wall and covered the distance between the hut and the watchtower in a matter of seconds.

5   As Orvin wiped the soot and sweat from
Marigween's pallid forehead with a wet cloth, behind
him the roof of the stable finally collapsed in a cloud
of smoke and sparks. The old man wanted to move
Marigween to the relative safety of the forest on the
other side of the dirt road, but she was in no condition to be going anywhere. She lay on her back,
groaning horribly. Her fight with the Saxon had
induced labor, and there was no one else around to
help Orvin deliver the child. The fact that the cut on
Marigween's face had temporarily stopped bleeding
offered only minor relief. Orvin would still have to
stitch it, scarring her tender cheek. But it was her
baby he worried most about now.

The old sky watcher cleared his thoughts, bit back the various aches and pains he'd acquired from the recent combat, and began to make preparations. He had never seen a child born before. No midwife had ever let him in the room. Suddenly he was angry at them. If he could have seen, he would know what to do now! But sheer anger would not help him. First, he guessed, he had to get something clean under Marigween. His gaze assayed the surroundings: a pile of black, ember-filled rubble that was once a stable, a nearby well—with saddle blankets draped over its edge. They had been washed by the hostlers and left there to dry. He stroked Marigween's good cheek, stood and strode to the well. He shouldered the blankets, which were still slightly damp, and figured that while he was there, he should draw a few buckets of water. He found the wooden pails behind the stone wall, filled both, then carried them back to Marigween.

"I want to slide these blankets under you," he told her, his bass voice lifting to a broken tenor. He had to sound more sure of himself. He had to dispel her worries. But he was as fraught with fear as she, perhaps more.

Marigween lifted her buttocks and Orvin slid the blankets under her. "I am ashamed," she said between moans. "You will have to undress me." And then she let out a wail that wrested Orvin.

"Easy, I'm here. I'm here." Orvin lifted and pulled back her woolen kirtle to reveal her pale white linen shift. "I have seen many unclothed women, young lady. I was a roaming cavalier in my youth. Most find the body ugly, but I do not. I neither despise nor love it. It simply is and I accept it. So your shame is wasted on me. Besides, I kneel her with my shirt off revealing to all the most wrinkled, soft, gruesome

belly most will ever set eyes on. It appears I, too, will
have a child of my own soon!"

Marigween tried to smile, but her lips fell back into
the stiff, inverted grin that was her grimace.

Orvin peeled back Marigween's shift to expose her
swollen belly and privates. For a moment, a flash of
heat hooded the old man's head. The world narrowed
to a tiny black speck then returned. He needed to
avoid looking at her down *there,* for the sight might
cause him to collapse. But how would he monitor the
baby's progress? He had to bare her privates, and
forced another look. Another flash hit him, a shovel
over the head. He grimaced and took another look.
And then another. And another.

"Sir Orvin, it hurts so much!" Marigween cried.

Tenderly, Orvin once again wiped her forehead,
and then dried the perspiration that puddled in the pit
of her neck. "I know," he said softly. "I know it hurts.
But you must not think about it. I'm going to tell you
a story about Christopher, and I want you to forget
about the pain and the smell of those fires and everything else, and let my voice take you away from here."

"I'll try," she panted.

"He had just come to us and I had stitched up a
wound on his leg. My son insisted he stay in the keep,
which, of course, had sent the chambermaids buzzing
with gossip. Why would the lord of the castle attach
himself to a mere saddler's son? To this day I do not
know why my son was so taken by Christopher. I
only know there is something special about him, a
feeling one gets when one is around him. He does not
have to say anything, just be in your presence."

"I have felt that," Marigween said.

"Now there had been a mare in labor," Orvin continued, "and no hostler had been able to ease the ani-

mal's pain. Everyone had feared that she and her unborn foal would die. But as I am trying to comfort you now, so did Christopher limp down to her stall and stroke her head. He has no particular affection for horses, but Christopher saw the agony of the mare, and it had been he who had somehow gentled her condition. Even beasts recognize something about him, something that must make them feel as warm and calm as we do when he's here."

"If only he were here now!" Marigween's plea was closely followed by a long, crescendoing bellow.

"Close your eyes and think of the way he calmed that mare."

Marigween obeyed.

Orvin slid his fingers gently through her hair. "And feel his hand now on your head."

Marigween's vocal torrents subsided, and her breathing steadied. Then her torso stiffened.

Orvin looked down. The baby's head appeared, faceup, covered with blood and a thin, milky white fluid; its eyes were tightly shut.

"I feel the baby!" Marigween cried.

"Stay calm calm and push, push the child out." Orvin set himself back and watched as the shoulders of the baby emerged. He wanted to help the child out, tug its shoulders, but thought better of it. He might injure the tiny, frail body.

Between new pants, Marigween groaned deeply from her diaphragm, and the more she groaned, the farther along the baby came. Once the waist was free, Orvin guessed it was only a matter of seconds before the rest would slip out. He flicked his glance up to Marigween: her face was soaked in sweat, her eyes bloodshot and tearing. Then he looked down, and realized the baby was free, lying there on its back, its cord snaking back up into Marigween's womb. Then the afterbirth arrived and Orvin had to turn his head away.

"It's here, isn't it?" Marigween barely managed to ask.

Orvin forced himself to look at the child. It wasn't moving. Why? Was it dead? He didn't think so, it looked pink and alive. Then he remembered. He needed to spank the child's bottom to make it draw breath.

He shuddered as a question played through his mind: *What if I don't spank the child? What if it dies here?*

Christopher's life would be so much simpler without the child. The baby would irrevocably link the young saint to Marigween, when Orvin knew the boy loved Brenna.

All I have to do is nothing. Just sit here.

No! That would be murder! You know how to make the child breathe, and that knowledge makes you guilty if you fail to act!

But what if I weren't here?

You are!

Then it is true. I cannot change what will be. It is Christopher's life, and though I want to, I cannot— must not—interfere. I am here. I must act accordingly.

He lifted the baby by its legs and spanked it once, twice, three times. A tiny cry came from the child, and then another, much louder.

He turned the baby and cradled it in his arms. Never had he seen life so fresh and close, so raw in its beauty. The tiny form made him reel with feelings he didn't know he had. Only a moment ago he had thought of letting it die. Now he could not imagine that notion ever crossing his mind. With blossoming pride, he held up the baby for Marigween to see.

Covered with sweat and out of breath, she smiled, and then relinquished her pent emotions in a burst of laughter.

Orvin set the crying child down on Marigween's chest, blessed himself, and thanked God for giving him the stamina to be with her. There was still more to do, the cord to cut, but his mind was already racing ahead of that matter. There was a place he would take Marigween and the baby now, a place he prayed the Saxons would not find.

6 Arthur's dilemma consumed him. The speech that Christopher listened to him deliver was not only halfhearted, it was woven with anxiety and with utter contempt for his own, and the army's abilities. His noble modesty had rotted into depression. Arthur repeatedly referred to the men as "you who will give your lives today," and that only scared them, only deepened their wounds of uncertainty.

Because Arthur's voice did not carry to the back of the army, those who could hear turned and repeated the king's words to their neighbors. But after a while, they stopped. Arthur's face was devoid of the luster, the vitality it once had. His past dicta were always full of animated gestures, of shouts of emphasis, of fists pummeling the air. But now, Arthur stood, as bored and bereft of enthusiasm as any man drafted into the peasant levy. Even Lancelot's face mirrored his burgeoning concern for the king. It appeared Arthur was already defeated, Excalibur never unsheathed.

As the king stepped down from his supply cart

dais, Christopher turned to his liege. "I wish to talk
to the squirearchy now."

"There isn't much time," Arthur said sadly.

"I will hurry!" Christopher was emphatic.

By the time the sky above the western slopes was
stippled a pale orange, and the bright green of the
slopes appeared something more akin to brown,
Christopher had assembled the six junior and two
senior squires serving the battle lords, and invited
Doyle and any archers and varlets that cared to listen
to a knoll southeast of the Rearward Battle.

In all, nearly twoscore young men circled
Christopher. Doyle was there, lending his confident
winks and encouraging shouts. It was the first time
that Christopher employed his title. He would
address them as squire of the body, as a leader who
answered to Arthur. There was a sense of formality to
the gathering that was not Christopher's doing, but was
created by the others. They referred to him as "Sir
Christopher"—the "squire of the body" being a bit
clumsy, the "sir" recognizing his rank above regular
senior squires. Indeed, it was a knight's title, and perhaps for the day Christopher would have to be a
knight.

For most of the squires, varlets, and a few of the
archers, this was their first battle; and as it drew
closer, Christopher knew the unseen future waned
into cold, tight knots in their stomachs. The blood
fled their faces, leaving their complexions linen
white. But they did their best to hide these afflictions
from Christopher, and instead conveyed to him only
their hope, and their bravery—though that was born

of their innocence. They all were, for the most part, like Leslie and Teague: they wanted to fight, but were afraid of what they would find. Would the grass really be strewn with entrails? It was an evil, possibly true thought he knew none of them could suppress.

Christopher would never forget his first battle—as these boys never would. He wanted to go up to each and every one of them and say, "You will fight valiantly. You will find courage you didn't know you had." He wanted to do that for himself. As he looked at them, he tried to see which ones would die and which would survive. He had never played soothsayer before and already hated the role. Teague, it appeared, didn't have a chance. Leslie fared much better. Doyle, if he kept his hands off his flagon and his position in line, would be fine. He hoped. Each of the others scored low or high but all of it meant nothing. What mattered was that he stood in the center of a circle of boys whose plated and scaled armor made them look much older than their years; a group of sons lonely among the greater burdens of the world; a tiny, insignificant speckle of humanity that, at the moment, needed Christopher more than anything else in the realm. He was the center of their lives. He was their reality. And he could not let them down. St. George help him, he could not let them down.

"Brothers . . . and you are my brothers this day," he said. "The king has not taken our predicament well, as I'm sure you heard in his voice."

The boys murmured their agreement. Christopher chanced a look at Doyle; the archer nodded: you're doing fine. And yes, Arthur's words were bleak.

"But we are *all* afraid now. From what hill will the first invaders rise over? When the battle begins, it will seem they are everywhere—and they will be. Listen to me now when I say I served in a Saxon army under a Celt leader. You may already know that. But think me not a traitor, but as the best advisor you will ever have, for I know their ways. They are trying to adopt to our style of fighting, but there are many things that are and will forever be barbarous about them.

"Now let me tell you how they fight. They fear traversing the battlefield alone and always travel in numbers. If you are caught by yourself you may find two or three against you. It is rare to engage a single man, but it does happen. I want you to watch them. See how their strokes are not measured but the products of rage. See how they howl to frighten their opponents. I urge you to howl back! See how frightened a Saxon becomes when he realizes *you* are the barbarian! But above all remember this: despite their differences, they are just like us. Just as young, as scared, as innocent. Kill them, for that is what we must do now. But hold in your hearts and minds a sacred day when peace reigns throughout this land and Saxons and Celts live under the same sky and drink from the same well. Man cannot murder himself forever. For if the sacred day never comes another will—a day scorched by the fires of God.

"You know your training. Use the ways. Act, do not think. Sometimes the body knows better than the mind. Know you are a part of a brotherhood as loud and mighty as a thousandscore coursers, as bright as a forked bolt from the sky, as swift as a leveret, and as wily as a fox! Each of you is a link in our honorable chain and together we will never be broken! Do let the glory of this battle run through your veins! Feel your heart pump for Britain! Raise your fists in the air with me and know that we are the greatest fighters the world has ever seen!"

Christopher wished Orvin was here to see these young men punch the sky and cheer so loud the heads of as many as tenscore men craned their way. They might be innocent fools, but they would die honorably, knowing who they were, why they were present. Their souls would rise on a golden beam, and be freed into a cloud-filled eternity.

How wrong the war was did not matter anymore to Christopher. If he died with these boys, then he would wend his way up a path of light and be back in the gentle arms of his mother, witness again the kind smile of his father, the sly wink of Baines—all alive in Heaven! He would wait for Orvin and Doyle, welcome Marigween and Brenna, and the ladies would forgive him and both be able to love him. His sins would be laved away, for he carried in his heart the right thing. He did what he must in the world to survive, but he, above all, never abandoned the truth, the great redeemer. He would be squire of the body to Christ.

"Go now to your positions," he told the boys as their arms lowered. "Serve your hearts, your minds, and God well. You squires, varlets, archers—you are the life of this army. Breathe your courage into those around you and fight well, dear brothers, fight well. God be with you all!"

The group dispersed, leaving Christopher and Doyle alone on the knoll.

Doyle fell to his knees, took Christopher's hand, and kissed it. "You are *something.* I didn't know you could speak that way. Even the king—"

"Rise, Sir Doyle, before you utter more. Besides, you look like a jester on your knees before me. No wonder why *you* are not a knight!"

"The bow is my weapon of choice," Doyle answered, then rose.

"Use it well this eve. And this," Christopher tapped the flagon at Doyle's side, "you won't be needing."

"You're right," Doyle said. He unstrapped the flagon, removed the hemp, then guzzled the contents before Christopher. "My stomach is a better flagon!"

Christopher frowned; he wanted Doyle to take the coming battle more seriously, but was infected by the archer's humor. He smiled, then a bitter thought took hold. He embraced his friend.

Doyle broke the embrace then bounded off. "See you once the fires have cleared!" he shouted over his shoulder.

"Once the fires have cleared," Christopher repeated in a soft whisper to himself.

7

Seaver caught up with Ware and stopped the scout before he got to Kenric. Together they went to Kenric's small tent, pitched one hundred yards south of the castle under the shade of several beech trees.

Excitedly, they reported to their leader that most of the sentries defending the curtain walls of the castle were dead. The Saxons controlled the outer bailey and all watchtowers along the walls—except those behind the keep. The keep, with its own surrounding curtain wall linking six watchtowers, still posed a considerable problem.

The battering ram had gotten stuck in the keep's moat, and so the keep's portcullis could not be smashed in like the one safeguarding the main gate-

house. Saxon archers had set up a perimeter along the
moat and had built a cover wall of mantlets. But the
Celts gave them few targets to shoot at. They popped
in and out of their watchtower loopholes and windows, fired arrows and bolts and retreated too swiftly
to be picked off. Any Saxons who reached the berm
outside the walls were met by immediate showers of
Greek fire dumped from huge cauldrons over the wall
top. Saxon infantrymen, their heads, arms, and shoulders blistering in flames, went yelping toward the
moat and threw themselves into the turbid pool.

There was a greater force protecting the tower than
Seaver had originally estimated, and if the Saxons
could not penetrate the keep, then they only ruled
half of the castle.

But Kenric had a plan. And Seaver and Ware
worked with Manton and the rest of Kenric's battle
lords to initiate it. A score of men were positioned
on both the east and north curtain walls and fought
their way toward the northeast corner of the castle
behind the keep. While the Saxon archers provided
plenty of diversionary fire from the south side of the
tower, the invaders on the wall behind it were met
by only a handful of bowmen manning the battlements on the roof, and only an estimated half score
more behind the loopholes. Iron treble hooks
attached to long, wrist-thick ropes were thrown onto
the keep's upper parapets, and their barbs bought
purchase in the cracks where stone block met stone
block. Of the twenty ropes thrown, twelve were successful. The Saxons swung from the wall and crashed
into the side of the keep, then muscled their way up
the ropes. They had to reach the upper windows of
the keep, for those were the only ones wide enough
to fit a man through.

As they climbed, they were not subject to arrow fire from the loophole bowmen; those Celts could not shoot their arrows straight up or straight down, and the Saxons were careful to swing their ropes away from the narrow slits in the stone. But the men manning the two battlements that cornered the roof of the keep were able to drop missiles on the ascending Saxons. Those Celts were, however, under the steady fire of a group of twoscore Saxon archers twenty yards outside the main curtain wall. Occasionally, the Celts managed to release a stone, but with every offensive move, they suffered more casualties. Soon, the men behind the battlements fled.

The first two Saxons who made it to the upper windows were doused with pitch by a pair of chambermaids. As one of the invaders fell back, hot tar devouring the skin on his face and neck, he snatched the kirtle of one of the chambermaids and pulled her through the window. Gagged by terror, the maid fell with the Saxon. The only noise emitted from them was the sound of their bodies hitting the dirt and gravel of the inner bailey, a nearly imperceptible *ka-thump* under the cacophony of the siege. The next wave of Saxons breached the windows and encountered no resistance.

Once two dozen of his men were inside, Seaver, his heart racing, took the rope, climbed up, and joined the attack. He came into one of the eight sleeping chambers on the fourth floor. His men had already ransacked the rooms, which made him angry. The castle was going to be theirs—why destroy it? But the heat of the battle melted reason into aggression, and destruction was the only way for his men to cool down. Before descending to the third floor, Seaver had to do something. Something he had promised himself. He ran up the spiral staircase of the western battlement and burst onto the roof of the keep. He beheld the entire siege, painted copper and silver by the fires and waxing gibbous moon. What a magnificent display of power it was! In the distance, he saw Kenric's tent, and then the man himself standing next to it. Seaver waved to his lord. It took a moment for Kenric to notice him, but when he did, he returned a fist in the air. If glory were rain, then Seaver was soaked. He spent another moment watching the ever-firing archers and the cavalry plowing into the bailey. Then he turned and descended the staircase to the third floor.

The killing would be systematic now. Most of the keep's defenses were on the ground floor, built under the assumption that an attack would be mounted there. A threat from above was only a minor consideration to the architects of the castle of Shores, and for the castle's inhabitants, that strategic deficiency would prove fatal.

Seaver ordered Woodward's solar and the great hall to be spared, explaining that Kenric would take them both for his own. Then it dawned on the thick-headed infantrymen that they had just decimated their own chambers above. Destroy men, not the treasures within these walls, Seaver urged them. The fires outside could not be helped, but the keep—it was a gem to be saved and polished.

Barely a score of Celt garrison men attacked them on the third floor, and the Celts were routinely piked or knifed or axed within a quarter hour.

The second floor garrison quarters and wellhead were divided in half by a wall that had only one central doorway. A thick oak door, double-bolted from the other side, stood between them and the rest of the garrison.

Seaver ordered torches to be taken from the walls and put to the base of the door. It would take some time, but they would burn the wooden barrier down.

8

"My liege! They are coming! Just over the next rise!"

The scout grew from the shadows of the jagged hillock and came into the radiance of over a hundred war torches.

"To the earth!" Arthur ordered.

Christopher joined his king in dismounting, and simultaneously every man in the Main Battle knelt, drew the sign of the cross on the ground, bent and kissed the earth, then took a piece of soil in his mouth. All stood and picked up their arms. The cavalry remounted.

Arthur was a much more religious man than Lord Hasdale, and this ritual made Christopher feel a bit more at ease in the seconds before the attack. Everything was in order: the men were ready, the ground they may die on blessed, and the sky a dark, metallic blue for war.

"We fight four battles at once," Arthur said, staring pensively at the hillock above the archers. "I'm sorry."

Christopher could only guess why Arthur had apologized, but he sensed the king was sorry for not listening to him earlier. He respected Arthur, knew his pain, and was smart enough to realize that Arthur, though king, was still only a man. Christopher fumbled for a reply. To say nothing might be telling Arthur, "Yes, you should be sorry." To tell Arthur he need not apologize would only be falsely modest and the king would read through that. Perhaps if he admitted how he felt, Arthur would appreciate his honesty.

"My lord. I love and respect you. You could not know of this future, and I only glimpsed a shadow of it. You did what you thought was right, and I will forever defend your decision. I cannot help but advise you when I sense danger, and I must continue to do that. I hate being right at this moment. I hate it."

"Merlin said I might plunge into the rash ways of my father. And here I am. If I had spoken less and listened more . . . I have learned something already. God, I pray I live long enough to use it."

"You will, my liege. You will."

"When I made you squire of the body, I told the crowd: Here is the most loyal squire I'll ever find. And in recent moons I doubted my words. All your talk of peace made me suspect treachery. But you have been faithful."

"Thank you, my lord. And know that yes, I will die for you. But let's speak not like mourners at our pyres, but like fighters."

"Indeed," Arthur said, his voice a notch closer to sounding brave.

A glassy yellow glow appeared in the sky above the hillock, and then Christopher heard the hollow roar of the Saxon cavalry. It sounded like an approaching storm. Saxon torches rose into sight, a freckling of small white orbs among the shifting silhouettes of the horsemen. The sound accompanied by the vision was out of the blackest of Christopher's sleeps, and he could not have consciously imagined a more impressive, more horrid sight.

Then Christopher envisioned what the Saxons saw as they charged:

Two wedge-shaped groups of Celt archers, each of fifty men, barred the Saxons' path. On either wing and curving slightly forward, thus making the whole line concave, were another hundred, sharp-eyed bowmen. Their job would be to let loose a steady hail of arrows until their ranks were broken by the cavalry. Once separated, they would advance beyond the horsemen and fire randomly into the column of invading infantry that surely lay behind.

Any Saxon horseman who made it beyond the archers would encounter the fivescore men that made up Arthur's cavalry, including the king himself. If that horseman was lucky enough to advance farther, he would run straight into the infantry: nearly a hundred professional men-at-arms and another hundred in the peasant levy, all brandishing picks or bills or spears or halberds, or any of the other lethal pole arms used to stab and hook knights from their mounts.

If the Saxon made it past the infantry, he would find himself trapped approximately two hundred yards away from the peasant levy of the rear guard.

Judging from the fact that the Saxons had chosen to put their cavalry in front, Christopher assumed that their archers were in the rear. That strategy was smart and counterstruck their own. Arrows would continually shower their ranks until their cavalry made it to the Saxon bowmen. And that, Christopher knew, would be Arthur's plan.

"Banners advance! In the name of Jesus, Mary, and St. George!" Arthur barked.

The cavalry divided in half, one group flanking around the archers to the left, Christopher and Arthur's group to the right.

The archers, under the command of the boisterous Sir Michael, set down on one knee, drew back their bows, waited for their signal horn, then unleashed their first whistling shower of arrows.

Christopher snapped the reins of his courser and tightened the distance between himself and Arthur. The sound of hundreds of hooves impacting the earth droned steadily, and he wondered how he would hear commands from his lord. Besides Christopher, the banner bearer and hornsman were with Arthur, and Christopher could do little to assuage them. They were unarmed and staring at a pack of Saxons bearing down on them. Christopher reviewed how useful their jobs would be in the darkness and din of the battle. Had he been king, he would have given each of them a spatha. But Arthur insisted on protecting his sense of order—even if the world around fell off the edge of a gorge and into chaos.

They galloped, fifty men ten abreast, attempting to circle around the Saxon cavalry to hawk the archers.

But the enemy cavalry reacted to this dispersion of men, and they, too, deployed their ranks into a long fence that not only extended to the archers, but continued on to the flanks.

Then Christopher heard the unmistakable shouts of the Saxons mingle with the hammering of hooves. He wished he did not understand what they said, for their total confidence and sheer might was intimidating. And the group was smart. Tactical. They were not the arguing cavalry of Garrett's army, but a smooth, lubricated team of mounted killers whose speed, flexibility, and split-second reactions were a gloomy surprise to every Celt who witnessed them. They were wolves. And their bellies were empty.

Arthur *sringed!* Excalibur from its sheath, raising

the sword in one hand while holding his reins and
escutcheon in the other. The shield was painted with
the same likeness of the Virgin Mary that was on
Arthur's banner, his surcoat, and Christopher's surcoat as well. The king slammed down the visor on his
helm, and was as ready as he would be for the
onslaught.

Christopher made his own preparations; he pulled
his broadsword from its sheath, then slapped down
the visor on his salet. The salet was a new helmet
forged for Christopher by Brenna's father, and it
tapered back behind his head, creating an oval lip of
steel that protected the back of his neck. The visor
had a two-fingers'-width slit that Christopher was not
happy with. The helmet cut off a lot of his peripheral
vision. But the last time he'd fought on the Mendip
Hills he'd caught a cat-o'-nine-tails with his face, and
had the streaking scars to prove it. This time he would
suffer with limited vision to preserve what complexion he had left. As for his bulky suit of armor, he'd
grown accustomed to it and felt agile. It had only
taken him about a dozen moons to break in the suit.
But the piece of gear he hated most was his shield. He
would never get used to the heavy escutcheon, or the
fact that he had to steer his horse with the same hand
in which he carried the shield. Though he knew the
escutcheon might save his life, he wouldn't panic if he
lost it. He would parry an attack with the sharp movements of his horse and blade, and not rely on the
shield. Besides, he was prone to dropping it anyway.

The two-and-one-half score men of the right-side
cavalry collided with the left flank of the encroaching
Saxons.

A shortness of breath came with the familiar
klang! of blade on blade, blade on shield, blade on

armor. Christopher licked his lips and drew back his sword as a heaving barbarian galloped past him and Arthur on their right. Christopher was nearest the dark-haired man, and had the advantage of the pass. The Saxon held his spatha in his left hand, apparently his stronger one, and would only be able to defend a blow from Christopher. Unless he changed sword hands—which he did as Christopher neared him.

Christopher pictured his arm as a piece of bent steel attached to the sword. He lifted and came down on the Saxon's hoisted blade. *Klang!* He felt the vibration of the impact shudder up his arm, then saw that the Saxon had lost his weapon.

"Circle back and finish him!" Arthur ordered.

But Christopher knew it was not prudent to leave the king unattended. "My lord—"

"KILL HIM!"

Christopher wheeled his horse away from Arthur and pursued the unarmed Saxon. He shot a glance back to the multiple entanglements of men and horses, and among the individual fights he spotted Arthur, who reined his steed to a stop, looking for a challenger. Two Saxons a hundred yards north shot from the night gloom and galloped toward the king, their torches flattened in the breeze. Christopher returned his attention to his own Saxon, wanting very much to get the killing over with and return to the king. He could already hear Lancelot: "You left the king—and now he is dead! How could you do such a thing!" The fact that Arthur had ordered him away meant nothing.

As he spurred his courser on to speeds that tested the animal's abilities, Christopher's intellect took over. Maybe he could reason with the Saxon. Ask him to leave the hillocks peacefully.

Why can't I just accept that this Saxon has to die?

There he was, thinking again, and the thoughts put doubt in his mind. Yes, it was true: hesitation would kill him. And so there could be no thinking. He would slay the man quickly so that there would be no time for the image to etch itself in his memory. To kill and forget. It was the only way.

His buttocks bounced on the saddle, and Christopher knew if he kept up his pace he would be very sore come morning. If he saw morning. He rode thirty yards more and thankfully arrived at the Saxon's side. He threw down his shield, then popped up his visor. Now he could fight.

The Saxon attacked with a surprise spare sword, and Christopher deflected the blow with his own. The clanking of metal alarmed his courser, and the animal sidestepped away from the Saxon. Christopher wheeled his mount around, pressed his boots against the horse's ribs for support, then came into another swipe from the barbarian. It was supposed to be kill and forget, but Christopher found himself wanting—needing—to talk to the Saxon.

"I admire your army," he shouted in the invader's language. "This is the best effort I've ever seen by your people."

Christopher followed his words with a potent horizontal cut that nicked the Saxon's shoulder, but his blade did not penetrate the invader's link-mail hauberk. The blow did, however, unbalance the Saxon. Yet from the look on the barbarian's face, it appeared Christopher's words unbalanced him even more.

"You're Arthur's squire. You're Christopher. We have in our ranks a man who once served with you: Owen. He told me you were kidnapped long ago by a small band of rogue Celts. He and a few others tried to rescue you, but they were unsuccessful."

Garrett's men, though probably spread among the many Saxon armies, were still on the land and still fighting. They had not gone home across the narrow sea. Christopher lowered his sword. And then the Saxon tentatively lowered his own.

"It is strange," the Saxon added, "to be *speaking* to my enemy."

"We are the future. This is what *must* come."

"I have no desire to kill you," the Saxon said.

"Nor I you," Christopher assured him.

"Then what do we do?"

"Ride back to our masters and report each other dead. May your Gods be with you!"

"And yours with you!"

The Saxon heeled his mount into a gallop toward three pairs of clashing men. Christopher sheathed his sword, turned his courser around, then started off.

A mystical string of burning lights, as if the stars had organized themselves into ranks, crested the left rise less than a hundred yards from Christopher. As he strained for a better look, the image became lurid, pitching into the running, howling, sworn-to-draw-blood Saxon infantry. At least tenscore men now bore down on him. Christopher looked for Arthur, but saw only the silhouettes of a countless number of mounted men. He veered his courser right in retreat, then saw that in the distance he would come upon the peasant levy of the Vaward Battle. Alone, he could not stay where he was, and he did not know if Arthur lay ahead. He continued on his present course toward the Vaward, swearing over an impasse that once again took him away from the king's side.

Christopher threaded through the farmers, sweepers, grooms, sawyers, bakers, and the other men whose occupations numbered as many as fifty in the peasant levy of the Vaward Battle. Disorganized and disgruntled, the levy resembled the last-resort company it was. The men were armed but not trained, and presently cringed and cried as they held up shields against the sporadic arrow fire that arced under the stars.

He needed to warn the men-at-arms ahead that the Saxon infantry in the north had divided and the eastern company was marching to attack the Vaward from its most pregnable point, its rear. Craning his head and tossing wary glances over his shoulder, Christopher rode on. He heard a *ping!* on the top of his helmet, and his head jerked backward involuntarily. He guessed he had just been shot by an arrow, but the shaft's velocity had weakened from its launch point and the metal of his salet was—thank Saint George and Brenna's father—thick enough to divert the iron tip.

As he left the peasant levy and neared the rear of the Vaward's infantry, Christopher saw something that made him pull hard on his reins.

Teague and Arn, another junior squire, were mounted and thrashing four Saxons who assailed them from the ground. A pair of abandoned war torches spewed shimmering light from the grass, and reflections of the flames lit the squires' armor.

If they are here, what has become of the rear guard?

Christopher threw back his visor. "Arrant knaves! Why have you left your positions?" Christopher expected no answer from the boys; he knew they were slightly distracted.

He assayed the situation and decided to ward off the two invaders who fought with Teague. The one swinging the battle-ax was giving the squire the most trouble. Christopher rode behind the man and reacted without thinking. His blade came down askew, hit the Saxon's head, passed through hair and skin, fissured bone, then penetrated brain. His tight grip on the blade kept it in his hand as the forward momentum of his horse tore the sword free of the infantryman's head. He braked, tugging the courser's head right to arc toward Teague.

As the other Saxon guided his halberd, about to hook Teague off his mount, Christopher hacked a jagged chunk of flesh from the back of the man's hand. Caterwauling like a mouser whose paw had been run over by a supply cart, the Saxon dropped his pole arm and turned in time to witness the millisecond image of the tip of Christopher's broadsword as it rammed its way past his lips, broke his teeth, and pierced the soft, wet skin at the back of his throat. Christopher closed his eyes, thrust harder, then pulled back. He nearly dropped the broadsword as his courser neighed, stepped back and then forward. Christopher wiped his incarnadined blade on the bottom of his mount's saddle cloth, then resheathed it. He would not look at his victim.

Teague, though only a junior squire, proved smart enough to take advantage of his freedom. He circled, held his spatha high, then aimed for the Saxon plying a spear on Arn's right.

Christopher didn't wait to find out if Teague's effort would be successful, for he wanted to help Arn with the Saxon on the boy's left, one of the tallest invaders Christopher had ever seen. The long, hooked bill with which the Saxon feinted and jabbed was Christopher's first target. As he stormed behind the Saxon, the man turned. Christopher dropped his reins as the giant thrust his bill. With his left hand, Christopher locked onto and wrested the Saxon's pole while simultaneously spurring his courser into a gallop. He tucked the bill under his arm and dragged the Saxon for a moment before the man lost his grip. A jolt of the sudden weight loss told him that it was time to hit his second target.

But as the Saxon ran from him, and Arn circled around to block the invader's path, a squeal of agony came from Teague's direction. Christopher's gaze left the tall Saxon, swept over the smoking landscape, and found, just beyond the perimeter of torchlight, the silhouette of Teague slumped backward on his courser. The squire's boots were still locked in their stirrups, and his chest was impaled by a spear that stuck straight up into the night like a banner pole. The Saxon who had gutted Teague lay on the ground near Teague's courser, the squire's spatha wedged between the Saxon's ribs. At least Teague had killed his killer. But on second thought, that meant nothing. A burst of numbing cold ripped through Christopher. His hand went slack, releasing the Saxon's bill.

Arn panicked. He urged his courser in Teague's direction, and, as he did so, the tall Saxon ran at him, leapt up, and knocked the squire sideways off his mount. Arn's head hit the ground, but the rest of his body did not impact. He was still caught in his jingling stirrups and hung precariously upside down on his courser. Pained from the blow, the horse hooved itself into a canter as the tall Saxon rolled on the grass, came up, and chased it.

Doggedly, Christopher goaded his courser toward the scene. The Saxon unsheathed Arn's spatha, which hung from the squire's saddle, then slipped it under the boy's gorget. A thrust. Arn's blade scraped against his collarbone as it killed him. The Saxon withdrew the spatha and spun to face Christopher.

A closer proximity revealed the barbarian to be gargantuan, only half resembling the man he was. His face glistened menacingly with sweat, and his eyes owned a vigor Christopher had seen in few men.

Employing a sudden idea, he slid his boots out of his stirrups, dropped his reins, then clutched the saddle's pommel. He would have to time it right. When his courser was almost on top of the Saxon, Christopher pushed his knees back up onto the saddle. From this kneeling position, he leapt sideways onto the invader.

Both went down in a wind-stealing *frump!*

The Saxon tried to wrestle Christopher off with one hand while he fumbled for the spatha he had dropped on impact with the other.

Christopher unsheathed the anlace he kept bound under the metal greave that protected his right shin. Every sinew in his body flexed as he dug his left elbow into the Saxon's chest and thrust the dagger with his right hand. His blade cut through the Saxon's gambeson and pierced his belly.

The Saxon flinched, cursed, then summoned a demon from the underworld to kill his oppressor.

Christopher stabbed him again. This time he struck closer to the invader's heart. The Saxon swore once more, but was silenced midway by his own blood. Christopher wrenched the dagger free, screamed, punched it home again, then pulled it out. The dead man emptied himself into his breeches.

Christopher stood, breathless, death on his hands. He sheathed his dagger without cleaning it, then spotted his courser. He made a clicking sound with his tongue, and the courser responded, trotting to him. He stroked its head and the horse whinnied with pleasure.

"We go now," he whispered to the beast.

He spent a last grim moment eyeing the carnage before him. Once thinking, breathing, feeling, magnificently complicated creatures, Teague, Arn, and the four Saxons were now fleshy bags of blood, water, and bone. And as he had observed his first time on the battleground, these young men were like broken swords, ready to be tossed away and forgotten.

Christopher's cheeks sank in nausea. He averted his gaze and mounted with haste. He snapped his reins and started toward the nearest hogback, away from the dark valley.

From his perch atop the hogback, Christopher overlooked a new valley. He could see the Vaward Battle's archers combating at point-blank range an equal-sized force of infantrymen. These Saxons were part of the eastern force, and gave the archers a hard enough time as it was. Christopher didn't know if he'd have the heart to tell Lancelot that another force of infantry from the north was headed their way, plowing through the rear of his division.

What Teague and Arn had been doing in the Vaward Battle still remained a mystery. Had the rear guard been swept eastward by the Saxons in the south? Or had Teague and Arn joined Doyle's private, rogue-of-the-battlefield club? And what of Leslie? He and Teague were supposed to remain together. Was he with Arn's partner? And most importantly: was King Arthur all right?

Christopher would make his report and then fight his way toward the east side of the Main Battle, where he had left Arthur. He descended the slope, his movements guarded, his breath running wild. The only comforting notion: Doyle was among the fighters; maybe Christopher would see his friend and be assured that Doyle was all right.

If one covered one's ears, the battle from Christopher's distance might be mistaken for an all-night festival—a shifting crowd under the smoky haze of fivescore torches. But the conspicuous sound of metal on metal and the hysterical shrieks of dying men, of men suddenly bereaved of their brothers, unshrouded the truth and purged ambiguity from the scene.

The valley bathed in blood.

Christopher pried off his salet and hooked it on his saddle, then removed his padded coif, placed the link-mail under cap inside the helmet. He doffed his gauntlets and slipped them into the small riding bag behind him. He was sweaty, vaguely dirty, physically and mentally exhausted from killing. He shouldn't have fooled himself into believing he could come on the campaign and not kill. It only made matters worse now. If coerced, he would have to deal out more death. He repeated that to himself as his mount's legs found level ground. He beat a path around the perimeter of the battle to search for Lancelot.

A frenzied Saxon infantryman materialized from a cloud of torch smoke, brandishing a pike. Another Saxon swinging a battle-ax succeeded him. Christopher ducked and spurred his way out of a conflict with these men.

He found Lancelot dismounted, his face rosy with anger, his body spinning like a mill blade gone berserk as he cut down four Saxons in a single stroke. Lancelot was mad with courage, gripped in the arms of a beast named strength, and his feats were marred only by his epithets. Each time he butchered he cursed the enemy, hating him with sword and mouth, killing him with syllables and steel: "Damn you! Damn you to the pits of bloody, stinking, foul, dung-caked, urine-washed Hell, you pieces of hairy, lice-infested filth!"

Not knowing how to react to the display, Christopher found himself smiling dumbly. Lancelot, the great, chivalrous knight spoke like an ill-bred innkeeper. Christopher levered himself off his saddle and swung down to the grass.

Lancelot cocked his head and directed his blade in Christopher's direction. The knight's expression softened with recognition. "Christopher! Why are you not at Arthur's side?"

The sight of him alone always brought the same question—which Christopher now decided to avoid. "I come to report that half the infantry we fought in the north moves through your peasant levy."

"Foolish boy! I already know that. You left the king's side to tell me that!"

"No! I was forced here by the foot soldiers."

"Get back to the king at once!"

"I will!" Christopher marched toward his horse, slipped his left boot in the stirrup and climbed up. Before leaving, he shouted to Lancelot, "Have you seen Doyle?"

"Get back to the king!" Lancelot repeated, then leapt from the path of a galloping Saxon cavalryman drawing circles in the air with a long, spiked mace.

He turned away as Lancelot bent his knees in preparation for another swooping run by the Saxon.

Christopher steered his mount toward the western fringes of the battle, whence he would break through the melee and streak toward Arthur. The landscape grew more ghastly as the war beat on. Bodies waiting to be looted lay bloodied, twisted, and mangled everywhere. The smell of dust and fresh blood clotted his nose. Several times Christopher's courser kicked its way through the human debris, and the ugly noise made by hooves on exposed muscle and bone made Christopher's nausea return.

Where the air had once been clear, the visibility at least one hundred yards, it was now grainy and draped with acrid smoke. Forgotten torches had started fires all over the slopes. He rode through a fog, only hotter and thinner, and the clouds of grayness whipped past him. He traversed a small gully, then climbed and reached the crest of another hillock. The air smelled fresher, and he could see down into another, narrower valley. As many as threescore of Lancelot's archers took defensive stances on the hillside, firing down into the Saxon-infested lower ground. There was no method to their madness, as much farther beyond, another group of archers fired from the opposite bank at the same Saxons, but too many of their arrows fell long, and one landed just a yard away from Christopher and his mount. If the archers continued their strategy, they would kill themselves long before the Saxons ever reached them.

"Christopher!"

Leslie cantered up from the gully. The junior squire arrived at his side and Christopher immediately noted the filth of war on the boy: the right sleeve of his link-mail hauberk was stained with blood; the squire's nose had bled, and his upper lip was crusted in crimson; his eyes were glassy and red, irritated by the smoke; and his hair was besmirched with dirt, for he'd fallen at least once from his mount. These things, though they made Leslie look haggard, also made him look older. Already, he was a veteran of combat, be it for only a few short hours.

"I won't even ask you what you're doing here," Christopher said, "for confusion is the order of this eve."

"You never said it would be like this!" Leslie exclaimed.

"Yes I did!"

"Have you seen Teague?"

With eyes still keen on the knots of fighting men below, Christopher deliberated Leslie's question. Was it time to put sorrow in Leslie's heart? Then, dismissing his intellect, he answered, "He's dead. On the morrow he rides on a beam to heaven."

Leslie bit his lower lip, and the air that came through his nose was the short, hard exhalations of a sob.

From the corner of his eye, Christopher viewed the approach of another horseman. He turned his courser around and snicked free his broadsword. He heard Leslie do likewise with his spatha. As the figure moved from dark silhouette into color, Christopher relaxed in his saddle.

It was Doyle, with a body lying facedown slung over the rump of his confiscated Saxon rounsey.

"He brings Innis," Leslie said darkly.

"Innis?" Christopher asked, having almost forgotten about his feud with the varlet.

"I saved you the prize!" Doyle shouted, his voice too loud, his ability to judge sound apparently gone.

As he drew closer, Christopher saw by the way Doyle bobbed in his saddle that the archer was drunk. "What happened?"

"He's dead," Doyle said with a smile.

"It's nothing to grin over," Christopher replied.

"Especially when Doyle killed him," Leslie added.

Every emotion that brought with it a sense of fulfillment instantly exorcised itself from Christopher. In the blink of an eye he was empty. And that emptiness was pregnable. In another blink shock entered. Then horror. Then a state of paralysis.

Somehow, a scintilla of hope sneaked back in, the hope that Leslie was mistaken. He regarded the junior squire, demanding to know more.

Leslie sighed and lowered his gaze in contempt. "I saw him do it. He put an arrow in Innis's back when he thought no one was watching."

"You lie!" Doyle screamed, then climbed clumsily down from his horse and ran toward Leslie.

Christopher maneuvered his courser to block Doyle, but the archer palmed his way around the horse. Doyle yanked Leslie off his mount and wrestled him to the ground. A scant boot's length away from the two, a stray arrow thunked the earth. Christopher hopped from his mount and fell to his knees before Doyle and Leslie. He had to pry them apart and sort the rest out later, for the battle in the valley was snarling and clawing its way closer.

His friend fought voraciously, but Christopher tugged him off Leslie and rolled him away. He pinned Doyle's arms under his knees, then smacked him across the cheek. "Did you do it?"

Doyle closed his eyes and tightened every muscle in his face. Christopher felt Doyle's knees hit his back, then the archer's boots connect with his ears. Doyle locked his heels under Christopher's chin and slammed him backward. Christopher fell onto Doyle's legs. Stunned, he felt Doyle climb out from under him.

"I killed the wretch," Doyle confessed as he stood. "I've been waiting too long for this. He would've killed me and then you if we had let him live. And

you didn't have to listen to him for these past moons.
The very sound of his voice drove me mad!"

"It was wrong," Leslie said.

Christopher sat up, rubbed the fire under his chin,
then fingered his sore ears.

"Let's go," Doyle said. "It's too late to know if it
was right or wrong. He's dead and I'll find a pyre to
dump him on." He turned his fiery gaze on
Christopher. "I just wanted you to see him. He's
dead. Aren't you glad?"

"I'm going to report this," Leslie promised. He got
to his feet and brushed himself off. "And if you try to
stop me, Doyle, I'll fight you."

Doyle ground his teeth and nodded. In the gloomy
light that flickered with dust motes and cut the angles
of his features with shadows, Doyle looked demonic.
The archer was a man so thoroughly engrossed in his
actions, so thoroughly numbed by ale that he had lost
who he was. And whatever it was that drove Doyle,
Christopher knew at least part of it was evil.

"You go ahead and report it. Go now," Doyle told
Leslie.

"I will," Leslie snorted, then jogged to his horse
and mounted.

Doyle stomped toward his rounsey as Christopher
rose. "Was this your plan all along? Did you know
from the beginning you were going to kill him?"

"Our problems with him are over," Doyle hissed.

"They've just begun!" Christopher cried.

Doyle reached his mount and lifted his longbow
from its saddle hook. He drew an arrow from the
quiver tied to one of his riding bags.

"What are you doing, Doyle?" Christopher's heart
leapt into a dash as Doyle nocked the arrow and
pulled back at least sixty pounds of draw.

He turned to spy Doyle's target, but had already guessed it. Christopher bolted toward Doyle, his arms outstretched, his fingers itching to grab the arrow and bow from the archer's hands.

Fwit! The arrow tore through the night air as Christopher tackled Doyle.

Their arms became twisted in the bowstring, but Christopher ignored that. He cocked his head and strained for a glimpse of Leslie.

The junior squire, the thirteen-year-old boy, slumped forward onto his horse's neck, Doyle's arrow embedded a finger's length below his right ear-lobe. In the seconds that followed, beads of blood trickled down the wooden shaft, soaked the fletching, then dropped to the cool, dampening earth.

Christopher rolled off of Doyle and collapsed onto his back. He gazed absently at the blinking, uncaring void above and wished it would take him, hide him, lose him in its endless bowels. All the hope and desire he had for Doyle conquering his problems was lost an instant ago. There was only blood now. And pain. *How could this have happened?*

He felt Doyle fumbling with his bow; the archer freed the weapon from Christopher's arm, then sat up.

"We have to move," Doyle said. "Now." There was not even a feather-thin trace of remorse in his voice.

Christopher flexed to a sitting position, then cocked his head to face Doyle. He seized Doyle by the collar of his blue surcoat and drove the archer onto his back. He sat on Doyle's belly and pressed his thumbs under his murdering friend's chin, ready to bury them in his neck.

Doyle choked as Christopher's rage expelled from his lips: "WHAT ARE YOU DOING? WHO ARE YOU? YOU KILLED THEM! YOU KILLED BOTH OF

THEM!" He paused to catch his breath, and shuddered through it. "What if others saw you kill Innis? Are you going to kill them, too? What about me? I know all about it!" Then his words came slower, softer, laced with sorrow. "And I watched you kill Leslie. Do you have to kill me now? Do you have to kill everyone, is that it? Do you want to kill the whole world?"

Christopher released his thumbs from Doyle's neck, but the archer still gagged. Isolated tears leaked from his eyes. "Maybe I do. Maybe I want to murder everyone."

"No, you don't," Christopher said. "You don't know what you're doing."

And then Doyle bellowed. A resounding cry—not of pain—but perhaps of guilt.

Doyle wrapped one arm behind Christopher's neck, the other around his back. He pulled Christopher down and held him there, crying into his chest.

Christopher was frightened for his friend. Doyle was married to his desire to prove himself on the battlefield; to the guilty and lost feelings his inability to have a relationship with his parents extorted; to ale, that faithful friend who always listened, never criticized, and turned past and present pain into a truthless bliss. He was alone, needing acceptance, and most assuredly, love. He lacked these assets, and that hole in his heart was sieged by violence. And he killed. He should have never come on the campaign, for all the world of good that realization did Christopher now.

What to do about the mess? Leave the bodies and blame stray arrows? That would save Doyle from the gallows tree. But it would be a lie. How much did he value his friendship? He had always said he would never be able to cope with Doyle's death. Orvin and Doyle were the only family he had left in the world.

Could he lose Doyle as he had his parents and Baines? He had so few left, so few who loved him.

Christopher would do it. He would help Doyle. There would be no more killing. But win or lose, this had to be Doyle's last campaign.

An arrow flew past the muzzle of Doyle's rounsey, and the animal neighed its fear and surprise, kicked up its forelegs, then retreated a few yards.

"Archers! Fall back! Fall back!" The voice was pitched with fear.

Christopher pushed Doyle away from his chest and shifted to see a jagged ribbon of dirty, terror-struck longbowmen wildly retreating over the top of the hogback. The bowmen were so intent on their escape that they regarded Leslie and his mount as merely an obstacle, rushing past the dead squire without a second glance. It was foolish for Christopher to even think they would suspect something. This was a war. This was havoc realized. Dead men were as much a part of the landscape as the grass, the jagged limestone, the stands of oak and beech.

Doyle and Christopher joined the archers in their breakneck withdrawal. Innis's body was dumped on the dew-slick grass not far from where Leslie still sprawled on his horse. Stray arrows. Damned, horrible stray arrows.

Poor Leslie, you big-eared squire. Doyle, you killed him. You killed Innis. And now I must protect you because I don't want to see you die too. But how could you do it? You make me feel as guilty and as miserable as you do right now. Maybe you deserve to die—no, no you don't. You've just gone mad for a while. It will pass. And I will try to help you. But now you make me live with this bloody secret. Is this the true test of being a blood brother?

9

The door, a scorched, flame-riddled, crumbling mass, its hinges heated to a dull orange, was smashed in by a trio of Seaver's men. The garrison on the other side had soaked the door in defense, but the Saxon-induced fire had gone too long unchecked.

Four Celts across the hall of the quarters fingered the triggers of the their crossbows. Bolts flew and found the foreheads of the first two Saxons coming through the door, and they died before having a chance to scream. But in the dusty cloud of sparks and ash, ten more of Seaver's men rushed the crossbowmen, drove them back into the wall, then thrust their spathas into the Celts' leather-covered chests. The blades passed through the men and chinged the wall behind them. As the Celts wailed and slumped, a broken dam of Saxons poured into the room and swept away the lives of the remaining garrison holed up there.

Blades arced and heads tumbled.

Knifed men gurgled and raised arms that were hacked off.

Celts cursed and Saxons answered with spears.

Death yelps split the air.

And as the slaughtering inside the tight quarters continued, Seaver took four men with him to the first floor supply rooms. There, they cornered the squires, hostlers, and chambermaids hiding behind the grain sacks and ale barrels. The squires came into the open, raised their thin arms, steadied their spathas, and flexed into fencing positions. Seaver was delighted. The game was on. He left two of his men to try to remove the squires' weapons without killing the boys—a challenge, indeed—and took the other two down a moldy staircase that led to the dungeon.

The deep, wheat-colored hues cast by a pair of torches picked out the butlers, pantlers, leather-dressers, cooks, ewerers, cupbearers, mat weavers, pages, spinners, grooms, sweepers, armorers, and every other serf who worked in the castle. Nearly fourscore men, women, and children had jammed themselves into the cells and had locked the doors behind them. The serfs sent a clear message that they wished to be spared, and if Seaver could, he would tell them that they would enjoy serving their new master. But he could only walk up and down the narrow hall that divided the cells on either side of him, and simper his overwhelming delight. Once again, for a little man, he felt very big. He left his other two men to convince the serfs to come out. His men frowned. How could they do that without knowing the Celt language? Seaver chuckled. Another amusing game. He strode out of the cellblock.

He met Kenric in the great hall, where a score of bowmen who had surrendered stood in a line under the vigilance of four Saxon guards.

Kenric sat in his newly plundered high-backed chair before his rectangular dining table, a meat cleaver clutched in his right hand. As each bowman on the line came forward he was blindfolded and forced to place his right hand—palm down—on the table in front of Kenric.

Seaver knew Kenric had been deprived of combat, and this practice was his lord's form of release. Kenric did not risk himself in battle, as Garrett had. No, he was too smart for that. But Kenric possessed the same desire to inflict pain. And he could not satisfy his appetite for blood by standing in the rear and watching. Yes, any one of Kenric's men was capable of this bloody task, but Kenric *needed* to do it himself.

The Saxon leader lifted the cleaver and brought it down in a perfect swipe, expertly chopping off the bowman's thumb and forefinger so that he would never draw a bowstring again. Moaning, writhing like an oak buffeted by a squall, and still blindfolded, the bowman was escorted to the hearth in the middle of the hall. A rag was stuffed into the Celt's mouth as his raw wound was slapped onto a cherry-hot spatha. Blood boiled and flesh *hiss*ed as the wound was seared closed. The bowman fainted and was dragged out of the room by one of the two Saxons attending the hearth.

"Next man!" Kenric yelled.

Seaver paralleled the line of pale Celts, rounded the table, and arrived beside Kenric, just as he cleavered another pair of fingers from another bowman's hand. Kenric swiped the fingers off the table into a basket that sat on the stone floor. It was a curious sight, that basket, half-full with a pile of fingers that looked almost like sausages to Seaver.

"If, by chance, Lord Woodward survives on the Mendip Hills, I want to see his face when he returns here." Kenric looked up, eyes distant, reveling in the vision.

"His mouth will hang open," Seaver said.

Kenric nodded, then regarded Seaver. "Are the serfs in the dungeon?"

"As expected."

"Good. Now send a messenger to West Camel. I want to know if Durwin has taken the castle of Rain."

"Done."

Kenric was distracted by the next bowman in line, seeing how the Celt sweated, trembled, swallowed, wrung his hands, and paused to stare at the two fingers he was about to lose. This delay in his pain brought tears to the Celt's eyes. Kenric hemmed, then assured the man, "Do not fret, you'll get your turn!" He followed his words with a cackle.

The Celt did not understand Kenric, but the Saxon leader's laugh menaced him back several steps.

Kenric regained his composure. "Little man, Seaver. Not such a little man anymore, eh? I entrusted the duties of a battle lord to you during this siege, and you have done better than my best. Manton is dead. Now you will be my second-in-command."

Seaver exhaled very hard, sheathed in sudden thrills that bore into the very core of his being. This was his greatest moment *ever* since coming to this land. It was *his* epoch, his time to rule. This was the night he would pillow his head on a mountainside, pull down a piece of the heavens, and sleep under a gleaming blanket of stars. And when he snored, it would rumble as thunder to those in nearby villages, those whose entire bodies would fit on one of his fingernails. And when he awoke, he would eat a field of corn for breakfast and wash it down with a lake. By midday, he would scoop a bit of honey out of the sun and savor it on his tongue. By nightfall, he would do it all over again, only this time he would be joined by a woman, a lady as perfectly proportioned as he; a woman whose breath carried the scents of powder and dayflowers, whose eyes shone like sapphires in moonlight, and whose sole existence was to love and worship him, to tend to his every need. He could have anything he wanted now. Anything. He controlled the world and the world snapped at his every command. Oh, the power he had now. The control. Kenneth had told him how delightful it was, how much larger than life it would make him feel. But to experience it! To live it now! He was drunk with glory.

"Have you nothing to say?" Kenric asked.

Seaver, looking down on the castle from a thousand yards up, the stars tickling the backs of his ears, suddenly found himself back in the great hall. "Yes!" he blurted out. "Thank you. Thank you, my lord. I will be your best fighter. I will."

"I know." Kenric scratched the stubble on his chin. "Take care of one last bit of business. Once the serfs are removed from the dungeon, tell them they will prepare a feast for us, as lavish as any given by Lord Woodward. Now be off, Battle Lord Seaver." He tipped his head toward the Celt on line. "Our friend waits very patiently here."

Seaver bowed in respect, spun on his heels, then paraded toward the doorway. With his wings of greatness spread, he could not feel his feet touch the stone as he walked.

10

If the sun had a choice, it would not choose to birth a new day over the Mendip Hills. To illuminate such butchery was an act against nature.

But nature would have to be forgiving.

Groans of the wounded echoed around Christopher and Doyle as they galloped toward the heart of the now-dying battle. The clankings of sword and shield, pole arm and link-mail had diminished with the night. A mist prowled the lower valley and created islands out of the tops of the taller hogbacks, hillocks, and slopes. The scents of wet grass and leather, horse dung, and his own perspiration combined into a rank miasma. His mouth tasted of something bitter and dry, and his thighs and rump ached from riding.

Doyle was the same, silent, his mount in perfect alignment with Christopher's courser.

Everything that had passed seemed a lifetime away. Both had seen so much, been through so much that they were physically and mentally conquered by the very experience. If they decided, they could reflect on it now, shiver at how unreal it all was. But all they could do was ride.

And then they saw it. It came from the west, dawn's lambent glow flittering effortlessly over it: a wall of men-at-arms, the expanse of which shocked them. Christopher looked right, then left, and could not see where the horizon of Celts ended.

Nearby, the ground began to quake, and Christopher knew it could not be from their horses. It might be from the myriad of men ahead. But they were too far off. He looked over his shoulder.

A rampart of cavalrymen from the east descended the slope behind them, and in seconds they were swarmed by lance after lance, score after score of Celts. The men rode with such furor that they nearly dismounted Christopher and Doyle.

Now, even if Arthur's forces had been defeated, Lord Wyman and his Saxon comrades would not escape. A new day produced the fresh armies of Leondegrance and Uryens closing from the east, Woodward and Nolan from the west.

"The messengers got through!" Doyle shouted, new life in his voice.

The sudden rush of horses and men rejuvenated

Christopher's weary bones, and lifted the fatigue from his head. "Yes! Yes!"

One of the cavalrymen, whose red surcoat inscribed with a silver cross marked him as a member of Leondegrance's lance, a senior squire, reined alongside Christopher. "Is the king alive?" he asked.

"I don't know. But we're searching for the Main Battle. If Arthur is alive, he should be there."

"Has your force won the night?"

Christopher shrugged.

"Certainly the battle is won now!" the squire boasted.

Probing from side to side, Christopher saw that he and Doyle had joined a barrier of men as vast as the one that lay ahead. The squire's boast was deserved. At least four thousand Celts hemmed in the central slopes where Arthur's army had mounted its defense. Never before had so many fighting men come together in one place. It was a dazzling spectacle of absolute force that Christopher and Doyle found hard to witness. It all but frightened them.

The two great walls of men-at-arms slammed into the remnants of the Saxon army and flattened it into oblivion. Some of the Saxons chose to take their own lives, while others surrendered. But the Celts were merciless. No prisoners were taken.

Finally, word got to Christopher of Arthur's survival and whereabouts, and he breathed a deep sigh of relief. *Thank St. George! He's alive!*

They discovered the king sitting on the back of a supply cart, blood leaking from cuts on his hands, neck, and face. His hair and beard where matted and oily with sweat, and his eyes wore the burdens of battle. He sipped cautiously on a tankard of wine, as if imbibing too much would increase his pain. He set the mug down on the flatbed beside him as Hallam, the former monk from Queen's Camel Abbey who served as doctor to the Main Battle, dabbed at a fine cut across his forehead with a rag.

Christopher and Doyle dismounted. Christopher's footsteps on the soft, spongy grass were tentative, and his nerves jittered over Arthur's unknown reaction to him. Would he scold his senior squire for not returning?

They dropped to one knee before their king, and Christopher took Arthur's hand, found a clear spot among the cuts, then kissed it. "My liege, the sight of you overcomes me."

"What happened?" Arthur asked weakly.

"I could not get back to you because—"

"No," Arthur interjected. "Did we win the eve? Is the battle ours?"

Christopher's attention was tugged away by the sight of Uryens and Lancelot strong-arming a man, assumedly Saxon Lord Wyman. The invader was grayer, and sported more armor than any of the other Saxons in the valley. "See for yourself, lord." Christopher indicated that Arthur turn around.

Uryens and Lancelot shuffled the last living Saxon on the Mendip Hills past the cart and presented him to Arthur.

"We suspect he is the leader," Lancelot said. "He is the miry demon who promised to beat us. All of his followers are dead."

Wyman arched his back, brought himself as close as he could to Arthur despite the men holding him, and spat. The Saxon's saliva hit the king's breast-plate, then oozed down his chest.

Christopher and Doyle exchanged incredulous looks, and wondered how the king would parry the blatant display of contempt.

Before Arthur could say or do anything, Uryens balled his left hand into a fist and pummeled Wyman's temple. "You will die shortly, ogre."

Wyman called Uryens something Christopher would not repeat, but was aghast to hear. He could relate to Wyman's predicament, for he, too, had found himself in the hands of the enemy. But he had not been as bold as this Saxon. No, Wyman already knew he would die, and his last breaths would damn his slayers. He would not submit to death. It was the warrior's way.

"Let him go," Arthur said, his voice weary but still able to carry the cadence of an order.

"He is the last one, my lord," Lancelot said. "Why not complete the job?"

Arthur shook his head no. "Send him to warn his brothers on the isles of Wight and Thanet that no Saxon army shall conquer this land."

Lancelot and Uryens beamed with the idea.

"Two of my men will escort him there personally," Uryens said.

"Take him." Arthur coughed, then rubbed grit from his eyes.

As the two battle lords turned with their prisoner, Lancelot found a moment to shoot Doyle a scornful look, a look that asked, "What are you doing here when you belong with the rest of the archers?"

It was the path of their lives on the battlefield, Christopher mused. Both he and Doyle were never where they were supposed to be, yet both had been through two battles and come back alive. Maybe they would not change this chaotic, but ultimately life-granting method. Perhaps Doyle's rogue-of-the-battlefield club wasn't so bad after all. But it was against orders, and they would forever suffer disciplinary action.

"This is a great day," Arthur sighed. Christopher sensed that the king wanted to stand and extol everyone, but was just too exhausted to do so. Arthur's condition stole the feeling of victory from all around him.

"It is," Christopher agreed somberly.

Then Arthur looked at Doyle; it was a look Christopher could not discern. "You," Arthur said, shaking a pointed index finger, "you fought bravely I suspect?"

Doyle, expecting to be chastised, was surprised by Arthur's question.

Christopher could have stepped in and told the king that yes, Doyle had fought bravely, but he did not. Doyle had murdered.

He flicked a glance at his friend, saw that Doyle nodded and ever-so-slight reply to the king.

"And you, Christopher," Arthur said, shifting his attention, "I mourn for you."

"May I ask why, lord?"

"Because you believe in peace, and had to go out in darkness and abandon your belief."

"Not all Saxons are killers. If one leader would feel as I do . . . "

"He is a man I would reason with, be it cautiously. But I would speak with him."

"Garrett was such a man," Christopher said.

"He was a Celt," Arthur qualified.

"Peace will come." Christopher was sure of it.

"I have no doubt of that." Arthur hefted himself off the supply cart and stood, then flexed his muscles as the bones in his arms and legs cracked. He raked his long hair back over his ears and inhaled deeply. "For now, though, I think the Saxons will not bother us. We can go home." Arthur smacked his lips with a new idea. "And I think I will spend some time with Lord Woodward, Christopher. That would keep you in Shores for a while. You would like that."

Christopher grinned. He missed the village of his youth, though it was a rebuilt one now. But the place still had *that* smell; it carried for miles, that scent of gorse and humus cut with the stench of leather. It would never change.

"Then we eat," Arthur added, "gather the fallen arms, strip and burn the dead. That done, we start the long journey to those emerald fields and towering ramparts."

Arthur's words painted the tableau so clearly in Christopher's head that he felt he could step out of his body and into the mind picture. He could run across the field amidst the tender zephyrs and lunge into the open arms of . . . who? Brenna? Marigween?

At home he would have to make a decision between the young ladies. But his love was excruciatingly torn between the raven maid and the orphaned princess. If he continued courting them both, it would break all hearts.

His problem with Innis had blossomed into a black rose, with Doyle trapped in its petals. And he knew how the guilt would haunt him:

Arthur's wraith would come in black sleep and tell Christopher how sinful it was to harbor Doyle's secret, how his own hands were bloodied by his aiding such a person, a person who had done such unspeakable acts. What fool would leap onto a runaway rounsey as it hooved toward a cliff?

Yes, he missed the village and castle of Shores, but going home meant facing the demons and decisions. It had been easy to hide in the hills, to forget about everything and fight. What awaited him was pain, perhaps more than he had borne the brunt of thus far.

But at Shores there was good food, better company, and the security of familiar surroundings; they would be his tabard and shield him from the night chill that was his future.

He took a moment to explore the young sky, asked it the same question he had many times before:

What will be?

As always, the powder blue dome hung reticent.

PART THREE

CRACK IN THE CRYSTAL BALL

1

The cave to which Orvin took Marigween was three days' ride east from the village of Shores. A single tortuous cliffside road descending one wall of a wide gorge led to the musty quarters.

Orvin sat opposite Merlin around a circular stone hearth at the mouth of the cave. The night was clear, the stars points of radiant silver, the moon nearly full. Had it not been for Merlin's presence, Orvin would have found the moment blissful.

"So, you've become a coward," the druid accused Orvin, looking up from the fire.

"In my village, a man who saves a woman and child is regarded a hero," Orvin shot back.

Merlin finger-combed his long, white beard and smiled, dull yellow teeth revealed to the molars. Then he chuckled.

Piqued, Orvin's jaw muscles tightened. Then he heard a faint cry from within the cave. Another cry. The baby. Then sweet Marigween's tender voice shushing the child.

"I seem to recall a day many, many moons ago. The day we first met. And the first words out of your mouth to me formed a wild boast." Merlin's smile mocked all that Orvin stood for, all he cared about.

"Had I a dagger in my hand, I would do a hero's justice right now," Orvin said calmly, repressing the crazed demon inside him.

"I, like you, am just too old to kill," Merlin observed. "I fear we shall both live forever."

"Then may God bless us and keep us apart."

Merlin tugged thoughtfully on his beard, bit his lower lip, then furrowed his brow. "Hmmm. Why is it you hate me so? I, over the years, have developed a tolerance for you. Why can you not do the same?"

"Do you wish me to cite incidents where you have embarrassed me, jeopardized my life, and tried to undermine all I stand for?"

"You claim to be a teacher now, or at least you act like one," Merlin said, "but you have yet to learn the lessons I tried to teach you in your youth."

Orvin smirked at the memories of Merlin's lessons—the potions, the roots, the berries, the "magic" of the wood. What good were they to a young knight in the service of Uther Pendragon? Merlin had tried to turn him into a wizard, but Orvin had always known that the future would reveal itself in its own way, and he did not need a mortar and pestle to summon it up. The sky held the mystery. The simple, blue sky. When he looked at it, he could feel what would be.

Orvin pushed a hand through his hair, then extended both palms closer to the fire, warming them. "Your lessons were and still are useless to me."

Merlin shook his head, his expression of pity cast in a golden hue from the dancing fire. "The narrow-minded man lives a bleak, empty life. He travels a single desolate road and sees no farther than the wood on either side. And he is consumed by loneliness.

"How can *you* speak of loneliness?"

"I venture out now and again," Merlin replied.

"To misguide the man who is our king! A lovely service you do for mankind—druid." That word was something bitter on Orvin's tongue. The druids—all of them—were nothing more than mad soothsayers.

Uther Pendragon had placed all his faith in Merlin. Uther Pendragon had died a miserable death, his kingdom divided. And now Uther's son was making the same mistakes. Orvin winced as the future unfolded; it repeated the black past. Merlin had claimed he could help mankind move forward with his "magic." But to Orvin's eyes, mankind remained a stagnant moat. Merlin argued that it had been Uther's shortcomings that had led to his demise, his lust, his impetuous behavior. But Orvin felt differently. He knew who was to blame. If Merlin stopped tampering with the minds of men, perhaps the land would someday be united. Arthur's dream was a noble one, but it was flawed by the mere presence of Merlin.

"Are we to begin, once again, a debate of methodology?" Merlin asked.

A burning log in the hearth weakened, rolled off its perch on another log, then hit the earth bottom of the fire. A spiraling flurry of sparks rushed upward. Orvin's gaze followed the minute points of light as they diminished into the night sky. He brought his palms together and rubbed them, and then finally regarded Merlin. "In my youth, you wanted me to be a wizard as well as a knight. A fighting man of magic. I rejected that notion. I am a man of this realm." Orvin gestured broadly with his hands to the cave, the cliff, the gorge behind him. "This, the real world, is a harsh, unforgiving place, a place where faith should lie within one's self, not in a spell."

"I agree," Merlin replied. "You are a pragmatic man. But you fool yourself. Old age has brought with it a faith that lies in the heavens, not the heart. I deal with things of this world. My power is harnessed from the land."

"What does any of this matter now," Orvin asked bitterly, "when our land is being taken from us?" Slowly, he rose to his feet, leaned over, then rubbed his sore knees.

"What does your sky tell of the Saxon invasion of Shores?" Merlin asked.

Orvin ignored the questions and moved past the fire into the deeper shadows of the cave.

A single candle burned in a simple iron holder in the back of the quarters. The candle sat atop a trunk at the foot of a particularly wide trestle bed. Save for the bed, the trunk, and a few clay pots, two sacks of flour and a burlap bag full of apples, the cave was empty. Where was the elaborate room where Merlin mixed his "famed" potions, his love serums, and his truth brews? Was there another cave? Perhaps . . . but it didn't matter.

Marigween sat up on Merlin's bed, her back resting on a pillow propped against the uneven stone wall. She wore a black cloak Merlin had given her, and cradled the swaddled baby in her arms. She lifted her head at the sound of Orvin's sandaled feet scuffing along the cave floor.

"He is kind to let us stay here," Marigween said softly. "Do you truly hate him as much as you say?"

"More than I've admitted," Orvin grumbled. He moved to her, then ran a wizened finger along the stitched cut that had ruined one of her perfect cheeks. The work was good; Orvin had become adept at mending wounds over the years. And it seemed the better a doctor he became, the more wounds there were to close. He turned away, circled around the bed to the trunk, pushed the candle to one corner, and sat. Then he added, "Some men simply do not get along."

"Some men could learn to get along."

"He and his people pretend to know more than all of us. But they are just men."

"Like you. Just a man."

"Am I so terrible, to have saved your life and brought you here?"

Marigween sighed. "I know how much this bothers you. I am just trying to help."

"He's a fool. And if someone doesn't watch him, he'll be the ruin of us all. Again."

"How do you know?"

Orvin exhaled loudly, then absently smoothed the long hairs on his upper lip. He wished to speak of Merlin, the feud, no longer. He did not reply. Instead, he stared down at the candle and watched as a rivulet of melted wax crept down the stick onto the holder.

"Perhaps we shouldn't—"

"How is your son?" Orvin blurted out.

"He's sleeping now." Her tone changed. "Orvin, can I tell you something?" Fear laced her voice. "I never . . . learned how to . . . "

"Instinct," Orvin replied, leveling his gaze with hers, "will show you the way. As a knight on the battlefield you must simply act and not think. If you *feel* the child needs something, do it. Do not consider it for a second. Act."

He watched as Marigween stared lovingly down at the little face hooded in the scraps of linen he and Merlin had collected from the druid's supplies.

"He doesn't have a name yet," Marigween said with a trace of sadness. "I don't . . . I don't want to name him without Christopher."

Orvin only watched her. There was nothing to add to her words. He wondered if Christopher had survived on the Mendip Hills. Even if Arthur's army was victorious, their triumph would by an empty one upon their return. As for Christopher, he was in for an unforgetable welcome home.

Here is your home: under siege.

And here is . . . your son!

Orvin thanked the Lord he was not Christopher. To be so young and confronted by such shock, such sudden responsibility, and on top of that, to have your home wrenched away twice in your lifetime. Dear St. George—it was too much. Orvin would have to be the boy's solace. But he, too, would find it hard to keep his spirits up in such gloomy times.

A new thought forged inside, one he unfortunately voiced to Marigween before realizing the consequences. "How will you and Christopher explain the child to everyone, especially Lord Woodward?"

Marigween kept her gaze on her child. "I don't know," she said faintly.

The church condemned children out of wedlock, and condemned those responsible for such children. Condemnation took the form of a burning at the stake. How would Christopher, Marigween, and their child avoid such a fate?

The child would have to remain hidden. No one must know of its existence.

"Perhaps," Orvin said, "it is better not to explain the child to anyone."

"What do you mean?"

"I think you know."

"What kind of future will my son have? What will he think of me when he discovers I kept him hidden? He will think I hated him, that I was ashamed of him." Marigween shivered as tears, glistening in the candlelight, slid down her cheeks.

"What other alternatives are there?" Orvin asked,

his mind groping for new paths of escape for the ill-begotten family.

"We could say I found the baby. Christopher and I could be married, and then take the child as our own."

"Are you going to tell Christopher the truth?"

"Of course," Marigween replied quickly. "Do you think I would tell him I found this child, that it is not his?"

"He is a very young man, with a great many burdens, alone in the world and without a family. If he does return, what is he going to find? Chaos and ruin. And out of that . . . a son. My God . . . "

Marigween's expression grew dark, and her aroused temper was evident in the tone of her next: "The truth will not cause him as much pain as a lie. And now he will have a family." Marigween nodded to herself. "Yes. I will tell him the truth. No matter *what* you think is right. *I* know what I will do. I think I've suffered much already. This child is part of Christopher—and he must share the burden . . . and the joy."

The soft shuffle of leather soles on rock caught Orvin's attention, and he cocked his head in the direction of the sound. Merlin slipped deeper into the cave, steadying himself with a gnarled, wooden cane, the end of which was worn smooth from use. He came from the shadows into the dim, flickering light. His gaze found Marigween and her baby.

"What do you want?" Orvin asked, an edge in his voice.

"I wish to be alone with Marigween and her son."

"For what purpose?"

"Simply to talk."

Orvin rose from the trunk. "Another reason why I despise you, Merlin. Your secrets. Everything must be in private. All whispers and spells and magic."

Orvin started toward the moonlight that lit the mouth of the cave.

He heard a conversation begin behind him, but instead of straining to hear it, he picked up his pace and arrived before the flaming hearth outside. He sat, brooding as he stared at the gold and orange and red blades leaning in the night breeze.

2 They swam in the clear, pure lake.

Christopher's head popped out of the water and the sun glinted off his hair. He seemed a living gem to Brenna as she planted her feet on the sandy bottom and rose above the water, exposing her breasts to the air. She felt her skin roughen with gooseflesh.

Christopher's gaze did not lower to her breasts; instead, he looked into Brenna's eyes with an expression she knew could only be love. If there was lust, that was fine, but the love was most important, most powerful. And it was there. She could see it, feel it, taste it, touch it, even somehow smell it. There was an aura around him that enticed her every sense. He moved closer to her, bobbing his way through the water until he was only inches away. But he did not touch her. He stood facing her, looking at her, smiling, eyes shining, shoulders broad, muscles taut and dripping with water. She ached to have those hands on her, to caress her, to touch her in ways she had never been touched before. He could do anything to her. He could have her. She would willingly surrender to him. He was a god before her.

"I love you," he said, his voice as sweet and tender and musical as a lute.

"And I you," she answered, feeling a nerve wrestle in her neck and make her swallow.

And then, oh then, his hand lifted from the water and his thumb and index finger touched her cheek. She felt herself shiver and tried to suppress it, not wanting him to know how nervous he made her.

"You're shaking," he said.

"I'm a little cold," she said, knowing he knew better.

"Let me warm you."

He slid one arm around her neck, the other around her waist, and they embraced. Her breasts pressed into his chest. She felt the scratchy sensation of his pubic hair on her belly. She wanted to kiss his neck. And she did so, melting into the skin that felt very much like—

—a pillow.

Brenna flickered her eyes open, then squinted at the morning sunlight flowing into her chamber and splashing across the floor. She released the pillow from her arms and threw it across the room. "When are you coming back?" Her words echoed hollowly. She collapsed onto the mattress and stared at the rafters, forcing herself to replay the dream in her mind, to see his face again. But it was much harder now, and his handsome features would only congeal into a nondescript lump of flesh, a faceless figure devoid of love.

Come back to me, Christopher. Please come back.

In the outer bailey, a herald's horn blew, and the pounding of hooves drew closer. Brenna heard the chatter of men, and after a few moments there came a shout: "To arms! To arms! Sentries! Raise the drawbridges!"

Brenna sat up, got out of the bed, then crossed the room to the window. From the two towers on her side of the castle she could see bowman after bowman storming from the doorways, hustling along the wall-walk and taking up positions along the parapets. The drawbridge leading from the outlying land to the gatehouse began to rise, as well as the other drawbridge connecting the gatehouse to the outer bailey. She saw the pair of giant spindles begin to turn, spooling link after link of clanking chain. Timbers complained, and finally a *cha-chud!* reverberated throughout the castle as the outer drawbridge locked into position. Then another *cha-chud!* as the inner one stoppered the bailey. Brenna's gaze panned the landscape beyond the castle, but she did not see an attacking army.

"What's happening?" Brenna shouted to anyone below who would listen.

A sentry on the ground called in response, "Get back inside, maid!"

Suddenly, Brenna heard her door push in and someone bounded into her room. She turned to see Mavis and Wynne, her best friends in the world. They looked scared and both, like Brenna, were barefoot and still in their linen nightgowns.

"Brenna! Have you heard?" Wynne cried, her lithe form visibly rattling. "We're under attack!"

"What are we supposed to do?" Mavis asked, moving away from Wynne. She strode into the room past Brenna to the window and studied the scene of the soldiers readying themselves on the wall-walks, the peasants dashing madly through the inner and outer baileys.

"Look beyond our castle," Brenna told Mavis. "I do not see an army out there."

"Perhaps they come from the other side," Wynne suggested.

"Let's find out," Brenna said. She turned from the window and headed for the door.

They left Brenna's quarters and moved across the hall toward the chamber on the opposite side of the keep. From the levels below them, they could hear the cacophony of the keep's inhabitants preparing for the possible attack: shouts; rattles; the ringing of a shield being dropped; the cry of a baby; the pounding of many leather soles on the stone floors. It was a mad atmosphere, one none of the girls had ever experienced.

Instead of a door, the chamber opposite Brenna's was partitioned by a thick wool curtain dyed black. Brenna swiped the curtain aside and stepped into the small, drab room. They found an empty bed, a nightstand supporting a single candle in holder, and a medium-sized trunk below and unshuttered window. On the floor next to the trunk was a pile of soiled kirtles and shifts.

"Please don't kill me! If you don't, I'll serve you well." It was an older woman's voice, slightly muffled, the tone high and fraught with tremors.

Brenna looked around, but she could not find the person who belonged to the voice. The room seemed empty. Mavis and Wynne shrugged.

"Please, I beg you . . . spare me."

Brenna moved to the bed, dropped to her knees, leaned down, then picked up the woolen blanket that covered the bed and extended down to the floor. She peered into the dark recess.

And there, recognizable by the blue kirtle she loved to wear, was Evelina, the senior chambermaid of the castle. She was a sight, cowering under her mattress like a child.

"Evelina!" Brenna gasped. "Come out."

Behind her, Brenna heard Mavis and Wynne giggling.

"Is that you, Brenna?" The old woman's face was away from Brenna, and her lumpy body barely fit under the bed.

Brenna stood and threw herself onto Evelina's bed,

elbowed her way to the opposite edge, then stared down as the old lady dragged herself out into the open air, panting, her eyes closed, her forehead damp with sweat. She rolled onto her buttocks and clutched her heart, unable to speak, only to breathe.

"Are you all right?" Brenna asked, not able to ward off the smile that so deftly attacked her lips.

"I . . . couldn't . . . I couldn't breathe very well under there."

Mavis crossed the room and stood on the trunk to shoot a glance out the window. "There is no army on this side either." Beyond her were the slopes that tapered off into the patchwork of fields below the castle, slopes that were, indeed, devoid of infantry.

"Let's get her up," Brenna said. She rolled off the bed and circled around Evelina. Mavis and Wynne joined in, and they hoisted Evelina to a standing position, not without groaning themselves. She felt as heavy as a courser.

"There now," Brenna said, out of breath, "you're up. And there's no need to hide."

Evelina's gaze lowered to her sandals. "I apologize to you, girls. I instructed you in what to do in case of an attack, and now that the time has come, look at my behavior. My cowardice. I'm ashamed."

Mavis took one of Evelina's hands in her own. "We're just as frightened as you. Don't be ashamed."

"Yes," Wynne chipped in. "We might have done the same thing!"

"Well, we may still have time to behave like women," Brenna said. "Perhaps the army that will attack is still a few days away. We can begin to prepare now."

After several hours of waiting, nerves began to calm, perspiration ceased and dried up, and voices grew steady. The attack, it seemed, wasn't coming.

Rumors spread like fires on thatched roofs, and word trickled back to Brenna that the castles of Shores and Rain had fallen under attack and were now possessions of the Saxons. Rumor also had it that King Arthur's army was on its way to Shores along with Lord Woodward's army. No one knew if the king was aware of the two lost castles. Upon hearing all the news, Brenna made a decision. She would tell her friends about it, and hoped they would agree; but even if they didn't, her mind was set.

With the attack either delayed or not coming at all, Brenna, Mavis, and Wynne resumed their daily tasks. Working individually, they made the beds of the five noblemen Lord Uryens had left in charge of the garrison, accomplishing this with the aid of a long stick to reach across the vast breadth of the four-poster beds. Cushions were shaken out, chamber pots emptied, and sconces were refilled with fresh candles. They swept each of the five quarters and laid fresh rushes on the stone floors. That done, they took the dirty laundry outside to a pair of wooden troughs near one of the inner bailey's curtain walls. They dumped the livery into a mixture of water, wood ashes, and caustic soda. All three girls fetched wooden paddles from under the troughs and began to pound the clothes.

"Certainly an exciting morning," Mavis noted as she worked.

"I hope we are not attacked," Wynne said fervently.

"I'm going to Shores," Brenna said.

Both Mavis and Wynne stopped their work and regarded Brenna, their mouths open.

Brenna continued working her paddle. From the corner of her eye she saw her friends. "I know," she added, "I just know Christopher is alive. And he's with Arthur. And they are going to Shores. I must see him."

"But *now*," Mavis asked, "after you have become so accomplished in waiting, having already shunned three perfectly good young men simply dying to court you?"

Brenna shook her head negatively, then worked her paddle a little faster. "I cannot see his face anymore in my mind. In dreams I see him, but when I awake he is gone. The longer I stay here, the farther away he gets. I realized that this morning. I must go to him. Now. And I need your help."

"This is madness," Mavis said. "You'll be riding into land now held by the Saxons."

"I don't have to be alone," Brenna suggested.

"You want us to go with you?" Wynne asked incredulously.

"If you wish. I would love your company."

"I won't," Mavis said, "and I won't change my mind."

"At least help me acquire a horse, some riding bags, and provisions for the journey," Brenna pleaded.

Mavis threw her paddle into the trough and stepped away, putting her back to Brenna.

Brenna released her paddle and regarded Mavis, who shook her head. Brenna didn't have to see her friend's face to know it was a mask of disbelief.

"You need to speak to the abbot," Mavis said. "Satan has taken over your mind."

Wynne shifted quickly to Brenna's side and rested a hand on Brenna's shoulder. "You don't really want to go there, do you?"

Brenna turned her gaze from Mavis to Wynne. "Yes." Her answer was piercing, definite. Wynne backed away from her as if she were a girl with some illness. Brenna sighed, lowered her gaze to the ground, and pursed her lips.

"You're going to do this, even if we don't help you. Is that it?" Wynne asked.

Brenna nodded. It was true.

Mavis spun around, and yes, disbelief stained her face. "A young woman traveling alone—into Saxon territory no less!"

"If I cannot find someone to accompany me, then yes," Brenna said. She had never been as sure about anything else in her entire life. It was a quest now, one she would clutch tightly to her breast.

The beating of a farrier's hammer on his anvil somewhere in the outer bailey distracted Mavis a moment, but then she answered, "After vespers, we will take you to see the abbot."

"I will be gone before then," Brenna reported flatly.

Wynne, looking about to cry, said, "Brenna, I'll . . . I'll go with you."

"No you will not!" Mavis shouted; it was an order, as Mavis had suddenly appointed herself in charge of Wynne's life.

"It's my decision to make!" Wynne parried.

"You don't have to," Brenna told Wynne, "just help me collect what I need."

"I'm going to the abbot now," Mavis said, then marched off.

When Mavis was out of earshot, Wynne assured Brenna, "She won't go to him. She just doesn't want you to leave. I, too, don't want you to go." Wynne embraced Brenna. "But if you do, I will be at your side—despite whatever happens."

Brenna held her friend, envisioning herself astride a galloping courser, riding bags bulging, the wind and sun at her back. Then she tried to see Christopher. Nothing but a blur. And the desperation to leave became even more real to her. She would not finish her chores, but begin to prepare for a swift departure.

3   The armies of King Arthur and Lord Woodward
were on the last leg of their trek home to Shores. Filthy,
hungry, wounded, and exhausted, the men could not
wait for the pleasures the village and castle promised.
Simple pleasures like a bath and hot meal, but dire
necessities in their tattered state. They had but a few
more hours to wait until those pleasures were theirs.

Christopher shared the same pain and needs as the
rest of the men, combined with tremors of trepidation that rocked him as he rode.

Staring absently at the rolling fields sparsely dotted
with beech trees, he imagined his homecoming:

Marigween would be standing in the outer bailey
of the castle, a basket of fresh, sweet loaves hung
under her arm, a shift flowing like ivory honey over
her lithe frame. Her eyes would light on him, and a
lance of adrenaline would impale his being as he dismounted before her.

For many moons his hands had touched rough
things: the chapped leather reins guiding his horse;
the unpolished hilts of swords, battle-axes, and
lances; the uneven, pitted plates of armor; and the
jagged surfaces of link-mail. Now he could reach up
and caress something so tender that it would frighten
him. Would he be able to touch her without shattering such perfection? Could his callused skin connect
with the supple smoothness of hers?

Yes. She would lean into his hand as he stroked
her cheek, then drop her basket and embrace him.

And suddenly a hand would slam down on
Christopher's shoulder and he would spin around
and look into the eyes of . . .

"Christopher?"

He snapped out of the mental homecoming and turned to see Lord Woodward cantering behind him.

"I'd like to have a word with you," Woodward continued, then spurred his courser, putting himself at Christopher's side.

He knows! But how can he know! Doyle is the only one who knows! Did Woodward see us? If he believes Marigween and I are . . . then this it! He's going to challenge me to a trial by arms. He'll tell me that Marigween is his and that I deserve to die!

There was something caught in Christopher's throat as he answered, and he knew it was his fear. "Yes, lord. How may I be of service?"

"I wish to speak frankly with you, Christopher. And I demand your privacy. It's hard for a man to admit . . . " Woodward's voice waxed melancholic.

This is odd.

"I assure you, lord. Your words will be kept in utter confidence."

Woodward stroked his horse's neck as he spoke. "I have concluded that Marigween will never love me. It is true that the law states she must be my bride, but how are laws supposed to govern love? They cannot. Therefore, I've decided not to force Marigween to marry me. I'm sure her shunning of me is not news to you or the rest of the castle."

"I have heard Marigween express that opinion on more than one occasion," he said.

"I know that you and she are—"

Christopher's heart staggered.

"—friends," Woodward finished. "And that is why I have a favor to ask."

Oh, praise St. George! He doesn't know!

"What is it you request, lord?"

"I know there is a young chambermaid in Gore who is the apple of your eye, Christopher. But—"

"Lord," Christopher interrupted, the conclusion in his mind startling him with irony, "you cannot be asking what I think you are . . . "

Woodward looked at Christopher, the knight's countenance full of resignation and sorrow. "I'm not asking you to court her, though I believe you would be as suitable a man for her as any." Woodward reined his steed closer while reaching out and grabbing Christopher's wrist. "Stay at Shores with me, and become my squire. And you could . . . watch out for Marigween. Become her protector. I am too busy for the job. She has no family—and someone must look after her. There are far too many men in my garrison with loins that ache for her." Woodward released his wrist.

Christopher thought about Woodward's last remark, smiling inwardly. Yes, it would be easy to become Marigween's protector, oh-so-easy to be around her all the time. And it would be grand to be home for good. The offer was brilliant, but if he took it, the deal would be sealed in deception, for once Woodward discovered he and Marigween had been courting all along, then . . . then . . . Christopher did not know what would happen. Better to refuse, and he had the perfect excuse.

"My lord, I doubt King Arthur would release me from his service. Not to boast, but I believe he values my services. And until he settles into a fortress of his own, I will travel with him."

"Messenger! From the south! Ho! A messenger!" one of the banner bearers spearheading Arthur's army shouted.

Woodward diverted his attention to a lone, galloping horsemen tearing up the field as he bounced toward the army. Christopher craned his head and observed the same, sensing that something was not right.

The rider was a messenger from one of the scouting parties leading the army. Frequently the messengers would appear with reports on sudden changes in the landscape ahead, but most often they blew the all clear horn and returned with haste to their brothers-in-arms ahead.

"Trouble?" Christopher asked, his tone betraying his concern.

Woodward snapped his reins. "Let's find out."

Christopher and Woodward galloped ahead to join Arthur and Lancelot.

There was a feeling inside of Christopher, in the pit of his stomach, not unlike the one he had felt when the news had arrived moons ago that Arthur's army was surrounded on the Mendip Hills. He tried to comfort himself. It was probably nothing. Perhaps a river had overflowed its banks and the army would have to divert around it. Yes, that was it. A simple change in course that might delay their arrival in Shores until nightfall.

Why am I always fixating on doom? Why must it always be bad news? Why am I forever looking at the dark side of things? Come now, Christopher, it's nothing! The messenger's report will be so routine that it will be boring!

Christopher and Woodward reached Arthur's side. Christopher studied the messenger; he could not be more than twenty, his beard thin, his face the color of freshly cut oak. When he spoke, his words poured out quickly, emphatically. "Your Majesty, I bring grievous news!"

Christopher's stomach dropped farther, widened to an infinite void, and his mind whirled and spun and leapt to a million premature conclusions. What could have happened? Were the scouts attacked? The problem, whatever it was, lay ahead, and that could only mean . . .

"The village of Shores has been pillaged and burned," the messenger continued. "The castle walls were breached by Saxons, and they now occupy it. We fled before we could get an estimate of their numbers."

Arthur shot a worried look to Lancelot, who gritted his teeth, spat on the ground, then raged aloud. The king craned his neck farther to glimpse Christopher.

Not able to contain his pain, Christopher averted his gaze and rubbed away the fresh tears forming in his eyes. He was embarrassed, but the terribly unexpected news was simply too great a weight to bear after all he had been through. Memories of the day he and Baines had ridden into Shores and found it burning and under attack struck as bolts of lightning in his mind. Vivid pictures of carnage, of the deaths of his mother and father flashed between the darkness, evoking those very same feelings of complete pain, of complete loss. And the feeling of being totally alone in the world returned. Would it be Marigween's charred body he would find now? How could the future be so unfair?

"Christopher," Arthur said, "you weep for your home. But you will not weep long. If there is any group of soldiers who can answer a challenge like this, it is *these* men."

Christopher lifted his head. He swallowed, sniffled, then bit his lower lip. "Yes, my lord. We will drive them out."

Arthur returned his gaze to the messenger. "Where are the rest of the scouts?"

The messenger's face became more despondent. "Fallen prey to one of their border patrols. I suspect I am the only one still alive."

"My liege, if I may," Woodward interrupted.

Arthur nodded.

"It appears we've been hoodwinked. In my opinion, the goal of that Saxon Lord Kenric was to occupy my castle. The armies he amassed on the hills were simply a diversion to draw us away."

"Blast these foul brigands!" Lancelot shouted. "I'm going to skewer many a head in the days to come!"

"That is only conjecture," Arthur told Woodward, "but if it is true, then where were these castle-robbing Saxons hiding? Our scouts searched the territories from here to Brent Knoll and found nothing."

"I do not know," Woodward answered. "But there *are* the Quantock Hills."

"To camp an army in that wasteland would be mad," Arthur said. Then he tugged on his beard, as he was wont to do while thinking. After a moment, he added, "But, indeed, the Saxons are mad. We may have been checked . . . but we have not been mated yet!"

By this time, the rest of Arthur's battle lords had joined the king, forming a circle of mounted men. Christopher watched as Arthur rattled off orders to his knights. He instructed them to break the news gently to the soldiers and peasant levy, and he assured them they weren't going to attack until fresh provisions were procured from the neighboring village of Falls, providing it had not been attacked. If so, then they would turn to the abbey at Queen's Camel. The monks would not be able to provide

enough supplies for both armies, but any help would
be better than none. Siege machines would have to
be secured, and those they might be able to borrow
from Lord Nolan at the castle of Rain. If not, they
would have to transport them from Uryens's castle in
Gore. It would take nearly a moon to move the tre-
buchets, mangonels, and ballistas that far.

All the while Arthur spoke to his battle lords,
Christopher could not help noticing the calm in the
king's voice. Arthur was a changed man. Christopher
remembered how the king had reacted to the news of
being surrounded by the Saxons; he had been a lost
soul, about to fall down and surrender. But now, in a
time when Christopher himself felt ready to concede
defeat, the king blazed with determination and a self-
assuredness that was infectious. Christopher felt his
spirits slowly rise as Arthur spoke, and the doubt
began to ebb.

Christopher detected the clatter of hooves over his
shoulder and cocked his head to steal a look.

The scaled armor of the galloping rider identified
him as an archer. The man charged out of the
Vaward Battle group toward the south, whipping his
steed's flank with the palm of his hand.

It seemed the rumors of Shores's fall had torn very
quickly through the ranks of the army, and now
someone opted to take on the enemy single-handedly,
perhaps over a loved one. Christopher squinted to get
a better look at the rider's face, the late day sun dic-
ing the image with blinding white light. For a second
he caught sight of the man. "Doyle," he whispered
aloud.

Arthur broke free from his battle plan, his eyes
wide over the sight of the mad rider. "Someone stop
that archer!"

"I will!" Christopher shouted, then reined his courser out of the group and heeled the strong horse in pursuit of Doyle.

4   Brenna and Wynne borrowed two rounseys from a hostler who fell easily under their charm. Though Brenna had imagined herself astride a mighty courser, the rounsey would do. It was not the time to be picky.

With their hastily packed riding bags weighted down with provisions, and their hearts beating a cadence of excitement in their chests, they rode out of the castle of Gore's outer bailey and into the cool shadows of the gatehouse. They were questioned by the sentries in the fore towers, but easily managed to pass with a story about a delivery of fresh linens to the inn as a favor to Lady Griselda, the reeve's wife. The sentries smiled flirtatiously and let them go.

Brenna was not comfortable with lying, but it was a necessary evil if she was to see Christopher.

Once out in the open country below the castle, Wynne drew in a deep breath and said excitedly, "I cannot believe we're doing this!"

"Well, we are!" Brenna answered. "I wish I could see the look on Evelina's face when she finds the note on her bed." Brenna's grin was wide and magical.

"What did you tell her?"

"Oh, nothing but the truth."

"You didn't . . . "

"Oh, yes," Brenna said loftily. "Wynne and I have

gone on a journey to Shores. We are not sure when we will be back, but when we do know, we might send word by carrier pigeon. But then again, we might not!"

"You didn't say that," Wynne argued.

"I should have," Brenna said with a chuckle.

"What about your parents?" Wynne asked. "I . . . didn't even say good-bye to mine. I knew I couldn't."

That reminder evoked a shiver of pain in Brenna. She tried to blanket the feeling, make herself and her friend feel better. "Don't worry about them. We'll be back home so quickly they'll have scarcely missed us."

Brenna pictured the face of her father upon receiving the news from Evelina. He would become red as a beet, and the sweat on his head would start to boil off into vapor.

I can't think about this! I have to ride!

They cantered on for a silent moment, and soon they were each eyeing the landscape with a newfound wonder, a newfound freedom, forgetting about the problems behind them. Then Brenna suggested they kick into a gallop.

With the wind rushing through their hair, and the hooves of the rounseys thumping rhythmically on the soft, sun-withered grass, they arrowed toward the town of Glastonbury.

Joy was a flame inside Brenna's body that caused beads of sweat to dapple her forehead and upper lip. Her perspiration was also attributable to the summer sun and hard ride, but Brenna considered it solely due to anticipation. She could feel the certainty of her reunion with Christopher. And the joy of knowing burned hotter inside.

She took the lead while Wynne followed. This was,

after all, her adventure. She had suggested all of it and had dragged Wynne along. Well, not dragged. Wynne had chosen to come of her own free will, and Brenna was more than thankful for the company. But the burden of being responsible for Wynne was there. It was a minor weight, one she could easily shoulder, but if anything should happen to Wynne, Brenna did not know if she could forgive herself.

She purged all the doubt and misgivings from her mind and rode on, concentrating on the slowly changing countryside.

Ahead, a line of four ox-driven carts reached the crest of a small slope. As Brenna and Wynne drew closer, Brenna saw that the lead cart was driven by a pot-bellied farmer, the others by three boys who were undoubtedly his sons, all pale-skinned with flaxen hair. They had a delivery of vegetables and fruit for the castle. Brenna slowed her horse to a canter and Wynne did likewise. In a few moments, they were upon the caravan. The strong aroma of the basketed harvest awakened a pang in her stomach. She and Wynne nodded to the farmer, then moved on to the three sons. The oldest was their age, each after him a year or so younger. Brenna felt their gazes on her, and she turned away shyly.

"Ho!" the oldest boy yelled as his cart moved behind them.

Brenna turned around and the boy threw a bright red apple. Brenna thrust out her hand and, at the very last second, caught the apple, a slight sting rippling through the skin on her palm.

The boy smiled.

Brenna turned away and felt her cheeks flush.

Wynne coaxed her horse next to Brenna's. "I believe he likes you, Brenna," she said teasingly.

"Here," Brenna said, handing her the apple.

"But it's yours."

"I don't know why, but by eating this apple, I feel as if I'm making a pledge to that boy. And we both know that is not possible."

"You are an odd one," Wynne announced.

"If we're to reach Glastonbury by nightfall, we'd better make haste." With that, Brenna drove the heels of her sandals into her rounsey's side.

She had never been to the town of Glastonbury, but her mother had told her about it. When they had left the castle of Shores and had moved to Uryens's castle at Gore, they had considered stopping at Glastonbury to rest, but Brenna's father had not allowed it. He had been too afraid of a Saxon attack and had pushed the family like a mad dog to Gore.

Under the dying remnants of an orange-and-mauve sky, Brenna gazed upon the town from their perch on a hillock. She thought the hillock might be Windmill Hill, a sacred place of prayer used by the monks of the abbey below, but she could not be sure.

Thatched-roof houses were the common structures, save for the church and the abbey house which were, of course, made of stone. Flickering candlelight painted rectangular dots of color on a scene that could not be more peaceful. They heard a dog howl in the distance, shattering the restful quiet. But silent order fell once again.

Brenna sniffed. The grass was already damp with dew in spots, and the thick scent was not pleasant to her nostrils. "Come on," she urged Wynne. "Enough admiring the view."

Wynne hesitated. "Between us we've only six deniers. I doubt we can afford to stay at the inn—if there is one."

"That abbey must have a barn. We'll find it and sleep in the loft," Brenna said, the notion having brewed in her mind from the moment they had crested the hillock.

"What if we're caught?" Wynne asked.

"Then our necks will be warming the gallows tree ropes," Brenna said with mock seriousness.

Wynne's jaw fell slack.

Brenna *tsk*ed. "Come now, I jest. If we are caught, we will use our smiles and our wits and talk ourselves out of punishment or fine or anything else."

"What if we cannot do that?" Wynne challenged.

"It is either that or we sleep out her, vulnerable to anyone or any*thing* that might *crawl* along." Brenna knew her last was adequate persuasion.

"All right then," Wynne said with lukewarm agreement. "Let's ride down."

"After you." Brenna gestured with her hand.

"No, I think you should lead."

Brenna complied, smiling over her friend's indelible uneasiness.

They descended the slope for the dark, still avenues of the town.

Brenna did not know what her bravery was born of, but she did enjoy flaunting it in front of her friend. She felt very powerful, able to take on the realm in a single breath. She had finally, for the first time in her life, acted upon one of her desires. For too many moons she had longed for things that had never come, put her hopes and dreams into things that had never satisfied. All of her life she had relied on other people for her happiness. She knew being with Christopher would make her content; now she had acted upon that wish and would fulfill it. The sheer fact that she had acted at

all made her feel wonderful. And brave. Ah, yes, her
bravery was conceived of her ability to seize control of
her life. To finally stand up for something she believed
in. She was ready to fight for what she wanted—and if
anyone stood in the way of her goal, she would cut them
down and push them aside. She hadn't taken the anlace,
sheathed and strapped to her side, for nothing.

Upon reaching the first road, they dismounted and
towed their horses by the reins. Brenna had never
seen a path such as this; it was similar to the wall-
walks of a castle, but different. Stones were set into
the road, turning its surface into a fairly even sheet of
solid rock. The shoes of their rounseys *click-clacked*
off the stones, and Brenna prayed that no one would
come out of their house to investigate. But as it was,
the noise was apparently common, and they were not
accosted. They rounded a corner and found themselves on a street that paralleled the great stone
abbey. Yes, there it was: a wide two-story building
standing behind the abbey. Indeed, the abbey barn.

Brenna's rounsey neighed softly. She reasoned the
animal caught the smell of the fresh hay, carried on
the night breeze from the barn. "Quiet. You'll be fed
soon enough," she told the beast in a stage whisper.

"I don't like this," Wynne said.

Brenna glanced over her shoulder and saw her friend
spying every window, doorway, crack, and crevice of
the buildings around them, apprehension twisted
around her like an angry vine. "What are you saying?"
Brenna asked. "It's perfect. Our horses will be fed, our
minds and bodies will be rested. And we'll be gone
before the hostlers even open the doors to the barn."

Wynne began a rebuttal, but stifled it.

"You see? You cannot argue," Brenna said.

The full moon broke free from its grapple with a

cloud and cast a pale, silvery hue over the two sliding doors of the abbey barn. Brenna exploited the sudden light and found a leather tie that bound the doors together at their thin, iron handles. She untied the leather strap and slowly slid the right-hand door open. The wooden rollers were well waxed and the timbers moved effortlessly and silently.

As many as a dozen occupied stalls lined the rear of the barn, a surprising number. Brenna guessed that the monks and their abbot must do a lot of traveling, for even the abbey at Gore, a much larger town, had a barn that housed only four steeds. The horses in the stalls began to shift nervously. Brenna reacted, pulling her rounsey inside, then waving Wynne to do the same. Brenna slid the door closed and the horses began to quiet.

A single shaft of moonlight beamed in from a lone loft window on the right side of the barn. Navigating in the gloom, they tethered their rounseys to the support poles of a wall, fetched and mounded piles of hay before the steeds, then unfastened their riding bags. They looked for a ladder to get up to the loft and, to their good fortune, discovered a sturdy staircase constructed against a sidewall of the building. The abbot of Glastonbury, like most abbots, spared no expense—even in his barn.

Brenna sat down, falling back onto a pile of hay below a wall of stacks. She stretched her arms outward and felt the stiffness in her shoulders give way. The hay scratched her neck and the backs of her ears, but that didn't matter. It was great a relief to take the weight off of her body.

"I am a weary traveler," she announced to Wynne.

"I am a weary traveler's even more weary companion," Wynne said with a giggle.

"Feeling safer now?" Brenna asked.

Wynne was seated and nudged her way closer over the timbers, one of them groaning loudly in objection. She stopped, and Brenna heard the sounds of Wynne's breathing cease.

"Do you think someone—"

"No," Brenna said. "Now we have to eat and then sleep; otherwise, we won't be strong enough for the morrow. And we cannot do either of those things if you're to worry all night."

"I'm sorry. It's just—"

"I know. Neither of us has ever done this before. But that doesn't matter. We have to grow up sometime, and it might as well be now."

Brenna sat up, pulled her riding bag closer, unbuckled the flap, and threw it open. She withdrew a flagon of cider, twisted out the cork, then took a long pull on it. The warm liquid slid down her throat and reached the dark, empty cave that was her stomach, flooding it delightfully. She pulled the flagon from her lips and proffered it to Wynne, who accepted it heartily. Brenna reached back into the riding bag and wrapped her hand around a bundle of pork ribs, salted and wrapped in linen. She hoped Wynne wouldn't finish the ale, for the meat would summon up her thirst all over again. As she unwrapped the meat, she heard one of the barn doors begin to slide open.

Wynne gasped.

5 Standing on the wall-walk of the northeastern tower of the castle, Seaver gazed down upon the murmuring forest. He was crestfallen, guilt having pierced his armor and gone on to his heart. In the air of victory, he had been too busy to feel any grief, any loss. But days had passed, and the consequences of battle had settled in, like a tankard of hemlock juice, a horrid poison.

He shouldn't feel miserable. He shouldn't. Why, he was Lord Kenric's second-in-command now! He was a man of tall responsibilities, looked up to for direction, perhaps even admired. Why should he care about some young scout, some young, clumsy buffoon?

But Cuthbert had tried. The boy had tried very hard to please, to be accepted. But at both, he had tried too hard.

Was his death my fault? Maybe I did not train him well enough. . . .

When the boy's body was brought in on the back of a flatbed, Seaver could hardly believe what had happened. How could Cuthbert let himself be killed so easily? It seemed he had never defended himself.

Perhaps it was *my fault!*

Seaver remembered feeling embarrassed for the boy. It was a dishonor to be slaughtered in such a way: without, apparently, putting up a fight. At the time, Seaver had focused on his censure of the boy's actions; Cuthbert's inability to stay alive. Now the time had come for grief, for guilt, and these feelings would haunt him for many moons, he knew.

What was the music on the breeze? Seaver did not know. It was a whistling sound through the parapets that he read as a dirge. Or maybe it *did* sweep up from

the great hall, the newly indentured musicians exhaling
into their odd instruments and banging on their drums.

Why had he come here at all? With preparations
already made to defend the castle against the
encroachment of the Celt armies, there was little left
to do but wait for their attack. He should have
retired to his chamber, or perhaps learned to play
that game that enchanted Kenric so much, the game
called chess. Yes, he should learn to play, and per-
chance recruit Ware, teach that callow scout to play
as well.

*What am I thinking about? What's wrong with
me?*

Seaver was tired, but he could not sleep. He was
hungry, but he could not eat. He was thirsty, but he
could not drink. He had to *do* something, but he did
not know what.

Leather soles padded over stone, and though the
noise was barely discernible, Seaver's honed senses
picked it out among the din of insects and night creatures. He whirled around.

"Halt!" a Saxon sentry on the other side of the
tower shouted, brandishing his pike.

"It is only I, Darrick."

"Very well," the sentry said, then was swallowed
back into the shadows.

Darrick stood before Seaver. The man was partially
eclipsed in darkness, the veins on his brawny arms
bulging and covered with a fine layer of dirt. His
hands bore the distinctive calluses of a mangonel
operator, and he reached up with a stubby finger to
scratch a bit of dust out of one cold, dark eye.

"What is it?" Seaver asked, irked by the intrusion.

Darrick opened his mouth, revealing a pair of gaps
in his lower teeth that made him look as if he'd been

defanged. Seaver knew the man's temperament, and
determined that yes, the fangs had once been there.
"I come here representing at least twoscore men who
disagree with Kenric's decision making you second-
in-command. We will no longer hold our tongues."
His tone was low, the words breathy, the threat clear.

Seaver took a step back from the man, his hand
going instinctively to the hilt of his dagger, at home
belted around his thigh. "I'm overjoyed you've told
me this. First, I shall bleed the names out of you,
then round up the traitors and bathe them in Greek
fire—you along with them!"

Darrick flipped a grin of defiance, then raised an
index finger. "Pay no heed to your threats or your
dagger, but to what I say. I wasn't sent here to kill
you. We supported Manton, and feel that Renfred
deserves his command. For more than a score of
moons did Renfred serve under Manton, and what
reward does he get? He gets to see a dwarf assume
his rightful role as second-in-command."

"I am *not* a dwarf!" Seaver screamed. "My body is
of normal proportion as you can plainly see. I am
simply shorter than most men. But that hasn't
stopped me—has it?" The question was rhetorical,
and Seaver added quickly, "Why do you take this up
with me? Why not go to Kenric?"

"We already have," Darrick said. "He seems certain *you* are the best man for the job. Ha! A runt
such as yourself." Darrick continued to chuckle, a
sound that would send dogs running.

"I suppose it's quite easy for Renfred to relax in his
chamber while you're up here doing his bidding for
him and the rest of his supporters. I wonder why he
does not confront me himself with his lust for my
command. Or is *he* the runt?"

Darrick glowered and took a step toward Seaver, restoring the distance between the two. Then he took another step. Seaver could feel the man's hot breath on his cheeks when he spoke. "Renfred is a greater man than both of us. He respects Kenric's wishes and will not argue with him. But in this, I tell you, Kenric is wrong. We'll go above Kenric if necessary."

"And what will make that necessary?" Seaver asked.

"Your refusal to willingly step down," Darrick said. "All you have to do is resign and recommend Renfred for your command."

"And if I don't?" Seaver asked, already knowing the answer to the question, but wanting to hear it come out of Darrick's mouth to be certain.

"If you don't, I promise you, you will die."

Another figure appeared behind Darrick. The figure stepped forward, and the moonlight picked him out as Ware. "We've caught a Celt, my lord," he said. "An archer who charged the gatehouse. Kenric wants you to question him."

"I'll be down immediately," Seaver replied.

Ware nodded, spun on his heel, then whisked away.

Seaver regarded Darrick, shaking his head with disdain. Then he turned his head in the direction of the sentry. "Guard. Come."

The young man marched over, his leather and armor rattling along the way. "Yes, sir?"

"Take this man into custody. We are all going to the dungeon."

Darrick shot Seaver a black look, but said nothing.

The guard led Darrick at pike point along the wall-walk, with Seaver trailing close behind.

Darrick craned his head, then smirked over his shoulder at Seaver. "My imprisonment is your answer to them. And they will kill you."

"Guard? Shut his mouth," Seaver ordered tersely.

The man relished the liberty Seaver gave him. With his free hand balled into a fist, he hammered it into Darrick's mouth. One quick punch, and the fat mangonel operator's lips were split.

"Are you going to speak again?" the guard asked Darrick.

"You dog! You've drawn my blood!" Darrick's steps became staggered. He turned toward the guard and raised a hand.

The guard delivered another punch into Darrick's mouth. This time there was a crunch. Darrick nearly choked, then spat a wad of bloody phlegm mixed with a long-rooted tooth into his palm.

"You'd best be silent," Seaver warned Darrick, "for you cannot afford to lose any *more* teeth . . . "

They shuffled under the archway that led to the tower's staircase, then mounted the stairs and began their circular ascent.

6 Christopher lay in the damp brush opposite the northeast curtain wall of the castle. Three hours prior he had watched the Saxons pull Doyle from his mount, strip him of his armor and weapons, then cudgel him mercilessly. The gatehouse sentries had taken turns with their clubs while Christopher had looked upon the scene feeling helpless and horrified.

He had trembled with the desire to aid his friend, but
to do so would have meant being captured along with
Doyle.

*There was nothing I could've done. I have to keep
telling myself that.*

While waiting for night to cloak his retreat,
Christopher questioned Doyle's actions. Why had his
friend charged the castle alone? It was beyond reckless, beyond foolish. It was senseless and altogether
unexplainable. What did he hope to gain? What
could he have possibly been thinking?

Or maybe he wasn't thinking clearly at all. His
senses could have been numb. Christopher had
rarely seen that flagon leave Doyle's side, and Doyle
was quick to refill it when the brew ran out. Numb
with ale, Doyle had probably decided to charge the
castle. But the reason still remained a puzzle. A suicide run? Was Doyle so distraught over his problems that he had finally given up all hope?
Christopher had not detected this from their conversations, though they had in past days carefully
avoided speaking of Innis and Leslie. Maybe Doyle's
guilt had smothered his hope. He could have
decided that he didn't deserve to live after killing
Innis and Leslie. Maybe he didn't have the strength
to kill himself and wanted to leave the task up to
the Saxons.

But Christopher knew the Saxons wouldn't kill
Doyle. Christopher had served in a Saxon army and
he knew all too well what happened to archers who
were taken prisoner. . . .

He looked down at the thumb and forefinger of his
right hand, touched them with the fingers of his left,
then shivered at the thought of having them hacked
off.

A scuffling of leaves and shifting of branches brought Christopher around on his belly. He drew his dagger and held his breath. Shadows. Silhouettes of trees and limbs and brambles and bushes. It was hard to distinguish a man's form amid the confusion of the forest. He squinted against the night and stared until it burned in the direction of the sound.

Then the figure came into view, hunkered down, sword drawn. The figure prowled forward.

His anxiety stoked, options sprang into Christopher's mind. He could call out. But in what language? Saxon? If it was a Saxon out there, then he would be taken for a friend. But if it was a Celt, then he would be mistaken for an enemy. If he called out in Celt, he would be playing the same fifty-fifty odds, and he was not much of a gambler.

Christopher decided that calling out was *not* an option after all. He would have to flee, hopefully undetected by whoever it was, or get close enough to identify the figure. If the man was a Celt, they would flee together, if he was a Saxon, Christopher might have to kill him.

Better to flee undetected and not have to kill. Gingerly, he lifted himself to his hands and knees, pushed his knees forward, then got to his feet, careful to keep himself as low as possible; he stooped over like an old man.

But then Christopher saw the figure charge, a black demon with a liquid ebony blade raised high over its featureless head.

Christopher sprang right, but the figure altered its course and came at him. He was close enough to the figure now to distinguish the man's livery: that of a Saxon perimeter guard.

"You fool! It's me!" Christopher shouted to the

man in Saxon as he darted behind a beech tree. Furtively, he peered out from behind the trunk.

The guard broke off his advance and stood poised, shifting his head, searching for Christopher. "Farman? Is that you?"

"You would have killed me!" Christopher said, feigning his anger.

The Saxon took several steps closer toward Christopher—too many, Christopher reasoned, so he shot off.

He should have removed the rest of his armor before tethering his horse to the boundary of the forest and threading in toward the perimeter. But as it was, he still wore his hauberk, greaves, poleyns, and heavy riding boots; they were enough to announce his every move to the Saxon and burden his every step.

Christopher ignored the weight and rustle of the armor and dodged around columns of oak and beech. Sleeping larks and pipits in patches of nearby briar were rudely awakened; they fanned out from their nests in chirping clouds, leaving a rush of air in their wake. Christopher stumbled into a bush and fell forward onto his chest. His leg armor protected him from the thorny limbs of the bush, and his link-mail–covered arms were only soiled with dirt. He felt the impact echo through his body as he scrabbled with his hands to right himself, pushed up, then resumed his run.

So strong was the notion of getting back to his horse that Christopher barely felt the thump on the back of his head. Had he turned around to look, he would have seen the Saxon guard's dagger lying useless on the forest floor behind him, its hilt end having hit Christopher's head.

An owl hooted, heralding Christopher's arrival at

the edge of the forest. His courser was not there. This was not his original point of entry. He gazed north, then south, and in the distance saw the wagging tail of his grazing horse some hundred yards away.

Behind him, in the forest, he heard: "You'll not escape, Celt! By the blood of my father I will kill you!" The Saxon guard's voice carried with it a fervor and intensity that chilled Christopher to his bones, and inspired his feet to move. He knew his escape would be a great insult to the guard. The man would report the incident to his superiors and receive, at the least, a gauntlet in the face, and at the most, a dagger in the heart. Most Saxons were fiercely loyal and uncompromisingly honest.

Christopher quickly untied the reins of his courser from the trunk of a wide oak. He slipped his left leg into a stirrup, then swung himself onto the horse. He wheeled the steed around just as the Saxon sprinted up, swinging his sword.

"Dismount and fight, yellow swine!" the guard screamed, then charged toward him.

Christopher's courser reared, nearly throwing him out of the saddle. He struggled for control and gained it, bringing the animal down and tugging him right as the Saxon came in for the kill. Christopher's mount slammed into the man and knocked him onto his back, though he held fast to the blade in his grip. Christopher spurred forward, leaving the stunned guard behind him.

As he brought his steed to full gallop, he heard a screaming cry behind him: "You'll not die this night, Celt! But on another, I promise!"

The shrill voice faded into the din of his horse's hooves and the drone of the wind.

•   •   •

Christopher did not realize how hungry he was until
he drew near the camp the two armies had estab-
lished along the River Cam. The tall reeds that
extended from the bemired shores into the surrounding
fields made for ideal cover, and though Christopher
could smell the meat roasting over cookfires, he saw no
trace of the glowing flames as he dismounted.

"Halt!" The voice shot through the night.

"Hold!" Christopher shouted back. He couldn't see
the guards through the reeds, but he knew their crossbows were windlassed, loaded with bolts, and aimed
at him. He raised an open palm. "It is I, Christopher,
the king's squire!"

A tall man bearing a crossbow slipped from behind a
cluster of reeds. "Only a dolt or a Saxon would approach
without announcing himself," the bowman said.

Christopher let out a deep sigh. "An error I apologize
for. I've just come from the castle, and from a small fray
with a Saxon guard. My thoughts are still jumbled."

The bowman's gawk was exactly what Christopher
wanted to see. The man was either impressed with
the fact that Christopher had returned alive from an
enemy-occupied castle, or he thought Christopher
was twice a fool for being there in the first place.

In either case, the bowman let him pass with a
slack-jawed nod, then called after: "You're to report to
the king's tent at once. So say my orders to tell you."

Christopher gazed over his shoulder. "I will."

He walked his horse down a narrow path freshly
cut through the reeds that opened up into a broad
portion of shoreline where a long row of tents was
being pitched. The smell of the meat was dizzying
now, and Christopher viewed a young boar revolving

on a spit over a raging cookfire. He needed to fill his belly before he reported to Arthur's tent, where the king would fill his ears with questions.

Moving through the team of peasant levy tent pitchers, Christopher found a groom and turned his horse over to the lean, weary-looking man. Weaving through several infantry and cavalrymen ambling to their tents or returning to the fires for more food, Christopher spotted Lord Woodward seated on a woolskin with a pair of his lieutenants. The banner knight tore away on a juicy, sweet, roasted leg of a leveret. Christopher's mouth watered at the sight.

Woodward looked up, and his brow lifted. "Christopher." He stood, navigated around the seated men, then placed his free hand on Christopher's mail-covered shoulder. "We feared the worst. Why did *you* choose to go after that mad archer?"

Staring at the remains of the leveret, sitting on a carving board atop a traveling trunk, Christopher said, "If I may share in your catch, I will tell you."

"Of course, of course, come, sit down. This'll be our last great feast for a while. I suspect the wood will be hunted out in several days, and who knows how long it'll be before fresh provisions arrive." Woodward gestured toward an empty place on a woolen blanket laid out before the fire. "Fetch yourself something and sit down."

Christopher picked off a hunk of meat from the breast of the leveret, then another. He took a bite and began chewing as he crossed to the blanket and sat with a loud clanking of his leg armor. He swallowed the meat and took another bite, chewing without thinking, just doing it quickly like a hard-driven horse after a day's ride. One of the lieutenants thrust a tankard of cider toward Christopher, and he took it without looking up and sucked down a heavy gulp of the warm liquid. He knew he ate as loudly and quickly as Sir Orvin, but he did not care. His belly screamed for more.

"He's famished," the lieutenant said to his cohorts.

"Now tell me, young man, before you go running off to the king, which I know is where you're headed now, why did you risk your life for some peasant archer?"

Christopher stopped chewing and set down his tankard. "He's no peasant. His father is Lord Heath, Uryens's steward. And he is one of the best archers in the Vaward Battle. He is also my friend. We became blood brothers."

The murmuring of the men fell off into the crackling of the cookfire flames.

"I'm sorry, Christopher," Woodward said. "They captured him, did they not?"

Christopher nodded. "Cudgeled him, then took him prisoner."

"There is not much information they can get out of him. But you're aware of what they'll do. He's lost now, Christopher."

Christopher lowered his head, gritted his teeth, and felt the pain of tears build in his eyes. "No. He is *not* lost."

"Look! Look who it is!" The shout came from an archer squatting before a cookfire adjacent to Woodward's. The boy added, "Why I thought he was . . . "

Christopher tilted his head up, and through a billowing cloud of cookfire smoke there emerged a familiar, endearing face. Sir Orvin. The old man's breeches and linen shirt were wrinkled and dirty, but the tabard he sported was new, and it fanned out at his ankles as he walked. Swatting men out of his way,

Orvin cleared a path for himself that led to Christopher.

Never had Orvin arrived at a more-opportune moment. Christopher felt dark and heavy-hearted over his fallen home and fallen friend. And he had yet to discover what had happened to Marigween, and the confirmation of her death lay like some predatory creature inside, waiting to strike his vulnerable heart. At last there was Orvin's wonderful shoulder to lean on, his wise mind from which to seek guidance. He had left Orvin behind and had gone into battle once before, only to return many moons later brimming with questions and a heart as weighty as a mangonel stone.

Nothing had changed. He felt the same now, all the emotions and all the questions built into a single force that lifted Christopher and drove him past Woodward and the lieutenants, out onto the shoreline, and toward the old man.

They met, and Christopher said nothing, only took the old man into his arms and embraced him, burying his head into Orvin's shoulder, feeling the coarse wool of the tabard on his cheek. He began to weep, for there was so much to weep over.

"The young patron saint cries as we all should in this bleak hour," Orvin said solemnly.

Remembering where he was—among his peers— Christopher broke the embrace and fought for control of his grief. Breathing deeply, wiping away his tears, he took a long, hard look at Orvin. The man looked no worse for wear. Once you were old, Christopher figured, how could you get any older? What did another wrinkle mean among many? What did another white hair mean among the gray? It was gratifying to see that Orvin had not changed. He was the only thing about Shores that had remained constant.

"What happened? How did you—"

Orvin put a finger over Christopher's lips. "I've come here with . . . *Merlin*," he said, uttering the name of the king's druid-advisor as if it were anathema. "He feeds Arthur his meal of misinformation as we speak. And while the king is busy, you and I have much to talk about." The old man considered their surroundings. "But not here."

"You know Merlin?" Christopher asked, impressed.

"It is no pleasure of mine. Now come." Orvin turned and started off down the riverside.

Christopher jostled his way through milling soldiers, squires, and the like, back to Woodward's cookfire. He told the knight he would finish their conversation later, that he must speak with Sir Orvin. Woodward nodded, but before Christopher could dart off, the knight reminded him of his offer to become his squire and to protect Marigween; that was if they found the orphaned princess alive once they breached the castle's walls. Christopher replied as he had before, saying the offer was tempting, but that Arthur would probably not cut him loose. Woodward said he would see about that.

Once he caught up to Orvin, Christopher walked north with the old man along the Cam. The river reflected the moon and splayed a copper-and-tin light across their path. They came upon a place of relative quiet that struck Christopher as familiar. He let his gaze play over the muddy soil to where small clumps of low-lying weeds grew and meshed into the wall of reeds. Among the weeds he spotted a dirty, torn, lump. He moved closer to the lump and saw it was an old woolen blanket, probably abandoned many moons

ago. He leaned down and picked up the blanket with
his index finger and thumb, then shook it out.

Images of the past shimmered and woke in
Christopher's mind. He was on the same shoreline
with Doyle's brother Baines, watching the squire
unwrap a stolen broadsword from a woolen blanket
that protected it. And here now in Christopher's
hand was a piece of his past, the very same blanket
that protected the sword. The blanket had been abandoned, but the sword was at this moment sheathed
and fastened to Christopher's mount.

"What rubbish is that?" Orvin asked.

"Baines and I came here once. He showed me the
broadsword he'd stolen from your son. He hid the
sword here, wrapped it in this blanket."

"Memories. They're a wonderfully disquieting
thing," Orvin said. "The boy who was once here has
become a man. A true servant. But he has yet to face
his greatest challenge. And I know not if he's ready."

Christopher dropped the blanket. "Tell me what
you mean."

Orvin stepped slowly to the water's edge. "Perhaps
you are not ready yet. Perhaps this old wag has
opened his trap one too many times. Then again,
maybe it is none of my business at all. Who am I to
be directing the young patron saint's life? If I am
directing it, then what am I? Nothing more than a
silly druid staining the future land with blood?" He
turned his eyes up to the blue-black heavens. "What
am I, dear God? What is it I am supposed to do?"

Christopher was taken aback by Orvin's conduct.
Never had he seen his mentor as troubled, as . . . distracted. What was it that drove Orvin to turn to God
for answers? For a moment, Christopher was glad he
was not Orvin, for a least he had someone in the

flesh to turn to for help. Orvin could only rely on
God—a much greater force than any man, yes, but a
much more mysterious one. Faith in God required
great patience, and Christopher had only a small
pouch of that to expend. He believed in God. But he
did not have time to wait for miracles; he wanted to
help them along.

"What's wrong, Orvin? What is it?" he asked.

Orvin's gaze left the sky and lowered to the the
water. But Orvin didn't seem to be looking at the
water; he stared into depths of nothingness. "You
fought bravely as a boy when your village was
attacked. You saved yourself. And you came to me as
the skies foretold. And there was something.
Something undeniably special about you, Christopher.
My son saw it right away. It took me time, but then I,
too, knew you would grow up to become an extraordinary man. Your life thus far has been full of challenges, all of which you have met head-on and
conquered. Now, I simply cannot understand why
God has impeded you so? What is it he wants from
you? And what can I do to help you?"

Christopher crossed over the mud and reached
Orvin. He draped an arm around the old man's back.
"My life is not that terrible, Orvin. Yes, my parents
were taken away, along with my home. But time
heals the wounds as you've said, yes? Shores will not
be in the hands of the Saxons for long. I've seen a
new light in Arthur's eyes, a new calm. It excites me."
Christopher swallowed as thoughts of Doyle let
themselves into his mind. "The greatest pain I feel
right now is for Doyle, who threw himself to the
enemy. Somehow, I must get inside the keep and free
him, along with the rest of the nobles who may be
held prisoner."

Orvin turned his head and leveled his soft, gray eyes on him. "A noble quest, young patron saint. But is it also sparked by another desire?"

"What do you mean?"

"Do you suspect young Marigween is behind those walls?"

Orvin knows. But how could I hide my relationship with Marigween from him? He probably saw it in a cloud, or in a fork of lightning! He may be hurt that I never told him. But I knew what he would say: "Young patron saint, you embark on a path of evil, one from which there is no turning back." But I'm not perfect, and it felt *so perfect. What was I to do? Doyle admires me for it. But I know Orvin does not. Brenna is safe and waiting for me at Gore. But Marigween . . . if she's alive, she needs my help. It's too late to consider whether courting Marigween was right or wrong. I must act. Admitting it to Orvin will not make a difference; admitting I was wrong to keep it from him will.*

"There are no secrets I can keep from you, Orvin, though I have tried. I should have told you about Marigween. I was wrong. And I'm sorry." Christopher could not meet his mentor's gaze.

"I have told you this before, but it seems you have yet to heed my words. Do not let love blind you—as it always does. You looked too deeply into Marigween's eyes. Your love for her destroyed your balance of mind and heart. You've run wild for too long. It is time to come home now, home to yourself, to the responsibilities of being a man, of *loving* like a man."

The silhouettes of a pair of archers appeared on the shoreline ahead. "Who goes there?" one of them shouted.

"Arthur's squire Christopher. And Sir Orvin of Shores," Christopher called back.

"As long as you're not Saxons," one of them said with a weak chuckle; then he and his partner turned and vanished back into the reeds.

The interruption reminded Christopher of an earlier question he had posed to the old knight. "Orvin, you have yet to tell me what happened to you when the Saxons came. Where did you go? What did you do?"

Orvin reached around his torso and fingered the small of his spine. "My back grows weary. I wish there was a clean place to sit down, but this tabard is borrowed, and I've no scrubboard to clean it before its return."

"Your back does not hurt that badly. You avoid the question." Christopher was not usually this curt with his master. Was it the moons on the battlefield that had taught him directness? Indeed, there was no time for coy banter with a spatha-swinging Saxon galloping toward you. He came. He died. No conversation. Except once. And any talk between Christopher and the other knights and squires was, for the most part, clipped. It was simply his environment.

"What do you know of my pain—boy?" Orvin retorted with a snort. "Do you possess the power to climb inside my body and experience my misery? I think not."

• Christopher bit his lip. He wished he could pull his words back out of the air and swallow them. "I'm sorry. My manners are as rusted as old armor. It seems *I* have been left too long in the rain."

Orvin ambled away from the water and moved through a gap in the reeds wide enough to meet his girth. It seemed to Christopher that he did not care if the squire followed him or not. But Christopher did, and Orvin said nothing as he fought his way clumsily through the dew-slick reeds, alive with the buzzing and snapping of insects. A frog turned a gear in its throat and let out a short triplet of calls. Christopher was not comfortable with all of the noise he and Orvin made as they struggled to break free of the tall grasses and emerge onto the flat, open field. The nerves of the perimeter guards were pulled taut. Christopher could have been shot when first returning from the castle, and could have been shot while talking with Orvin on the shoreline. He prayed that if they were heard, the guard would call out before he nocked his arrow and let it fly. Most did. But all it would take was one bowman bent on a kill.

Orvin broke free onto the field with a deep sigh. Christopher followed, then paused to brush himself free of mud and pull a few blades of grass that were caught in the creases of his greaves and poleyns. That done, he surveyed the scene. The smoke from the continuously burning cookfires obscured a large portion of the sky to the west. On the other side of the field lay the thin forest that bordered the castle's tourney ground. At the moment, there were more Saxons in that wood than squirrels, and though they were a mere two hundred yards away, none of those enemy soldiers would dare attack. They were defenders, and Christopher knew they would obey their orders.

A plow lay not far from where they stood, its long main beam an inviting bench that Orvin did not let go unwarmed. He hastened to the farm tool and moaned softly as he took the weight off his feet. The warped wood creaked, then settled. "Ah, the little pleasures of life are often found in the strangest of places . . . "

Christopher joined Orvin, but he did not sit down, for fear that the plow might not hold the both of them. A night zephyr picked the hair off his forehead

and raked it back. Christopher turned into the breeze
and inhaled deeply. He smelled home, the gorse, the
humus, the faraway tanning of leather. Then a
remembrance impaled him; he cocked his head
toward Orvin. "I'm supposed to report to the king!
Surely Woodward will tell him I've returned, and I
wager he is looking for me!"

"I thought *feeling* more comfortable would make
what I have to *say* more comfortable, Christopher.
But as I sit here and ponder that, I see it will not. Go
to the king, then."

"What is it—"

"Never mind, saint. Go. The king waits for no one."

"All right. Sorry, Orvin. We'll talk later, yes?"

Orvin nodded, a sad wave washing over his leathery face.

*What's the matter, old friend, dear mentor? Why
the mystery? What do you have to tell me?*

Christopher turned and rushed away, striding
along the path where reeds met field, searching for
the right spot to cut through and find the king's tent.
Orvin's long face and somber tone were obviously
part of some heavy burden he shouldered, and that
burden somehow involved Christopher. With each
step, Christopher tried to guess what cross it was that
Orvin carried, but it could be anything. To guess anymore would drive him insane. He elbowed into the
reeds and saddled his mind with new thoughts of
what he would say to the king.

7

Brenna clutched her heart as she watched the young, lanky monk slide the stable door closed. She gazed a second at Wynne, who trembled, and tears flowed freely from her eyes. Brenna brought her index finger to her lips, and though Wynne understood, it seemed compliance would be a difficult task for her. Wynne's fear looked as if it would burst from the young chambermaid's lips.

The monk stepped into the moonlight a moment. He had the hood of his robe down on his shoulders, and Brenna was afforded a view of his thick beard and pale, gaunt cheeks. He looked like an amicable fellow who might not give them any trouble. After all, he was a monk. But, she reasoned, it would be best if he did not discover them.

The monk opened the door on one of the horse stalls, and Brenna watched as he stroked a pale gray rounsey that neighed softly and somewhat contentedly. "Why do you not sleep? You must get your rest. I know your leg hurts, but the poultice will help. Let's have a look at it." The monk leaned down out of view.

There. He's just checking on his wounded horse. Nothing to worry about.

Wynne let out a soft whimper. Brenna whipped her head around and glared at her friend.

The monk came out of the stall and stared up in their direction. Thankfully, the angle obscured them from his view, but Brenna pushed herself slowly back anyway—and knocked over her uncorked flagon, its contents spilling onto the floorboards of the loft and seeping through the cracks. The cider dripped from the bottom of the loft and fell some twenty feet to the earth floor. Brenna didn't look, but she expected that the monk was investigating the sound.

The monk said nothing. He did not call out. And that frightened Brenna even more. He moved, and she knew he was nearing the dripping cider. What he would do next, she could not even guess. Another look at Wynne proved to be a mistake. Her friend's watery eyes, shivering frame, and fidgeting fingers served to further agitate Brenna. She had been the leader, the confident one. Now she was scared out of her wits with no one to assure her it would be all right. And Wynne must think her a fool. But did that matter now? Could they really talk their way out of trespassing?

She heard the monk mount the stairs, and his climb was deliberately slow. Yes, he was probably as frightened as they were. A confrontation was inevitable. Would it be better if she called out to him? Allay his fears and possibly her own?

"Friar, we are two maids who sought rest here!" Brenna blurted out.

He appeared at the top of the staircase, a hasty weapon—a pitchfork—held in his hands.

Wynne took one look at the monk brandishing the sharp, steel fork and burst up, bolting forward toward the edge of the loft.

Brenna knew what her friend was about to do and screamed, "No!"

But in a frenzy, Wynne leapt from the loft and plummeted toward the earthen floor.

Brenna scrambled to the edge of the loft as she heard Wynne shriek and hit the ground with a brutal thump. She looked down.

Wynne lay on her side near the center of a puddle of moonlight. She did not move. Brenna could not tell if she was breathing. "Wynne!"

"Dear, Lord," the monk said, dropping his pitchfork. He turned and raced down the staircase as Brenna rose and hurried to follow.

Wynne was still not moving when they got to her. Brenna fell to her knees and turned her friend's head toward her. "Wynne, wake up! Wake up!"

The monk put his palm on Wynne's neck and held it there, closing his eyes and concentrating on something. Then he said, "She lives."

Brenna lifted her gaze to the monk, his face reflecting what looked like genuine concern for Wynne. Brenna's thoughts were in chaos, her body leaping with adrenaline, and she found her mouth working, but was not aware of what came out of it. "We were just . . . I wanted to see Christopher at Shores. We were not going to take anything. We didn't want to cause . . . I'm sorry," and with that, Brenna began to sob.

Mavis had warned her about coming. It was mad. It was a fool's trek, and now Wynne, poor, sweet, frightened Wynne lay here, her eyes unwilling to open.

It's my fault! It's all my fault! Curse love! Curse Christopher for going away! Curse everything! Why did this have to happen? All I wanted to do was see Christopher. All I wanted was to be happy! Oh, God, please let Wynne be all right. She is my friend and she is young and she only wanted to help. Do not punish her for that. Do not punish her for being scared. Punish me. It was my fault. Do something to me. Hurt me in some way. I want Wynne's pain. I deserve it now.

"Let us worry about your friend now," the monk said. "I once saw a mason fall from a scaffold. They did not move him until a doctor arrived. I think it best we do the same. Stay here, and I will fetch a doctor."

Tearfully, Brenna said, "Thank you."

The monk slid open the stable door and ran off across the yard toward the abbey house as a bell atop the highest tower knelled the commencement of matins and lauds.

Brenna stroked Wynne's cheek, looked down at her hand, then noticed that it trembled. "You will be all right, Wynne. He's gone to fetch a doctor. You're going to be all right."

8

Seaver scowled at Darrick. The mangonel operator sat fingering his bleeding gum behind the corroded iron bars of a dungeon cell. Seaver had already decided he would kill Darrick, but he would learn the names of the traitors first. That, he knew, would take time. A very *painful* time for Darrick. He would enlist Kenric's aid in Darrick's torture, and make sure that he and Kenric confronted Renfred with the news. Renfred would make an appeal to the men to stop their rebellion and stand behind Seaver. Renfred would do that, or, Seaver suddenly decided, he would die as well.

They will know my wrath. They will fear me!

He shifted away from Darrick's cell and strode down the hall toward the chief guard, who stood before the cell of the captured Celt. Save for Darrick and the Celt, the stone boxes of pain and suffering to his left and right were empty—the way they should be. There would be no one serving "sentences" as long as the Saxons reigned here. There would only be slaves. It was not a matter of tyranny; it was a matter of economics. Manacled prisoners were unproductive. Slaves produced something.

"Here he is," the guard said, opening the door. "And he reeks of ale."

Seaver stepped into the cell. The Celt archer lay naked on his side, bruises purpling his cheeks, neck and arms. His eyelids were swollen, and blood was dried and crusted throughout his thin mustache and beard. His nose was dark blue and leaning slightly off center. Seaver looked at the archer's hands; both were uniform, perfect.

"Fetch me a hatchet and hot spatha. This archer has yet to be humbled."

The guard bowed, then ran off.

Seaver leaned over the Celt, fumbling in his head for the right words. The memory of a spring day flowered in his head, the sun gleaming down on his former lord's head. Garrett had been a great soul, though a poor battle strategist. He had been the only Celt Seaver had ever admired. He had taught Seaver the Celt tongue, and now Seaver saw Garrett's mouth forming words, sentences, phrases in his head. It had been too many moons since Seaver had spoken the words, but it was essential that he practice now, since he stood on lands once occupied and still surrounded by Celts.

"Am I to understand correctly that you came here alone?" he asked the Celt, pausing haphazardly as words came to him in clumps.

The Celt made the tiniest of moves, turning his head, flickering open a fat, crimson eyelid. He stared at Seaver with a face too raw to form an expression, and uttered faintly, "Kill me. Please."

Seaver frowned, then shook his head no. "We need young men such as yourself to defend this fortress. Killing you would be a waste." The foreign language was alive in Seaver's mind. He had reached far down into his well of memory and the bucket had finally risen to meet his hands. With growing confidence he added, "This was probably once your home. It still is. You simply serve a new king now, King Kenric of Shores, the first Saxon ruler of Britain."

The Celt turned his head away and closed his eyelid. "I serve only God."

Seaver snorted. "Your God has failed you. You should pray to our many gods, most of all to Woden. Only he can help you now."

"You can help me," the Celt said, his voice thinning. "Put your dagger in my heart."

"You came here alone in the hope that we would kill you, is that it?"

"Yes."

"How unfortunate." Seaver hunkered down, trusting that the Celt would not attempt to strike him. "But tell me. Why do you want to die?" Seaver was glad he did not have to kill the boy. He was an interesting lad, not at all what he expected. Here was an archer who had thrown himself not on their mercy, but on their butchery. But he did not know everything about the Saxons. Their butchery could be more accurately described as selective slaughter. And captured Celt men-at-arms were presently not on the slaughtering list.

"What care is it of yours?" the Celt said, bitterness flooding his throat and befouling his words.

"It is no care. Only a curiosity. I have been a scout for most of my life. It is my nature to probe, to find."

Footsteps echoed off the dungeon walls, announcing the approach of the guard. Seaver stood, turned, and watched as the guard set down the hatchet in his right hand and unlocked the cell door. He moved inside and handed Seaver the hatchet. In the guard's other hand was the scalding, orange-and-red spatha Seaver had requested.

Turning the blade of the hatchet toward him, Seaver ran a finger along its edge; recently honed, the battle-ax would perform to perfection.

The Celt's bloodshot eyes were trained on him now, and he dragged himself slowly toward the rear of the cell. "If you're going to use that, I beseech you, use it on my head, or my chest."

"Why?" Seaver asked. "Why do you want to die?" He reasoned that maybe the hatchet would draw an answer out of the Celt.

"I betrayed my oath as an archer. I betrayed my oath as a member of King Arthur's army. No man who has done what I have should live."

"There are easier ways to die than coming here," Seaver noted. "Perhaps you still have a thirst for glory, and a desire to preserve your memory—and what I know you believe is your soul. I kill you, you go to that, that place of peace. The clouds. But if you kill yourself, ah, yes, you burn in the fires of a pit. I remember now." Seaver brightened with the notion that he had finally figured out why the archer had let himself fall into their hands. "I'm right, am I not."

The Celt reached the rear wall of the cell and pressed his bare back against the mossy stone. "Just kill me. For if you do not, I promise you will live to regret it."

Seaver let out a laugh, then turned to the guard, whose face was also split by a grin. "Look at this poor oaf. He begs to die and then he threatens me. It's true, he has yet to be humbled. Set down that spatha and hold him for me."

The guard placed the heated blade on the stone floor and joined Seaver. They converged on the bat-

tered Celt, whose eyes were blank with fear. The
archer's breath came in loud, short bursts as the
guard knelt and grabbed the Celt's left arm with one
hand, reached around with the other, and pulled the
boy's face into his chest.

Seaver seized the archer's right hand and pinned it
palm down on the floor. He felt the boy's arm convulse
and listened to him whine faintly as he reared back
with the hatchet, aiming for an imaginary line across
the archer's hand that separated the boy's thumb and
forefinger. But the fingers were not positioned right,
and he would have to take them off one at a time.

Something pure and heady coursed through
Seaver's veins. There was no true joy in inflicting
pain, but there was that tremendous feeling . . . the
power. He controlled the boy. *His* life dominated
another's. There was nothing in the realm that could
replace the feeling, give him the same kind of chills
or take his breath away in the same way. But there
was a gnawing guilt—nothing that would prevent
him from carrying out his duty—but a sense that he
was, in some diminutive way, linked to the archer. He
did, after all, understand the lad. And with that
understanding came a small measure of respect.
Indeed, the boy had made a plan. Be killed by the
enemy, save himself from the grief of life, and save his
soul from what he felt would be damnation. He was
no oaf. He was a man. A man who had made some
dire mistakes. A man whose life had reached a cliff,
and Seaver was the only one who could abet him.

But he was an enemy archer. And his talent must
be taken away.

Seaver would do it as quickly and as mercifully as
possible. He fixed his gaze on the archer's forefinger,
then brought down the ax.

Chomp!

"Ahhhhhhhhhhhh!"

The Celt continued to scream as Seaver, grunting and gritting his teeth, slammed the ax onto the archer's thumb.

Chomp!

The fingers lay separated from the Celt's hand, pieces of flesh and bone that were still pink and warm.

"Spatha now!" Seaver ordered the guard.

The crying Celt's hand bled profusely; the puddle grew and he had to stop it. With a stiff hand and vised grip, he lifted the archer's wounded hand from the stone, received the spatha from the guard, then pressed it onto the Celt's wounds.

Though the rank scent of searing flesh and blood had found his nostrils before, this time, being so close, it made Seaver gag. And the noise produced, like water thrown into an empty, glowing cauldron, added to his nausea. With a single tug, he pulled the blade from the archer.

It was over. Whimpering, the archer pulled the charred, deformed lump that was his hand to his chest, gripping it with his other, rocking and trembling with pain. Then, after a few breaths, he lapsed into unconsciousness.

Seaver pushed back from the archer and rose unsteadily to his feet. Still pulsing with power, horror, and nausea, the combination raging havoc inside him, he said, "Get him a pack for that hand, and a mattress to sleep on. When he wakes I want him fed." Seaver eyed the fingers and the pool of blood. "And fetch a maid."

He turned for the door, making the mistake of inhaling again through his nose. He dropped the hatchet and shifted quickly out of the cell. Once in the hall, he found himself breaking into a sprint, but then he stopped, dropped to his knees, closed his eyes, and emptied the contents of his stomach onto the floor.

9

The night zephyrs grew into stubborn gusts as Christopher walked past tent after tent. Each of the thin shelters rattled loudly, their pitching twine pulled taut, their stakes threatening to pop out of the earth. Up ahead and farther away from the Cam, in an oval region of shoreline that fought back into the reeds, Christopher spied the king's blue banner whipping high above a tent top. He bustled forward, his gaze trained on the image of the Virgin Mary ornamenting the flag. He inadvertently bumped into someone, then heard his name called out. Averting his gaze, he saw it was the bird, Phelan. Stripped of armor, Phelan wore only a ragged shirt and breeches with holes in the knees. His dirty feet were wrapped in sandals as frayed as his livery.

"Phelan. You look . . . a mess."

"Our trunk was lost somewhere on the Mendips, and we have yet to find a generous soul willing to part with a simple shirt or pair of breeches."

"That's true," Neil chipped in, moving around a pair of peasant bowmen and arriving at Phelan's side; he, too, looked as scruffy and haggard as a bailey sweeper. "But we have washed them, though I'm afraid the harsh water of this river has all but worn them out."

Christopher smiled, affected by their playful tone. "You two are in good spirits, considering your appearance."

"A man with a full belly can always smile," Phelan philosophized, patting his lean gut, which, judging from the looks of it, didn't take much work to quiet.

Neil, on the other hand, was pregnant with a millionscore past feasts. He tapped his lips. "You'll only get a half grin out of me," he complained. "It takes a lot more than boiled cabbage and a few pork ribs to satisfy this dragon." He set a palm on his belly, the dragon flapping out beneath his shirt. "But a labor of love it is."

Phelan took a step closer to Christopher and lowered his voice. His expression grew serious. "I assume you couldn't stop Doyle."

Christopher nodded, an uncomfortable charge listing on his spine, a force generated from his helplessness, his failure. "They have him. We all know what they'll do. And if he doesn't obey them, then he's a dead man, sure enough."

Neil pursed his lips as though resigned. "All we can do then is hope and pray he survives until we breach the curtain walls."

But what if he doesn't survive that long! What if we get inside and find him dead because we didn't act sooner? He's alive now, I feel that. I don't know how, but I do. And there is no time to wait!

An odd thing happened to Christopher. Though he knew that all of it was unreal, his senses experienced every bit of it as reality. He stood facing the bird and the barbarian, among the racket of army and the howl of the wind. But those noises dropped off into silence. If there was activity in the background, he could no longer detect it. All was at an eerie stand-

still. And in the quiescent moment there was one
thought that burned so brightly that *it* had to be the
thing numbing his senses.

He would not wait for the siege to begin. He would
assemble a group, breach the walls himself, and get
Doyle out. He had confessed the desire to Orvin,
then just a wild notion, but now, now it was real in
his mind. Possible. And maybe, just maybe, he would
find Marigween.

"Christopher?"

"Christopher, are you all right?"

The archers spoke to him? Yes, they had spoken.
He was with them on the shoreline of the Cam. "I'm
fine. I was just, well wait now. You two grew up in
Shores, just like me."

"What does that have to do with anything?" the
barbarian asked.

"Then you might know the castle as well as I, yes?"

The bird smiled. "Better. There are passages within
the curtain walls I believe the architect did not even
know about. Neil and I have discovered them."

"Do not sit too high on your throne of secrets,"
Christopher said, "for I, too, know of those passageways, and of the tunnel under the north curtain wall.
Remember Regan, the big jailer? He showed them to
me once. I wonder if the Saxons have discovered
them. . . ."

Neil took a step back from Christopher. "I know
what you're thinking and I won't do it. Besides, the
king would never approve."

Phelan pitched Neil a quizzical look. "What is he
getting at?"

"Why don't you tell him?" Neil asked Christopher,
his voice burred with doubt and skepticism.

"The plan is simple. We dress like Saxons. Enter

the castle by night, then find and rescue Doyle and anyone else we can."

"Oh, that sounds simple," Neil groaned. "And if we're spotted we'll simply take on their entire garrison. Let's see, that's probably about two hundred men for each of us."

"How do we make it to the north side of the moat without being spotted?" Phelan asked Christopher.

"We don't," Neil answered.

"Perhaps we'll have the aid of the king for a diversion. I'm on my way to see him now." Christopher beat a fist onto his thigh. "Come on. Doyle is as much your friend as he is mine. We *must* help him."

Phelan looked at Neil. The barbarian shook his head negatively, his lips forming the word no.

"Despite this dumpy mule's cowardice," Phelan said, returning his gaze to Christopher, "I will go with you."

The barbarian slapped a beefy claw on Phelan's shoulder and yanked the wiry archer around to face him. "Dumpy mule? Coward? I know what you're trying to do. You're trying to shame me into doing this. I'll tell you one thing. If we have the blessing of the king, I *might* consider it."

"We'll have Arthur's support," Christopher said. His confidence was buoyed by a foundation of doubt and could crumble at any second, but his friends needed to see a sure, stone wall before them, and Christopher had masoned himself into such a rampart.

He told the bird and barbarian he would meet them after his talk with the king, then bid them a terse farewell. Neil continued his plainting about the dangers of the rescue attempt, and Phelan answered his friend's reservations by calling him once again a dumpy mule.

And a coward. Christopher chuckled inwardly as he strode away from the bantering bowmen.

A pair of heavily armored and heavily armed infantrymen stood guard at the entrance to Arthur's tent. Two more men were posted at the rear of the tent. A wide, rectangular hearth lay opposite the shelter, the wood within charred, pinpricked with glowing embers. The air still wore the rich scent of cooking. The king had dined heartily, something Christopher should have done instead of rushing his meal. The burning sensation in his throat conveyed that truth.

He came near the entrance of the tent. One of the guards leaned over and pushed his head through the flaps. He said something softly, the words muffled to Christopher. The guard pulled his head back and said, "You may enter." Both guards stepped aside and let him pass.

Slicing through the flaps, he immediately noticed a new smell, one that was much different than the aroma of roasted game; it was a sweet odor that Christopher had never experienced before. Along with the smell came the warmth of the tent, and the cozy feeling the small trestle bed and traveling trunks created. All his lord needed was a fireplace, perhaps a four-poster bed to replace the trestle, some straw rushes for the floors, and a hound that would sit to be stroked at his side. Rank doth have its rewards and privileges.

Arthur lay on the bed, his head propped up by a pair of goosefeather pillows. He wore a knee-length nightshirt, and beneath, a layer of long underwear that extended below the hem of the shirt. Excalibur lay sheathed and at the ready, resting upright at the foot of the bed. The king had his fingers knitted over a belly that, unlike Neil's dragon, was surely full. His eyes wore the fog of one too many pulls on the flagon.

This is perfect. He's been fed and aled. He's comfortable and susceptible, open to plans of rescue.

"Christopher. I'd get up, but I'm afraid I've allowed myself too much boar and too much ale."

An understatement.

"Not necessary, lord. We fought long and hard. You deserve an eve like this, and the hills were no place to rest." Christopher stepped farther into the tent, turned, and with a nod from the king, sat down on top of one of Arthur's chests. He looked to his right and spotted a small metal bowl from which burned a brown lump of something—the thing that produced the wonderful scent.

"It's nice, isn't it?" Arthur asked. "It's called frankincense. A group of traders came from across the sea and sold some of it to Sir Lancelot, who in turn gave some to me. It's much sweeter than the incense used by our abbots. Perhaps they should change their suppliers."

Here we are, talking about incense. I must get this conversation back on the right path. I might as well be blunt.

"Lord. The Saxons have Doyle."

"Spare me your report. Woodward has told me everything. Though I should punish you for rushing off before Doyle's lieutenant could pursue him, I will not. Your friend is a young man of fire. He is quick with the bow and his tongue. I know you're trying to help him . . . but what he's done I cannot understand."

Christopher sank a little. "I believe he threw his life to them."

Arthur tightened his brow. "But surely he had

everything to live for. Or perhaps he didn't. You're his friend, Christopher, you would know." Arthur fingered the long tuft of hair under his lower lip. His forehead was furrowed, and his eyes were distant, pensive.

How much would Christopher tell Arthur? Would he report the unabridged truth? Tell the king Doyle's history, how he had been kidnapped as a small child by a jewelry merchant and raised by the man until he was fourteen? Would he tell Arthur about how Doyle had been reunited with his parents, but didn't feel like they were his own? Explain how Doyle's father wanted him to be a steward, and Doyle only wanted to be a bowman? Would he inform Arthur about Doyle's heavy drinking, about how Doyle had murdered Innis and then murdered Leslie? Could he piece together a small part of the puzzle and reveal it to the king? Or once he started, would the king be able to fit it all together and discover that Christopher was lying?

He sat next to the king and wanted desperately to confess it all, but he knew that if he did so Doyle would swing from a thick rope until he was blue and dead. He could tell the king that Doyle had killed Leslie and Innis—but by accident; however, once the web started, Christopher knew he would become entangled in it.

What part of his internal truth would he murder?

Would he betray his oath as a blood brother or his oath as squire of the body?

Doyle, why did you do this to me! I know you didn't mean it—but look at what has happened!

He must answer questions truthfully, but not volunteer any information. He had to protect his friend. He had to save his friend, not only from the enemy, but from himself. One thing was certain. He must never lie to the king. *Never.*

"Doyle does have a lot of pain in his life," he told Arthur.

"So he did want to die," the king concluded.

"I'm not sure."

"Was it over honor. A woman?"

"If I may ask, Your Majesty, why the curiosity?" Christopher thought his last a smart question, putting Arthur on the defensive, steering him away from the particulars, the details, the truth. It was a bold move, yes, but the king was relaxed and would hopefully not take offense. The more Arthur pried, the more Christopher would be forced to tell him, and then he would eventually betray his oath as a blood brother to Doyle.

"Any bowman that inspires my squire to risk his life is a concern of mine," Arthur retorted quickly. "And besides, Lancelot has told me that Doyle might have become one of this army's greatest archers."

Christopher licked his lips, then swallowed. His next words would not be easy; he had to drag them out of himself. "I must confess, lord, that Doyle's capture has inspired me to risk my life again. Only this time, I will have help. And I pray to St. George that I will have yours, and your blessing as well." Christopher shuddered. He had said it, and it felt wonderful to be released. But then the sudden fear of Arthur's response clutched him.

"You have a plan brewing in your mind?"

Christopher lifted himself off the trunk and went to Arthur's bedside. He knelt and placed his elbows upon the bed. Arthur regarded him with a questioning stare. Christopher closed his eyes and spoke. "I've spoken to two archers, Phelan and Neil. We believe we can get Doyle out and perhaps save a few others as well. There are passageways in the castle that I'm sure the Saxons have not discovered. I know a way into the castle. But I need your help, lord. Perhaps we can move together, we three, and the rest of our armies."

Christopher heard the trestle bed creak and opened his eyes. Arthur had brought himself to a sitting position, and now eyed him with fatherly contempt. "Christopher, I'm appalled. You sound as foolish as your friend who threw himself to the Saxons. Laying siege to a castle is a costly, long, drawn-out affair that must be done right, and with the proper tools. On the morrow a team will be in the easternmost forest cutting down trees to build scaling ladders. Once we get word from Nolan, we'll find out whether we can use his siege engines or have to haul Uryens's down from Gore. I've sent messengers to Falls, Rain, Glastonbury, and Queen's Camel, announcing that we're hiring diggers to undermine the curtain walls. Don't you see, Christopher? This is the *way*. This is not a tournament with some rogue knight you can slay. This is a very different battle. And there is no room for youthful heroics. They will only result in your death. And you are far too valuable to lose. I learned something from a young man, from *you*, up there on the Mendips. I learned humility, a trait most uncommon in my family. And now faced with another challenge, I'm not wallowing in my mistake, but thinking clearly and fighting to correct it. But now the tables have turned, and it is you who have become rash. I know all about your passageways inside the castle. And I'm sure the Saxons do too." Arthur's eyes grew wide, as though something else had hit him. He put a hand on Christopher's shoulder. "By the way, Woodward told me of the offer he

made to you. And you were right. I will not let you
serve him. Moons ago I told the people of Shores I
had found the best squire in the land, and it was not
a lie. But purge your mind of this rescue. Just pray
that Doyle listens to the Saxons and keeps himself
alive."

*That is not good enough! I will go without your
blessing then, King Arthur!*

Christopher opened his eyes. He wanted to scream,
but battled the desire back into his throat. He would,
however, voice his concern and disappointment. "It
may seem rash, lord. But I fear the longer we wait,
the closer Doyle comes to death. He will not obey
them."

"Christopher," the king began, his voice soothing,
comforting, "for all we know Doyle may already be
dead, and then your rescue would be for nothing."

"We could bring out some of the peasants, the
cooks, the hostlers, anyone."

"We will. The right way. When we're assured of
victory. Now rise and go. I sleep alone this evening.
There is a tent for you, and you'd best bed down
now. You've a long journey to make on the morrow."

Christopher furrowed his brow. "New orders?"

"Sir Orvin has not informed you?"

He shook his head no.

"Well, it is not my place. Tell him I've given you
permission to ride out of Shores with him and
Merlin. He will tell you where you're going." Arthur
fell back onto his bed and draped a hand over his
eyes, then sighed deeply. "I turn my thoughts now to
a young virgin of Cameliard whom I have not seen in
many moons, but whose smile is still vivid in my
head."

Christopher stood. "By your leave."

"Good evening, Christopher."

"Good evening, lord." With that, he left the tent.

Don't worry, Doyle. I'm coming for you. . . .

10

The doctor was an ancient man, bald, with only a few trace gray hairs hemming the sides of his head. A plague of sun freckles dotted his forehead, and when he raised his brow they rippled as the skin did. He wore his long nightshirt, over which was an open, woolen cloak. Slung over his shoulder was the long strap of a leather bag that bulged with hidden remedies. He stepped into the barn barefoot, moving gingerly over the straw and dirt.

The monk followed the doctor, his face offering reassurance to Brenna. She gently let go of Wynne's head and eased it onto the earth. She crawled back as the doctor bowed ceremoniously before his patient, then seated himself on the ground.

As the doctor began to unbuckle his bag, he said, "She has not moved since she fell. True?"

Brenna sniffled. "I can hear her breathing, but she has not moved."

From his bag the doctor drew a sandglass. He pressed his fore and middle fingers onto one of Wynne's wrists and turned the glass over. He mumbled numbers to himself.

"Can you help her?" Brenna asked.

"Shush," the doctor ordered.

Brenna swallowed, lowered her head, then closed her eyes. She felt a hand on the back of her head and looked up to see the monk hunkering down next to her. "Say a prayer with me," he whispered in her ear.

Tightly, they held hands, and the monk began a musical chant Brenna had heard many times before, but one she had never taken the time to learn.

The melodious voice of the monk carried her thoughts away from the terrible moment and eased her into peaceful thoughts. Light surrounded and engulfed her, lifted her up and propelled her through the sky. Was it a vision of death? Maybe she had asked too fervently for God to punish her for Wynne's accident. Was God taking her now? If he was, then she would go. She would not try to fight Him. She would go in place of Wynne—if her friend was to die. But did she really want to give up life? She had come this far and was not even allowed the most infinitesimal of moments with Christopher. All she had to show for her efforts was a friend, lying somewhere between life and death.

The sound of coughing. It was not the doctor!

Brenna snapped her eyelids open. The doctor sprinkled a rust-colored powder under Wynne's nose. Wynne was awake, her eyes wide, her mouth open, her back arched. The doctor whisked the powder away with his fingers as Wynne relaxed her back. Her breathing was jarred by more coughing, but her eyes remained open. And then she sneezed. Once, twice, a third time.

The doctor regarded the monk with a wan, though to Brenna wonderful, smile. "She was not coming back until you began praying, friar. Thank you."

"Is she . . . is she all right?" Brenna asked.

"Let's get her up and see." The doctor gestured with his head for the monk to help him. The two lifted Wynne carefully to her feet.

Wynne stood composing herself for a moment, and then, with vigilance, the doctor and the monk released her.

"There," the doctor said. "Move your limbs."

Wynne frowned. "I beg forgiveness. I do not understand—"

"Your arms, maid," the monk said. "Move your arms and your legs. Walk."

Wynne obeyed, and thank St. Michael she was fine. But then she flinched, staggered, and grabbed her left side. The doctor and monk rushed toward her.

Some hours later, Wynne slept in a trestle bed in the vast rectangular dormitory of the monks. The doctor told Brenna one of the bones that protected Wynne's heart might be cracked, and it would take some time to heal, but Wynne would fully recover.

While sitting in the cloister court, Brenna sipped on warm tea given to her by the careful brother, the first monk awake in the morning. As the brother rang the bell of prime, and rays of the rising sun drew a jagged pattern of shadows across the yard, she thought about the immediate future. The right thing to do was stay with her friend until Wynne recovered, then abandon the journey to Shores and return home—to face punishment by her parents and the abbot. They could conceal Wynne's injury, but the fact that they had run off would be enough to keep her in misery for many moons. If they revealed Wynne's injury, then Brenna would face an even heavier sentence. It seemed that no matter what, going home, though the right thing to do, meant anguish.

Then how can going home be the right thing to do if it

*will ruin my life? Did I not gamble everything by rid-
ing out and trying to better my life? Am I not trying
to make myself happy? If I am, then why should I go
home?*

*But what about Wynne? I cannot ask her to go on.
Even if I had the time to wait for her to heal, I would
not want her coming. I cannot bear the burden. The
thought that something else could happen is too
much for me. It is not fair to subject her to more—
though I know she'll want to come. Her journey has
ended here. She'll face punishment. But she knew
that when she came with me. I wish there was some
way out of it. But there is not.*

The decision was made. Brenna would go on alone,
providing Wynne would be cared for and escorted
back to Shores by one of the monks. That was a tall
order, but she would offer the free services of her
father to the monk who brought Wynne back. Her
father was the best armorer in Gore and could produce for the monk whatever he requested. She rose,
drained the last bit of tea from her cup, then moved
toward a long hall that would take her to the quarters
of the abbot.

11 Christopher had never fallen asleep. All
night he had wrestled with his rough blanket, fully
aware of every clack and bicker of the small, one-man
tent. Though his eyes were now closed, the cry of
crows, the yawning of men, and the crackle of freshly
flinted cookfires all messengered morning.

He had never found Orvin the previous night, and
that had been one link in a chain of things that had
shackled him awake through the wee hours. He knew
he would ride out with Orvin and Merlin. But why and
to where, he did not know. Or would he? Maybe he
would not agree with whatever it was they wanted of
him. He still had to do something about rescuing Doyle.

He had been honest with the bird and the barbarian after his meeting with Arthur. Phelan had insisted
he would still go, despite violating the king's orders.
Neil had looked at his friend as if he were a heretic.
Neil held fast; he would not do it unless Arthur
approved. Christopher began to wonder if the king
was right. Maybe the whole idea was impetuous and
ill conceived. He needed Neil, but was not willing to
lie about Arthur's approval to get the archer to go
along. He would have to find someone else—or
change Arthur's mind; the former was a much
smaller mountain to climb. Then again, who would
volunteer for the rescue?

In the hours of sleeplessness, he had had time to
ponder Marigween's fate. Bloody visions of her
demise at the hands of the Saxons had rocked his
body with jerks and shivers. And her face had
blended into the tear-soaked face of Brenna, who
waited too long for him back at the castle of Gore.
He had seen Brenna in a candlelit chamber in bed
with another, crying out in passion as the other made
love to her. The other had turned his face . . . and it
had been Innis on top of Brenna. Innis, back from the
dead to steal Brenna away again. Christopher had
curled up and pulled his hands through his hair, trying to yank the image from his head.

"Hello inside," a creaky voice called out.
"Christopher of Shores, the wind whistles your name.

It beckons you out to greet one who has waited moons to meet you."

Who is that? And what manner of speech is that?

Christopher sat up, rubbed his eyes free of sleep grit with the heels of his hands, then stood. He pulled his linen shorts up to his belly button, then shivered. Summer roamed the land, but her mornings still held the accursed reminders of winter. He found a scruffy though functional nightshirt and slid his head and arms through it. There was a large hole in the front of the shirt that exposed one of his nipples, a strange pink eye peering out of his chest. Self-consciously, he adjusted the shirt to hide the hardening nipple beneath it, then padded outside.

It was cold! The dew on the grass stung the soles of his feet. He was so intent on fighting off the ice of morning that he barely noticed who stood before the tent. Hopping up and down, he took a look at the man.

Never had he seen a beard and hair as long and as white. Nothing man could produce would equal the color. Merlin was framed in strands of what resembled tearings of clouds. His face bore the deep canyons of age, but Christopher did not focus on them. His gaze was commanded to the old man's eyes, which were of a color that Christopher could not describe. They seemed to contain every color and no color. When he first looked at them they appeared a bit green, blue, brown, and yellow. He blinked, and for a second they looked white, then spilled into blackness, then back to the rainbow of hues. Was it some trick of the druid's?

"Don't stare at me, boy," Merlin croaked. "Say it is an honor and a privilege to meet the great Merlin!" The old man laughed, his version of the act more aptly described as a cackle.

"I have seen you from afar. But now, indeed, it is a privilege and an honor." Christopher extended his hand.

Merlin slapped the hand down. "Hate that custom. No need for it. A look. A word. They are enough to know we are already friends."

Insulted and puzzled, Christopher withdrew his hand and shielded his chest with his arms as a gust bid him a frosty tiding. "Arthur told me I was riding out with you and Sir Orvin this morning. He wouldn't say why. Why?"

Merlin extended his arms to the heavens. His tabard billowed in the wind, and he looked powerful and sinister. Someone not privy to the conversation would think the druid evil . . . and mad.

Come to think of it, I'm privy to the conversation, and I think he's mad!

"You must come with us, Christopher. You have no choice! It is matter so grave, so important, so meaningful to you, that if you were to miss it, why, your whole life would be . . . " Merlin thought a moment, then: "Nothing!" Merlin moved in close to Christopher and grabbed him with long, gnarled fingers by his shirt collar. His next came in a tone that evoked strange portents. "It is a matter of blood."

Still clutched by the druid, and feeling as awkward and cold and confused as ever, Christopher asked, "Where are we going?"

Merlin released him and stepped back—so that he could wave his arms again for emphasis. "Well, we're going to a place most fantastic. Hidden away from the cares of the world, it is a place few have seen a place where the power of the land is fully realized. We're going to my cave!"

A cave. Most fantastic? Christopher didn't think

so. It was probably cold and cluttered with coveys of sharp-toothed bats, and he was sure it reeked of mildew. And the nearest caves to Shores were at least three days' ride away. What were they supposed to do there? Also, it would be a minimum of six days before his return. Would Doyle be alive that long?

"He's awake. Good." Orvin's voice came from behind, and Christopher craned his head to see his master round a tent corner and shuffle toward them. The old knight arrived, not completely out of breath, but nearly so. "What have you told him?" he asked Merlin, his voice honed with accusation.

"Simply the *where* of our journey. That is all, fretful knight."

Orvin had told Christopher that knowing Merlin was no pleasure of his, and that fact was now boldly illustrated before Christopher's eyes. Yes, these men openly despised each other, but Orvin's hatred was in the fore.

"I hope you are not lying, as is your practice. Remember our covenant." Orvin sneered at Merlin, but the look had no effect on the druid.

It was fortunate for Merlin that Orvin was unarmed; Christopher would have to make sure to keep his weapons out of reach whenever these two were together. But what was it that Orvin said?

"What covenant do you speak of, master?" Christopher asked.

"You're freezing. Get cleaned up and dressed. Pack your bags. We travel for three days. I'm going to fetch our mounts. We'll meet here." Orvin looked at Merlin. "If that is all right with you, oh great soothsayer."

"The petty details I leave to you," Merlin answered. He spun and ambled off, then called back,

"Remember, Orvin. If there is any problem, you *know* what to do."

Christopher watched Merlin shuffle by passing horses and men, then become obscured by the rest of the army. He looked to Orvin, and stiffened. He would get answers. Now. "Why are we going to Merlin's cave?"

Orvin sighed. "There is no time to discuss the whys of the world, young patron saint. Trust your master."

Christopher shook his head negatively, uncomfortable with his sudden rebellion but holding his ground. It was the first time *ever* he refused Orvin. "No. Tell me why—otherwise I am *not* going. My friend most assuredly lies in a dungeon cell, and he will die if I do not help him. Now you ask me to go on a journey? To leave him? For what? For no reason! Unless the king is in on this as well? Has he asked you to take me away for some reason? How can you expect me to go without knowing why? How can you expect me to leave my friend to die?"

"Curse that druid's insight," Orvin said, then stepped quickly toward Christopher, pulling something out of his pocket, something wrapped in a linen rag. He pushed it into Christopher face and the smell was horrible, worse than a dung pile as high as the curtain walls of Shores! Frantically, Christopher tried to pull Orvin's hands away from his face, but as he inhaled through his nose, he felt himself become numb, weak, and he sensed his arms fall away from his face. Suddenly he felt very pleasant, very light, and the muscles in his legs and back were no longer contracted and supporting him. A cool wave of darkness rolled in, and there was nothing more to see or hear, smell, taste, or touch. There was only the void.

•   •   •

He felt the up and down rhythm of a horse under him and detected the sound of its hooves clattering over a rocky road. He knew he was prone, but in exactly what position he couldn't tell. He opened his eyes, but sunlight launched its painful arrows of light, and he shut them tightly, globes of whiteness flashing in the blackness within himself. He opened his eyes again, this time forcing them to stay open. He blinked repeatedly, then caught sight of the road, and the hooves and tail of the courser. It was his courser, carrying him fifteen hands high above the ground.

Christopher hoisted his head, then realized it was full of blood and throbbing with near-dizzying pain. He winced, then took a look ahead.

Merlin cantered on a charcoal gray mule, his hair tossed gently by the canyon updrafts. Christopher saw that the reins of his courser were spindled around the aft peak of the druid's saddle so that the druid could escort him down the narrow, winding road ahead. Winding was an understatement. The suicide path was a hair-raising, cliffside affair that promised at least a half dozen switchbacks.

As he eyed the druid and the road, a shock wave broke free in an alcove of Christopher's mind. The wave rattled with the news that he was not in Shores, far away from it, in fact. Days away.

Then he remembered. Orvin had done this! How could he? And what was it that he had used to make Christopher sleep for so long? A potion of Merlin's?

He whipped his head right and saw Orvin atop a brown jenny behind him. "Orvin!" he shouted, his voice echoing sharply off the rock. He decided to hop off of the courser. He pulled his arms up, but found

his wrists tied together with leather straps and bound
to his boots. His pulse skipped a beat, then made up
for it by leaping into a sprint as panic and desperation breached the walls of his heart.

*What's going on? What are they doing to me? Are
they impostors or something? Is this not my master
behind me? Is this not the man I've grown to love
and respect and honor? Has some incantation been
cast over him by Merlin?*

"Orvin! What happened? Why did you make me
sleep?" He realized the throbbing in his head was much
worse, the beat of his own heart a menacing drum that
clogged his ears. No matter what Orvin's reply was,
Christopher needed to be untied. He had to sit up.

"You left me no choice," Orvin said, lifting his
voice above the hoofbeats of the mules and horse. "I
was going to tell you on the field, but two things held
me back. Fear. And a promise I had made." Orvin
had tried his best to comfort him, Christopher knew,
and he must—he'd better—have a good reason for all
the secrecy. But relief would only come when he was
untied and delivered the truth.

"I cannot stay like this! My head rages!" He hadn't
even mentioned the wolf of hunger that howled and
tore bloody hunks out of his stomach.

"Ho. We stop here."

Christopher watched as Merlin dismounted, then
walked gingerly toward him. The old man jammed
his sandal on a stone and nearly fell face forward, but
caught himself at the last moment.

"Foul road! Foul road!" the druid cried. Christopher
sensed that Merlin's ego was bruised, but that his foot
was fine. The great wizard had looked ridiculous, however, Christopher was in too much pain even to grin.

Merlin unstrapped him and helped him down from

the horse. Christopher stood. The towering walls of
the canyon swayed around him—or was he swaying?
The road would not stay still; it, too, rolled like
waves across the Cam.

"How long have I been on this horse?" he asked
Merlin.

"Three days," Merlin said matter-of-factly.

"Three days!"

"Not continuously, young man. We took you down.
Watered your throat and kept you warm at night."

As the realm slowed and collected itself into the
rock-solid place Christopher knew it was, he contem-
plated the news. Three days of his life had been taken
away. Three days in which Doyle might have been
killed. Three days that he could have done so much
with. And these two old men, did they really know
what they were doing? He could have died, strapped
to his horse for that long! Didn't they know that?

And exactly where was he? Probably east of Shores,
but that was all he could guess. Maybe that was the
plan. He was not supposed to know the cave's loca-
tion. Perhaps Merlin feared he would tell others.

"Now that you're awake," Merlin continued, "I suspect you realize it's much too late to run away. My
cave is less than a quarter day's ride from here. So
you might as well come along now."

Orvin scuffled over the dusty rock to Christopher's
side. Christopher grabbed his mentor by the collar of
his tabard. "Promise me something, Orvin. Promise me
that when we get there you will explain everything."

A strange light, a light of knowing, filled Orvin's
eyes. "I may not have to."

Christopher ripped his hand off the tabard and
sighed loudly for their benefit. "Damn the mystery!
Damn the deception!"

"If it is the truth you so desire, then let's stop wagging our tongues and ride," Merlin said. He turned and walked back to his mule, this time carefully measuring his steps over the obstacle course of small stones.

They rode in silence. After downing a small portion of overcooked pork, Christopher finished up his desperately needed meal with a large cluster of wine grapes, plucking them from the small vine with his mouth. The grapes were ripe and sweet, unlike Christopher's mood, which was sour through and through.

I had better get the truth when we arrive! I had better get the truth—or I don't know what I'll do!

He followed Merlin around a sharp bend in the road, careful not to look over the edge of the cliff. He'd made that mistake a few turns back. The sheer drop-off and the image of the river so tiny, so very far down below, clinched his throat and nearly made him drop his reins. From that moment on, he steered his courser close to the canyon wall, hugging it as tightly as possible without chafing the animal's flank.

Around the bend, the road became much wider, and a great mouth of stone yawned in the canyon wall. Before the cave entrance was the ring of stones of a well-made, heavily used hearth. As Merlin guided his mule around the hearth, Christopher turned his head to peer into the shadows of the cave.

Out of those shadows came an angel. She wore a pale linen shift that flowed like ivory honey over her lithe frame. Her eyes lit on him, and a lance of adrenaline impaled his being. Without thinking, only reacting, he dismounted and ran toward her, calling, "Marigween!"

She was a dream. A dream made real.

12 Men dealt with torture in different ways. Some took it in silent defiance. Others held conversations with themselves that were diversions from the suffering. Others had no pride at all, fell to their knees, then appealed for mercy.

Seaver had little tolerance for the prideless ones; those he gutted with extreme repulsion. The talkers were a rung braver than the silent ones. He usually let them live for a while, then rewarded their semicourage with a merciful death as they slept. The men he held in highest esteem, the men he feared most, were the prisoners of reticence. These were men who would flinch and bleed and tremble, yet remain silent. There was something unsettling about a man who took his punishment without protest. It was as if he had some deep, dark, powerful secret buried in a place that only he and the gods knew about. Perhaps in death, he would dig up this power and unleash it on his oppressor.

Seaver stood with Kenric in the middle of Darrick's cell. The poorly lit room was now a grotesque melange of dirt, sweat, and blood. Seaver and Kenric looked as if they, too, had been tortured, but it was only Darrick's vital fluid that stained their livery. When Kenric had broken the fat mangonel operator's nose, a piece of the soft bone had burst through the skin and a fine, warm mist of blood had showered the two Saxons. After Darrick had fallen, Kenric had used the heel of his heavy riding boot to drive the fat man's eyes into his skull.

Darrick had taken his death in silent defiance.

Kenric had demanded the names of the other traitors for the past three days, a relentless period of questioning that had evoked a black passion in

Seaver's leader. Seaver had seen the anger in his lord as it had festered, the way the veins at his temples had bulged and pulsed. Finally, Kenric had snapped.

Darrick had not even cursed his slayer, had not even defended himself. He had died as Cuthbert must have, without a struggle.

But Seaver knew Darrick was no young oaf. The man had had a plan, and now he might have his revenge. With the names of the traitors still unknown, they all still posed a threat to Seaver's life. They could move unfettered throughout the castle and close in on Seaver until it was too late. Darrick must have known that. He must have reasoned that it was better for him to die, for he would get his revenge. To live and give up the names would only mean he would not die alone. And so, in death, he had vengeance to gain.

"Lord. I am here as ordered." The deep, resounding voice came over Seaver's shoulder.

Seaver whirled to see Renfred standing on the other side of the iron bars.

Why don't you cut your hair, Renfred? It's so long and brown and straight. You look like a tavern wench. Do you accidentally sit on that hair when you mount your horse? And what is that loop of silver I see dangling from your ear? The tip of an anlace could catch that nicely and take off your lobe with it! You appear to spend more time plucking the hairs between your eyebrows than you do honing your skills as a lieutenant. But, that mistake of yours has already cost you. Look upon this scene with fear. You are next if you do not obey!

"I had hoped it would not come to this," Kenric said. "I cannot understand it. Darrick had always been loyal. Why did his loyalty wane? Do *you* know, Renfred?"

Good, lord. Make this coward sweat.

Renfred frowned. Seaver hated the look. If Renfred had smiled, Seaver would have hated that, too. "I insist, lord, that this man acted entirely on his own. I had nothing to do with him, or the others. He received no direction from me."

Kenric waved a hand. "Come in here, Renfred. The door is open."

With distinct trepidation, Renfred clenched his fists at his hips and slowly stepped into the cell. When he crossed in front of Seaver, Seaver accidentally smelled the man; the perfumelike odor wafting from the lieutenant made him want to gag. Renfred reeked of that soap many of the men had found in the chambers of the Celt nobles.

As he pulled at his nostrils, trying to stifle the odor, a question regarding Renfred's last statement occurred to Seaver. "Lord," Seaver began, "how is it that Renfred knows there were others involved? Darrick's imprisonment is well-known by now, but only you, the chief guard, and I knew there were other conspirators."

Kenric turned his head to Renfred, then raised his brow in a query of his own. He took a threatening step toward Renfred. Seaver did likewise.

Hemmed in by the walls of the cell, the bars behind him and the two encroaching men, Renfred could do little more than tremble. And that delighted Seaver. He noted the way Renfred kept swallowing, wringing his shaking hands, and shifting his weight back and forth between legs.

"Answer the question," Kenric ordered curtly.

"They c-came to me. They w-w-wanted my support. I told them n-n-no."

Shake, you dog! Rattle in fear!

"Did you?" Kenric asked, prying for the truth.

"Y-Yes, lord. I know why you chose Seaver to second you. His scouting and then his leadership during the siege of this castle was remarkable. Many despise him because of his stature. But I admire him. I aspire to be a leader such as he."

Seaver tried to read under Renfred's words. He knew the Saxon lieutenant would say anything to get out of being killed. But Seaver had to admit that the surface meaning of the words was most pleasant. It was grand to listen to the tall, lean, strong man speak so humbly. But was any of it true?

Does he really aspire to be like me? I don't know. The fact is, if I'm murdered, and Renfred is not involved, then Kenric will logically choose him to succeed me. Blame the murder on a few rogues and Renfred gets his command neat and clean. That could be his plan. Deny he's involved, and have me murdered just the same.

But why warn me? If Renfred is that thirsty for power, why did he send Darrick to issue me an ultimatum? The only reason I can think of is that Renfred, or whoever is behind this, has a conscience. Why kill me when I might just step down out of fear? But they underestimated my courage.

Seaver could conjecture all he liked, but it was to no avail. Renfred's fate was not in his hands. Kenric would have to decide. He could only pray to Woden that his master would make the right decision.

Kenric buttoned his lips and scratched an itch behind his ear. He squinted into a thought, then took a deep breath. "I don't know what to believe, Renfred. Let's begin again. Who came to you with the idea of taking away Seaver's command?"

"I said 'they,' but it was Darrick. He told me he represented many. He didn't tell me who they were."

"Then it is conceivable that Darrick plotted alone, is it not?"

Renfred beamed with the notion. "Yes. Yes, it is."

"Lord," Seaver interjected, "there are those who have served with me whose respect I have earned. But you must know there are many whose envy and whose prejudices dictate their actions. I believe Darrick *did* represent others."

"What you believe and what I believe are not necessarily the truth," Kenric said. "Therein lies our dilemma. We do not know anything, and all we have"—he leveled his steely gaze on Renfred—"is your word to go on."

Seaver thought a moment, then said, "I do not wish my life resting on assumptions, lord. I suggest we give the traitors the opportunity to come forward, with the promise they will only be banished and not killed. Meanwhile, I suggest that Renfred be kept under guard in his chamber. It may not be his fault that some have acted on their own—if they have—but the fact that he is involved makes it a necessary precaution."

"Done," Kenric said, not even thinking about it. That was what Seaver liked about Kenric. No hesitation. No indecision. When he heard a good plan, it was implemented. Period.

"I am deeply sorry about this," Renfred told Kenric, lowering his head. "My honor and my name have been defiled. That is already punishment enough."

Kenric answered in earnest, stealing a last look at Darrick's gore-laden corpse. "I hope I do not have to kill you, too."

•   •   •

The passageway to Seaver's chamber was a dark
stretch of stone intestine, lit by only two torches, one
at each end. There were no windows allowing entry
of the warmth and light of the afternoon sun. It was
one of only two halls in the entire keep so constructed. Save for the dungeon, it felt like the darkest
place on earth. Seaver and Kenric had chosen such
chambers for protection. Centrally located on the top
floor, they were seemingly Celt-proof, or at the least
provided ample time for escape if the Celts were to
reach the perimeter windows. The depressing gloom
was unavoidable.

The sound of his footsteps was too loud. He
wished they had been able to save some of the
tapestries that had once hung in these halls and had
muffled the noise. Flame-happy infantrymen had put
their torches to the dry, colorful fabrics, and all that
remained of them were their long, scorched hanging
poles.

He reached his chamber door and pushed it in,
expecting to find Ware waiting for him. He had
ordered the scout to meet him, for he would now
serve as Seaver's personal guard until the conspiracy
was over.

Blackness clogged the room. A small wedge of light
from the hallway pyramided across the floor, but left
the corners of the chamber in gloom.

The feeling was small, a whisper somewhere within
Seaver. Then, like a beast whose young were in danger, the feeling abruptly roared.

He was not alone.

Seaver craned his head just as someone came from
behind and shoved him into the room and slammed
the door shut.

A thin puddle of light leaked under the door, and

though it was meager, it was enough to cause a shadow. And as Seaver turned around while backing away, he saw and heard the shadow lunge.

Seaver dived right, knowing his poster bed could not be far off. He crashed into the bed pole near the trunk at the foot of the bed, elbows and shoulders impacting on the wood-and-iron column. He repressed a groan. He rolled and looked up, rubbing the heat of pain from his arms onto his thighs. Eyes adjusting to the darkness, he saw the silhouette of the attacker and was able to pick out the daggers the person clutched in each hand. The assassin sniffed, shifted his head right, then left, as though all senses save for sight probed for Seaver. There was nothing distinguishable about the traitor's clothing; it must have been dyed in a deep hue.

Seaver knew he would not make it across the room to the corner where he stowed his weapons. He was on this side of the chamber and would have to find something, anything to defend himself with. A vision of the recent past came to him, and he silently cursed his wandering mind for summoning it up. It was the most trivial of things, and he could not understand why he had thought about it. He had a stack of woolskins inside the trunk that needed to be dyed. It was a notion he had had back on the Quantock Hills, for he could not wear the light-colored, though exceedingly warm garments at night. An enemy would spot him easily. Yet dye was a commodity the Saxons had little of, using it up as quickly as they plundered it. The Celts knew how to make dye; the Saxons had yet to discover the method. Then it dawned on him. He had set two large pitchers of black dye on top of the trunk and had ordered one of the Celt maids to take his woolskins out to be dyed. The other Saxon lieu-

tenants were quick to confiscate and use the dye, and
Seaver had reserved his two pitchers by taking them
to his room. If the maid hadn't dyed the skins yet, the
pitchers would still be there. He reached over. His
hand was met by smooth, hard clay.

"I'm right here, traitor. If you dare to come."
Seaver gripped the handle of the dye-filled vessel.

The assassin came slowly, furtively, his footsteps
almost undetectable, his silhouette vague, though
enough to betray him.

Seaver heard him breathing, hard and heavy, and
knew the man's heart must be rumbling in his chest—
as Seaver's was. He thought about stone. He thought
about himself as stone, stiffening every muscle in his
body. He took in a very long breath and held it.

The traitor was only a yard away. He cocked his
head and kept himself erect. He would not expect an
attack from below. The assassin turned right, display-
ing his profile to Seaver.

Now I move!

Horns of advance resounded in Seaver's mind. He
lifted the pitcher from the trunk, thrust it up toward
the assassin, then jerked it back.

No, the assassin did not expect an attack from the
floor, nor did he expect to be doused with the cold,
slimy mire that was the dye. As the liquid cloud fell
over the man, he cried sharply in surprise.

Seaver would not wait around for another reaction
from the traitor. He sprang to his feet, dodged
around the man, then scrambled toward the line of
light that marked the entrance door. His hand found
the latch and he yanked the wooden barrier open.

Something tore hard across his shoulders, and a
warm, tingling sensation quickly followed it. He staggered into the hall and turned to see Ware rounding

the corner at the other end. Then he whirled around to view the assassin, whose face was completely masked in the black dye.

Dousing the traitor had bought him the moment to escape, but now there was no way to identify him.

Seaver shouted to Ware, but he didn't have to. The scout, upon seeing the black, knife-wielding assassin, broke into a sprint down the passageway.

The traitor looked at Ware, then back at Seaver. The movement of the man's eyes was highlighted by the dye, the white of those globes the only color on an otherwise swarthy face. He repeated the action, and Seaver knew the man's mind ticked with decision. He had yet to lunge, and Seaver continued to back away from him in Ware's direction. If he was going to make a move, he would do it now.

The assassin turned and darted off toward the opposite end of the hall.

"I'll get him, lord!" Ware yelled as he neared Seaver.

"No. Let him go," Seaver said. "I need help." And then he felt himself hit the floor and his gaze focused on the long wooden support beams that crisscrossed the ceiling. The back of his shirt was warm and damp; he'd been cut. He shivered as he wondered how deep the traitor's blade had sunk.

Ware hunkered down, then stared at him, his eyes bulging, his face riddled with deep concern.

"Don't look at me," Seaver said weakly. "Fetch the doctor."

"I won't leave you!" Ware countered.

"Then I might die. Go."

Clearly, Ware was torn. And the young man had a point. The assassin could return—but that was not likely. It was better that Seaver be left momentarily alone. The risk had to be taken. And it was good that Ware reasoned that out, stood, then jogged off, yelling for help.

Seaver closed his eyes and listened to himself breathe.

13

Brenna knew that by now, Wynne whimpered like a child. That was always how her friend reacted to bad news. The abbot would have told her she was staying at the abbey until she healed, and then would be taken by Friar Peter, a scribe of the abbey, back to Gore. Peter had business with the abbot in Gore, and it would be no trouble at all for him to escort Wynne.

Though she knew she had hurt one of her best friends in the world, Brenna did not let her guilt put an end to her journey. She knew what she did was selfish, but it was time she did something for herself, instead of always tending to the needs of others. And besides, she had already agreed that it was too dangerous and too great a burden to take Wynne any farther. Her conscience would not allow it. Then why was she second-guessing every move she made? Was it because she had never done anything like this before, never acted so quickly and rashly? That had to be part of it. She felt as if all of it was a fever, and she sweltered with the desire to go on, to see Christopher, no matter what the cost.

Even the dense fog that now shawled the land and lurked at her rounsey's hooves would not stop her. A few hours after she had left the abbey, a terrific rainstorm had pelted Glastonbury and the surrounding farms, and the rain continued to track at her heels. She continued evading it, and had retreated into a roiling mist. The path paralleling the farmlands toward the Cam was gone, replaced by a gray, vaporous wall. The occasional oak, beech, or fruit tree came into view only at a few yards' distance. She would have to pay close attention, to mindfully steer her horse. This part of the journey was supposed to be routine; now it proved anything but.

A chuckle sounded in the distance. Did it come from in front of her or behind? Another laugh. And then a deeper voice shushing the giggler. She strained to see into the fog, but the effort afforded her nothing. People were out there. Were they watching her? Following her? Who were they? What did they want?

Though reckless, Brenna snapped her reins and heeled her rounsey out of its trot into a canter. Her face moistened with sweat. The nerve-racking, hollow cries came from everywhere and nowhere.

More shushing. Then the bellow of a wolf that was not a wolf came from somewhere in the fog. If terrorizing her was their goal, then they had already attained it.

A row of wheat that shouldered the narrow dirt path sprouted out of the mist. The field to her left lay harvested, but the opposite one was untouched. It was from there that the voices must have come. Surely, they hid in the wheat, watching her through the thin, golden stalks with eyes fixed, hearts intent on causing her harm. They were going to kill her. Whoever they were, they were going to kill her.

Stop it, Brenna! Don't think like that! They could

*just be farm boys having a bit of fun, jesting with me.
Yes, that's who they are. They're boys as sweet and
kind-looking and generous as the ones Wynne and I
passed while riding to Glastonbury. Maybe one of
them will offer me an apple as well!*

*Think about it Brenna. They giggle. They howl. It's
not what they're going to* give *you. It's what they're
going to* take!

*Maybe they won't bother me at all. If I ride away
quickly enough, maybe they will leave me alone.*

Thought turned to reflex, and Brenna snapped her
reins again then drove her heels into the rounsey. She
reached to her side and drew her anlace from its sheath.

They smashed through the wheat, two of them,
young brigands not much older than herself. Then
another one popped up from behind a plowed ditch
on the harvested field. Shocking her rounsey with
cackles and blocking the horse's path, the highwayboys caused the animal to neigh in protest and rear.
Brenna slid backward out of her saddle, felt her sandals leave the stirrups, and then was falling backward
in the air. Her dagger slipped from her grip.

She felt the wind blast out of her lungs as the sudden vibrating jolt of the earth tore through her. She
had tried to put her hands back to break her fall, but
somehow they had missed the ground. Her only fortune was that the path was soft; had it been dry for a
few days, it would not have been as forgiving, and
her rump would truly be burning with pain.
Presently, her posterior stung mildly and her vision
was blurred: everything gray and unfocused. She was
aware of movement around her. And sounds. The
continuous cackling and chortling. Much too close to
her. She lay on her back a moment, fearful even to
breathe.

Seconds passed, and finally she reasoned she had to move. Brenna sat up, then moaned softly. She felt the mud caked onto the back of her head and kirtle, then looked down at her fingers; they were covered in the muck. She leaned forward and felt as if a bed-making pole was jammed up her spine, one she would be forced to live with for the rest of her life. As she oriented herself, she thought of her rounsey, and the provisions in her riding bags; those were what the boys were surely after.

Three of the youthful robbers were at her mount, one holding the reins and calming the horse, the other two rummaging wildly through the bags. There was nothing distinct about the three. They were a seemingly natural part of the landscape, mirroring its saturated filth perfectly. She had been taught not to judge people, but in this case, the boys were as they appeared: the lowest form of rabble in the realm.

With a noisy stomping of feet through the wheat, a fourth brigand broke into view, using one of his thick arms to clear a path for himself through the stalks. He stepped onto the path.

Brenna could not bridle the shiver that quaked through her head and neck as she took in the garish, ugly splendor of the fat, middle-aged man. He wore silver and gold rings on each of his fingers—including his thumbs, and the rings bore the flickering colors of many gemstones. His hair was dark and as greased as a cart axle, the long, flat mane kept in check by a head band as bejeweled as his rings. His shirt, Brenna knew, was of the finest linen, but its days of purity were moons gone. His breeches were expensive as well, but one of the legs was stained a deep crimson from either blood or wine. His eyes wore the luster of a king, his walk as lofty and ceremonious.

He approached Brenna, reached up past his mustache, and stuck a fat finger very unkinglike into one of his nostrils. Still picking his nose, he spoke, the words ringing oddly, suggesting he was not from Britain but somewhere very far off. "Well, what do we have here? A young lass who has fallen from her horse. Allow me to assist you, dear." The thief took the finger out of his nose and proffered that very same hand to help Brenna to her feet.

Brenna grimaced, then refused his aid with a quick, short shake of her head. She pitched her body forward, pushed herself up onto one of her knees, then stood. A large chunk of mud clung to her kirtle where her knee had driven it into the ground. She shook the kirtle and the chunk fell off, leaving a deep stain in its wake. She had never felt so dirty and scared. She tried to channel her fear into a preoccupation with her clothes, examining them, brushing herself off, trying to purge her body of the filth. If there were only a way she could purge herself of the men.

She knew he watched her. She felt his gaze touch her, and wished she had something to hide behind. She continued to wipe herself off, reaching down to her sandals. She checked the ground for her dagger, but it was gone. She straightened.

They're not going to go away, Brenna. You cannot clean yourself up forever . . . and you have no weapon.

"I'm Montague, lass. And those are my three traveling companions." He gestured with his head toward the boys plundering Brenna's riding bags. "I'll let themselves make their own introductions, if they so desire."

"Please, don't hurt me," Brenna said, cursing herself for the way the words had come out, making her seem absolutely helpless and frail. It was true she felt that way, but she didn't have to let him know it. Her courage wasn't completely gone; it just lurked behind a tall fence of fright. She summoned it out repeatedly, but it shied away. It was just a matter of time. Hopefully it would not be too long before she could unleash the strength she knew she possessed.

"My poor lass. I apologize if we've frightened you. It's been a very slow day, you understand, and what with this rain and fog, there haven't been any travelers out on the road. Your business must be very important for you to venture out in weather as disagreeable as this." The headband on Montague's forehead lifted as he crinkled his brow.

What business is it of yours where I'm going, foul man! You just leave me alone before I . . .

Her courage stood on the top of the fence that prisoned it in her mind. But it wouldn't leap over. "Just take what you want. But leave me my horse."

Montague edged closer to her; his every shift forward, no matter how slight, made Brenna flinch and worm in retreat. Harnessing a tone of command, he said, "You haven't answered my question."

"I'm heading east," she reluctantly confessed, dropping her gaze to Montague's slightly bowed legs, then farther to his mud-covered riding boots that must have belonged to a knight. A now unfortunate knight.

"East," Montague said, not believing it. "To the Cam?" The fat king of the brigands was nonplussed. "Why, the armies of Arthur and Woodward are holed up there. Don't you know that the castle of Shores has been sieged by Saxons?"

Brenna nodded.

"Poor lassie, you're riding into a battlefield!"

Brenna looked away from Montague and spied his three accomplices hungrily chewing on some of the food given to her by the monks at Glastonbury: boiled chicken, assorted fruits, three flagons of spiced cider, and a loaf of sweet bread. The boys chugged the cider and chomped on the chicken, leaving the fruit and bread untouched.

Montague must have noticed her looking at his boys, for he shouted to them. "Save some for your master, greedy lads!"

The boys continued eating; one of them, the tallest, nodded, a drumstick held to his mouth. He was the only one who acknowledged Montague.

"Ah, they are getting more unruly by the day," he added with a small measure of disgust.

She resumed gazing at him and, ignoring the urge to swallow, asked, "What are you going to do? I said you could have my provisions. Just give me my rounsey and let me go. I won't mention this to anyone."

"Oh, I wish that I could do that, but it's for your own good that you spend some time with old Montague." Without warning, he moved in quickly and draped his arm over her shoulders. Brenna did not breathe through her nose, for fear Montague smelled as bad as he looked. He continued, "We cannot have you riding into the middle of a castle siege now, can we?"

"I'll be safe—if you'll just let me go." She was emphatic, but he shook his head against it as she finished the sentence.

Ironically, as Brenna concentrated on not getting a whiff of him, he commented on her odor. "Lass, you do smell heavenly. It has been too long for me. Much too long." He shot a look to his apprentices. "They can have all the food. But they cannot have you."

Brenna whirled to get out of his grip, her thoughts locked onto running, onto escape; but Montague was surprisingly swift in his reaction. She spun out of his arm, but he managed to grab the collar of her kirtle, and, as Brenna pulled, she found herself being choked. Montague exploited her delay and tugged her in as he came from behind her, then slid his arm around her neck in a deft, practiced motion. He dropped the hand clenching the kirtle and wrapped it around her waist. Then she felt him bury his hairy face into the side of her neck, his coarse hairs scratching her. She felt something wet and realized it was his mouth on her skin. He let out a soft moan, the mating call of some awful beast. Brenna fought against his grip, pushed herself forward, kicked and connected with his legs. But he was too massive, too strong. She wouldn't give up. She fought on, straining each muscle in her tiny frame. She tried to lean down and bite him, but the arm around her neck tightened and she felt an agonizing weight on her throat.

He is just too strong! He is!
Don't give up! Don't give up!
I can't break free! I can't!
Do you know what he's going to do to you?
But he's holding me so tight!
Break free, Brenna. Try! Try! Try!

And she tried. But his grip held. And his tongue, a wet, slithering, probing snake, found her earlobe. And the others rushed over and chuckled and spat at her and told her they would have a festival once night fell. They said she would not need her clothes.

From the tree to which she was strapped, Brenna looked upon her surroundings. The fog had slunk away into the caverns and dark hiding places of the earth, had laved the land to a rich luster, then bur-

nished the heavens to a shimmering ebony. An air of
quietude and peace filled the shallow valley. She
looked over at the five horses which stood tethered to
a pair of oaks, then let herself drift into the countryside. She ran the short distance to the horses, vaulted
onto her rounsey, wheeled around, and escaped.

Brenna pulled on her wrists, ready to mimic the
waking dream, but the leather that bound them was a
rough, tight reality.

The breeze was cool—uncomfortably so considering there was nothing shielding her body from it. She
stood exposed, bound on the tree, her nipples hard,
legs pressed together, crotch held firm against the
horrors to come. They had stripped her, tied her, and
now waited. For what?

The brigands had argued who would set the cookfire and it had taken them almost an hour to do so.
They had offered her some bread they had warmed
over the flames, but she had refused. Her stomach
was as knotted as the thong that constrained her.

Leaving his boys encircling the fire, Montague rose
with a flagon in his hand and lumbered toward her.
She was far enough away from the fire to be in
shadow, and she was thankful for that. There was no
more shame in the world than being seen nude.
Montague had told the boys to remove her clothes—
and when she began to shed tears, he had ordered
them not to stare at her. One of the boys had gagged
upon seeing the whiteness of her skin, and another
had mentioned something about how true it was
about the body being ugly. Montague, on the other
hand, had eyed her with a lust that bubbled over.

As he drew closer, she watched as his gaze fell
upon her breasts, then flicked down to her crotch. A
nerve in one of Brenna's eyes throbbed uncontrol-

lably. She knew she was at a point where terror now took hostage of her body, abusing it with chills and wild nerves and tremors at odd times and in odd places. And terror demanded no ransom. She was its slave.

Was this it? Had he come over to have his way with her? In a sick way, she almost wanted him to do it. At least the waiting, the anticipation of horrors probably greater than actually existed would be gone. It would be terrible. But it would be over. As she stood now, there was only her imagination to go on, and it sketched scenes of her rape, torture, and death, lengthy images that went into great detail, exploring her pain and misery.

No. No. Her fear tricked her; it tried to make her justify what would happen. She didn't want to be violated at all! It shouldn't happen at all! She should not concede so easily to the situation. She had to keep her mind fixed on getting away and not give up hope. To shrink into Montague's arms, to willingly open her legs to him, would release forever everything she held true and sacred. Mother had told her that virginity was a gift, a gift she reserved only for Christopher. To give it up so easily was not right. No, it was not right at all.

She would fight. She would kick and scream to the end. He might have to kill her.

"Saved you a couple of swigs of cider, lass," he said as he lifted his gaze to hers, then thrust the flagon forward. He smiled. "Oh, you cannot take it, can you."

"No, I cannot," she answered darkly. "And I do not want any."

"You must have something," he said. "Here." He stepped up to her and pressed his beefy gut to hers,

jammed the lip of the flagon to her lips, then began
to pour the cider down her throat.

Brenna swallowed a bit of the liquid, admitting to
herself that she was very thirsty, very hungry. But
then principle took over and she began to spit the
cider up, showering the fat foreigner.

Pulling the flagon away, Montague swore under his
breath. The words he used were peculiar and Brenna
could not repeat them if she tried. "Where are your
manners?" he asked, his face creased in disgust as he
wiped himself off.

"Where are yours?" she parried. "I told you I did
not want any cider!"

He dropped the flagon, marched up to her, and
pawed both her breasts with his filthy, thick hands.
He slid his thumbs and index fingers to her nipples
and tugged on them, moaning again as he had done
while kissing her neck. She knew of no sound more
repulsive. Then he lowered his head to her left
breast, wrapped his lips around the nipple and began
sucking on it like a nursing newborn.

Brenna drove her leg up toward his groin. She
could not get the proper angle to drive her knee
into his crotch, nor could she use the sole or tip of
her foot to pound it. She had to settle for using her
shin like a hammer to pound him. The blow felt
hard enough though, and Montague tore himself
away from her breast, his teeth scraping over the
nipple as he did so. He staggered back, clutching
his groin.

Brenna throbbed with her own pain. Her nipple
was swollen and red and covered with saliva. The
breeze stung it. She looked down to see if he had
drawn blood, but none was visible. She wanted very
badly to clutch her breast with a hand, to minister in

even the most feeble of ways to the pain. She silently thanked the Lord Montague had not bitten her.

A chorus of laughter erupted from the boys around the fire. Montague, still hunched over and gripping his privates, flipped them a look, then fired a glare at Brenna. "Shut up!" he screamed to his followers, keeping his gaze aimed at her. "You," he said to Brenna, "you and I are going to have a private festival."

Montague hobbled a few steps toward her, then removed his headband. He slid it over Brenna's head.

"Now what?" she asked as the world went dark.

He adjusted the headband, tightening it around her eyes.

This was different but no less worse than her imagination of the event. She was back to the waiting and wondering, not knowing what would happen, not even being able to prepare mentally for the worst.

I am sixteen years old—and this is how I will lose my gift.

Stop feeling sorry, Brenna. Don't give in! Remember? Escape. You have to get away!

She heard Montague circle behind her, and she felt him grab one of her hands. She flinched, but he strengthened his grip. Then suddenly her hands snapped free. He had cut her loose! She turned, pulling her free arm forward. She brought her hand up to the headband, began to tug it off, but heard him shuffle around. Her hand was slapped away from the band and twisted behind her back. Straining aloud, he started retying her wrists together. She pulled her body forward, digging her feet into the dew-slick grass but finding little traction there. She slipped and fell; the icy, wet blanket of grass came up with rude speed. She forced her wrists apart and discovered that

Montague had not finished fastening her bonds. With a considerable abrupt tug, she freed herself and rolled over once, twice, then sat up, slid both of her thumbs underneath Montague's headband, then ripped the foul thing from her head. She opened her eyes.

And almost wished she hadn't.

Montague came at her, panting, drooling with lust, and charged with an anger that illuminated his eyes.

Brenna retreated on her back like one of the crabs she had once seen at the market of Falls. She kept her face to Montague and her hands and legs moving. After a yard, she guessed she would not escape.

He kicked one of her legs, then bent down and grabbed the other; she writhed out of his grip, but not before pulling him off-balance. Montague went down with a howl.

Brenna rolled and stood. She looked right and saw one of the boys around the cookfire pointing at her.

"Don't play shy, lassie," Montague said between groans. "If you run away, I'll let the boys have their way with you as well."

She could do it. She could outrun them. She could escape. Brenna gathered saliva in her mouth and spat at Montague, hitting him on the cheek. "God will punish you." She spun around and sprinted away, the cries of Montague's boys not far behind her.

It had come. The waking dream had fleshed itself into reality. She ran toward the horses tied to the pair of oaks. In her imagination she had vaulted onto her horse, but now the twinge of forthcoming pain across her thighs told her she had better swing up onto it instead. Knights in armor were often injured vaulting onto their mounts. Naked chambermaids would wear the scratches and bruises of the act for moons.

Brenna's rounsey neighed softly as her trembling

hands unfastened its reins from the tree. She slid a
bare foot in one of the stirrups and pulled herself
onto the mount. She had thought the saddle fairly
smooth when she had first sat on it, but every imper-
fection in the leather was exposed to her skin now.
The saddlemakers had never expected nude persons
to be sitting in their seats. Ignoring her sweat and the
tiny cuts across her arms from the grass, she smacked
her rounsey on the rump, dug in her heels, then
cracked the reins. She knew the highwayboys would
mount up to pursue her, and so she didn't look back,
but focused her gaze on the forest ahead. She would
have to negotiate the wood while still at a full gallop,
but it was not that dense and the opportunity to lose
the boys in there was one she could not ignore. The
notion to skirt the forest had entered her mind but
had been discarded in a millisecond. If she could
thread her way through enough of the shielding trees
she could stop, hide herself and the horse there, then
wait until morning. There was still the question of
clothes. She could not ride into Shores naked!

*Brenna, you haven't even escaped yet. Worry
about the clothes later.*

The forest opened its arms to her.

14

"Marigween! You're all right!"

Christopher had never thought that the secrets
Merlin and Orvin kept from him involved
Marigween. The entire journey he had considered a
diversion from her, and from Doyle. How could he

have known that one of the very things he desired most had already been taken care of by the two old men? As he looked with sore eyes at Marigween, then reached up and touched a rough finger to her smooth cheek, he could not for the life of him figure out why the wizard and the ancient knight had kept her presence at the cave a secret. Why not tell him she was safe?

He would get answers to his questions later. There was only now. The moment. With her. She slid an arm over his shoulders and the other around his waist, then tilted her head back and pressed her lips to his.

Oh, did he swim in the kiss! His longing for her melted into the intense satisfaction of having her. He bathed in her and was showered by the feeling of her body against his. And the undamned river of emotions took him back to their first night in his chamber, the first time they had made love. Christopher cursed the fact that his memory was not cohesive, no more than a string of pictures and feelings stitched loosely together in his mind, images and senses that stood out and had burned impressions into him:

Marigween on her back, her great mane of red hair spread out like a halo around her head . . .

Her legs sliding along his sides, her heels pressing into his back . . .

The cool, sweet flavor of licorice on her tongue as his mouth devoured hers . . .

Her whimpers, her cries, her low, throaty groans, and the way she moaned his name, broken by desire: Chris . . . topher . . .

That peculiar odor of sweat and heat, the fury of their passion as their lathered bodies slid effortlessly back and forth against each other. . . .

In truth, the moment had not been as spectacular. He had been nervous, and had felt extremely awk-

ward. But those less-than-romantic elements were
erased by a heavy dose of fantasy in his mind. This
was the way he would remember it.

"I'm out of breath!" she said, pulling back.

He felt the heat of his blush. "I'm sorry. It's just I—"

"—I know."

She turned her head, and on the cheek he had not
touched there was a long, narrow scab. "What happened?" he asked, studying the mark.

She put her hand to the wound. "It's healing. Orvin
stitched it up. He removed the stitches, but the cut
opened up again. We let it heal without stitches this
time." Her voice was smooth and explanatory, and did
not carry any of the expected horror and dread a vision
such as herself might feel upon her beauty being
marred. Her cool acceptance of the scar was most odd.

Christopher gently grabbed her chin and turned her
head so that he could better view the scar in the light that
edged into the cave's entrance. "How did it happen?"

"When she saved me!" Orvin shouted from behind
them. Christopher turned from Marigween and
regarded the old man, lifting an eyebrow.

"Yes, young patron saint. I did battle with a Saxon
at my stable and Marigween helped. We slew the
dog, but not before my home was lost."

"You make it sound as if I helped," Marigween
said with a laugh. "I only tried and got this cut."

"So you escaped and came here," Christopher said.

"There is no safer place in the realm," Merlin said,
teetering up to Orvin's side.

For a second, Christopher caught Orvin communi-
cating something to Marigween with his eyes. He
flicked a quick look to Marigween and saw that she
nodded a response. "Is there something I should
know about?" he asked them, jarring both.

Merlin turned and looked west to the sun, which flirted with the rocky horizon. "Orvin. You will help me build a fire."

"Oh, I will?" Orvin's tone said he would not.

"If you want to eat," Merlin said.

Orvin signed, then nodded. When it came to food, the old man would forever surrender.

Marigween tugged Christopher's shirtsleeve. "Let's go inside."

She led him into the entrance tunnel, its floor smooth but uneven, its ceiling rooted with scores of teeth. The tunnel jogged right and opened up into the main room of the cave, where a single candle burned atop a trunk. The quarters were dusty, Spartan.

"You've been staying *here?*" he asked.

"What does it matter so long as it's safe?"

Christopher realized she was correct. He was used to living in places such as this, his cave a thin tent on a cold hill. He made that sacrifice to preserve the splendor of the castle for women like Marigween. He fought for her safety and comfort, and it seemed ironic that she would wind up within the confines of a dusty rock.

She crossed over to the narrow trestle bed where a small bundle of wool lay propped up against a pillow. With unusual care, she picked up the bundle and cradled it in her arms—as if it was a child.

"What's that you have there?" he asked.

She did not answer him until she was close, and then she began to push back the wool.

Christopher already suspected what it was. The way she held it. The way she had to push the wool away to reveal it to him. It must . . . it must be a child. Hers? No. It was probably an orphan. An orphan of the siege she had taken in. Or maybe, just possibly, it was a child—but not a human. A baby something or other. Bird? Cat? Dog? Still, he could not shake the idea that it was a human child; the notion clung to him.

A tiny, pink, sleeping face, framed by wool, appeared within the bundle. More of the wool parted to reveal the swaddling bands wrapped loosely around the newborn. Christopher had seen babies before, but never one so . . . so familiar-looking. He was not the type of person to spend hours in front of a mirror, and often used the blurry reflection of his shield to comb his hair. He kept himself as neat and clean as he could, but was not overly concerned with his appearance, such as the varlet Innis had been. He knew women found him pleasing to the eye, and that was enough. He had, however, spent enough time gazing at himself to know—to know that this baby bore an uncanny resemblance to that young man who stared back at him from within the waves of a river, from within the hard steel of a shield, from within the smooth glass of a mirror.

No. No. No. It was impossible. They had told him the tales. The men of the garrison and various knights he had questioned had told him the same story: a woman must be loved six times before she can bear offspring.

He and Marigween had made sure to count the number; they had stopped after the fifth time.

Had the knights and garrison men lied to him? They had taken his question very lightly and had chuckled as they had delivered their answers. Yet all had answered the same. Had it been some cruel joke they had played on him? Was that what older men did to younger men who inquired about lovemaking? Had it been some kind of crazed initiation into the world of loving?

No, it couldn't be. The knights had been right. His
fear was unwarranted. The child was an orphan. It
just happened to look like him.

"Christopher," Marigween began, her voice soft
and wavering with nervousness, "this is our son."

Christopher took a step back. He felt one of his
legs begin to jitter. "No, no, he can't be."

"He is. And he's beautiful. Look at him."
Nervously, she lifted her arms to bring the baby into
full view. "It is truly God's will that he looks so much
like you." And now she beamed with pride.

*What do I do now? What do I do? I'm a father? A
father? Wait, what about Woodward? He can never
find out about this child, for if he does, he'll kill all of
us! But how can we live like that? Do we have to
stay here inside this rock, in hiding, forever? How do
I tell the king about this? Is this what I want? Do I
even have a choice? Now I suddenly have a family?
And what about Brenna? What do I do? How do I go
back to Gore and tell her about this? I'm sorry but
we'll never . . . you see, I have a son now. I have a
son! I made him! He grew inside Marigween! He's
my blood!*

Even though there was no foul-smelling rag shoved
into Christopher's face, he felt faint. And it had come
on like a Saxon army enfolding his head.

The bed. There it was, only a few steps away. He
shambled toward it, turned, and collapsed onto his
rump. His cheeks sank in nausea. His tongue
drowned in a rush of saliva.

This was not how he was supposed to react! He
was a father! It was a joyous occasion. He remembered when the vice president of the saddler's guild
had had his daughter. The man's wife had nearly died
delivering the child, but, ultimately, woman and baby

had survived. The man had been ecstatic. Christopher remembered asking his father why the saddler had jumped around so wildly and had invited everyone to his toft for tankards of ale. Yes, it was because he had been blessed with a child.

Christopher knew his reaction hurt Marigween. He knew she would want him to react as the saddler had. But he couldn't—because this was not entirely a blessing. It was unexpected, shocking even. And dangerous. It posed a problem without an easy solution. He remembered Orvin's words on the field about how he had met many challenges but had yet to face one of his greatest. As usual, the old sky watcher had been right. Christopher had a little boy would look to him, call him father, seek his guidance.

I cannot believe it!

The nausea reached a climax, and his recent lunch was ready to explode from his mouth. He swallowed repeatedly. How could finding out he had a son make him want to vomit? It was his nerves, he reasoned. Yes, all the mystery, the waiting, and the incredible shock; they all took their toll on his flesh.

Marigween crossed to the bed and sat down next to him. "I know this is . . . unbelievable. I didn't expect it either. But we can make it work out, Christopher, I know we can. Here."

She set the baby into his arms, adjusting the way he held the child so that he supported its head. He could fight back the nausea, but not the tears that battered the walls of his eyes; they painted cool lines across his dusty face, and he saw them drip from his chin onto the wool. He wasn't sad. He wasn't mad or even perplexed now. He could not understand why he cried. Perhaps in the face of such a tiny, magnificent miracle—his son—that was the only thing he

could do, and it was simply involuntary. Or were they
tears of joy? There was a sense of joy, yes, but it was
tempered, shadowed, by fear. Fear of the unknown
future. And fear brought the return of anger. He had a
family now. He would have to wed Marigween. They
would somehow have to explain their child. Those
were the things he would have to do. He would *have
to do* a lot. He would have to react to the new path
his life had taken, instead of being able to choose it.
He should have been able to decide when and with
whom he would have a family. Now he just knew.

*But you made the mistake, Christopher. You
looked too deeply into Marigween's eyes. You let lust
capture your heart. And now you have changed your
life forever! Fool!*

Why did it have to change? Why should he succumb to Marigween, to this child, to this whole new
life that he had never thought about? Parenthood
was somewhere far off into the future. He did not
suspect he would have a child until he was at least
twenty-one. At sixteen, the duty was already his.

Christopher softened a little as he considered his
son. The child was strong, and his eyes, now open,
shone brightly even in the candlelight. He was calm
and wrapped one of his little hands around
Christopher's index finger. Christopher was drawn to
the baby; the power was indescribable, and the
longer he held the child, the stronger it became.

*No. I cannot do this. I won't do this. It's not hap-
pening! It's not!*

Christopher shoved the baby back into Marigween's
arms, stood, then double-timed toward the cave
entrance.

"Christopher? What's wrong? Where are you
going?"

Her plea was a sharpened arrow; it hit hard, and
his heart could not parry it. He felt miserable as he
finally emerged from the cave.

Orvin and Merlin had finished piling timber into
the hearth. Orvin worked the flint while Merlin prepared an iron tripod, cauldron, and chain to be set
over the hole. Christopher looked at them, then let
his gaze find and lock upon his courser, leashed with
the mules to a cluster of thick vines growing on the
canyon wall. The horse chewed indolently and noisily
on its hay. He strode toward the mount.

"Young saint, what is it you're after? I have the
riding bags over here," Orvin called.

Ignoring his master, Christopher reached his
mount and began angrily to rip the reins from the
vines.

"He's leaving, Orvin. Your squire apprentice is
running away—just as I said he would."

Christopher heard Merlin's confirmation to Orvin;
it only made him swing hard onto his mount and kick
the animal into a trot west, away from the cave,
toward Shores.

Orvin called after him, but the old man's words
were clouded by Christopher's steadily mounting
rage. He had to get mad to be able to leave, to be
able to live with himself for the moment. Yes, he was
running away. He could not slough off the disbelief.
And he was too confused. Slapped in the face with
the news, what did they expect of him? How did they
really expect him to act? To say, oh, yes, this is fine?
I guess I have to learn how to be a father now? I
guess I have to face Woodward and tell him the
truth? Didn't they realize how hard those things
were? Didn't they realize that he was unprepared for
all of that? He was only sixteen years old! A man by

some measure, but he still *felt* like a boy. He still had many of the same cravings and desires he had when he was ten or twelve. He still longed for adventure, loved to take risks, loved to just do nothing and everything, and dream. It seemed like he couldn't do any of those things anymore. Adventure was for the young. He wasn't young anymore. He was a father, a man. He had a son to think about, and could not take risks. He had a responsibility to the boy, to feed and clothe and protect him. He could not lie around and dream. It sounded like a horrible life.

"Easy now! Easy!" His courser came too close to the edge of the cliff, and a look down proved, as before, a mistake. He pulled the animal closer to the wall as one of its hind hooves tore free a bit of rock. The stones tumbled over the edge and splashed seconds later into the river.

He hated the path. He hated having been brought to the cave. He hated the uncertainty of everything. So many problems and not a single answer. Already, his heart beat in his head and put a pressure on it worse than his thick, battle-scarred salet. He had a headache coming to Merlin's home, and one now as he left it. That was all the place was good for: pain.

The trouble with charging off lay in his conscience. He knew it was wrong. He knew what he was doing was childish—but wasn't that the point? He didn't want to grow up so fast; he didn't want to know he was a father all of a sudden. Why should he? But how long could he run? Surely one of them would come to find him and pull him back into his forced life. But how could he think of it as forced when he made the mistake? He had made the choice to love Marigween. But the knights had lied to him! It was their fault! He should blame them. Blame them for what? His own naïveté? They would only laugh. It probably only took one moment of loving for a woman to become seeded with a child.

He simply could not accept his mistake. He could not acknowledge his responsibility. And until he could, he would have to run.

15 It was called the stone forest, for many of the trunks of the trees growing there were white. There was a name for the type of trees, but Christopher had long ago forgotten it.

Wild berries and mushrooms had been dinner, and as he lay, staring at the stars through the treetops, he tasted their dryness and sweetness again. He burped and swallowed, took in a deep breath then exhaled a sigh.

When he had entered the wood and settled down on his courser's saddle cloth for the night, he had been overwhelmed by a sensation of death; it lingered still. Maybe he would die among the dead trees. That would solve all of his problems, wouldn't it? He knew that was a coward's desire, one step even below the running. He would never kill himself, no matter how horrible his life became. Or at least he thought so at the moment.

Two more days until he arrived back in Shores, that is, if he rode at a normal pace, which he would not. He wondered how Doyle was. He'd been tortured, of course. Doyle could withstand punishment, though; that Christopher had already seen.

But how much of it? Six days' worth? He wasn't sure.

Insects made sounds that split open the quiet of the forest. The tiny creatures had too many friends who also loved to screech and chirp. Christopher felt comfortable with the rhythmic and soothing call of the crickets. But there were rogue bugs out there whose calls were abrupt and impossibly loud for such tiny things. He longed for the hoot of an owl, for its presence would make him feel safe from the curious, scampering field mice who might explore his sleeping frame. The owl would carry the rodents away to its nest, then dine on them throughout the night.

Christopher could not get comfortable, and he could not drift to sleep. The events of the day, combined with his lack of a tent and lack of a decent meal, had turned him into a stiff, hungry demon who would lie on the border between dreams and reality all night. Too many sleepless nights had already ruined his demeanor. He had to get some rest. He closed his eyes and forced his mind to think about darkness. He stared into the black, focused everything on it, thought only of it.

Christopher did not know how long he had been asleep when he found himself sitting up, backed against one of the bone white trees.

Orvin was opposite him, hunkered down, an unusual position for the old man, his ramshackle back somehow permitting it. The old knight fixed Christopher with a gray, penetrating stare. "Make me understand what it is you are doing, young saint."

Dumbfounded, Christopher asked, "How did you get here so fast? Once I left the canyons, I galloped all the way here."

"You can never run away from me, saint. I'll

always be up here." Orvin tapped his temple and smiled; oddly, his teeth were as white as the clouds, not the yellow Christopher knew.

"Is this a dream?" he asked his master.

"What is real?" Orvin asked.

"Dream or not, you've come to take me back, haven't you? Where's Merlin? He's here too, isn't he?"

"No. I come alone for knowledge. And to offer you guidance. That is all."

"There is nothing you can do to help me, Orvin. My life is in ruins."

The old man frowned. "What's so terrible about it?"

Christopher snorted. "Place yourself in my boots!"

"In your shoes," Orvin corrected.

"Shoes, boots, whatever the saying is! Can't you see what's happened to me?" Christopher closed his eyes, rubbed them hard with his fingertips, then reopened them. No, Orvin had not vanished. He was, however, blind to Christopher's problems. Or was he?

"When a father loses a son, or a son loses a father, it is a great tragedy. Of this, I can assure you." He leaned closer. "Has your son already lost his father?" Orvin was not shy about the challenge.

"I don't know," Christopher fired back.

Orvin slid smoothly into a standing position, turned and began slowly to pace in a circle around Christopher and the tree. Christopher craned his neck to keep his master in sight. What was the old man up to?

Over the years, Christopher had grown accustomed to Orvin's odd behavior, his secrets, his cryptic answers, and the questions answered with questions. But ever since · returning to Shores this time, his tolerance for the old man's whimsical ways had reached its end. He'd been brusque with his mas-

ter, and realized he thought of the man more and
more as an old fool than as a wise teacher. Why?
Was his ego becoming so large that he no longer
needed guidance? That couldn't be true, for he
needed it more than ever now. But he doubted
Orvin's ability to help. Was the old man so out of
sync with Christopher's life that there was no way he
could help? Christopher could only pray that wasn't
true. Yes, he had reasoned that the battlefield had
hacked away a lot of his patience, but his respect for
Orvin should have remained intact. But it had been
many, many moons since Orvin had had to deal with
any of the problems facing Christopher now, if he
had dealt with them at all. Was that it? Was it simply
the man's age that distanced him from Christopher?
Once he had looked upon Orvin as a sage, a prophet
and teacher, the man who had rolled out the carpet
for him to step upon and become a knight. The man
had taught him humility, taught him how to be a true
servant, to realize where he was best suited among
the vast numbers of Britain. And in that position,
squire of the body, he had become the best. The
other young men looked up to him for an example.
Indeed, he owed that to Orvin.

Then why the bitterness? Why the challenging of a
man who had done so much for him? Was he taking
out his own shortcomings on his master?

"If I could read your mind, young patron saint,
what would I find there?" Orvin was behind him,
hidden by the tree.

Christopher huffed. "At this moment, you wouldn't
want to know."

"Perhaps you've come to doubt me." A short, hot
breath was immediately on Christopher's neck as
Orvin continued, now into Christopher's ear. "Does

that strike a chord?" The knight stepped around the tree to face him. "Your eyes betray you, Christopher. You've forgotten about your first lord already? My son took you into battle. There, he died. I spent a good part of my life raising that boy. My father died before he could teach me how to be a father. But I learned. And as much as I hate admitting it, I learned from Merlin. I will pass on to you what I know."

"I don't even know if I want to be a father, let alone need instruction on how to do so."

"You are a father, no matter how you look at it," Orvin said.

Orvin, why are you so right?

Christopher relinquished a slow nod. "Tell me, is there any way to learn that kind of skill? Even from Merlin? Is it not something you . . . I don't know . . . just do?"

"Why is it you ask? I thought you were not interested in knowing."

Orvin wanted to take Christopher's doubt and stretch it out until there was nothing left of it. Christopher knew that and would not fall into the trap. He clutched his doubt, for it was a part of his old life, the life he didn't want to leave behind.

But he could not get that tiny face out of his thoughts.

"Just tell me, Orvin," he answered.

"Experience is fatherhood. Love is fatherhood. Understanding, compassion, and sacrifice. Those are fatherhood. And so much more."

"They're all just words lost to the wind," Christopher said. He felt the desire to stand, to even his gaze with Orvin as they continued to talk. He tried. His limbs were locked. "I cannot move!"

"You're bound in your misery," Orvin said.

Christopher cocked his head sharply away from Orvin, then squeezed his eyelids shut. "How could I be such a *fool?*"

"Stop asking yourself that and get on with your life." Orvin's tone suggested the act was as simple as honing a dagger or choosing between ale or wine to have with a meal.

"I don't even know what my life is anymore."

Orvin pursed then smacked his leathery lips. "You've lost balance. Begin again. Consider where you have come from, where you are now, and perhaps those will tell you where you are going."

Christopher thought aloud. "Where I come from, where I am now . . . I come from Shores. I am the son of a saddlemaker who was killed in a Saxon invasion. Now I am a squire, squire of the body, King Arthur's squire. My best friend is in an enemy prison, and I have just found out I have a son. That's where I am." Christopher strained to find an answer to where he was going; if there was an answer at all, it was too well hidden in his mind for him to uncover it. "I don't see how those things will tell me where I am going. And besides, why can't you tell me? Haven't you looked into the sky lately?"

Thank St. George his bitterness was ignored by the old man. This was a kinder, gentler, healthier Orvin who stood before him. "You were not born to lead a craftsman's life. Look at how your life has changed. At thirteen, you had already resigned yourself to the saddler's bench. Then a scant number of moons later, you stood on the practice field, ready to begin training as a squire. And unlike the craftsman, your life is ever-changing. That is one sure destiny of yours. It is time to assume another role. Saddlemaker, squire, and now father. Welcome the change. Welcome your new life."

"Don't you realize how hard that is? Do you know how many other problems I have to deal with because of all this?" He knew he whined, but what else could he do? He was frightened, so frightened of everything to come—whatever would come.

"You worry yourself with details, with petty things that may resolve themselves without your intervention." Orvin's face became rigid. "They are not your priorities. You must not worry anymore."

"How can you tell me not to worry when you offer no answers? I've had a child out of wedlock with a woman betrothed to the lord of my castle! Granted, he is freeing Marigween, but when he finds out that I courted her behind his back, he's going to challenge me. Besides that, no one will accept my bastard son!"

"You will wed Marigween."

Christopher smirked at the ease of Orvin's reply. "The church will not approve—and that will not change my son's place in this world."

"You will get the abbot's approval, trust me. The people of Shores will be most forgiving in these turbulent times."

It was easy in the beginning to do that, Orvin. But now, now I do not know . . .

With disgust, Christopher sighed. "I'm beginning to think the only one I can trust is myself." He looked up, ready for Orvin's argument to the contrary.

He was alone in the forest.

"Orvin?"

Christopher rolled over on the saddle cloth and shuddered awake. It was a dream. And at the end of it he had dreamed he had awakened—but never had. Was it a dream within a dream?

What was dream? What was reality?

In this reality he lay by himself. He was afraid to fall

asleep, for fear his troubles would now take him into a black sleep of nightmares; but he was too tired to stay awake. He closed his eyes. Heat and light both vied for control over his body. They had come on suddenly, along with the sensation of a hand on his cheek.

His eyelids yawned open into daytime. Arthur leaned over him, his expression hard to read. Concern? Anxiety? Anger?

Christopher pushed up with his arms, then shifted into a sitting position. Arthur sat down on a carpet of twigs and leaves. "You've been sleeping a long time," he said. The king reached over to a nearby bush and plucked himself a handful of berries. He popped one into his mouth and chewed slowly.

His senses dulled, it was only now that Christopher realized it was the king, the *king* who sat next to him. "I beg your pardon, my liege, I don't know how—"

"—Relax. Untie the knots in your muscles. You rode very hard to get here."

"How do you know that?"

Arthur frowned, and then he turned his head a little in thought. "I don't know. But I do. And that seems fine with me. Is it finc with you?"

Christopher shrugged. "I'm not sure. Yes, I guess."

"There are so many other things I know as well. Would you like me to share them with you?"

"Please do, lord."

Arthur considered another berry before popping it into his mouth. "Mmmm. These are sweet. Would you like one?"

They did look good, but Christopher's belly cut off the desire with a sharp pang. "I think I've had too many of those already."

"All right. So, where were we? Ah, yes. I know all these things about you, and it is very strange to be talking to you about them. For instance, I know Doyle killed Innis and Leslie. And I know you and he are keeping it a secret from me . . . "

How could Arthur rattle that off so matter-of-factly? It was inconceivable that the king would regard the murders in such a way—unless he had known about them from the beginning. But how?

"Lord, I beg of you, please, how do you know? And please . . . what's to become of my friend and me?"

Arthur smiled. "I don't know how I know. I don't know what's going to happen to you."

The king's smile was impossible, not to mention inappropriate. If he meant it, then it was a sinister smile.

"We should talk more like this, Christopher. You know, if I ever have a son, I would be proud if he lived up to your ideals."

"But how can you say that, lord—when you know I've kept a terrible secret from you?" Christopher found himself rocking back and forth on the saddle cloth, his nerves lording over his body—the order of things for the past moons.

"I know you wanted to tell me, Christopher. I know you're afraid of what will happen to Doyle if you do. Listen to your heart. Then listen to your mind. Do what they tell you."

"But lord, my heart tells me not to tell you and my mind tells me to do so!" From the moment Christopher had decided to shield the truth for Doyle, his heart and mind had mounted their attacks on each other. They fought bitterly, and would continue to do so until . . .

"What about Doyle? What does he want you to do? Have you ever spoken about it with him?"

Christopher realized he hadn't. They had avoided the subject altogether. "No, lord."

"Why don't you ask him what he wants you to do."

"Isn't that obvious, lord?"

Arthur steepled his brow. "Maybe it's not."

Something scurried across Christopher's ankle. He looked down and saw nothing there. He realized he was not sitting up anymore, but lying down. The heat of the sun was no longer upon his face; it was replaced by a cool breeze. He moved to look at his ankle again, then realized his eyes were closed.

He sat up, and as he opened his eyes, he felt something shoot across his calf and over the hand he'd pressed onto the saddle cloth for support. It was still night in the stone forest, and it was difficult for him to see what had probed him, but he had a good idea. As he had feared, some form of rodent had found him as he had slept. His linen shirt lay nearby. He picked it up and pulled it on, shivering.

He was sure he had been dreaming. He knew he had seen Orvin and Arthur. But what had they said to him? He could see their lips moving in his mind's eye, but no sounds came forth from their mouths.

Christopher moved to the nearest tree, sat against it, and pulled the blanket over himself. He huddled against the cold and blinked hard to keep his eyes working. To his right, his courser remained undisturbed. He wondered if the horse dreamed. If it did, it probably dreamed of a more sympathetic rider who would not drive it as hard. Christopher was determined to be in Shores by the next evening, and he hoped the animal would accomplish the task.

Sleep well, gentle mount. On the morrow you will feel my spurs. I will try to be merciful.

With nothing else to consider besides his discomfort, he turned his thoughts back to the dreams and attempted to extract some detail from them. What

had Orvin spoken to him about? It surely had something to do with his running. And why did he dream
of Arthur? What was it the king had said? It got
closer, neared reality . . . there. There it was, he
remembered. The king had told him that he should
speak to Doyle, to see if Doyle would allow Christopher
to inform the king about the murders on the Mendip
Hills. That was mad! Doyle wouldn't allow it!

Would he?

The king had suggested that Doyle's reply might
not be that obvious. If Christopher could tell Arthur
the truth, he would walk across the land a much
lighter man. It would be up to Doyle. If Doyle still
lived, he would ask him. If he had died, then
Christopher would make his confession to Arthur.

Perhaps Doyle would want to tell the king himself. . . .

With that door open, and a course of action laid
true, Christopher diverted his thoughts to Orvin.
Why had the old man come, or rather, why had he
dreamed of his master? The obvious reason was that
he needed help. Had Orvin provided some? He
couldn't remember.

*What good is dreaming of you if you cannot help
me?*

For a frosty second, Christopher thought he heard
his question being answered, but it was only the
scraping of branches against each other, forced into
intimacy by the breeze. He pulled the saddle cloth
over his head and continued to think about Orvin as
he rocked himself slowly toward morning.

16

Two hours outside of Shores, on the rim of the eastern forest that stretched all the way to the village, Christopher's horse slowed from its gallop into a canter, then into a trot, a walk, then stopped altogether. All the spurring in the world would not budge the courser.

"Orvin once had a mule like you," Christopher told the courser as he lifted himself out of the saddle. "But she was a mule. She had an excuse. You're a courser." Christopher ran a hand over the horse's flank. "Look at your muscles, how strong they are. You should be able to take me all the way home." He crossed to the animal's head and stared into its large, blank eyes. "I won't force you. You can walk with me if you like. Or stay here and rest."

Christopher dropped the reins and started off. After a moment, he looked over his shoulder and saw that the courser followed him. Good. If he left the horse behind, it would surely be stolen.

The eastern forest was a deeper, darker, denser place than the stone forest, and much more familiar. Christopher and his old friend Baines had trained in the closer, thinner forests that paralleled the tourney ground of the castle, but this was the place they had spent the majority of their time. If he searched hard enough, he could probably find the carvings they had made with their daggers in a trio of oaks; but now, the shadows of night would shade those memories. There was no time to reminisce. He would move his saddle-sore legs as quickly as he could, circle wide around the castle, then slip down to the Cam to find Phelan and Neil.

In less than an hour, Christopher stood looking at

the lights of Queen's Camel Abbey; they burned in the distance like stars resting on the ground for a spell before they resumed their places in the heavens. Christopher turned his gaze from the abbey to his courser, slid a boot into its stirrup, then swung up onto the mount. The horse had followed him all the way and he sensed that the animal was rested enough to carry him for the last leg of the journey home.

When he arrived at the camp along the Cam, he saw that something was wrong. Nearly all the men wore grim, sullen faces. Even the guard who let him pass was dour, barely able to answer him. He felt as if he rode into the camp of a defeated army, and he quickly prayed that was not the case. A few heads lifted to acknowledge his presence and to regard his battered state. He had barely eaten in the last two days, had worn the same clothing, and had slept in the forest with only a saddle cloth for cover. His arms were scuffed, and lines of grime outlined the wrinkles in his skin. He could only imagine what his face looked like. The fine layer of hairs that was his budding beard were surely caked with dust. He must eat and bathe and rescue Doyle—not necessarily in that order.

He found a lieutenant he knew was a member of the Vaward Battle group and asked him if he had seen Phelan or Neil. The lieutenant directed him upriver, where a large gathering of men stood for matins and lauds, directed by a brown-robed monk from Queen's Camel.

He spotted Neil standing near the rear of the crowd. As Christopher dismounted, a young page offered to groom his courser for a denier. He agreed and handed his reins to the boy. He would have to ask Phelan or Neil for the money; his coin pouch was in his saddlebag back at Merlin's cave.

Christopher came from behind Neil and gently rested a hand on the shorter man's shoulder. Neil looked up, and his eyes registered the surprise. He stage-whispered, "Where have you been?"

"Too long a story to tell now," Christopher answered. "Where's Phelan?"

"He's back at our tent. He hasn't been feeling good. A problem with his bowels. He hasn't been able to pass his meals."

"That sounds serious. Has Hallam had a look at him?"

Neil sneered. "Yes, he has. And his remedies have done nothing."

A tall, lean archer in front of them turned around and put a finger across his lips, shushing them.

Christopher gestured with his head that they move away from the crowd of worshipers. As they did so, once again, Christopher was met by the somber looks and the lazy, halfhearted steps of the men as they dragged themselves to their destinations.

"What is wrong with everyone?"

"That's right," Neil said, "You've been away." He sighed. "Are you sure you want to know?"

Christopher had heretofore been unnerved by statements like that, but after being told he had a son, nothing would surprise him. He nodded.

"The Saxons have taken the castle of Rain. Lord Nolan and his army won't be able to help us. He's a little busy, you understand."

Christopher felt a cold knot tighten in his gut. "They have two of our castles? What about Uryens? Can he help us?"

"He's transporting his siege engines down now, but they won't be here for a while. It doesn't look good."

"What about diggers? Have we recruited any?"

"I'm not sure. You'd have to ask Arthur about that." Neil pointed to a row of tents set as far back from the shoreline as possible. The reeds that had once surrounded the shelters had been hacked away, and a large pile of them was nearby. "That first one is ours."

Neil leaned over and slid into the tent. Christopher followed.

There was barely room enough for two inside the shelter, let alone three. Christopher sat down with his back pressed against the entrance flaps. Phelan lay on a pile of woolen blankets to his right, the bird's face a faint shade of yellow. He lifted his head, the effort clearly a strain for him, and smiled when he saw Christopher. "Where have you been?"

"He says it's too long a story to tell now," Neil answered. "I suspect he doesn't think we're close enough friends to tell." Neil's barb was good-natured; it seemed his mood was much lighter than the last time they had spoken, arguing over whether to save Doyle or not.

"No, it's as I said. It's just too complicated. There's just too much to tell. What I really want to talk about is freeing Doyle. Phelan, it appears you are—"

"We're not talking about Doyle anymore," Neil said annoyedly, cutting Christopher's sentence off at the knees. "He's dead. Accept that." The barbarian's good mood had dropped like a mangonel stone.

"How do you know for sure?" Christopher asked.

"Come on, how can he not be? We both know him. He spat in their faces and then they knifed him."

"What if you're wrong?"

"I'm not," Neil snapped.

Phelan pushed himself up onto his elbows. "You can't be sure about that," he told the barbarian.

"You're only certain because it makes you feel better. I think Doyle is alive. I won't be able to live with myself if I don't try to help him."

"You're not doing anything," Neil replied. "Look at you. You're . . . sick!"

"I don't care." He turned his glossy eyes on Christopher. "I still want to go with you. When do we leave?"

Christopher opened his arms to his fate and made a resigned acceptance of the fact that anything that *could* go wrong in his life *would*. He had returned to Shores, had run away from the responsibility that lay waiting for him in Merlin's cave, and simply wanted to bury himself in the idea of saving Doyle. He had decided that even if Neil still refused to go, that wouldn't stop the bird or himself. But Phelan was ill. Again, he was alone to face everything.

"Neil's right," Christopher told Phelan. "You won't even make it into the first passage. I'm sorry. I'll go alone."

Phelan pushed off his elbows and sat up, then threw off the blanket covering his lithe frame. "No, you won't." The bird's legs, visible below his breeches, were that same unnatural tint of yellow as his face. Phelan considered the color of his legs, then looked at Christopher, a smile taking hold of his lips. "If nothing else, I'll scare the Saxons to death with the color of my skin."

How Phelan could keep a sense of humor at such a moment, Christopher did not know. It had been too long since he chuckled, and he found himself still unable to do so. He stood, bumping his head on the tent top.

The bird became anxious over his move to depart. "No, Christopher. I'm coming with you I tell you."

"I'm sorry."

All the while, Neil said nothing. Christopher had to respect the barbarian for sticking to his decision, though wishing fervently he would change his mind. That event appeared to be something just short of a miracle.

He could use a miracle at the moment.

Phelan continued to call after him as he left the tent. Christopher heard Neil try to settle the bird down, and then found himself in the middle of a swarm of muttering men. Matins and lauds had ended the soldiers ambled back to their quarters.

Christopher became lost in thought, and he stopped in the middle of the crowd. What would he do next? Bathe and eat were still on the agenda. Then he would need to procure weapons. His broadsword was hopefully still in his tent; he had not seen the blade during the journey to Merlin's cave. He also wanted a crossbow, a hauberk, and light sandals for running. The Saxon livery he needed would come from an unlucky guard. It was a shame he hadn't taken the time to discover what Orvin had used to make him sleep. He could use that on the Saxons instead of having to hit or kill them. Too late to find out now.

What about Arthur? And Woodward? Christopher had been seen by a lot of men, and one of them would report his presence.

No matter. He had already decided to disobey the king and rescue Doyle. What was there left to talk about? Arthur's plan to free the castle seemed to be at a standstill, for the men seemed to be doing little more than wallowing in the bad news of the fall of castle Rain. They needed some hope. If Christopher was able to rescue Doyle and a few others, the men would cheer his accomplishment and know that it was possible to defeat their seemingly unconquerable enemy.

As men elbowed and shoved their way around him, Christopher lowered his head and closed his eyes.

Lord, ease my fear and give me the strength to help my friend. And please help me somehow. I'm so afraid of my future, of what to do about my son. You know I don't want to think about him now, or about any of them back there. I don't hate them. I don't hate what's happened. I'm just not sure how to act. I sometimes think, maybe the rules of combat apply to this: do not think, just act. But I don't know how to act now, and the more I think about it, the more frightened I become. I want to do the right thing. But I'm scared. Help me.

Christopher stood alone near the shoreline. The crowd had passed, leaving him, like their muddy footprints, behind. Heart pounding, he started off in search of his tent.

17

Brenna was safe. She had escaped Montague and his highwayboys. The brigands had scoured the forest all night but had not found her. By morning, they had given up the chase. Wrapped in her rounsey's saddle cloth, she had ridden for a day, and had encountered only the small animals of the field: the crows, larks, and pipits that had wheeled and darted overhead; the brown and gray squirrels who had studied her with curious eyes from their perches on tree limbs; and a fox, who, upon seeing her, had scampered off into a thicket.

She had come to a pair of small huts huddled

among the tall gold and green grasses along the Cam.
The huts belonged to an old man his wife. Once a
tanner in the village of Falls, the old man had opted
to spend his twilight years along the cool waters. His
wife had been kind enough to loan Brenna a shift and
kirtle, which had been big on her, but that had hardly
mattered. She had told them of her escape from the
brigands, and had lost her breath as she did so. They
had listened, deeply intent, their faces reacting to
every dip and turn of the story. Shocked by her
ordeal, the couple had resolved to take care of
Brenna, and even escort her back to Gore. Brenna
had insisted she was returning to Shores, but in a
snipped reply, the old man had said that was out of
question.

She had been there only a short time, yet the couple had taken her in like a daughter. Brenna had
appreciated their kindness, for without the clothing,
food, and shelter they had provided, she would not
have been able to go on. But the time had come.

In the middle of the night she left them. Both old
man and woman slept deeply, answering each other
with loud, drawn-out snores. She walked her horse a
hundred yards down river, mounted the rounsey,
then trotted off. A frog *ribbited* its good-bye.

She wished she could have written the couple a
note of thanks, but they had no quill, and that probably meant they did not read or write anyway. She
hoped her earlier thanks to them was enough, and
she prayed they didn't think she had used them. She
was truly grateful for their help. But the old man
wanted to undermine her plan to see Christopher.
She could have fought with him, but this way was
better. She was able to avoid the confrontation, and
at the same time ride into Shores well after midnight,

when the battle did not rage. Soldiers needed to sleep
like anyone else.

The river wandered left, and as Brenna followed
the gradual curve, the distant torchlights of the army
rose out of the darkness. She had thought the army
would have encircled the castle, but the old couple
had told her that they camped down river, near the
shoreline. It would be easier than ever to find
Christopher—providing there were no problems at
the camp, such as a Saxon attack.

She had come very far to see him, and had made
many assumptions. Part of her was filled with anticipation, the other part with doubt. What if she was
wrong? What if Christopher had died on the Mendip
Hills? What would she do? How would she act?
Would she be able to go on—to live with that shattering fact? She had risked everything in the belief
that Christopher was alive and at Shores. If he
wasn't . . . then maybe, maybe she couldn't go on.
There had been a time, it seemed like a millionscore
years ago, when Brenna was ready to end her life
over him. But that had been a brokenhearted girl
who had thought those thoughts. Brenna was a
woman, a woman who had decided what she
wanted. It was Christopher who made her happy,
who brought into her life all the joy she would ever
need. There was nothing he could not provide for
her. Few men in the realm were as considerate, car-
ing, and deeply feeling as he. For a man-at-arms he
was unique, able to fight with one hand, caress with
the other, doing each exquisitely, agilely, not letting
the brutish side of his personality plunder his sensi-
tivity. She would never find another young man like
him. Once, she had thought she could replace him,
and had found herself drawn to the varlet Innis, a

highly polished gem among the rough-faced fighters.
But behind all of his gloss had been an empty, selfish, spoiled boy with a violent streak that knew no
bounds. No, she could not replace Christopher. No
man would ever come close.

What if he's dead?

Stop thinking that, Brenna. You have to believe.

What if he doesn't want to see me?

Why would he not?

*I don't know. Maybe he'll think I'm intruding. Maybe
he'll tell me the battlefield is no place for a chambermaid and send me away. Maybe he'll yell at me!*

*If he does that, it's only because he loves you and
doesn't want to see you hurt. So be prepared.*

*There's something else. I thought about it once.
What if he is alive but he's not . . . whole.*

Do you love him?

Yes!

Then you'll love him no matter how you find him.

I will. Yes, I will.

Temporarily lost in her fears, Brenna did not realize
she had come upon the perimeter of the makeshift out-
post. Two wide-eyed, slack-jawed guards accosted her.

"Maid! You don't belong here!" the stouter one
shouted, brandishing his halberd, the tip of which
he kept only a few inches away from Brenna's chest.

"That is a matter of opinion, sir," she said,
unsheathing a force in her voice meant to command.
"I am here to see Christopher, squire of the body.
Please take me to him."

The guards exchanged a look that meant nothing to
Brenna. The taller, clean-shaven one asked, "What
business do you have with him?"

*He's alive! He's alive! Thank you, Lord. It wasn't
all for nothing! He's here and I'm going to see him!*

"It is a private matter that brought me all the way from Gore. If you let me pass now—without further delay—I won't have to mention your impertinence to him. If you know him, then you know he tends to tell King Arthur everything, being his squire. I wouldn't want you two to suffer any disciplinary action for delaying me."

"Are you threatening us?" the fat guard asked, more insulted than not understanding.

With a confident calm, she replied, "Not at all."

Again the two looked at each other, and this time Brenna could see each man silently asking, "What do we do?"

The clean-shaven guard tightened his lips and shrugged, then he nodded.

The fat guard snorted disgustedly, then switched his glance to Brenna. "Pass. And if you have lied, the punishment we receive for letting you come through will be in turn taken out on you."

"You are a smart man," Brenna said as she heeled her rounsey past the guards.

Ha! What a joy it is to be strong, to exercise some power! And to know he's alive! If we do marry, I will be able to use my authority all the time. Granted, Christopher is not a knight, but he's certainly no peasant.

Brenna's bravado leaked quickly away as she entered the main area of the camp. The soldiers had obviously not seen a woman in some time, and their gazes followed her every movement. From wherever they were they watched. Some even woke their snoozing brothers so that they too could have a look at the young, pretty maid atop the horse.

She felt as if she were on display outside a butcher shop, a piece of pork or poultry to be pinched and squeezed.

A few of the men howled. Others whistled. Brenna lowered her head and urged her rounsey forward.

A young man, partially clad in armor, ran up to the side of her horse. "Hold, maid."

Brenna obeyed.

"What are you doing here? How did you get past the perimeter guards?"

"I'm here to see Christopher, King Arthur's squire." By uttering his name, she felt she had recovered a small measure of confidence. His name carried weight, and to be associated with him made her feel strong, no matter to whom she spoke.

"I am the lieutenant of this watch, and if you want to see Christopher, you'll have to get permission to do so."

"How do I go about that?" Brenna asked, agitated by the sudden delay.

"He will have to be notified and then, if he does wish to see you, we can establish a time and a place for the meeting." The lieutenant spoke with a practiced authority, his voice devoid of feeling. He only knew his orders.

"You mean to say I need an appointment to see him?"

"Maid. You have just ridden into the middle of a battlefield operation. Do you understand that?"

No, Brenna did not—would not—understand. She didn't have to. Christopher could not be more than a few hundred yards from where she was, and the only thing that stood between them was a dull oaf and his orders.

"He's probably just up ahead. If you'll go fetch him, I know he'll want to see me now. I know it! Please!"

The lieutenant wagged his skinny little empty head no.

Brenna cracked her reins and jammed her stirrups home into her horse's ribs. The animal leapt forward.

"Stop!" the lieutenant cried. "Stop her!"

Brenna galloped down the main path of shoreline that divided the river and the tents of the army. "Christopher!" She called to him loudly, putting everything she had left into his name. "Christopher!"

18

A sergeant of the Main Battle group swiped one of Christopher's tent flaps aside and leaned inside the tent. "Christopher, did you hear about that crazed maid who just rode into camp?"

Christopher indicated he hadn't, then pushed past the sergeant to join the man outside. He adjusted the hauberk, crossbow, and quiver of bolts he carried in his left hand, then rested his right hand on the hilt of his broadsword that was sheathed and bound to his belt. "I'd love to chat about it, but I haven't the time."

"Where are you going at this hour?" the sergeant asked.

"I thought I'd sneak into the castle and rescue a friend."

The sergeant began to chuckle, and he continued until his laughing came so hard he choked.

"Easy there, old man," Christopher said, slapping the man-at-arms on the back, "I've been told before I'm an accomplished jester, but never has my humor brought one so close to death!"

The sergeant swallowed, then wiped the tears from his eyes. "I'm all right. Yes, yes, I'm fine. Oh, I needed that, Christopher, I truly did. Thank you. It's been too long since I've had a good laugh."

"Glad I could help. Well then, good evening." Christopher turned toward the tall grass behind his tent.

"Oh, Christopher," the sergeant called, "I never finished telling you about that maid."

Christopher paused, craned his head, then smiled. "Some other time." He turned away, stepped into the many damp blades, and was soon walled in by the marshy landscape.

The grass grew taller as he moved on, and there were other plants around him as well, the thin leaves of which extended over Christopher's head. He withdrew his broadsword and hacked a path toward the field beyond. It would have been much easier to take the path already cleared to the field, but it would have been much harder to convince the guards at the end of that path that he was just out for a bit of hand-to-hand practice. They would have wanted to know why he was headed in the direction of the castle, and with whom he planned to practice. Better to forge his own path.

After fighting his way a score of yards through the grass, Christopher knew that he was close to the field. He could no longer make as much noise. He stepped gingerly, sheathed his sword, and elbowed through the foliage, a slower but quieter method of travel.

It was interesting, he thought, how firmly his mind was set. His doubt was beaten down by a powerful sense of certainty. He *knew* Doyle was alive. He was not a soothsayer, there was no magic up his sleeve, no crystal ball gleaming back in his tent. There was a connection between him and Doyle that could never be broken, a link of blood forged moons ago that

bound them to each other no matter what stood in
between. The curtain walls of the castle were a mere
physical barrier. Their link was extraordinarily beyond
the physical; it was generated from their hearts and
would exist as long as each was alive. The closer
Christopher got to the castle, the more he understood
this. Yes, he had doubted, but no more. With the link
came the peace of knowing, and there was nothing
that could relax him more. He had never done anything so dangerous, never submitted himself to something so ambitious, and at the moment his heart ought
to be pounding and his steps ought to be uneven.

But he was calm. Confident. Resolute.

Doyle was there. He knew that no matter where his
friend was inside the castle, he would figure a way to
get him out. He would have liked Phelan's help, but
he didn't need it. What was it that Hasdale had told
him about a man going into battle? If a fighter's heart
and mind are right with God, then his apprehension
and fear are allayed. He rides toward his fate with a
calm purpose. He seizes the poetry of the moment
and lets his body do the work. As Orvin had taught,
he acts; he does not think. If he is true to himself and
his quest, he does not have to think.

It would be grand, Christopher thought. The cries
of the Saxon sentries as he took them out one by one
would be music to his ears. His crossbow would soon
sing, and his sword would soon conduct a song of
hope and victory. As he had already dreamed, he
would emerge from the castle with Doyle and a
stream of freed peasants. His blade would rise in the
fresh, crisp air of morning and signal to every fighter
in the army that the castle was theirs again.

Quit dreaming and get on with it, Christopher!

He came to the point where the reeds and grass

broke off into the field. He hunkered down to survey the scene.

A quick fifty-or-so-yard dash would put him into the forest that divided this field with the tourney/practice field of the castle. There was no way to tell if Saxon perimeter guards were in that forest, though he assumed they were. The many shadows cast by the trunks, brambles, and limbs made the thin forest appear much denser. Christopher let his imagination run wild, seeing a Saxon posted behind every tree. He would have to contend with each, and when he was done, all the killing would make him so ill that he would not be able to go on. He wouldn't listen to those thoughts, and refused to see those images again. There were two, maybe three guards in the forest, all unfamiliar with the territory, all tired and cranky and miserable over being stuck on the wee hour watch. Their senses would not be alert. Christopher would exploit their heavy eyelids and hard dispositions.

The trouble was, he had to run the fifty yards to the cover of the trees. That run would leave him vulnerable. He had a plan for crossing the tourney ground to get to the next forest, but the first field left him baffled. The only way to do it was run outright. Simply put everything he had into a mad dash for the forest, and whisper to his old namesake, St. Christopher, to protect him on the short but dangerous journey.

Ready . . . and go!

He hadn't realized how heavy his equipment was until he tried to run with it. Plodding along through the grasslands was one thing, hightailing it at full tilt over the field was another. And the noise—his crossbow banged onto his quiver, which repeatedly struck

the hilt of his broadsword, which thumped off his
knee, which cracked under all the exertion. He
sounded like an overloaded armorer's cart on a rocky
road, everything rattling—including his nerves.

Maybe I should have crawled the fifty yards. . . .

Christopher knew it was too late to turn back and
try it over. He was already halfway there. Only
twenty-five, twenty, fifteen, ten . . .

He fell in love with the widest, nearest oak and
darted for her cover. Behind the tree, he sank to his
knees and waited for his heavy breathing to subside. He
felt for his gear, the bow, quiver, blade, and hauberk;
all were accounted for. He tossed a look right, then left,
then, sensing it was clear, he stood. He took a few steps
forward, annoyed at how loud his sandals were on the
bed of dead leaves left over from last fall. He held his
weapons as steady as he could so that they would not
rattle and attempted to measure his steps from tree to
tree. Five, perhaps six to the next. He stepped as widely
as he could, the fewer steps, the less noise.

Was it pure luck that no guards had spotted him
thus far? Christopher didn't want to believe that.
What he liked to think was that it was, indeed, St.
Christopher who carried him home. But even if St.
Christopher was busy and not helping him, then it
was God who kept the eternal vigil. Luck was for the
gaming man, not the fighter. There were, however,
some things that would have to be, like the sentries
in the towers of the castle. There was no way out of
contending with them. They would be there and
would have to be eliminated, or at least stalled until
he made it to the moat.

A thin beech tree stood between Christopher and
the practice field. It was over two hundred yards to
the last wood at the bottom of the rocky rampart.

Once he reached that forest, he would parallel the
mountain path up to the castle, all the while keeping
within the forest, staying out of the clearings. Once
up on the rampart, he would have no problem getting
to the north side of the castle. Once there, the fun
would begin.

The plan to cross the practice field was simple, and
was born of an accident he had had while a squire in
training. This part of the field was dotted with grass-
covered ditches, some shallow, some as wide as three
feet across and equally deep. Christopher had been
riding hard and fast, trying to keep up with Lord
Hasdale. The knight had been trying to get a sense of
Christopher's riding ability. Christopher had not seen
a ditch until it had been too late, and he had taken a
hard fall. That fall stayed close to him. Even now he
could feel his leg scream. It was good that the pain
had returned. It reminded him of the ditches. He
would hide in them.

He jogged out of the wood, spotted an oval shadow
in the grass, and ran to it. He felt his footing go and
knelt in the first ditch. Excellent. He paused, scanning for the next shadowed hole. There it was, barely
visible under the starlight, twenty yards ahead. Run
and fall, run and fall. That was the rhythm he would
keep. As he got closer to the last forest he looked up
and saw the illuminated castle. Flickering candle and
torchlights fled through the cruciform loopholes and
rectangular windows, drawing long shadows across
the deep gray ashlar walls. Though it was small compared to Uryens's or Nolan's castle, Christopher
always thought it superior. It was not only a completely functional fortress, but it somehow belonged
up there. It was as natural a part of the landscape as
the rampart or the field. There was nothing obtrusive

about it. It existed harmoniously with the earth. Somehow, Christopher knew the castle would always be there. The Saxons might change it, and the siege might ruin a lot of it, but it would never go away. That warmed him. Home would always be home. No one could ever take it away.

He thought himself a cat as he moved, entering the last forest and slipping by a guard that he spotted only a few trees away. He had been right about the guards. They were as numb as ever.

Christopher had ridden up the mountain path countless times, but never had he tried to do it from within the adjoining forest. Briar bushes were everywhere, and their tiny thorns dragged across his legs. He felt blood leak from a few of the tiny cuts across his ankles and lower calves, but did not bother to stop and examine the wounds. The feeling of resolution was all-encompassing. He would make it to the top of the rampart. He would arrive on the north side of the castle.

At the top of the rampart, Christopher heard a sound from the forest behind him. A rustling that could only have been caused by something large, possibly a man.

Christopher sprinted off, keeping the trees to his right, the castle to his far-off left. The nervous run brought him to the north side of the fortress in far less time than he expected.

He knew, he just knew the wood behind him crawled with guards. One was posted at least every fifty yards. The trick was to keep their backs turned away from him, as they presently were. They guarded against men coming toward the castle, but Christopher had already slipped behind them. Silence was the order of the moment. He sat down, leaned against an ivy-covered trunk, and shed his weapons. He slipped on his hauberk, lacing the shirt of mail up the center. There was a specific reason why he needed the hauberk, other than the semiprotection it provided him in hand-to-hand combat. The hauberk was heavy. And for once he was thankful for its weight. It suited his forthcoming need perfectly.

He took up the crossbow and cranked the handles, windlassing the string into place. He inserted a bolt, but not before running his fingertip over the steel edge of the projectile. His heart began to feel heavy as the thoughts of killing struck. It was his internal contradiction. He wanted to be a fighter but he hated killing. More so now because he knew one day a Saxon leader would come and speak of peace. This war would not last forever. For the moment, he had to justify his actions. He had to tell himself there was no other way to get inside the castle and rescue Doyle. Men would have to die.

He knew what he had to do. He wished he felt better about it.

Christopher readied his gear for a swift departure. With one knee on the earth, he lifted the crossbow and dug the butt of the weapon into his shoulder. There was one guard stationed in each of the four towers along the wall. The object was to silently take out each of the four men. Ironically, if Doyle had been next to him with his longbow, the task would have been easy.

Christopher deduced that these Saxon had never seized a castle before. If they had, they would have known to extinguish all of their tower torches. You don't want your guards illuminated to those who might be shooting at them. The guards should have been trained to recognize each other in the dark, always to call before firing. They might as well have been standing in daylight, their halberds firing dazzles of reflected torchlight that drew Christopher's gaze to the target.

He fixed his sight on the exposed neck of the young Saxon standing idle atop the leftmost tower. A hit to the chest might prove effective, but he'd be gambling on the thickness of the man's link-mail. A reasonably thick coat might just stop his bolt. The arrow of a longbow would be far more effective no matter what kind of mail the man wore, but Christopher was not going to drag a cumbersome longbow around, and then attempt to fire it. Lifting and aiming a crossbow was one thing, pulling back ninety pounds of draw while keeping a longbow steady was another. He would be lucky if he could hit the tower itself with a longbow, let alone the guard.

As he steadied his crossbow, he knew he had to count on more than just hitting the man. He had to pray the man fell back quietly, or fairly so. If the guard fell forward, tumbled in the air, and hit the berm—or worse, the moat—then the noise he created would undoubtedly alarm the others.

Yes, now was when the fun would begin.

He had the Saxon dead, his sights locked onto the soft flesh covering the watchman's Adam's apple. He was not sure how the bow would react when fired; he hadn't taken time to practice with it. He eased down on the trigger, and before he figured the bolt would fly, it did.

He lowered the crossbow a bit as he gazed wide-eyed at the shot. The bolt hit the man exactly where Christopher had intended. He could not have asked for a better shot.

The guard's hands went to the bolt as he swayed forward then backward, each movement causing Christopher to stiffen a notch farther.

Finally, the guard fell.

Forward.

He swore aloud as the man's body turned over slowly in the air until it plunged back first into the moat. A terrifically *loud* splash followed.

Christopher loaded another bolt as the guard in the rightmost tower pointed a metal-covered finger and screamed.

He fired a wild shot at the wailing guard; the bolt fell pathetically short.

But the guard was suddenly hit in the shoulder by an arrow, an arrow that seemed to come from nowhere. The Saxon fell over the side of the wall to join his comrade in the moat.

Before he could load another bolt, Christopher heard another guard's cry. This man fell back with an arrow stuck squarely in his chest. Christopher rose, took a pair of quick steps out of the forest toward the castle, turned, then threw a glance down the field.

Barely visible at the edge of the forest, he saw the silhouette of a man drawing back a longbow.

I don't know who you are—but thanks!

He cocked his head, abruptly aimed, then fired at the remaining Saxon. The bolt found the man's bicep and rooted itself there, while simultaneously, an arrow from the longbowman struck the guard under his left ear and finished him off.

"Christopher! Come on! Let's go!"

It was the longbowman shouting to him, waving an arm. He recognized the voice, and was shocked.

He jogged down field to join Neil, knowing they had only a moment to move before the horn of attack sounded and as many as twoscore men appeared on the wall-walk. He could already see the shifting shadows of archers through the loopholes.

Neil tore off his quiver and threw down his long-bow. He drew the dagger sheathed at his belt. "Forget your bow. Come on," he urged, then turned away even before Christopher reached him.

Christopher abandoned the crossbow and quiver of bolts. His own dagger and broadsword would be enough once they were inside the fortress. As he ran, hard on Neil's heels, he shouted ahead, "Thank you, Neil! Thank you!"

"I'm not doing this for you," Neil called back. "I'm doing it for Phelan. And Doyle. And because I must be a little mad! Like you!"

What they were doing was mad, but Christopher was very sure about it, sure about his madness. A man had to toss away his logic to do something like this, otherwise the fear would overwhelm him. You didn't take on an occupying army of Saxons without surrendering to the absurdity of the act. You simply let the waters of fate carry you up the correct stream, and you prayed that stream would lead you to victory.

Neil did not test the waters of the moat before leaping in. He simply increased his sprint as he reached the correct spot opposite the northmost tower and launched himself into the air.

Christopher felt the cool mud of the shoreline on his toes as he watched Neil dive under the water. He inhaled as deeply as he could, cursing the decaying stench of the stagnant pool. He gripped the hilt of his broadsword to steady the weapon on impact. He extended his free hand to guide him and pushed off with his legs.

The icy rush of water never came. The moat was warm, the waters having been heated by a succession of clear days, with only a single, brief storm in between. He had forgotten about the strange texture of the water; it was uncharacteristically thick and made diving a bit more difficult than it would have been had they been in the Cam. Christopher knew his hauberk would help drop him deep enough, but he'd aid his descent with his arms and legs. He paddled down, eyes tightly shut. He knew Neil was ahead of him, and hoped the barbarian knew the way as clearly as he did. Christopher had to enter the castle literally with his eyes closed. He knew he could do it. But he wasn't sure about Neil.

He felt ahead, nothing but more water in front of him. Then his hand smashed against the slick, miry surface of a stone wall. He felt his way down the wall until his hand reached a sudden edge. He reached around the edge and knew this was it: the tunnel. Kicking hard with his feet and releasing a little air through his nose, he forced himself into the circular hole. The tunnel was constructed wide enough to fit a man, but just barely so. Christopher hit his head several times on the stone ceiling as he fought his way forward. He could only hold his breath for a few more seconds. A pain shot down from his throat and into his stomach. He had to hurry. He thought the tunnel was far shorter than it actually was. When was it going to end? He moved faster, began to panic, wanted to scream and suck in a deep, healthy breath.

Hands were on him. They seized his shirt and pulled him up. He felt the waters of the moat begin to pool off of him. He flickered his eyelids open and drew in a breath.

He was at the end of the tunnel where its ceiling opened up into the first passageway within the north-side curtain wall. Neil was hunched over him, soaked but smiling.

"You looked like you were in trouble. You

should've opened your eyes. You would've seen the light," the barbarian said.

There *was* light at the end of the tunnel, and it came from above, from a few of the loopholes. The sills of the holes had dropped out, and the light from the chambers fell within the wall. If any man ventured a gaze down, they might be spotted. But as it was, the archers were too busy racing around to find out who had killed the men in the towers.

Neil pulled Christopher from the watery floor of the tunnel to the dry surface of the passageway. Normally filled with flint and rubble, this part of the wall was hollow, but the exterior ashlar walls were still strong enough to deflect a mangonel stone.

"Ready? Or would you like another moment to catch your breath?" Neil asked.

Christopher found himself grinning. "Are you in a rush? You can't wait to get in there and face the Saxons, can you?. . . "

Neil tugged on his wet beard. "I just want to get all of this over with and go home."

"You are home, Neil."

Neil whirled around. "Let's go."

As Christopher followed Neil, he checked for his dagger and felt the empty sheath. He must have lost it during the swim. He still had his broadsword. That had better be enough.

At the end of the passageway, Neil leaned over and felt along the wall, tracing the edges of a square, base stone. Even in the half-light, Christopher could see that the stone was not as dusty and rough as the others. Neil had found their exit.

"Lend me a hand," he said, falling to his rump and digging his fingers into the corner of the stone.

Christopher knelt and put his fingertips to work,

forcing them into the crack and pulling inward as hard as he could. The stone budged. An inch, and then two, and then their leverage increased. In one yank, the stone came free from the rest of the wall. Thankfully, the wall was only a palm's length thick there, otherwise the stone would have weighed much more than it did—and there would have been no way in the realm to drag it across the floor.

Torchlight, tinkling with the dust of their efforts, entered the passage from the hole. The wall sconce was above, Christopher knew, and, unfortunately, would illuminate their entrance.

Neil stuck his head into the hole and peered around. He leaned back into the passageway. "It's clear. But once we're in there, I was hoping you knew a way out. Didn't you say that old jailer was your friend?"

Christopher nodded. "Go ahead."

Neil pulled himself through the hole and disappeared. Christopher unbuckled his sword belt and wrapped it around the sheath of his broadsword. He passed the weapon through first, then followed it.

As he rose from his belly to a kneeling position, Christopher laughed ironically to himself. He stood in a dungeon cell, last one on the left. The iron bars were shut. He and Neil had, in a sense, already been captured.

Christopher refastened his sword belt around his waist as Neil moved to the wall and reached into the hole. Getting the stone back in place would be easier than dragging it out. Set into its inner face was an iron loop to hold a manacle chain. Neil simply grabbed the loop and pulled the stone back into place within the wall. He stood, then wiped the rust from his hands onto his damp breeches.

Christopher checked the iron door. Locked, as expected. A simple rule he knew: never fumble for a way to get through a door unless you are certain that it's locked. Men have spent hours agonizing over ways to pick locks which were open all the time.

But even though the door was locked, Christopher would have it open in a minute. Old Regan the jailer had shown him a lot more than just the tunnel entrance. Regan never used the cell, for fear a criminal might discover the tunnel. And once he had accidentally locked himself in and had spent a miserable day and a half before he had been discovered. Never again would old Regan let that happen. The key to the door sat atop the highest crossbar. Christopher reached up and felt magic in his hand.

"You have a key?" Neil whispered, amazed.

"Of course," Christopher answered softly, with mock haughtiness. "What did you expect? Another secret tunnel?"

Neil rolled his eyes. "I'm glad you're taking this all so lightly."

"I'm not. I just don't want to think about being scared," Christopher said in earnest. "Would you like to say a prayer before we go?"

Neil shook his head. "I already have."

"Me too," Christopher confessed.

He unlocked the door, returned the key to its spot on the crossbar, then moved past the door. Neil fell in behind him. The barbarian eased the iron barrier shut, wincing as a final creak tore a hole in the silence of the hall.

Christopher figured there would only be one jailer on duty, and perhaps another at the upstairs entrance.

"First we check the cells," he whispered to Neil.

Neil acknowledged, removed his sandals, drew his dagger, then padded off soundlessly, checking cell after cell. Christopher began his own quiet inspection, drifting up the hallway.

If Doyle was in one of the cells, the whole rescue would be magnificently simple. Knock out the jailer, get his keys, remove Doyle from his cell, then take him out through the tunnel. They would encounter only minimal Saxon resistance. But Doyle was not in the cell block. Somehow, Christopher already knew that, but he wanted Neil to check the block anyway to be sure. When Doyle was close, he would know. Like drawing the right weapon for a knight, the sense would be there. He only felt damp and sticky, and suddenly hungry. He had forgotten to eat and bathe. Well, the moat had taken care of the bath, save for the fact that the water was foul. Somehow, somewhere along the line, he would have to satisfy his deprived belly.

Once Neil had finished his tour of the block, he joined Christopher. "They're all empty," he said incredulously. "I thought there would at least be a few prisoners here. I thought Doyle would be here. Maybe I was right. Maybe he is dead."

"No, he's not." Christopher thought a moment, something new occurring to him. "Did you see the jailer in the outer hall?"

"No."

Something tingled at the base of Christopher's spine; it grew into the kind of chill he only got when something was terribly wrong. "He has to be here. They wouldn't leave the dungeon unattended, even without prisoners."

"Maybe they would," Neil guessed. "They're Saxons."

"No," Christopher said. "Something's wrong. Back in the wall we go!"

The chill increased within Christopher as he sprang back toward the cell. The sense that they had just walked into a trap was so strong that it made his vision go blurry in the effort to escape. His legs moved, his heart pounded, his lungs filled with air and blew it out, but all he could feel was the ice of the moment, and all he could think about was that he had made a grave error. He was first back to the cell, first to see the two Saxon sentries smiling sardonically at him, their spears at the ready.

He shot a glance to the stone at the base of the floor; it had been moved. The Saxons weren't wet, yet they had come from the inside of the curtain wall.

There must be another passageway, one Christopher didn't even know about!

He tore his gaze away from the Saxons and brought it to bear on Neil. "Other way!"

Neil stopped short and turned around.

Christopher looked up the hall over Neil's shoulder.

A stream of guards poured down the stairs and began to flood into the cellblock.

Someone must have seen them dive into the moat.

Arthur was right; the Saxons knew all about the tunnels, and knew them better than they did.

Neil craned his head, his eyes glossing with fear. "I should've . . . forget it." His dagger fell out of his hand to the floor. The guards surrounded him, clutched his wrists, then brought them together behind his back.

Christopher resigned himself to the other Saxons as they ripped off his sword belt, then seized his wrists. He felt the rough steel of shackles bind him.

Someone shoved him from behind, and he said in Saxon, "I'll come. You don't have to push me!"

He knew the guards were surprised to hear him speak Saxon, but didn't bother to turn around and confirm it.

They were each escorted by a pair of guards down a chamber hall high in the keep. Christopher wasn't sure what floor they were on. He had been battling verbally with the Saxon who had first shoved him. The man had continued to do so, and Christopher had resorted to attacking his family, his friends, everything he stood for. So intent was he on stopping this man that he'd become oblivious of where he was going. That, in a small way, was good. If he was to be tortured, he didn't want to worry about it on the way there.

Before they turned and entered through an open chamber door on the left, Christopher noted how coarse and hostile the hall had become—all the tapestries were gone. It was a little thing, but it made him feel all the more cold inside.

A man sat up in a poster bed, two Saxon guards at his elbows. The man was shirtless, a linen bandage wrapped tightly around his chest. Christopher flipped a perfunctory glance at the man, expecting to find just another angry Saxon leader who would taunt then torture him. One look and his spirit rose out of the gloom.

The Saxon's hair was cropped much shorter, and his complexion was fairer, but it *was* Seaver, the little man with whom Christopher had served in Garrett's Saxon army. Seaver had taught him the ways of a scout. Once he had thought of murdering Seaver to get away, but he had become too friendly with the

man, and when others had ridiculed him, Christopher
had come to his defense more than once. Seaver
might be short, but he was very tall when standing on
his scouting abilities.

But what was he now? Was he the leader of the
Saxon army? No, that post was held by a man named
Kenric. Seaver must, however, now hold some posi-
tion of power.

"Kimball. It is you, isn't it?" Excitedly, Seaver
leaned forward in his bed, grimaced, then set himself
back down on the pillows propped behind him. His
eyes regarded Christopher with surprise, and perhaps
a trace of pleasure.

Kimball. That was the name Garrett had given
him. Christopher had refused to talk to the man
when he had first been captured, and so Garrett had
taken it upon himself to call him something.
Eventually, Christopher had revealed his true name,
but Seaver had obviously never learned it.

"It is me," Christopher answered in Saxon.

"Christopher, you know him?" Neil asked, trying to
tug his way out of the grip of the guards holding him.

"Yes, he does," Seaver answered in Celt. "We
served together."

Neil gritted his teeth. "I'd heard the stories about
you serving with the Saxons, Christopher, but I
didn't want to believe they were true. Now I see they
are. Are you a traitor? Did we come here for some
other reason than to save Doyle?"

"Your friend's no traitor," Seaver answered for
Christopher. "I can assure you, he will be humbled
and enslaved just as you will be." Seaver directed his
gaze to Christopher. "I see you go by another name
now. No matter. Whether you are Kimball or
Christopher, you will have to be punished. It is with

regret that I do this, but my duty is far more important than an old friendship. I'm not a simple scout anymore, Kimball. I cannot ignore my responsibilities."

Christopher's face grew hard, and his expression darkened.

"Have you nothing to say?" Seaver asked him after a moment. "Have you no plea to make?"

"Only one. I wish to see my friend Doyle before you maim us."

"He wouldn't be an archer, would he?"

Christopher nodded.

"You can see him. But he's not an archer anymore."

Christopher had suspected what they would do to Doyle; he'd seen it happen when he had been a member of Garrett's army. But there had been the hope that somehow Doyle would escape disfigurement. This confirmation made his shoulders slump. They had taken away Doyle's best talent, as they would Neil's and his. What would they do to strip him of his squiring ability? Hack off an arm, a leg, blind him, ram pokers in his ears? Perhaps all of those things.

When he had first seen Seaver sitting in the bed, he had guessed his situation was not as bad as it looked. He had thought that he could exploit his past friendship with the man. They had, after all, served together, had risked their lives together. He knew now that Seaver did not climb the Saxon ladder of leadership by dishing out succor and mercy to friends; he did it without feeling, with a bloodlust that consumed his heart. He could try to stir some emotion out of the man, but Seaver's face already told him that would be futile.

Christopher had been rash. He had made a mistake, and was now shackled to all of his errors.

"Take them to see the archer," Seaver barked to his men. "Then back to the dungeon. I'll meet you there."

Seaver dismissed the group with a wave of his arm. Christopher turned around with his escorts. They followed Neil and his two guards out of the chamber.

An extraordinary collection of pictures and feelings came alive in his mind as he walked. He wasn't worried about his own fate anymore. His mind swept back to Merlin's cave, to Marigween, to his son. They needed him. They could not afford to lose him. He had never felt like this before—but it seemed natural, instinctive, an epiphany of what truly lay within his heart. It was easy to let them into his mind; he no longer fought away the images. In this dire moment he needed something to live for, and there was no better motivation than love.

Why hadn't he realized this sooner? Why had he been so selfish, so confused? It was not right for him to take wild risks when he had a family. It was the battle between old life and new, and this time old had won. But it could cost him dearly. If he died, how would his family remember him? As a traitor, a coward who ran from his duty, a fool who threw his life away. And what about his son? The boy would grow up without a father. He tried to imagine what life would have been like without his own father, without Sanborn's instruction and guidance. Though his father had been firm, Christopher knew the man had loved him. Could he deny his own son that security, that basic need?

It was ironic, but he thanked God for being captured; it made him realize how important his family was to him. If he could mend his errors, trace his way back to the beginning of that new life he had once despised, he would be content with himself. He would be a man.

He had to survive. For them. He couldn't guess what would happen next. There wasn't even a sky to ask that venerable question: what will be?

PART FOUR

DUTY BOUND

1 The door was pushed in on the narrow, shadow-filled sleeping chamber, and at the back of the room Christopher saw Doyle. The archer sat on the edge of one of three scanty trestle beds, his bare feet resting squarely on the stone floor. On his lap was a large bronze breastplate which he had been in the middle of polishing, but the sound of the door had made him stop. Christopher pushed past Neil and ran toward Doyle, calling his friend's name. It seemed a lifetime had passed since he had seen Doyle, and despite the circumstances, Christopher felt heady with the joy of being reunited. Christopher's own guards grunted and ordered him back, but he ignored them, then tossed off a derogatory remark in Saxon, something about the promiscuity of the guards' mothers.

As Christopher neared his friend, he saw the linen bandage balled around Doyle's right hand. He saw how the hand looked smaller than it ought to be. And as once before, Christopher felt a burst of sympathetic pain rush through his own shackled hand and streak with the intensity of lightning up his arm. Doyle lowered his head and moved his butchered hand underneath the breastplate. The archer could hide the wound for now, but Christopher knew a day would come when his friend would have to confront what had happened. And if they survived, that day would not be far off.

Christopher had focused on the worst of Doyle's
injuries. Now he took into account the terrible beating they had inflicted on his friend. It was difficult to
find a place on Doyle's face, neck, and arms that
wasn't red, or a deeper, darker, much more painful
blue. Even with Doyle's head tipped forward,
Christopher could see enough of the bruises. The joy
of being with Doyle again was now marred. He felt
awkward. How could he console Doyle? He had
never seen anyone at a point so low in their lives. Not
only was Doyle's body broken, but his spirit was as
well. Doyle's polishing of the breastplate proved that.
They made him do menial tasks in order to break
him, like a wild horse. It was frightening to see Doyle
so lonely, so beaten.

Before Christopher could open his mouth, Neil and
the others surrounded Doyle, and Neil blurted out,
"Oh my God."

Neil's tone made him feel even worse. Christopher
did not want to address Doyle's injuries, but skirt con-
veniently and mercifully around them. That was what
he had been taught to do when visiting someone ill.
You never spoke of how terrible they looked or how
horrible it was for them to be sick. You only told them
they would get better and gave them hope for the
future. His mother had instilled that behavior in him.

Christopher shot Neil his darkest, rain cloud look,
then eyed the guards, addressing them in their
tongue. "Can you stand aside so we may have a few
moments alone with our friend?" His tone was harsh,
the anger born of Neil's remark and of the smirks on
the guards' faces. The Saxons did not move.
Christopher blew out a breath in disgust. "Is it too
much to ask?"

One of the guards pursed his lips and gestured

with his head for the others to move off, toward the back of the chamber.

Christopher crouched in front of Doyle, able now to look into his friend's bloodshot eyes.

Neil moved next to Christopher, then whispered in Christopher's ear, "I'm sorry."

"It's all right. I know how I look," Doyle suddenly said, his voice strangely unchanged from how Christopher remembered it. Somehow, he expected Doyle's voice to be bruised or disfigured like the archer's body, but the words flowed smoothly, the expected sadness or embarrassment absent. They resonated with fact, nothing more.

"I . . . I don't know what to say," Christopher said, swallowing deeply. "I cannot ask if you're all right because obviously you're not."

Doyle's jaw muscles flexed and the fingers of his left hand curled into his palm, forming a fist. "I came here to die. But God wouldn't grant me that wish so easily. I must be punished for my crimes. I know that now. What they've done to me . . . I deserve every bit of it."

"What are you talking about?" Neil asked. Christopher stole a look at the barbarian and saw how perplexed the archer appeared.

"We don't have to—" Christopher began.

"I killed Innis," Doyle said, overriding Christopher with his louder voice. "Leslie saw me do it. He was going to turn me in, and so I killed him, too."

"Dear Lord . . . " was all the barbarian could say.

"The Lord has not been so dear to me," Doyle added, "but it's just as well." He slid his bandaged hand out from beneath the breastplate. "I will never draw a bow again. Think about that, Neil."

Blood did not run through Doyle's veins; ice did.

Christopher knew that somewhere within his friend
there was a tiny part that wanted to reach out and
hug him, a tiny piece of Doyle that wanted very much
to cry. But Doyle would not allow himself the luxury
of tears. His stoicism was part of the punishment, a
punishment that God had not inflicted upon him, but
one he had inflicted on himself out of guilt. Doyle
tortured himself before their eyes, and Christopher
knew it would continue unless he did or said something to stop his friend.

"I don't know how long they're going to give us,"
Christopher said, referring with a tip of his head to
the guards standing near a floor sconce adjacent to
the door, "so I'm going to say this all at once and say
it quickly. We've come here to get you out. It seems
impossible now, but we're not ready to give up. If we
make it out, Doyle, I want you to do something for
me, something that will help you more than you
know. Confess your sins to the king. Throw yourself
on *his* mercy. Let the truth be known, and as we have
both heard many a monk say before, 'the truth will
set you free.' Don't ask me to keep your secret anymore. Please. King Arthur is a fair man."

Doyle took a long, decisive moment before answering. Then he raised his head, wiped his right eye with
the back of his bandaged hand, and said, "It will be
God's will if we get out of here alive. And if we do,
the very first person I will speak to is the king."

A voice was capable of conveying many things, and
often times Christopher could not figure out the
exact truth from the inflections of the speaker. But
there was no mistaking the regret in Doyle's tone,
and the softening of his voice.

"Thank St. Michael and St. George," Christopher
said. "We've both been running away from our

duties, Doyle. You from telling King Arthur the truth, I from the responsibility of my son."

Doyle's head jerked back. "Your what?"

"Yes," Neil chipped in, "now what are you talking about?"

Christopher felt his body stiffen, partly from being on his haunches with his hands bound, partly from the looks of his friends. He stood, and felt their gazes track him. He closed his eyes. "Marigween was pregnant when we left for the Mendips. While I was away, she had our son."

Neil nudged Christopher with his shoulder. Christopher opened his eyes and turned his head to look at the barbarian as he spoke: "She is betrothed to Lord Woodward! And what about you? I thought you were courting that maid from Gore?"

"Don't ask me to explain how it all happened. It simply did. And you must never repeat a word of this until I say you can. Will you do that, Neil?"

"We may all die, so you won't have to worry about that. If we live, I'll keep your secret—for a price to be negotiated later."

Christopher frowned at the barbarian's opportunistic acceptance. He was about to ask Doyle if he had seen any possible way for them to escape when one of the guards announced that their visit was over. Christopher looked at Doyle and mouthed the words, "Be ready," then turned to face the guards with Neil. He whispered to the barbarian, "We'll break as we exit through the door, push them outside and slam it shut behind them. Understood?"

"Sounds easy," Neil whispered back sarcastically. "What do we do after that? And how do we remove these shackles?"

"Think hard," Christopher replied.

Christopher didn't have to look at the barbarian to
know that he shook his head with skepticism. The
guards surrounded them and they all started for the
door. Neil deliberately stalled and let the first two
guards slip through. Christopher took the cue and
shot back behind his guard, buried his shoulder in
the small of the guard's back and then drove the
Saxon through the passage. Neil did likewise, but his
Saxon rolled off his shoulder and spun around.

That was all the time the other guards needed to
turn and dash back into the room. One particularly
scarred and hairy man grabbed Christopher by his
shirt collar and threw him past the door. Christopher
slammed against the opposite wall of the hallway outside the chamber and felt the wind escape from his
lungs. Neil was booted on the rump, the force of the
blow sending him through the doorway and crashing
into the wall next to Christopher.

"A most excellent plan, squire of the body," Neil
said, huffing and grimacing.

Christopher silently cursed to himself as the hairy
guard who had thrown him put an index finger under
Christopher's chin and forced his head up. "Try that
again, and your punishment will come much sooner.
Enjoy your healthy, perfect body now—while you still
can. In a little while, you're going to look even worse
than your friend in there.

2 Orvin left Merlin's cave in pursuit of
Christopher. He arrived at Arthur's camp along the

Cam only to discover that Christopher was nowhere to be found. The last person to see the squire a sergeant who had said Christopher had gone off for a little weapons practice. That had been was the previous night, and here it was, late afternoon on the following day, and still Christopher had not returned.

No, the squire had not gone off for weapons practice, and as Orvin sat on a weathered stump in the wood opposite the east wall of the castle of Shores, he knew exactly where Christopher was. The young saint was inside the fortress trying to save his friend. Blast the impetuousness of youth! Couldn't the boy understand what a foolhardy mission he had assigned to himself?

The boy did not understand, Orvin reasoned. And if he were Christopher's age, he knew he would have done the same.

But Christopher was now in the middle of much more than an enemy-occupied castle. He was in the middle of a siege. Arthur had moved the camp away from the Cam and now began the first stages of his attack to win back the castle. Orvin watched the grim spectacle unfold before his eyes:

Lance after lance of Arthur's men completely surrounded the castle to prevent the entry of any stores, in the hope of starving the Saxon garrison into surrender. The next step would have been the discharge of an assortment of missiles from the siege machines, but those Orvin had overheard had still not arrived from Gore. Instead, Arthur's archers hid behind their movable wooden mantlets and showered the battlements of the castle with arrows. No Saxon sentry would dare step out from behind a protective wall or loophole. Occasionally, a Saxon archer would venture an open shot, but twice Orvin had watched those men succumb to Celt arrows. Hollow cries abounded, mixed with the neighing of cart-pulling horses and the grinding of wheels as salvaged supplies from the remains of Shores were brought in to aid the fighting men. Under the cover of the archers, gangs of men Orvin assumed were hired from neighboring villages moved up to fill in a portion of the moat in order to make use of a makeshift belfry. The wooden tower on wheels would be rolled up to the castle walls so that the archers within it could rake the battlements, then lower a wooden bridge to allow a team of Celts access to the wall-walks, commencing the invasion. The filling in of the moat was a long process that Orvin guessed might take several days. Orvin also noted the presence of a peasant levy of diggers; these fourscore of men, when called upon, would undermine a section of a curtain wall and cause it to collapse. Orvin knew what section they would choose, a hollow portion that contained a tunnel that led to the dungeon—the route Christopher most certainly had used to enter the castle.

From his vantage point, Orvin could watch in reasonable safety. He did not wish to be with Lord Woodward or any of the other battle lords who had invited him to their tents scattered just beyond the range of the best Saxon archer and the strongest mangonel. The knights promised lavish meals, but Orvin ignored the tempting bait since he hated their company. He would rather remain alone with his small pouch of dried pork and his pair of apples.

Correction. He would rather remain alone, but with a lot more food than he had.

Woodward's constant badgering about how he should have moved into the castle had always been too much to take. And the present situation had given Orvin the perfect opportunity to chide the battle lord. "You see," he had told Woodward, "if I had moved into your castle, I might not be alive now!"

No, Woodward had not liked hearing that. But Orvin knew there were things he could get away with saying because of his age. Gray hair gave one a lot of free conversational ground. He could criticize the king if he wanted, but for the moment, he could find no fault in Arthur's siege plans. The king would not start making mistakes until Merlin arrived. If Orvin could keep the druid away, under the pretense that someone must stay with Marigween, then Arthur just might win the castle back. Thus far, the plan was working.

There was something Orvin had forgotten to do, and as he thought about it, he couldn't believe he had made such an error. He knew that Arthur suspected Christopher was inside the castle trying to rescue his friend, but he wanted to confirm that notion to the king. Arthur needed to know for sure that Christopher was inside, so that when the squire escaped he would not be accidentally killed by the Celt archers. The Celts needed to be on the lookout for young Christopher.

But Orvin could not tell Arthur he had physically seen Christopher go into the castle; he knew it only from the sky. Whether Arthur believed him or not didn't matter now. What mattered was that he should have told Arthur when he had first returned to Shores.

Yet it had slipped his mind!

Am I getting that old? Was I so preoccupied with getting a meal that I forgot all about the patron saint?

No! It was unintentional . . . but I must mend my mistake. Now. Yes. Now.

There, he had decided. He rose and stepped past a

line of low-lying shrubs and started down the dirt
road toward the king's tent, erected five hundred
yards south of the wood.

Orvin was a mere fifty yards into the journey when
he spotted her sitting idly in front of a dying cookfire,
staring with distant eyes into the puffs of thin white
smoke that rose like cold morning breath into the sky.

"Brenna? Is it you? The young raven maid from
Gore?"

Her hair was the same, perhaps a few inches
longer, but just as raven black as he remembered it.
Her face was a little leaner, a bit gaunt, even, as if
she had not eaten well for the past moon. The sun
had browned her skin and there were new lines on
her forehead and one near her right eye that Orvin
felt made her look not older but strangely wiser. She
was smart enough to get to Shores—and that must
have been a feat. Had someone helped her? Had she
come with her family? If so, for what purpose? To
see Christopher? No, that was lunacy. She had come
for some other reason and it was convenient for her
to see Christopher. But for what other reason would
she have ventured into the middle of a siege!

*Look at her, you old fool! She looks like she's just
been on a terribly rough and long journey. Use your
eyes to see, Orvin. My God, she's come for the saint!
Has she seen him already? Has he told her about
Marigween and the child? Has he broken her heart?*

*Or worse! Has Christopher lied to her? Would that
fickle boy try to court Brenna while sharing a child
with Marigween?*

*Orvin. Orvin. Have more faith in your apprentice.
Christopher is too smart to do that. If they have met,
he has broken her heart. Look at her now. She looks
lost. She looks as if she has learned the truth.*

Brenna stood, smoothed out her soiled kirtle, then raked the fingers of one hand through the right side of her hair, removing a pair of small twigs which had become tangled there. She was too aware of her appearance, and Orvin sensed that she was ashamed of it. The softness and timidity of her voice confirmed that: "Yes, Sir Orvin"—she let out a breath—"it's me. I've forgotten how long it's been. I thought you might visit Gore, but you never did."

Suddenly Orvin was on the defensive, staring into Brenna's lovely eyes.

Don't lust after the young girl like you did Marigween!

But I can't help thinking that!

It's fine to think it. Do nothing about it, and don't let it affect your conversation!

"I wanted so much to visit Gore, to see you and your family again, to see so many old friends who went there after my son's death. But my back"— Orvin placed a palm on his lower spine—"I'm sure it would have broken on such a long journey." It was not a lie, but a fear he had honestly had. Still, it was true he could have overcome the fear and gone to Gore. It wasn't that much farther away from Shores than Merlin's cave.

Brenna's smile was wan, but there. "We still have your mule."

"Cara?" Orvin asked, fervently wishing his old mount was still alive.

She nodded. "I'm afraid I sold the saddle Christopher had made for her, but I don't think she liked it anyway."

Orvin returned her nod. "You know Cara all right." Orvin felt the weight on his feet seemingly multiply, and knew he had to relieve the pressure. "Do you mind if I sit?"

"Here," Brenna said, circling around the cookfire and taking his arm, "let me help you."

She guided him down, and Orvin made what had become his ritualistic groan as his weight finally settled onto his rump. "There. Much better. Don't ever get old, Brenna. It is no fun at all."

Brenna sat quickly, her agility demonstrated before his immediately jealous gaze. "Do you know where Christopher is?"

He should have known that she brimmed with questions. Deep down he did, but despite that he wanted very much to be with her at the moment, to share a bit of the past that conjured up a lot of good feelings, and, of course, a lot of bad ones. Yes, they would talk about Christopher; he would dominate their dialogue. But were there still secrets to be kept? Orvin had to find out.

"Yes," he answered, "but first let me ask you a question and then I'll tell you."

"Please ask," she said anxiously, rocking back and forth with a new, burnished light in her eyes.

"What are you doing here? How did you get here? And have you spoken with Christopher recently?"

"Sir Orvin, that's three questions," Brenna said in a teasing voice. She was, indeed, jovial. "But I'll answer all of them just the same. I came here to see Christopher. I grew tired of waiting. I wanted to be here for him. I tried to bring my friend Wynne along, but she got hurt and I had to send her back home. I've come so far and so long to see him—and still we have not been reunited! Thank the Lord I was able to remind King Arthur who I am and explain why I'm here. After a lot of pleading, he finally granted me permission to stay, albeit far from the battle. And I told him I will help in any way I can, cooking, laundry, anything."

Orvin creased his brow in thought, analyzing the situation thus far. Christopher had not been able to tell her about Marigween and the child. Orvin could do it now and spare Christopher the anguish.

No, that would be wrong. He would be meddling. That very act would make him no different than Merlin. Telling Brenna was Christopher's duty. The boy would have to do it. A new question formed: "Did the king tell you where Christopher was?"

"All he said was that he had an idea but he could not be sure. I think he's very upset with Christopher, though. He said something under his breath that I didn't quite hear, but made me think that." Brenna sighed. "I hope Christopher is not in much trouble. Where do you think he is?"

"He is inside the castle," Orvin said, the matter-of-fact tone in his voice intentional. There was something about *knowing* when others didn't that always made him feel a little powerful, and always made him want to understate that power in the tone of his voice. Yes, the world's coming to an end. He would deliver that statement as if commenting on the salt content of a particular fillet of fish.

"Has he been taken prisoner?" Brenna asked, her eyes unable to widen any more with concern.

Orvin continued to deliver the facts, knowing he had become the center of Brenna's world. He liked that. When some thought him a mindless recluse, she saw him as a wise man, an esteemed knight who held the key to unlock her happiness. And her attention was undivided, her eyes so firmly glued to his that he could almost feel the connection. "Christopher went into the castle to rescue his friend, Doyle. There is a way in through the moat. If he's had any luck, he should be coming out soon."

"God, Orvin, how can you be so sure! They must've caught him! There must be scores and scores of Saxons inside the keep alone. Do not tell me you saw it up there." She pointed to the sky with an index finger, and as her gaze lifted, Orvin saw tears flood her eyes.

She was much harder, much stronger than the raven maid he remembered. No longer was she the shy chamber girl infatuated with a young, handsome squire. She was, in many ways, now a woman, hardened by the world and driven by her desires to a place of pain and death. The tears were of frustration, of a love Orvin sensed was so deep, so meaningful, that it scared him. It scared him because he knew Christopher would have to shatter it.

"Faith," Orvin said, beating the word out into the air. "I see *that* is still something that eludes youth. You've changed a lot, Brenna. You are . . . *almost* a woman. Faith is still the one thing you lack."

Brenna stood and turned away, lowered her head, then put a palm to her face. Orvin was not sure if she wept or not; she made no sound.

It was one of those moments in which, a countless number of moons ago, Orvin would have stood and gone to her side and held and comforted her. His physical inability to do so angered him. He had made no mistake, striking her with steely words, but at the same time he could, in a very small but significant way, relate to her pain. He had spent a lot of time separated from Donella and had many times been teased with the idea of them coming together, only to have it ordered away by another knightly duty. The strain on their relationship had often made him question whether knighthood was really what he wanted. But the course of his life had already been laid in heavy stones. And as he looked at Brenna, he imagined that long ago his own Donella had grieved the same.

"Brenna, believe he's alive and that you will see him again. Let that belief carry you now. But also remember, as I have seen a change in you, so will you see one in Christopher. He, like you, has become hardened by the world, or more precisely in his case, the battlefield."

It was important that he *not* lead her on. There must be some way to ease her into the events to come, but at the moment, a way to do that eluded Orvin. He could not even hint about Christopher's situation, for she might reach her own conclusions, which might be wildly false, or bull's-eye the truth. She would urge him for confirmation and they would drop into an argument. All he could do was say what he had, that the patron saint was *changed.* That would not prepare her for what Christopher would say. But all of the speculation on Orvin's part. He could not even guess how Christopher would handle her. He went on the assumption of how *he* would deal with her. *He* would confront Brenna and tell her the truth, knowing at his age that honesty was the only path to take. Christopher was young and raged with unbridled emotions. What he would do would only be known in time. The sky would not reveal it to Orvin; he had tried to conjure up the information, meditating after Christopher's departure from the cave. But his mind had remained blank.

Slowly, she pivoted back to face him and lowered her hand from her face. She had not shed a tear, but color had flooded her cheeks. "You say that Christopher has changed. Do you mean he doesn't love me anymore?"

Damn the insight of women!

Orvin conversationally leapt to correct her. "No, no, no!"

She sighed. "Then he does love me, thank goodness."

Orvin closed his eyes and rolled them back in his head. He could not tell her no. He could not tell her yes. The ultimate dilemma. His silence would convey a yes, yet that might be the truth. Indeed, Christopher might still love her. That probably had nothing to do with the fact that they simply had no future together. Orvin steadily realized that the more involved he became with her, the more dangerous it would be for his relationship with Christopher. Their ties were already frayed. The young saint lately questioned his judgment—something he had never done before. And if Christopher found out he had spoken with Brenna, the act might be mistaken for meddling.

Maybe he shouldn't have stopped to see Brenna at all! But it was too late for that and all he could do was bail himself out of the conversation in any way he could. He discarded the notion of confirming or denying Christopher's love for Brenna and let her believe what she would. "When you meet up with Christopher again, you will not only see the squire of the body, dear Brenna, but you may be surprised to see . . . a man."

"If he comes back," she retorted coldly. "I will never be as certain as you. You're right. I do lack faith, only because I have believed for so long that Christopher would return, and I grew tired of believing. *I* wanted to make that happen. I have faith, Orvin. Faith in myself right now. But as for Christopher. He may die. And to think I came all this way only to see his body burn on a pyre . . . " She broke off into finally released tears.

"Christopher has too many things left to do in his

life. If you could see what I have seen, dear raven maid, you would know. He's just like the king! Not meant to live an ordinary life, but to be a part of something extraordinary, something that will be remembered always."

Orvin's own words shocked him. Yes, he had always known there was something special about Christopher. But as he had just spoken, things had become oddly clear in his mind. It was not as if he stared into visions, as the sky often blurred into mind pictures, but as if his own heart had released feelings that were transformed into knowledge. The knowledge that the future, with Christopher as a vital part of it, would be something spectacularly grand! He was chilled by the thought.

Brenna stepped over to him and put her hand on his shoulder. "I pray you are right, Orvin. I pray you are right."

He lifted his gaze to hers. "I am," he said in earnest. "And I am also terribly hungry. I only took a few scraps with me today. Is there anything—"

"Let me help you up and I'll fetch you a large bowl of a stew I started this morning. I wager there is a line of cart drivers already forming around the cauldron, so we'd better hurry."

Her tone had risen a notch, and as she helped him up, Orvin felt content over their meeting. Yet he also detected a heat of guilt on his back. The knowledge of Christopher's family and what would come was a rising sun from which he sought shadow. The more things became illuminated, the more pain he knew Brenna would feel. He tried to ignore the heat and let her escort him to the food.

3   Christopher smiled weakly with recognition as
he looked around the cell. It was the very cell he and
Brenna had spent a brief time in during the first
moon he had courted her. It had been an innocent
midnight rendezvous that had almost landed him in a
lot of trouble. The trouble he had experienced had
come, thankfully, from Orvin, and though his master
had been the last person in the world that he had
wanted to let down at the time, at least Orvin had
been the most understanding.

Was there some kind of strange fate working that
had put him back in the same cell?

Neil seemed to think so. Upon voicing his memories
of the place to the barbarian, the pudgy boy began a
detailed inspection of the room, pressing his fingertips
into every crack and groove of the cell, searching for
another elusive secret exit. Christopher doubted Neil
would find what he was looking for. Regan had been
an expert jailer and had known the block better than
anyone. The man had shown Christopher every way in
and out of the place—save for one. Christopher
wished he knew where *that* exit was, the one the
Saxon guards had used to capture them. Christopher
did know where it wasn't—in their cell.

"Forget it," he told Neil, shooting the ferreting
archer a cynical look.

"I refuse to just stand here and wait to be chopped
up!" Neil shot back.

Though muffled by the thick walls of the cell and
the encircling earth, Christopher thought he could
hear the shouts of men. Something was going on outside. Perhaps Arthur had begun the siege. If that was
the case, escape would be even harder. Escape. That

word, that act, seemed a distant dream. Christopher *tsk*ed and sighed. As he absently rubbed the sore spots on his wrists left by the shackles, he attempted to open his mind to the other avenues of flight. But his mind was as locked up as his body. He felt his legs begin to shake and the tremor moved up into his torso, spilled into his arms, and rolled across his neck. And as the chills engulfed him, Christopher realized his confidence was gone. That fighting spirit he had been able to maintain even after being captured had finally left him. His hopelessness had become as thick and as sure as the iron bars in front of him. There was no escape now. He repeated that to himself. Seaver would come with his cohorts and they would hold down Neil and him and destroy their futures. His eyes grew heavy with tears as he considered what a fool he was.

How many errors of judgment will I make in my life? I've made so many already that it seems I may lose my life! I don't have any ideas on how to get out of this! There was always something, something that came to me right away. A plan. Sure, we can try to wrestle our way out of the guards' grips when they enter the cell, but there will most likely be too many of them. That idea is about as good as my last one up in Doyle's chamber. Here we are, behind these bars, and that is our fate. I have to accept that.

No! No, I cannot accept that! Marigween and my son need me. King Arthur needs me as his squire. The other squires and varlets of the army need me. Even Sir Orvin and Merlin need me, if for nothing more than to have something to argue over.

"I think I've found something," Neil said.

Christopher craned his head and saw that Neil knelt in front of a stone at the base of the floor, two

stones away from the right rear corner of the cell.
Christopher moved to Neil's side and fell to his own
knees, then he jammed his fingertips into the cracks
around the stone where it met its neighbors.
Christopher dug his nails in, and together they tried
to pull the stone forward.

It didn't budge.

"Let me try kicking it in," Neil suggested. He fell
back onto his rump, rested his palms on the floor for
balance, drew back one of his booted feet, then
kicked the stone. He repeated the action again, then
again.

Christopher rose, blowing out a breath of disgust
through his nose. "That's nothing but a stone.
There's no passage behind it, only rubble."

"Why don't you help me instead of giving up?
What's wrong with you now?" Neil shook his head,
his beefy face tightened in a frown. "Remember, it's
your fault I'm in here and you'd better help me get
out! You're responsible for me!"

"No, I'm not!" Christopher fired back, his desperation turned into headlong rage. He pointed an index
finger at Neil that might as well have been a sword.
"You came here because Phelan wanted you to. You
told me you did it for him! And for Doyle!"

"I lied about that. I did it for you, Christopher. As
much as I hate to admit it, I knew you were right in
coming here. Trying to save Doyle is the right thing
to do. It's a shame you didn't have a real plan for getting him out, and that our lives will be wasted now
for nothing. You're the squire of the body, you're
supposed to be the one who knows what to do. Look
at you now. I wish I had a mirror so I could show you
how scared you look!"

"Quiet! Hold your tongue!" Christopher screamed,

then he dropped roughly onto his backside, slammed himself next to Neil, drew back his leg, and proceeded to help the archer pound the stone. "You didn't do this for me," Christopher added between slams of his foot. "You just don't want to blame yourself for coming here."

A key went into the lock on the cell door behind them. In unison, they turned their heads to see a lone Saxon open the door and step into the cell.

Christopher hauled himself to his feet. Neil rolled and stood, his reactions much slower than Christopher's. They moved to opposite corners of the cell to stand poised and ready . . . for what?

There was something remotely familiar about the Saxon. Christopher guessed he had seen the man before, but could not remember from where. It had probably been only recently, inside the castle. That seemed logical, but then for some reason the explanation seemed unlikely. He had seen the Saxon before—but it might have been a long time ago.

Tall and bearded, the Saxon scratched an itch on the top of his sandy brown hair, which was parted in the middle and tied back into a ponytail with a leather cord. His face and neck were strangely darker than his hands, as if he had purposely darkened them with a dye of some sort. His pale blue eyes emitted a glow of experience that was far beyond the Saxon's years. He was probably about twenty, Christopher guessed, but he appeared to be a man who had seen many battles. If you served long enough in the field, you could sometimes recognize a fellow combatant, and the Saxon wore the unmistakable look of a veteran warrior.

Before Christopher could ask what the man wanted, the Saxon said in perfect Celt, "I don't

expect you remember me, Kimball. We met only
briefly when we served together under Garrett. I'm
Owen."

"Owen," Christopher repeated, letting the name
submerge into his memory in the hope that it would
release and float to the surface that part of his past
that the man fitted into. Owen, Owen, Owen.

*Yes, he had tried to rescue me when I fled the
Saxons after Garrett had died. He had tried to get me
back from Mallory, but his team of mounted archers
had failed.*

It had been very cold that day, and Christopher
shuddered with the memory. But this was not the
first time since that day Christopher had heard the
name Owen. There had been a moment on the battlefield moons ago, when he had left King Arthur's side
in pursuit of a Saxon. Instead of killing the man, he
had had a brief but memorable conversation with
him. He had told the invader that they were part of
the future. One day Saxons and Celts would coexist
on the land. The man had recognized Christopher
and had said that he knew a man that had served
with him—a man named Owen.

A man who now stood before Christopher.

"I know who you are," Christopher said warily.
"And surely you know my name is not Kimball."

"I call you that in honor of our old master, Lord
Garrett."

"A great fighter, but a troubled man. Had he lived,
we might not be standing here now. Why is it you are
here? Are you the one to punish us?"

"He can't be," Neil said. "They wouldn't be stupid
enough to only send one guard down here!"

"Anything's possible with *Seaver* as second-in-
command," Owen said, uttering the name of his

superior with a hatred as honed as the tip of a new anlace.

Christopher felt the muscles contracted in his shoulders begin to relax. There was obviously some dissension among the Saxon ranks; how far it went Christopher did not know. It was odd that a scout would rise so quickly to second-in-command—especially when Seaver did not offer the appearance of a great leader. He appeared like what he was trained to be—a spy, a ferret who retrieved information. Seaver a leader of men? Yes, that notion was odd. To Owen, it was apparently much more. It brought anger, and Christopher wanted to find out just how angry Owen was.

"He's not exactly one of your friends, eh, Owen?" he asked the Saxon.

"I have removed most of it, but I'm sure you can still see the traces of dye that I have on my face. Seaver threw it on me."

"Why?" Christopher asked.

"Well, he did have good reason," Owen said with a new smile. "I was trying to kill him."

That fact was good. No, that fact was excellent. Owen was an enemy of Seaver's. Christopher and Neil were imprisoned by Seaver's orders. Would Owen try to help them escape? But why would he do that?

Owen took a step closer to Christopher, who matched a step back. "Don't be afraid. I'm here to help you."

"I don't believe him, Christopher," Neil said. "What does he have to gain?"

Owen regarded Neil with a scowl. "If I were you, I wouldn't question my only way out of here." Then he returned his gaze to Christopher. "When our second-

in-command Manton died, we all assumed our next-
best fighter, Renfred, would become second. But
Kenric shocked many of us by bestowing the title on
Seaver, who is undeserving of it. I'm part of a group
who intends to unhorse Seaver. And anything we can
do to show Kenric what a fool that little man Seaver
really is will be done. You two are under Seaver's
wing. You two will escape with my help. If Seaver is
incompetent enough to let me *still* operate freely
within this castle, then what kind of a leader is he?
I'd rather pledge my allegiance to a boar; at least the
animal supplies man with something. Seaver is a lia-
bility to our army—not an asset."

Christopher looked up at the ceiling of the cell.
*Thank you, Lord. Thank you St. Michael and St.
George and St. Christopher.* "You may or may not
know this, Owen, but Neil and I did not come to the
castle for a visit."

Owen idly jingled the cell keys, and the sound
made Christopher's gaze lock on them as the Saxon
spoke: "Who do you think I am—Seaver? I know
you came for that archer who threw himself to us.
Why else would you be here? Surely you didn't think
just you and your friend would start the siege?"

"This is my home. And we will be rid of you. I care
not if you live in Shores, so long as it's not in this
castle. Build one of your own." Christopher had let
his anger change the subject and do his talking, and
he abruptly wanted to inhale his words.

"Don't enrage him," Neil said disgustedly. "He's
right. He's our only way out of here."

Christopher craned his head away from Owen, a
tad ashamed. "Sorry."

"Don't be."

Christopher looked up at the Saxon.

"Though I didn't know you that well, Christopher, I had heard of your tremendous courage and will. You stood up to Garrett when some of our bravest fighters twice your age would not. Your mind controls the heart of a warrior. Granted, there is no love lost between us, as we fight now on opposing sides. But you want to leave here, and your doing so will help my cause."

"We will not leave without our friend."

"He makes a fine bargain," Neil said. "Don't get greedy!"

Christopher stepped over to the barbarian and stared resolutely into the archer's dark eyes. "We're talking about Doyle's life, Neil. He's coming with us—or we're not going." Fanned to a high heat, the fire in Christopher's voice was irrepressible.

Neil's retort came quickly and unsteadily: "But all we have to do now is slip into the tunnel and we're out of here. I'll agree—if he can bring Doyle down to us."

Christopher craned his neck to regard Owen. "Can you get our friend down here?"

"I'm letting you out of this cell. That is all. If you want to rescue your friend, you do that yourself. It would be nice if you make it out of the castle, but getting you out of this room is enough to suit my purpose. The hand of Woden will pass over and guard you. I'll ask him to do that now."

Owen spun on his heel and marched out of the room, then paused in the hall outside. "We'll meet again, Christopher. It is . . . inevitable."

"Thanks."

"Don't thank me," Owen said. "Thank your old scouting partner Seaver for being such a foolish, undeserving leader." Owen turned and left.

Neil bolted for the open door, but Christopher

latched onto the back of the barbarian's collar, driving the front of Neil's tunic into his neck, choking him. "Forget it, Neil. We're going to get Doyle."

"Let go of me! Let go!"

Christopher complied, and the barbarian sucked down air in sudden relief. "How do you purpose to get through that locked chamber door?" Neil asked him between breaths.

"I thought you grew up around this castle like me," Christopher replied.

"I did! What does that have to do with the door?"

"Cell doors are one thing, my friend. Chamber doors are something else altogether."

The confidence was back. The plan was already formulated in his mind and he saw himself carrying it out with complete success. All they needed now were weapons. When he was caught in the dungeon, Christopher had lost the sword Baines gave him. The blade was somewhere in the castle and it would, as it had in the past, turn up. He wished he would trip over it now, but was not going to count on serendipity. That was something for soothsayers, not squires. What about the jailer? He probably carried a blade and Owen had probably taken care of him already. That was a start.

"God, I pray for your tender mercy. I pray that you guide my friend and clear his mind of the lunacy that now possesses it. If it is your will that I join you at the moment, then take me quickly and painlessly. I do not wish to die alongside a madman!" Neil's eyes were closed and his head was tipped up to the heavens.

"And God," Christopher added. "If we are to die, then let it be during a noble cause to save our friend; not fleeing like cowards through a hole in the stone; not swimming like bloated rats escaping from a sinking vessel; but with swords and bows in our hands, and our hearts and minds right with you."

"Oh, silence!" Neil said snapping his eyelids open. "Let's go get Doyle."

4 Christopher and Neil found the old Saxon jailer slumped over his small key desk, the rear base of his neck cherrying from a recent blow, his forehead cut open and bleeding from where it had hit the unforgiving wall in front of the key desk, or the equally merciless desk itself.

"Owen's got quite a punch," Neil said, observing the inert jailer.

"Don't give him all the credit," Christopher said. "See how circular the mark is? This man was struck with a weapon, perhaps the heel of a sword or dagger." Christopher checked under the lean, old man's tunic for a dagger belt. The belt was there, but the dagger sheath fastened to it was empty. "Blast. Couldn't he have left us a dagger?"

"Maybe he thought the man might rise and use his dagger on us," Neil suggested.

"Maybe."

Then Neil, the pinnacle of pessimism, began to shake his head negatively. "I don't think we should move into the stairwell without weapons."

"There you go thinking again," Christopher said. "Weren't you trained by Sloan and others like him? We act now. We *want* to be pursued."

"We do?"

"Yes. That's how we're going to get our weapons." Christopher turned and moved out of the small alcove toward the hall that led to the stairwell. It would be good to leave the dungeon, even if it was to engage the enemy head-on.

"All we need is one Saxon with a crossbow trained on us and we're finished," Neil argued, calling after him.

Christopher continued toward the stairwell, hearing the sounds of Neil's boots shuffling behind him. "One of us might be finished," he called back, "but the other will be able to get away."

"And seeing as how you have the luck of your saint, I'll be the one to stay."

Christopher mounted the stairs, taking them two at a time. He listened for Neil, but heard nothing. He stopped, craned his neck and saw Neil leaning against the wall at the bottom of the stairs, staring off into nothing.

"What's wrong?" Christopher asked. "Come on. We have no time to rest."

Without looking up, Neil answered. "I'm scared, Christopher, I'm really scared."

He descended the stairs and stood before Neil, then rested a hand of reassurance on the barbarian's shoulder. "The Saxons will think twice before shooting you. You look too much like them. They'll think they're killing one of their own. It's a good thing you're so hairy!"

"Stop jesting. I don't want to laugh before I'm going to die."

Neil had agonized over going up to save Doyle, and though he had already made the decision to go, he second-guessed himself now. Yes, Neil's fear was warranted, if not damned inconvenient, and

Christopher had to address it; humor was only a bandage, not a cure.

"You can't die," Christopher said, his voice even and never more certain.

Neil snorted. "One arrow, one sword. They make your words meaningless."

"You can't die because you're with me. Alone you will die. Alone I will die. Together we cannot be stopped. We have a power no Saxon can overcome. We have the power of love on our side, the love of our friend, the love of each other, the camaraderie we share as fighters, as Celts. No more jesting, no more thinking. Like falcons we will fly up these stairs, swoop into Doyle's chamber, and whisk him out. Any Saxon who gets in our way will not be looked upon as an enemy, but as a bearer of gifts."

Neil lifted one of his brows. "What do you mean?"

"Ah, any Saxon who comes with his sword drawn or his bow raised should not be looked at as a killer, but as a man who is offering his weapon to us."

Neil's lips curled into a grin, and a low chuckle began to rumble within him. His laugh rose and was finally expelled with great energy from his lips. His cackle was so loud that Christopher had to shush him.

"I'm sorry," Neil said, wiping the knuckle of an index finger across one eye and then the other. "I thought you weren't going to jest, but regarding the Saxons as bearers of gifts is so incredibly mad that it must be inspired!"

"And you didn't want to laugh before you die."

"It seems I don't have a choice." Neil reached up and removed Christopher's hand from his shoulder. "I'm all right now. Let's go. We have gifts to receive."

Christopher winked, turned, then began his ascent.

The staircase twisted up to the right as usual, the

ascender offensively hampered by the center post.
With only the narrow openings of loopholes cut into
the walls, and the wall sconces long burned out from
the night before, the well was laid deeply in shadows
that rose a full head above Christopher. That was
good. Their approach would not be seen on the wall
by anyone descending.

They made it to the first floor and stood a moment
in the long stone doorway, a bridge to the rooms
beyond. They encountered a boisterous conglomera-
tion of male voices and clanking armor that betrayed
its size to Christopher. Roughly fivescore men, he
guessed; without a look to be sure, that number
could easily be wrong. Present was a peculiar smell,
one which Christopher had always associated with
the kitchens, the bakery to be exact. The smell of
flour, or wheat, or some kind of grain. Oats perhaps?

Both of these things struck Christopher as very
odd. It sounded like a garrison quarters in there, but
those quarters, he knew, were on the second floor.
Had the Saxons moved them? Or were they using
both floors? Did they have that many men in the castle? The first floor was primarily the storehouse, thus
the dry tinge in Christopher's nostrils from the grain.
And considering the grain, never had the smell been
as powerful. Christopher remembered the odor from
the kitchen, and though he knew grain was also
stored where they were, never before had he actually
detected it. How much grain did the Saxons have?

King Arthur would want to know the answers to
those questions. If he could sneak a peek into the
room, the information he brought back to Arthur
would be invaluable, and, after all, he did need
something to soften his punishment. He'd come to
the castle against the king's wishes; by all rights

Arthur could have him hanged for treason, but Christopher gambled on the affection he knew the king had for him. Vital information about the Saxons' manpower and supplies might, in a small way, justify his actions to the king. No, they wouldn't really, but at least he would be doing one other constructive thing besides saving Doyle.

"I need to go out there to have a look inside the rooms," he told Neil in a stage whisper.

"Why?" Neil demanded in his own raspy voice.

"Numbers of men. Supplies. Arthur needs to know those things."

"Do you have to do it now?"

"When would you like me to do it, Neil?"

"I'm waiting here," Neil said. "They spot you, you'd better scream and let me know."

"They spot me, you'll hear them scream."

"Right."

Christopher peered around the edge of the alcove, all but his head and shoulder still obscured by a right angle of shadow. As on the other levels, a wall divided the floor in half. The near side was the supply room, though he could only see a small part of it in the light of a single torch mounted on the wall to his right. The back of the room remained a mystery. In the center of the dividing wall was an archway from which came a bit more light, and the thundering sounds of the garrison.

Christopher slipped from the alcove, hugged the wall to his right, and moved toward the torch. He slid it out of its iron holder and let it lead the way toward the back of the room.

As the dim glow brought the supplies into better view, Christopher gasped.

The entire wall to his left was obscured, stacked three deep from floor to ceiling with barrels of either cider or ale. Perhaps tenscore barrels in all, easily enough drink to take the Saxons through the winter. He turned left, and there were the telltale sacks of grain, they, too, stocked three deep. As Christopher tilted his head up to see the tops of the piles of grain sacks, noting they were only a mere yard from the ceiling, he spied something else. A network of wooden beams had been constructed, running parallel to each other from north to south, and from these beams hung sack after sack of what Christopher guessed were salted meats and fruit, apples probably. There were at least twenty beams with at least as many sacks hanging from each. Christopher lowered his head and glanced ahead to the rear wall of the storeroom. Wooden crates were arranged from corner to corner and rose up at least twice as high as Christopher. As he neared them, he could smell the strong scent of garlic and, through the slots in a few of the crates, saw the cloves. He also spotted carrots, potatoes, beets, and onions within the crates. Never in his life had he seen so much food gathered in one place. The previous lords of the castle, Hasdale and Woodward, had never fortified the room so heavily. It was disturbing but important news.

Feeling a pang of hunger, Christopher leaned over and slid out a carrot from between the slots of a crate; he bit down hard and chewed hungrily on it as he turned around and stepped lightly toward the archway.

A trio of partially armored sentries, their halberds resting back on their shoulders, moved suddenly through the archway; they chatted casually, and one of them chuckled loudly over something Christopher hadn't heard.

He slammed himself against the barrels to his right and fumbled with the torch, tipping it down and trying to smother it on the stone floor. But sparks and ashes floated up from the burning stick; they, however, weren't what the sentries noticed. Christopher heard one of them comment on how it had become strangely dark on their side of the room, the Saxons having grown accustomed to the torch burning on the wall—the torch Christopher held.

And one of them looked in Christopher's direction. "Ho! Who's there?"

There wasn't a second to think, and Christopher was thankful for that. With the torch still burning, he rushed forward toward the three Saxons, who stood some fifteen yards away. Knowing he came from the shadows, knowing that surprise was his, he let out a wild howl in the hope he would be mistaken for some dangerous, drooling, sharp-toothed beast, which he pictured himself as in his mind's eye.

As the torch began to illuminate the invaders' faces, Christopher noted to his satisfaction that they looked scared. He drove on, the torch pointed out, its fiery tip spearheading his escape. Once he came upon the men, he simultaneously thrust the torch into the face of the Saxon to his right and reached out with his free hand to lock it around the halberd of the Saxon to his left. The force of his momentum carried him straight on through the Saxon in front of him, the man flattened by the rushing beast that was Christopher. The burned Saxon shrieked and fell onto his side, clutching his face. The Saxon whom Christopher had disarmed grabbed the back of Christopher's tunic, but was dragged into his fallen comrade only to trip and go down himself.

The engagement was certainly heard by Neil, but Christopher shouted to his friend anyway: "Neil! Start running!"

Halberd in hand, torch in the other, Christopher stormed into the alcove and mounted the stairs. He looked up to see Neil disappear around the bend.

Then Neil came running down toward him, nearly knocking him over. "Guards coming down!" he shouted.

Christopher turned around, only to see two of the sentries he had driven past stomping into the alcove and brandishing the sharp tips of their pole arms.

"Can't go up! Can't go down!" He shouted back to Neil. "How many coming up there?"

"Two," Neil answered nervously.

"Armed with?"

"Spathas."

"Here." Christopher tossed Neil the halberd. "We're going up. You first. I'll burn and disarm the other."

"I hate when you tell me what you're going to do," Neil said, turning and stepping slowly up the stairs. "It means something else is going to happen . . . "

"Move and die!" one of the sentries ordered from below.

"If we *don't* move, we're going to die," Christopher shouted back, then followed Neil up.

The spatha-wielding guards rounded the corner too quickly, and Neil exploited their speed, throwing himself against the wall and lowering the long pole of his halberd to ankle height.

As the guards tripped, Christopher drove his torch into the neck of one man while simultaneously ripping the spatha from the Saxon's grip. The other guard not only tripped over Neil's halberd, but was sent airborne down the well—directly into the two sentries coming up. All three men went down in a pile. Christopher glimpsed the Saxons for a second, then faced Neil.

"You see," Christopher said, "I *did* burn and disarm him."

"Thanks to me." Calling Neil's grin cocky was an understatement. The barbarian lifted up his halberd and commenced his ascent. Christopher held tight at the barbarian's back, smiling at how Neil's fear had turned completely into confidence.

They came to the second floor landing, its alcove identical to the one on the first. Christopher heard men drawing water from the wellhead as they continued up the stairs. He also heard the busy racket of many more men. Another garrison of Saxons was there as well. He hadn't figured out an exact number of those on the first floor for Arthur, but judging from the sounds on both floors, their numbers were surely greater than Arthur had anticipated.

A heavy, buxom chambermaid, her gray hair pulled back tightly into a bun that was covered with a coif, nearly knocked them over as she waddled down the stairs.

"Oh!" she said, poising, her jaw falling, her eyelids yawning wide. "Who are—"

"Shhhh," Neil ordered. "Not a word."

"Lady, your service to the Saxons will not last long, we can assure you," Christopher said.

"Thanks be to God you're here. But you're so . . . young. How many others are there?"

"Sorry, we can't talk," Christopher said, ignoring her question. "Be silent. And go now."

"I'll pray for you, boys," she said, then resumed her steps downward. She looked back over her shoulder, nodded her head, then put an index finger to her lips in a show of compliance.

Up and up they climbed, and Christopher's feet felt as if they grew heavier with every step. His only solace was the light weight of the spatha. Had he been lugging along the Baines-given broadsword, he would look as out of breath as the barbarian did.

"I have a silly question," Neil said between huffs. "Do you know what floor Doyle's chamber is on?"

"Is it not the third?" Christopher asked.

"I thought that's where Seaver's chamber was and we went *down* to see Doyle. But that would put us on the second floor, which would mean we already passed it."

"No, I think his chamber was on the fourth, wasn't it?"

Neil stopped. "I wasn't paying much attention to where we were going. I was a little upset over being caught."

"What are you stopping for?" Christopher asked. "Come on, now, we'll find it."

"So which is it? Third or fourth?" Neil demanded, his agitation fully hatched.

"Third," Christopher said with a feigned aplomb that didn't last long. "I think."

"We did go down from Seaver's didn't we?"

"Who cares! Let's find out!"

"So we'll search the entire third floor of this keep, passing directly by the solar where the leader of all these Saxons is probably resting, and hope we're not spotted. And Doyle might not even be there!"

"I'm almost positive it's the third. Now if we don't start moving, we'll be caught right here." Christopher took the flat side of his spatha and smacked Neil across the rump with it. "Go!"

"Damn," Neil cried in pain. "All right. All right."

They resumed their trek, but scarcely a minute later Christopher detected something on the extreme limits of his hearing. He grabbed Neil. "Stop," he whispered.

They both froze. And listened. Footsteps shuffled

above, the sound echoing and spiraling down the well.

Finally, the noise drifted away. They nodded to each other and moved on.

Several minutes of rapid climbing brought them onto the third floor, the landing of which was well lit by a pair of blazing torches. With gingerly steps and furtive glances, they moved from the alcove of the stairwell into an intersection of three long, narrow halls. The sleeping chambers lay dead ahead, the hall jogging straight away from them for some thirty-odd yards, its rear wall illuminated by a simple cross-shaped loophole. Unlike the other unmanned loopholes they had encountered in the stairwell, this one was attended by a crossbowman.

That was problem number one.

As they ducked back behind one of the intersecting halls, and Christopher peered around the corner to espy the sleeping chamber hall, he considered problem number two; it was exceedingly more complex. He counted ten chamber doors on each side of the hall, all, for argument's sake, locked. Even without Neil's uttering a single word of skepticism, Christopher knew what they were about to attempt was well-nigh impossible. He would not be able to be open those doors bolted from the inside. Those locked from the outside, as Doyle's would be, he could get through. But there wasn't time to try every door, and there would be no way to do it without the crossbowman overhearing them. Besides that, who knew what lay behind those doors? An extremely angry, heavily armed Saxon battle lord, for instance. Trying every door would undoubtedly upset the chambers' occupants.

How far had we walked down this hall? Was it halfway? You have to remember, Christopher!

He knew it was not at his end nor the far end of the hall, but definitely somewhere in between. Excluding the first four chambers on each end left them with six chambers to examine. Still too many.

The *fwit!* of the crossbowman's weapon echoed once throughout the hall. Christopher watched him pause to windlass his bow, then let another bolt fly through the loophole. Strangely, there was no varlet to assist the Saxon in his loading. Christopher knew the Saxons employed such boys, but now shrugged away the incongruity. Probably none available. One thing was good: the archer was alone and busy. Thank St. George for the siege outside. It kept the halls almost empty.

A pair of horns blew, originating from somewhere below and inside the castle.

"They've started their search," Neil whispered, "and they won't be coming in pairs but in dozens. And by the way, have you figured out a way for us to even get *near* any of those doors—and then get through them?"

Just doing what he was doing was an incredible challenge, Christopher thought. But add to that Neil's immutable doubt, and he knew that if he made it out of the castle alive, he would have truly accomplished something much more grand than he could have ever conceived. He would have survived alongside the prophet of doom!

But if Neil hadn't complained, Christopher would have experienced a very strange, even fearful feeling about their next move. As long as Neil remained dubious and voiced his concerns, things felt right.

Go ahead, Neil, complain. Force me to ask myself those same questions. Push me to greater heights, you hairy ox!

He turned to Neil and studied the apprehension

chiseled into the bearded archer's face, the eyes forever glossed with a thick layer of dismay. It was interesting being partnered with such a fellow. Christopher had been used to the quiet reserve of Doyle, who only spoke of solutions to problems and never complained. Doyle was as much an advisor as a friend. Teamed with Neil, Christopher felt himself in the superior position, the barbarian looking to him for solutions, guidance, and assurance. Thankfully, a plan to goad the archer on had congealed in his mind.

"We're going to become friends with that bowman," he told Neil softly.

"I say we rush him and kill him!" Neil whispered tersely. "Why in the name of all the saints do we want to befriend him? And what if he doesn't want to be our friend? Wait a minute. What am I talking about? You've got me thinking as madly as you!"

"He's going to tell us what room Doyle is in."

The horns from below resounded again, this time closer.

"Then we'd better find that out now."

Christopher took a long look around the corner then ducked back to face Neil. "Follow my lead." He shifted around the corner and began to sprint down the hall.

Behind him he heard Neil mutter, "I've been following you ever since we've been here and look at what I have to show for it. You're going to get me killed. I might as well start accepting that."

Chamber doors blurred by on either side as Christopher ran. His heartbeat thundered in his ears and he felt his lungs threaten to burst; both discomforts were more from anxiety than the labors of running. He held his spatha upright in his right hand, steadying the sword as his sandaled feet carried him closer and closer to the crossbowman.

The Saxon archer turned as Christopher neared him. It would only take a second to run the enemy soldier through, and for an instant Christopher considered that, abandoning his plan to trick the man into showing them where Doyle was imprisoned.

"Haven't you heard, man?" Christopher screamed in Saxon, stopping short in front of the bowman. "Seaver has ordered that Celt archer out of his chamber. He's to be ransomed to the king! What have you been waiting for?"

Christopher's words were a bit choppy, he knew. All he could do was pray the man would attribute his broken Saxon speech to the fact that he was out of breath, and not discern that Christopher was a Celt. There was, however, another difficulty. This bowman was not the person in charge of fetching the prisoner; that was a duty for Seaver's personal guards. Christopher words, despite being broken, were militarily incorrect.

Realizing that fault, Christopher added, "We've been sent by Seaver, and he's promised death to any man who delays bringing the Celt out of his chamber."

The small mouth and deep-set eyes of the crossbowman made it hard for Christopher to read a reaction from the man. He lowered his empty bow and regarded Neil and Christopher with a look that could be curious, could be measuring. Then, in voice that sounded like it was mixed with sand, he said, "So what is the delay? Fetch the Celt. What business is it of mine?"

"We were told you would show us what chamber he is in," Christopher said. All of this thinking on his feet wore on him considerably; Christopher knew a headache was in his near future.

"Well, how should I know that? I'm a bowman with a duty to shoot arrows through that hole," he said, gesturing to the loophole with a thumb over his shoulder. "I know not, nor do I care, where Lord Seaver keeps the Celt."

Christopher felt something pressing at his back, driving into the thin linen of his shirt. He glanced to his left and saw that Neil prodded him with the tip of his halberd. A knotted look on the barbarian's face said: "Another great plan of yours crumbling like an undermined wall, squire!"

Thoughts flitting like pipits from branch to branch, Christopher had the answer. "All right, then, man. If you don't know where the Celt is, then help us look for him, for we'll all hang from a gallows tree if he's not in Seaver's presence soon!"

Christopher pitched a cocksure look to Neil, but Neil's scowl didn't flicker.

"I'll help you look, but how do we get in? I don't have the keys. Do you?"

"Ah, yes, yes we do," Christopher lied, then turned and hurried over to the first chamber door. He knocked twice on the thick oak. "Hello, hello in there. Hello, Doyle? Are you in there?"

The trouble with calling for Doyle was that Christopher did it in Saxon. The only thing Doyle would understand, if he listened from the other side, was his name. That, Christopher figured, would be enough.

All Neil could do was knock on doors. Christopher was thankful the archer had been smart enough not to open his mouth and call out in Celt. Christopher, the Saxon archer, and Neil knocked on door after door, and as they neared the opposite end of the hall, having no luck after more than half of the doors had been rapped on, another Saxon archer appeared in front of the loophole behind them.

"What are you doing?" he asked his comrade.

Christopher watched the archer lower his hand
from the door he was about to knock on, a door next
to Christopher's. "I'm helping Seaver's guards locate
the Celt prisoner. Seaver wants to see the Celt now."

That's right, you dumb bowman!

"Seaver has but one personal guard, and he is
Ware. Who are these . . . boys!" This Saxon, who
stood a full head taller than the other bowman, began
to step quickly toward them.

Christopher knocked on his door. "Doyle?"

Nothing.

He moved up to the door the first archer stood
before, shoved him out of the way, and knocked nervously. "Doyle?"

"Who is that?"

The voice was thin, tiny even, nearly completely
muffled by the door. But praise be to God it was there!

Christopher stole a look at the approaching crossbowman and saw that the tall man was beyond being
suspicious of them. The Saxon *knew* something was
wrong; it was written on his face, a lean, gaunt
glower that came rolling forward and augured imminent doom.

"Neil! Get over here!" Christopher shouted.

Damn, he'd spoken Celt.

Another look to the tall Saxon. The man brought
his bow to bear, its bolt waiting to fly.

"Stop them!" the tall Saxon yelled to the other.

Christopher fumbled with the door latch—locked,
of course. He'd learned an old trick from Regan
about opening locked chamber doors. You shoved a
piece of leather cord into the keyhole, applied
upward force to the door handle, gave a little shove,
and like magic it would open.

No time for magic.

The archer who had volunteered to help them turned on Christopher and Neil just as quickly. He came from behind Christopher, slid an arm over Christopher's shoulder, and proceeded to choke him. A second later, Christopher heard a short moan, and suddenly the pressure on his neck was gone, followed by the crumpling sound of the Saxon. Christopher whirled to see the now-whimpering man lying prone on the floor. Neil yanked the bloody tip of his halberd from the Saxon's shoulder blade.

"Throw down your weapons!" The tall Saxon was at full tilt now, and Christopher was shocked at how fast he could manipulate his giant frame.

"Onto the door. Now!" he ordered Neil.

"I thought you knew how to get by the lock?" Neil said frantically.

"I do!" Christopher said, rushing to the opposite side of the hall to get a running start at the door. "With me and you! Ready?"

Neil threw down his halberd and joined Christopher. This was one moment in his life that Christopher wished he'd been heavier. If not for Neil's presence, ramming the door would most assuredly *not* work.

"Okay," Christopher gasped, dropping his spatha. He started for the door.

Neil threw his stocky frame sideways onto the door with a force that Christopher guessed broke the lock instantly. Christopher turned his body and hit a fraction of a second later, but reasoned his assault was simply a good intention, that the real work had already been done.

The door swung open and both archer and squire collapsed onto the stone floor. Straw rushes dappled the chamber floor and aided Christopher's slide into

the leg of the nearest of the three trestle beds. His
forearm hit the leg with tremendous force, snapping
the support where it met the frame. He barely managed to lower his head so that it missed the bed
frame, but as it moved under the bed, his ear was
snapped back by the edge of the frame and dragged
under the hard wood. Once he stopped, Christopher
lowered his head. His ear flipped back into position.
It felt as if it was on fire. He let out a moan, tried to
reach up and rub the pain away, but realized he was
pinned under the bed. Then, hands clutched his
ankles and he felt himself being dragged into the
open.

"Doyle, quick, the door!" Neil shouted.

It was Neil pulling him out, and though
Christopher couldn't see Doyle, he heard his friend's
quick footsteps as he crossed to the door.
Christopher rolled onto his back and sat up—in time
to see Doyle begin to slam the chamber door in the
Saxon bowman's face.

The crossbowman dropped his weapon and
slapped his palms onto the door, applying increasing
pressure. Doyle struggled but couldn't secure the
door; there was still a hand's-length gap between
jamb and thick oak.

"Neil! Help me!" Doyle gritted out.

Neil crossed to the door and slammed his hands
onto the wood. His added pressure decreased the
opening only scant inches.

And then something was jammed at boot height
into the opening between jamb and door—the
Saxon's crossbow. Ear and forearm stinging,
Christopher rose, scrambled to the jamb, got down
on his hands and knees and tried to shove the
weapon back out into the hall. Yes, he tried. But the

Saxon was too clever. He had jammed the crossbow through, flipped it so that its T-shape was perpendicular with the floor, and then rested a foot on the firing end to secure it. The bow would not budge. Christopher even tried to pull it through into the chamber, but the Saxon must have hooked his boot onto it.

Three young men and one incensed Saxon, and only a door between them. *Why is this so hard?*

"I've an idea," Christopher said, standing to join his friends as they pushed on the door.

"Don't listen to him, Doyle," Neil said. "Unless, of course, you subscribe to lunacy—which is what all of this is!"

Doyle bared his teeth like a rabid dog, the muscles in his left arm bulging as he drove against the door. He kept his bandaged hand close to his belly, and Christopher could tell he wanted terribly to employ it, but knew the pain would be too great. He brought it up to the door once, twice, then pulled the hand back, swearing aloud. "What's your idea, blood brother?"

"No, don't even tell him, Christopher, I beg of you!" Neil was drenched in sweat, the front of his tunic stained in a dark oval. That, and the urgent plea on his face, made him appear much more than desperate and scared. It made him look already defeated.

"Enough, Neil! Do you want to get out of here alive? Even if we manage to close the door on this giant, what do we do then, eh?" Christopher didn't give Neil a chance to answer before continuing: "I say we let him in."

"Dear God . . . there! Don't you see, Doyle? He's mad, or possessed, I don't know which!"

Doyle's next remark came out with remarkable

calm, if one didn't know Doyle. "He's right." Doyle could talk casually about the tension of a bowstring in the face of death; it was his way with dealing with fear.

Neil's jaw, if it could have, would have fallen off his face. Instead, it hung down as far as it would go. "What? What?"

"Get ready to invite him in," Doyle said, then turned his grimace of exertion into a raised-brow question. "What's wrong with you, Neil? A problem with your ears?"

"No, no. I'm not letting him in," Neil cried.

"Get off the door and fetch a torch," Christopher ordered.

The barbarian hesitated.

"NOW!" Christopher's scream surprised even himself.

It certainly amazed Doyle, who gave Christopher a curious look as Neil complied. What was that look? Did his old friend think he had become a self-appointed sovereign? Or was there some admiration in those eyes? Perhaps Christopher's capacity for leadership was truly coming to the fore, especially in their present situation. As he had considered, being paired with Neil left him no choice but to lead—and Doyle had always assumed that role. Now that command was Christopher's, Doyle's ego might be bruised—along with the rest of his body. Christopher could not help that. There was no time for tact or emotional considerations. There was life. And death. And acting, not thinking. An ego was worth sacrificing to save a life.

"I'm leaving you alone for a second to fetch a torch of my own. Can you hold him?" Christopher asked Doyle.

Doyle nodded, then qualified: "For a second."

Christopher released himself from the door and darted right to the wall opposite from Neil, arriving under the torch. He removed the flaming stick from its sconce and then directed Neil, with a wave of the torch, to a position approximately two-and-one-half yards back from the door. Archer and squire stood on either side and at the ready.

Neil panted. "I don't know if I can do this . . . "

"Quit thinking about it!" Christopher said. If Neil continued to ponder what they were about to do, then it might make Christopher do the same—and when it came to killing, the more Christopher thought about it, the more he would hesitate, and that would lead to his death. The moment was, as much as he hated admitting it, a time to kill. The darkest hour. Black sleep come fully alive. Reality flooding into every sense with visions too awful to bear but ones that *must* be borne. The sight, the sound, the touch, the taste, and the smell of death would pervade the room and their memories.

"Here he comes," Doyle said.

With that, Doyle rolled away toward the door hinges, putting himself behind the barrier of wood.

In came the Saxon with the same sudden momentum that had carried Neil and Christopher into the room.

The bowman stumbled but caught himself. But that didn't matter. He wouldn't see the blinding flash of light and heat until it was too late.

Christopher thrust his torch into the Saxon's face; skin immediately smoked and sizzled. The invader wailed in horrific and sudden agony.

Neil simultaneously touched his torch to the back of the Saxon's tunic, which was exposed beneath the

leather straps that bound his breastplate to his chest.
The tunic was instant fodder for the flames.

Shrieking, the Saxon bolted up and his hands went
to his back in a desperate, awkward attempt to
smother the flames. He stepped forward, then one
hand drifted back to his melted nose, burned brown
cheeks, and seared-shut eyelids. There were few
things in the world that smelled worse than burning
flesh, but at the moment, Christopher couldn't think
of any of them. The smell, as always, was a powerful
emetic, and Neil was proof positive of that. Before
the archer could put his torch to the Saxon again, he
gagged, leaned forward, and began to vomit.

The Saxon's back continued to burn as he fell first
onto his knees, then onto his stomach, then rolled
over. Smoke, embers, and bits of ignited straw
wafted up around the writhing man. Christopher
stepped to him, closed his eyes, silently asked God
for forgiveness, then put his torch once again to the
man's face.

The Saxon gasped, and Christopher drove his torch
down hard, into where he thought the Saxon's mouth
was. He must have made contact with it, for the agonizing crossbowman was stifled.

Christopher felt a warm touch on his neck. He
opened his eyes and looked over his shoulder: it was
Doyle.

"Come on," Doyle said firmly, urgently. "And don't
look down."

Christopher released the torch from his grip, and
though the desire to inspect what he had done flickered across his mind, he wisely ignored it. He did not
want to end up like Neil. The fetid air had already
made him cross the border into nausea.

As Doyle raced ahead to fetch the crossbow lying

on the floor, Christopher crossed to the barbarian, who now stood wiping his mouth and nose free of his disgorge.

"Are you all right?"

Neil winced, then shook his head no. "I hadn't eaten enough to begin with. Now my stomach is not only knotted but it's empty, too."

Christopher draped an arm over Neil's shoulders and escorted him toward the door. "When we get back, I'll personally make sure you get a pork dinner the likes of which you have never seen!"

"Either that," Neil answered, "or you'll see to it that an arrow fills my belly—due to your wild schemes."

"You'll be full—nonetheless," Christopher quipped.

"Or dead."

At least Neil had spoken with a smile.

They found Doyle out in the hallway, standing near the Saxon Neil had gored with his halberd. Doyle had a quiver of bolts slung under his right arm, the crossbow held in his good hand. "There's a spatha. And a halberd," he said, referring to their abandoned weapons lying on the stone floor.

"They were ours," Neil said, then turned to Christopher, adding, "Gifts—from the Saxons."

"Well grab your gifts," Doyle suggested with an overobvious nod. Then he frowned, apparently thinking about what Neil had just said.

Christopher picked up his spatha, and as he tightened his grip on the hilt of the weapon, he realized he had fetched the blade because Doyle had ordered it. It was natural to hear Doyle give a command and then to obey it; Christopher took it as comfortably as an order from the king.

Twist of fate. Was it to be Christopher's ego that

would be bruised now? He had worn the gauntlets of command all the way into the castle. Could he hand them over to Doyle? Or should he fight to maintain them?

Orvin, dear old Orvin, had said something long ago that returned to Christopher's thoughts. The graying knight had taught that a good leader is a good listener. An even better leader knows when to step back and let his champion do the work for him. The greatest leader of all is the one who can do both, and still retain his pride, his ego not bruised but strengthened by the brothers-in-arms who surround him. A leader is but one man, built on a foundation of many. Without his men he is nothing. Without their leader they will fall into disarray.

Doyle and Christopher were both leaders. In the past, Doyle had ascended gracefully into the dominant role. Now Christopher was coming into his own, yet he had to be man enough to admit that Doyle had always given the orders, and would continue to do so in the future. That part of their relationship would never change. It had evolved too naturally, and to tamper with it would be to tamper with the friendship. Christopher knew he had to heed Orvin's words; it wouldn't be easy.

But it would make him the best possible leader, and build within him a powerful trust, a wisdom born of humility, and a sense of uncompromising honor. Few men possessed all of those qualities. Arthur, though he certainly had his faults, came very close in Christopher's mind.

"I'll never fire a longbow again," Doyle said, gesturing with the crossbow, "but I think I can one-hand one of these. Though one of you will have to windlass it for me."

Christopher nodded.

"Which way do we go?" Neil asked. "I wager the stairwell is crawling with garrison."

Doyle chortled. "That's what I love about you, Neil. You stand here in the bowels of a Saxon-occupied castle and you wager the stairwell is crawling with Saxons. I wager we're *surrounded* by Saxons!"

Neil *tsk*ed. "You know what I mean."

"Let's not stand here and debate it," Christopher said. "We've got to get down to the dungeon. We took the northeast stairwell. Let's try the northwest. No matter what, we must go down."

"Agreed," Doyle said, then turned to Neil. "We don't care what you think. You're coming or you're staying here, whichever you like . . . "

Then, with a slight grin, Doyle whirled around and strode toward the end of the hall.

Christopher looked at Neil. The barbarian muttered something unintelligible, but it was reasonable to assume it involved Doyle and contained expletives. Christopher tipped his head in Doyle's direction. Neil pursed his lips over gritted teeth then started off. Christopher hurried alongside his friend.

No one met them at the end of the hallway. But as they turned right and jogged down another barren, tapestryless corridor with nothing to absorb the thudding echo of their sandals on the stone, they began to hear the oncoming shouts of men.

"If you have any last requests to make of the Lord," Doyle said quickly, "make them now."

Neil made a noise: somewhere between a cry and a whimper.

Christopher felt every bit of air leave his lungs. An eyelid twitched—

—and then Doyle shouted, "To the wall!"

5   Seaver's physical wounds were not as great as
the mental ones he had recently sustained. The news
of the Celts' escape had made his temples throb, and
he had torn himself out of bed so quickly that he
ripped open the stitches in his back. The linen bandage wrapped around his torso was stained a wine-
dark hue.

But that pain was nothing compared to the rage and
sudden failure he felt. Ware stood next to him at the
narrow window, waiting for a reply, waiting for him
to say something, an order, anything. Seaver could not
utter a word. He trembled. Then disbelief hit him.
They were in the dungeon! How could they escape?

They had help! Yes, that must be it. But who?

Wait now. Seaver knew he had enemies, but would
they actually aid the Celts?

They might. That would explain a lot. But if they
hadn't, then Christopher was far too clever a boy to
be roaming around the castle. He and his two friends
must be apprehended immediately—before word of
the escape reached Kenric!

Or had it already? Ah, there was something to ask
Ware. And so he did.

Upon hearing the question, Ware lowered his head.
"Kenric knows. And that is why I am here. He wishes
to see you in his solar."

The dread bored into Seaver like an icicle, cold and
hard, merciless, and once embedded, it took control
of his entire body, freezing it instantly.

Without Ware's help, Seaver could not have made it
to Kenric's solar. The stitches bled—but not as badly

as his failure. The prisoners—all of them—were under his care, and they were to be turned into productive slaves, not into freed spies for the enemy!

The days of nibbling on clouds and resting his head on mountains and drinking lakes were gone. Once, Seaver's feet had barely touched the ground; now the weight of his own small frame was almost too much to bear.

Ware would wait outside. With a simple nod, the young man suggested that Seaver enter through the solar door, which was already cracked open.

Nervously tying the drawstring on his tunic, Seaver slid past the door and stepped into the room.

Since they had taken the castle, Kenric had never once invited Seaver to his solar. It took this defeat for Seaver to finally see where his master bedded down for the eves.

Seaver could have lived without the knowledge of what the room looked like, if being summoned there meant discipline, which he guessed it did.

Yet, faced with the facts, he was in the solar. And as his gaze took in the room, he could not find Kenric. There was the four-poster bed, with a mattress so thick that it made the bed appear very high from the floor. The woad blue linen blanket covering the mattress had not a single wrinkle, and the pillows above the blanket were overstuffed with goose feathers and looked highly inviting. Seaver longed to cross to the bed, lie down, and rest his heavy head on one of those pillows.

To his left, he viewed the four trunks stacked near the window alcove; those he knew were filled with Kenric's looted armor. Kenric's collection had grown from a single plundered traveling trunk to four. Besides the extreme comfort of the bed, and the growing collection of armor, everything else about the solar also reflected the distinct tastes of a Celt. Kenric had

changed the look of the room from the way
Woodward had furnished it, but as Seaver knew, his
master enjoyed the culture of the Celts even more
than the Celts themselves did. There was a standing,
wooden chessboard with a tessellated top of stone and
glass, its playing pieces composed of solid bronze.
Celtic pottery adorned the mantel of the hooded fireplace, and above it hung a painting of a meadow, with
birds circling overhead. For a fleeting moment, the
landscape made Seaver feel serene, and warm.

From the large wooden bathing tub, to the many
skins on the floor, to the stools, the sconces and can-
dlestands, the ewer and basin, and even the weapons
rack in the far corner, Seaver found it hard to find
anything distinctly Saxon. All of it said Celt, down to
the tiniest detail. Anyone who entered the room
would never believe it was occupied by a Saxon.

"I live like my enemy. And I actually enjoy the way
he lives. And I know him much better this way."

Seaver cocked his head, then turned slowly toward
the entrance behind him.

Kenric closed the solar door, then took a step forward and paused. He lowered his gaze to his hands,
an anlace in his right, the tip of it scraping dirt from
beneath the nail of his opposite index finger. Seaver
was accustomed to Kenric's nail-cleaning wont, and
he had observed that his master only did it on two
occasions: when he was impatient or anxious; or
when he was bored. It was safe to assume his leader
was not bored. . . .

Kenric continued, his gaze still on his hands. "How
well do you know your enemy, Seaver?" Kenric looked
up, and there were no other eyes in the realm that could
penetrate Seaver's heart more thoroughly than his did.

"As I told you, lord," Seaver began, realizing how

nervous his words sounded—and that made him even more nervous—"I served with the squire. I know him well. Or at least I thought I did. But hear me. I did not underestimate him. He is clever—but clever enough to escape through iron bars. I believe he had help."

"That occurred to me as well," Kenric said. "Perhaps one of Renfred's supporters aided in the Celts' escape." Seaver stepped forward, thrilled by the news that his master shared his belief. "All in an effort to cast a shadow over me, to make me look less favorable in your eyes. It has nothing to do with the Celts—everything to do with your decision to have *me* replace Manton." Seaver's step closer to Kenric woke a sleeping burst of pain in his cut back, a pain he could no longer restrain; he winced, held his breath, then bent forward slightly.

"Your wounds—"

"I am fine." Seaver straightened, swallowed, then tried to repress the inferno in his back. "I promise you, lord, the Celts will be caught. The knowledge of how they escaped will do us little good now, so long as you believe it was not due to my incompetence."

Kenric studied the nail he had finished cleaning. "What I believe does not matter anymore, Seaver. It is what the men believe. The news has already reached them. Now those who once supported you doubt your abilities. They may quickly join the supporters of Renfred. If they do, then I will have little choice. You will no longer be my second-in-command. I argued with the other battle lords to put you next to me; they finally agreed. If the Celts get away, I will no longer be able to control them. If you remain my second after that, those lords might even have me killed."

There was no fault in Kenric's logic. Once, Seaver had assumed it would be something personal with his

master, as had the traitors who had helped
Christopher and his friends escape. But Kenric was a
keen, reasonable man when his bloodlust wasn't
blinding him, and as much as Seaver despised the
facts, they were laid out very clearly before him. If
the Celts escaped, the garrison's faith in Seaver
would be gone, and that would charge Kenric with
the duty to strip Seaver of his command. One, two,
three, and he was back to being a scout—if the Gods
were kind to him. Somewhere along the path he
could be murdered. It was good that Kenric still
believed in him now. However, as Kenric had said,
that belief did nothing to change the facts.

There was one course of action left, and it would
be Seaver's sole reason for living: capture the Celts.
Then, after that, he must weed out his enemies in the
castle and destroy them before the eyes of the garrison. Then, and only then, could he restore faith and
be looked upon with respect.

Seaver nodded solemnly. "I know what I must do."

"Then go," Kenric said. "Go under the eyes of
every god."

Once outside the solar, Seaver had trouble containing
his thoughts; they darted, collided, scattered, combined, fled, and returned all in the seconds he regarded
Ware. "I want threescore of men added to those searching for the Celts. I want another score sent immediately
to the dungeon. The Celts will try to leave the way they
came. You and I will meet those men in the prison."

Ware moved behind Seaver and touched his back.
"Your wounds have bled through the bandage and
onto your tunic."

"There is no time for them to mend," Seaver replied with disgust. "And what should I care of them now—when I may very well die soon!"

Ware circled to face him. "No, you will not!" he said with angry resolve. "Not with me at your side."

Ware's pledge could not have come at a better time. If there was one man in the world Seaver did not have to prove himself to, it was the young scout. The man had seen him in action and owed his life more than once to Seaver. His loyalty was of a metal so strong that the hottest flame could not soften it.

Nodding and placing a hand of thanks on Ware's bicep, Seaver ordered, "Fetch me the squire's broadsword. Kimball will die by his own blade—a blade wielded by you. He chose to defy me, and if he knows anything about our ways, then he knows what a dishonor it will be for him to lose his life to the very sword once held in his possession. In his dying hour, he will know he was never a warrior. He will die in disgrace."

Ware bowed in compliance. "It will be an honor and a privilege to kill him. Now. You're safe here— but I will meet you at your chamber. You will not descend the stairwell alone." The scout backed away, then turned and hurried off.

Seaver turned in the opposite direction and started slowly down the hall. Though he was very secure on this floor, with guards searching and questioning every man who wished to come up, he could not ignore the desire to draw his dagger from its belt sheath. He kept the blade low at his hip, staring warily into the shadows at the end of the passageway as he shuffled toward them.

6 They had stood with their backs pressed against the hard stone for minutes that felt like moons. The barks of Saxons came from somewhere in the distance and echoed hollowly. There was no telling exactly where those men were. Doyle had ordered Christopher and Neil to leave the wall to extinguish some of the torches that lit the corridor. They had purposely left one burning at the end of the hall ahead, and another burning at the end of the hall behind them, illuminating a would-be attacker's approach from either direction. They, on the other hand, were cloaked in the darkness of the center of the corridor.

"How long do we stay here?" Neil stage-whispered.

"Can't you stop talking for a moment?" Doyle asked.

"The northwest stairwell is up ahead at the end of this corridor," Christopher said.

"That's where all the noise is coming from!" Neil said, making no attempt to douse the hysteria in his voice, nor regulate his volume.

"Shush!" Doyle commanded the barbarian, eyes emphatically wide, index finger vertical to his lips.

"We're waiting until it grows quiet," Christopher explained softly to Neil.

Without warning, it grew awfully loud. The thumping of many boots drew closer, and as Christopher swung his gaze forward, he saw four fully armored Saxon cavalrymen marching toward them in two lines, two abreast. The Saxons' sheathed spathas bounced off their plated hips as they moved, creating a rattle that accompanied the rhythm of their steps. All carried their salets in the crooks of their arms, leaving their perspiring faces and portions of their necks exposed. Judging from the mud covering their sabatoons and greaves, they had just returned from some sort of mission. Being cavalry, they had little use just then, for there was no way they would be ordered to leave the castle and engage the enemy. What their exact duties were, Christopher did not know. Their destiny, however, was something he planned to be a part of.

"Four on three. That leaves one free," Christopher said.

Doyle lifted his crossbow. "I don't like fighting when the odds are against me." He spun away from the wall, stepping into full view of the Saxons, aimed the bow with one hand . . .

. . . and squeezed the trigger. *Fwit!*

An unencumbered shaft of life-taking metal, Doyle's bolt wasted no time striking the front right Saxon in the soft tissue of his lower left cheek. The bolt passed through that skin and yearned to flee the man's body via the back of his neck, but there was simply too much flesh and blood in the way. The tip of the bolt did manage to appear under the man's ear, a scant thumbnail's length away from the rim of his gorget, but it stopped dead.

Christopher didn't wait to see the man drop. He cocked his head to Neil, who was deadlocked over the decision of whether to advance or not; Christopher could see it on the barbarian's face. Neil needed inspiration. Christopher cried, "You charge them now, Neil, or you *are* going to die!"

That, it appeared, was enough. Christopher's words implanted a rage within Neil that began with a deep bellow. As his war cry grew, Neil gripped his halberd, one hand high, the other low, steadied the shaft, then directed its silvery-sharp, hooked blade forward as he turned and drove his beefy frame toward the Saxons.

Christopher was only a step behind the barbarian, for the both of them had to give Doyle a chance to fetch the spatha of the Saxon he had shot. As it was, Doyle could not windlass the crossbow. He could shoot wondrously—but only once.

Neil's spatha connected with the breastplate of the heaviest of the Saxons, a bald invader with a silver loop dangling from one of his ears. The bald Saxon was driven back into the younger, hairier man behind him, and they both collided and dropped with a terrific *KA-KA-KRASH!* to the stone before they could unsheathe their weapons.

Doyle reached down toward the sheathed sword of the Saxon he had shot. He gripped the hilt and began to withdraw the blade—but the man's hand snapped up and latched onto Doyle's wrist. The cavalryman hadn't died!

Christopher started forward to help his friend, but while Neil had temporarily downed two of the Saxons, there was still a third to contend with, and his blade flashed before Christopher's eyes. Had he not peripherally caught sight of the sword coming at him, Christopher would already be dead. He took a wild step backward, and a cool wind blew across his face—the swipe of the attacking man.

As Christopher took three more steps back, adjusted the grip on his spatha, and breathed in deeply, he was able to scrutinize, if even for only a few seconds, his attacker. The Saxon was ancient, much too old to still be in service. What little hair he had left was thin, snowy, and wild, and the man's own sweat did nothing to tame it. He had a complexion of bark, and a neck that hung so loose that it seemed to pendulum as he shifted his head. But despite the decay he had remarkable speed, and a combination of thrusts that Christopher had never seen before—and had barely seen coming.

The old Saxon advanced, both veiny hands vised onto his spatha. He brought the blade across in a horizontal swipe.

Christopher squatted, and as the blade passed over his head he tumbled forward, came out of the roll, then brought his heels up into the Saxon's groin. Though the wizened invader's privates were partially protected by his tasset and a layer of mail, Christopher trusted that the angle and momentum of the blow would knock the man off his feet.

Grandfather knight went down as planned, and the resounding clatter of his armor on the stone made Christopher's blow seem all the more effective. Christopher arched his back and snapped himself to a standing position, not an easy move; he was glad he hadn't thought about it until after he was standing. Behind his fallen opponent, he saw Doyle engaged in a one-arm spatha fight with the young, hairy Saxon. Below the two swordsmen, the Saxon with the bolt in his cheek lay in a puddle of gore; several fresh stab wounds blemished his face and neck. There was no mistaking it this time: the Saxon was dead.

To his left, Christopher saw Neil parrying the strokes of the bald Saxon. Neil was, to put it mildly, in trouble. He was not able to turn his pole arm around and deliver a lethal thrust to the man. He was too busy defending himself. His defenses would wear thin and the man would finish him.

Though he knew it would give the old Saxon time enough to recover, Christopher decided to assist Neil. He leapt over the legs of his fallen combatant and rushed up behind the heavy Saxon battling Neil. He lifted his spatha high above his head, targeted the peeling, freckled

skin on top of the Saxon's bald head. He closed his eyes
tightly, gritted his teeth, grimaced, and, with a slight
exhalation, brought the blade down . . .

KLANG!

In the second that Christopher closed his eyes the
Saxon had shifted his position. Upon hearing his blade
connect with metal, Christopher flicked his eyelids
open.

The fat Saxon pivoted to face him. He noticed that
the silver loop that had dangled from the fat man's
earlobe was gone. Indeed, the entire earlobe and a
smidgen more of the ear had been hacked away by
Christopher. The Saxon brought one of his great
arms up and touched the wound with his spoke-thick
fingers. He withdrew his hand and inspected the
blood on it with growing horror contorting his face.

Suddenly, the Saxon glared at Christopher, opened
his mouth, and: *"Arrrggghhh!"* He wound up, arced
his blade, then brought it across, into Christopher's.

It was the kind of maneuver that should have cost
Christopher his weapon and his life. But the reflexes
of youth were on his side. Indeed, the blow did send
the spatha out of Christopher's hands, but it fell only
a yard away. Christopher dropped to his hands and
knees, fetched the blade, then rolled onto his posterior, able to parry.

The overblown Saxon collapsed forward before
Christopher, his jaw cracking like a nut as it
impacted on the same floor stone that supported
Christopher's foot. The sound of that jaw breaking
seemed more immediate to Christopher than even the
racket the man's armor made as he smashed to a
standstill.

The fat Saxon was down, hallelujah. But how?
What had happened? Christopher spied blood driz-

zling from the pauldron that covered the Saxon's
right shoulder blade. The darkening vital fluid spat-
tered upon his backplate. The ogre had been stabbed,
or rather halberded. Neil had lifted the Saxon's pauldron with the tip of his halberd and driven the blade
into the crease between backplate and pauldron. The
blade had more than likely pierced the man's lung,
which had in turn filled with blood.

Christopher's gaze rose to Neil. The barbarian eyed
the fallen Saxon with disdain. He gathered spit in his
mouth then hurled it onto the invader's back.
"Bloody pig. And I thought *I* was heavy . . . "

"You fight well for a fat man with no courage,"
Christopher teased, rising.

Before Neil could return a verbal jab of his own,
Christopher turned toward the sound of a skirmish
behind him—and was thankful he did.

While he had gone on to aid his friend, so had the
old Saxon to help his. Both young Saxon and old
were upon Doyle, whose single spatha arm shifted far
too slowly to ward off the multiple, unrelenting
blows that came his way. Like drooling, attacking
wolves in winter, both Saxons made guttural howls
as they tried to finish their prey.

At that twinkling, Christopher did not know if his
heart stopped—but something happened to it.
Perhaps it had taken control over his body. He bolted
toward his imperiled friend, fueled by something he
felt only rarely and had never been able to reflect
upon, for he could never remember the feeling once
it felt him. It was a feeling of the present. It existed
only in the rarest of moments, where life hung by
precious threads—and it was up to him to save those
threads and pull that life in, back home. He was
reminded of the tournament, not that many moons

ago, when he had fought Mallory. He had had to save
Marigween and the others from Mallory's cruel
blade. Now, leaping toward Doyle's attackers, barely
feeling his sandals touch the stone, he felt that presence, that power, all over again. There were others
times he had felt it, but not like this. His mind, nearly
shut down by his heart, relayed to him a single message: *If I do not intervene—my friend will die.*

What was that sound that escaped his lips? A cry
so loud and so deep that he barely recognized it as
his own. Was it anger? Rage? He didn't know. It just
came. The young Saxon responded to the sound and
turned away from Doyle, just as Doyle circled his
blade around the Saxon's to draw it away.

The joints in Christopher's arms felt well greased
as he, with his right hand clutching the spatha's hilt,
his left steadying its balled end, lashed out at the
hungry wolf. His blade met the Saxon's once, twice, a
third time, his strokes high, low, horizontal, vertical,
then horizontal again. By his fourth blow, a downward slash right, high from his left shoulder,
Christopher felt the strength leave the young man's
arm. So hard was the blow that it sent the Saxon's
blade skittering halfway down the corridor.

Christopher glimpsed—only for a fraction of a second—into the man's doomed eyes. He felt instant
sorrow. He could not kill.

You're making a mistake! Kill him!

*No! Why should I have to? I didn't want to burn
that bowman but I did! Why do I have to go on
killing? This man is defeated. Let him admit that and
run away!*

Christopher swung his blade around and thrust the
tip toward the Saxon's throat, carefully judging the
distance so as not to pierce the man.

Neil and Doyle engaged the old Saxon behind him, and though Christopher was aware of the sounds, they seemed a world apart from the moment. In Saxon, he addressed the cavalryman:

"You do not need to lose your life in a castle in a foreign land. Do you?"

"That is for Woden to decide!" the man spat back.

Christopher didn't see from where the Saxon had pulled the dagger, but suddenly it was there, in his gauntleted hand, and it came up and knocked his blade away from the man's neck. And continuing with that movement, the Saxon stepped toward Christopher, whirling the dagger once in front of the armor fauld plating his stomach.

In his effort to escape the Saxon's knife, Christopher stepped back—

—and found himself pinned against the corridor wall. He twirled right, and when he came around to face the Saxon once more, the man was upon him.

The Saxon's gauntleted left hand seized his wrist with a force that made him drop his spatha. As he looked down toward the fallen blade, he saw the Saxon's dagger advancing toward his chest. With his free hand he latched onto the Saxon's wrist—and stopped the blade short as it nicked the thin linen of his shirt.

Each man had a wrist; it was muscle and sinew against the same, and though the Saxon's will and strength felt unwavering, Christopher did not abandon hope. Instead, he slid his foot behind one of the Saxon's sabatooned feet, jolted his body abruptly toward the man, and, with nowhere else to go, the Saxon tripped backward.

Christopher tore his sword arm out of the invader's grasp and released his hold on the Saxon's

dagger arm. He dodged back, leaned over, and
scooped up his spatha. Jaw locked, an exhalation
coming hard through his nose, Christopher turned
toward the cavalryman.

The Saxon rolled onto his side and dragged himself
to his feet. Dagger against spatha now. When
Christopher had fought Dallas, a huge oaf and rogue
in Mallory's old band, it had been, as it was now,
dagger versus spatha. Dallas had thrown the dagger,
and the tremors of remembered pain phantomed
below Christopher's collarbone. He would not let this
young barbarian get away with the same; he would
not give him the opportunity.

The Saxon leaned forward into a fighting stance,
knees and arms bent, dagger hand eager to carve.

Normally, Christopher would have squared off
with the man and given him the opportunity to make
the first move. Christopher preferred a riposte as his
first move in hand-to-hand; it was a good way to feel
out the opponent's strengths and weaknesses. And
sometimes, he liked to warm up a bit before he let
loose with everything he had.

But Christopher had offered mercy to the Saxon.
The man had rejected his offer. Now Christopher
would offer him something else altogether—a journey
to the afterlife. Christopher would not fight like a gentleman, but as a Saxon—and he knew like no other
Celt how to do that. During his service to the Saxons
under Garrett, he had witnessed firsthand what bru-
tality and contempt for human life really were.

He strode toward the Saxon with his blade raised,
the very act throwing the man off guard. He hadn't
bothered to square off, hadn't bothered to assume a
fighting stance or even a defensive position. He was
all offense. Once his spatha was in reach,

Christopher drew back and came down in a vertical chop—but he didn't put any strength behind the maneuver. It was a carefully planned feint.

The Saxon went for the bait. He came up with the dagger to deflect Christopher's blade.

Christopher yanked his blade back, swept it around and under the Saxon's dagger arm, then came across with a horizontal stroke that could not have been more perfectly aimed or timed. The honed edge of his spatha caught the seam of the Saxon's gauntlet where it met the vambrace that protected the Saxon's forearm. The spatha pried into that groove and parted the metal. The blade drove past the link-mail beneath, cut through the flesh like butter, then tore through the bones in the Saxon's wrist as if they weren't there at all.

The Saxon's gloved hand tumbled to the stone, still clutching the dagger.

"My hand!" he cried, in a voice that belonged to a boy.

Moving swiftly, not bothering to look at the Saxon's wrist, which undoubtedly spurted blood, Christopher hoisted his blade above his head with both hands and then tilted the tip toward the Saxon. He blazed forward and drove his sword into the yelping invader's mouth, then continued on into the man, sending himself and the Saxon crashing into the opposite wall. He felt the tip of the spatha chip off on the stone behind the Saxon's head. The Saxon coughed—his last act—and his breath carried with it a mist of blood that Christopher felt dapple his face.

He let go of the sword and backed off the Saxon. The cavalryman, no longer under his own control, slid along the wall to his rump, leaving a blood trail in his wake.

The corridor was strangely quiet. The unbroken shouts of Saxons in the distance were there, like the steady rustling of leaves in the autumn zephyrs, but the closer sounds of the engagement were gone. Heart still racing, lungs doing all they could to take in more and more air, Christopher palmed the back of his neck free of sweat as he looked up to where Neil and Doyle had been.

They stood together, staring at him. Behind them, the old Saxon lay quivering, his armor newly reddened with his own blood.

"Remind me not to get you mad," Neil said. He had obviously intended it as a joke, but the intensity of the moment diluted the humor out of his voice. It came out like a fact.

Christopher flicked a glance toward the man he had just killed. The spatha still hung from the Saxon's mouth.

I will see you again. In black sleep, where you will rise to seek your revenge. But it is your *fault. I offered mercy. I did not want to kill you.*

"You have blood all over your face," Doyle said.

Christopher reached up and self-consciously ran fingers over his cheek; they came up bloody. Then he inspected his friends. Their clothes and arms soiled crimson, and they had blood on their faces as well.

A hatchet fell in Christopher's mind, severing his connection to the gruesome moment. "Gather up whatever we need and let's go," he said curtly.

"I was going to say that," Doyle answered.

"Sorry," Christopher said.

"Don't be. I'm glad you're doing some of the work for a change." Doyle fingered the fine hairs of his beard, then added, "And you know, I was thinking about the strangest thing when I was fighting that man back there. I was thinking that I cannot remember the last time I had a drink of ale."

"In your case," Neil growled good-naturedly, "that *is* an amazing feat."

"Close your mouth and gather the weapons," Doyle chided, without looking at Neil.

Christopher felt the walls press in around him, and he saw that they were covered completely in blood. A second, closer look proved him wrong. A ghost image. Something inexplicable. He had to leave. "I'll meet you at the end of the hall."

"Don't go alone," Doyle argued.

"I can't stay here."

"Just go up to the torch," Doyle suggested.

"All right."

As Christopher shifted away, he heard Neil ask Doyle, "Hey, where's he going? We need some help with these weapons."

"Let him go," Doyle answered.

7 Christopher shivered in the torchlight as he spat on his palms and rapidly wiped the blood off his face and out of his thin beard. He lifted his shirt and wiped some of it along the bottom, wiped his cheeks on his shoulders, and continued the process with an almost-manic determination, feeling he would never get all of it off. He asked himself why he trembled. It couldn't be because he had just killed a man; he'd done that before, and though he always felt miserable about it, he had never reacted this way before. Then,

he reasoned, it was the blood. Yes, that was it. Just too much blood all in one place. He had seen carnage far worse than what was down the corridor, but this time it had gotten to him. Why? He felt weak, and suddenly insecure. Thank St. Michael his friends were with him.

Then he realized why he was so overrun with this postbattle fear. Throughout the fight he had let his body work and, as taught, had not thought.

But there had been a mind picture that had shimmered to life several times: Marigween, in the cave, holding his son.

Lord, that is why. That is why I am so scared now. I came so close to death, so close to leaving my son fatherless, and Marigween, well, without me.

Say it. Say it to yourself. You're going to marry her.

I might. If I live.

You know you will. You love her.

I do. But how deeply? Do I love her because she is the mother of my child, or do I love her because she is the woman who means more than anything in the world to me, the woman I would sacrifice everything for, the woman who gives meaning to my existence? I should love her for all those reasons. But do I?

You know why you should love her. But not if you truly do? Why is that?

Brenna.

What am I to do about her? I don't want to hurt her?

Before Christopher could continue his internal argument, Doyle and Neil hurried into view. Neil sported a sword belt with sheathed spatha at his side. He carried with him another sword belt and sheathed spatha that Christopher assumed was his. Doyle wore a spatha and carried his confiscated crossbow, his quiver of bolts slung by a leather cord over his shoulder.

"Here," Neil said, handing him the sword belt.

"You didn't take any of the armor?" Christopher asked.

"I told him we should have," Neil said, referring to Doyle with a smirk, "but he said we don't have time."

"That's right," Doyle said firmly, then he regarded Christopher. "Get that belt on and let's make haste to the well."

They reached the end of the hall. Ahead was the alcove that led to the stairwell. A connecting corridor streaked off to their right. Both alcove and corridor were left unguarded. The siege was in full tilt on the opposite side of the castle, and that was more than likely the reason for the lack of security here.

Doyle was first into the well, his feet scampering over the stone steps.

"You're going too fast!" Neil cried.

"The wretches below will never know what hit them!" Doyle called back. "We'll blast right through them!"

Neil huffed. "I threw up and I haven't eaten since. I have no energy for *blasting!*"

"Just keep going," Christopher urged the barbarian, placing a palm on his back and pressuring him on.

Christopher put his sandal down, expecting the next step to be there, but in his haste, he misjudged the distance and his heel caught the lip of the step, driving him down not one, but two steps. As if buffeted by a gale, Christopher lost his balance, crashed into Neil, drove the gasping barbarian into the center post, and then continued downward toward Doyle—head first.

Doyle barely turned his head as Christopher

plowed into his left shoulder blade, throwing the archer sideways into the wall.

Wheeling forward, he felt his spatha catch on one of the steps, and his velocity caused the swordbelt to snap off his waist. His body found an odd, exceedingly painful rhythm as it bounced off the stone staircase, all parts vulnerable and taking turns at smacking onto the steps. He could barely see anything, but what he did glimpse was the floor and high ceiling spinning in the dim light of a twirling torch.

The landscape changed radically, and he felt himself rolling across level stone. Then his right arm and both knees hit what could only be a wall. He bounced off one of the great, rectangular stones, then remained still. He was on his back, breathing heavily. What he saw was unsettling: stone spiraled away into a blurry nothingness.

"Christopher!" Neil shouted, his voice floating down from somewhere above.

He heard the patter of steps coming quickly toward him, and then someone leaned over him. Out of focus at first, Doyle's concerned face finally sharpened into view. He reached down with his good hand and tapped gently on one of Christopher's cheeks.

"I'm all right," Christopher said.

"No, you're not," Doyle answered, "but you did beat us all to the second floor. We're here."

"Help me sit up."

Doyle complied, grasping one of Christopher's hands in his own and then pulling him to a sitting position.

Blood fled from Christopher's head, and the rush of it made the world rock a moment, blur in and out, and then become stable. "Oh, I'm dizzy. But it's gone already," he said, blinking.

Neil arrived on the second floor landing and squatted down to view him. "You're going to have quite a bruise on your shoulder," he said, then pointed with an index finger to an area barely exposed near the collar of Christopher's shirt. Christopher forced his gaze as far down as it would go and saw the red skin.

"That's not the only place," he added.

The full extent of the pain had not yet hit him. The minor bruises would reveal themselves on the morrow. Right now he would only have to contended with the major aches.

Lord, please don't let anything be broken.

He began to pull himself up, and Doyle offered his hand once again. Christopher took it and then rose, feeling the results of the many isolated blows to his legs and arms. He could move his limbs, despite the fact they were badly battered. It didn't matter whether he felt like he had spent some time on an armorer's anvil being pounded by the man's bloody hammer. What mattered was that he functioned. That was enough. He could still escape.

"You sure you can go on?" Neil asked.

"Absolutely," Christopher answered. "I'm as nimble as ever."

Doyle flipped a smirk to Neil. "What choice does he have?" Then he regarded Christopher. "And you're a liar. But I'm going to hold you to your word. Fetch your sword."

Christopher ventured slowly toward the staircase, and he was about to climb up the six or seven steps to where his spatha lay, but then it hit him: a thought, clear as an unmuddied lake, pure and precise and logical as anything he had ever pondered. It was not a complex notion, but a simple conclusion that for some unexplainable reason he had not come to sooner. Then again, there had been so much con-

fusion, so much blood and so much fear, that there
had been little time for logical thinking. But now it
struck him, as hard as each of the steps had.

By now, Seaver knew they had escaped. And where
would he assume they would go to exit the castle? Why,
the way they had come in, of course. It was the simplest
way out, and, once outside, they would be able to conceal themselves from the Saxon archers on the wall-
walks by holding their breath and going underwater.
They would have to pop up once or twice for air—but
only for one deep breath, and then they would be under
again, until they reached the shoreline of the moat.

A rather foolproof escape plan—except that Seaver
probably knew all about it. Where would most of his
men be? In the dungeon, waiting for them.

Christopher mounted the staircase and climbed to
his spatha. The thin brass buckle had been broken by
his fall, so he removed the spatha from its sheath and
abandoned the belt and sheath altogether. On the
way down the stairs, he could not help wincing as the
bending of his knees and the swaying of his arms
caused flashes of discomfort. He would wear the
scars of the fall for the rest of the moon, to be sure.
Perhaps Orvin or Merlin knew of a way to expedite
his healing. . . .

He rejoined Neil and Doyle on the landing, and, as
they turned their backs to him, about to round the corner and continue their descent on the next staircase, he
called, "Wait. We're not going to the dungeon."

Slowly, and nearly in unison, the archers turned to
face him.

Yes, they were both bowmen, but that was the only
thing similar about Doyle and Neil. They looked completely different, spoke differently, ate differently,
reasoned differently, and the list went on. There

were, in Christopher's opinion, no two men as dis-
parate as these two.

Yet at the moment, they shared a look that was
extraordinarily identical.

"What?"

"What're you talking about?"

Neil nudged Doyle with his shoulder. "He hit his
head. That's it. We cannot listen to him. He doesn't
know what he's saying."

"Listen to me. We can't go down there. It's no
good. Seaver and his men will be waiting for us.
That's just where he expects us to go."

"I care not if he's there," Doyle said cockily. "In
fact, I hope he is, so I can return the pain he inflicted
upon me." Doyle shook his bandaged hand as if it
were a raised fist.

"You really believe there will be a lot of men down
there?" Neil asked, the apprehension already flooding
into his voice.

"Where else would he expect us to go? There is no
easier way to leave the castle."

"All right then," Doyle said, "I'll play along. How
do you propose we leave?"

They had to get into the moat. That was a good
way to avoid the archers. Besides, there was no way
they would get the gatehouse drawbridge down; to
initiate that plan would require a score of men, and
the chances of its happening were slim. It could not
even be a consideration.

"How deep is the moat?" he asked Doyle.

Neil released a sigh. "I don't like where this conversation is leading."

Doyle furrowed his brow. "I'm not sure. I believe
its depth varies, though I'd venture to say it's deepest
near the gatehouse."

"That's too far for us." Christopher strained his thoughts, then remembered. "Wait a minute." He looked at Neil. "We swam into the tunnel on the north side, you and I, Neil. That water was fairly deep, wasn't it?"

Christopher was rationalizing all of it to himself, he knew; hearing Neil agree would complete the process.

"Who cares how deep the water is? Let's hurry up and decide what we're going to do! I don't like standing here!" Neil rubbed tense fingers over the hilt of his sheathed spatha, knuckles white, veins bulging. He backhanded sweat from his forehead, then exhaled. "I cannot believe this. I cannot believe any of this!"

"Let's go in the completely opposite direction. Seaver thinks we're going down. Let's go up."

"That's it," Neil said. "You do what you like. I'm going to the dungeon to get out of here." He pivoted to leave.

Doyle grabbed Neil by his tunic sleeve. "Hear him out," he said.

Christopher tightened the gap between himself and the barbarian; he fervently hoped the few steps closer would add a little weight and emphasis to his words. "Listen to me, Neil. We go up to the wall-walk. Sure, it'll be lined with archers. But busy archers. I believe the king has most of our men on the northeast side of the castle. There won't be as many on the northwest, where we'll be."

Neil frowned, then shook his head negatively as he had done so many times before—especially when listening to one of Christopher's plans. "Where do we go from there?"

Christopher grinned. And then he winked. "Home."

Doyle's distant gaze and narrowed eyes told

Christopher he was contemplating the plan, having already guessed their route to the moat.

"Home?" Neil repeated. "I don't follow you. We go up to the wall-walk and then go home?" Neil's brow suddenly lifted, and then his mouth yawned opened. "Oh. Oh, no. No. No. I won't do it!"

"The walls are not that high!"

"They're high enough!" Neil cried. "We're jumping from the wall-walk of the *keep,* remember! Not the curtain walls! They're twice as high, probably twenty times as tall as me!"

"That doesn't matter," Doyle told Neil. "Christopher's right. We get up there and jump into the moat. Then swim to shore."

"Do you know how many arrows are going to come our way?" Neil asked. "We'll be shot as we jump!"

Doyle didn't bother answering. He shifted past Neil and Christopher and started around the bend toward the staircase that led back up.

"Let's go, Neil," Christopher said. "You didn't want to stand here anyway."

"If we make it out of here, I'm never speaking to either one of you again!" Neil's face was flush. He stormed past Christopher in pursuit of Doyle.

If we don't make it out of here, you won't be talking to us anyway, Neil. Death tends to quiet a person.

8 Descending the spiral staircase was far easier than ascending it, Christopher quickly discovered—especially after his fall. He even had trouble keeping

up with Neil, and Doyle had long since disappeared around the stone bend. There was a stiff, vising pain that wouldn't let go of his shoulder, and if his right knee could talk, it would beg for rest, for every time Christopher's weight came down on it, it gave way a little more. Better to listen to the knee, treat it right and it might repay the favor.

Christopher paused a moment, put a hand to the wall, then shifted his weight to his left leg. He looked up. The stairs looked eternal, twisting into the flickering shadows of torchlight that were, like the path, unceasing.

"Christopher, are you back there?" Neil called, his footsteps betraying his unseen position.

"Don't stop. I just need a moment. I'll catch up."

"All right."

The echoing thump of Neil's footsteps fell off slowly into emptiness. It felt very good to just lean against the wall, to work his lungs and let his knee recuperate. They were between the third and fourth floors, having made it thus far without being accosted by a single Saxon. They had encountered an enslaved mat weaver and his two sons. The trio had joined them in the stairwell and had climbed with them. Christopher, Doyle, and Neil had winked and had put their fingers to their lips—as Christopher and Neil had with the chambermaid. Though brief, it had been a heartfelt encounter, as the weaver, upon seeing them and realizing who they were, had cried. Christopher had assured the man that the suffering would end soon, and he had embraced him, telling him to pray to St. Michael and St. George for the safety and victory of the king's army.

There were too many like the mat weaver who had become indentured by Kenric. They had, in the past, loved their lords. Hasdale, Devin, and Woodward were all fair, generous men who gave back as much as they took. They taxed fairly, and on holy days, held feasts in the great hall that were rivaled by no other lord in all of Britain. Christopher had seen men come from all over to serve those three men in any way they could. Hostlers of Queen's Camel came; armorers from Gore; chambermaids from as far away as Glastonbury. It seemed that all lords who resided in the castle of Shores were just and fair—all those except Kenric. Was it simply a coincidence that Hasdale, Devin, and Woodward were exceedingly unselfish? Or was it something about the castle itself, something contained within its walls that infected those who inhabited it? If that were the case, then Kenric would eventually reconsider his taking of the castle. He might give it back. The castle would demand it.

Don't be ridiculous, Christopher! All right. It is a crazy idea, but I am allowed to think it!

He wished he had lived in the days before the Saxons had invaded. Oh, how different his life would be. Oh, how splendidly boring it would be! But then again, he would probably be a dreaded saddlemaker. Even though the magic of squiring had worn thin, and nearly always turned into a life-and-death struggle, there was no other post he could think of that he would rather hold. He wanted peace. But he also wanted excitement. Somehow those were opposing forces. One day he would discover a way to have both.

He pushed off the wall and mounted the next step. His knee felt better, but was far from healed. To his delight, it was only a dozen steps until he reached the fourth floor landing. Though he truly wanted to pause again, he continued on up to the landing that would lead onto the wall-walk and the battlements.

As he trudged closer to the landing, telling himself, one more, one more, just another step, one more, he heard the whispering of his friends. Five more steps revealed the archers, huddled just inside the oval archway that led outside, the framework of stone concealing them perfectly. Raw sunlight drew an even rectangle across the landing, and Christopher stumbled into one of its blinding, ninety-degree corners. He squinted, having been in the dim torchlight and resulting shadows for too long.

From outside came an angry shout to halt firing. The command came from a sergeant or lieutenant, Christopher assumed, a man much too close to the archway for comfort.

"Get over here," Doyle called to him.

Crossing from the light to the shade paralleling the right wall, he moved up behind Doyle and Neil, then got down on his haunches.

"How does it look?" he asked Doyle.

Neil offered his darkly sarcastic evaluation first. "This is where it ends. This is where you get me killed."

"It's really not that severe," Doyle said. "The sergeant's right here, just beyond doorway. He's got two longbowmen on either side of him, facing west. You were right about the king's army. They're mounting their attack from the south and east."

Christopher nodded. "Arthur would be a fool to attack from the west or the north. Too little land between the ramparts and the castle. We'd have our backs against a cliff."

Neil craned his head toward Christopher and smirked. "You're quite a military scholar for a squire. That's the most obvious thing I've ever heard."

"Will you please?" Doyle asked Neil, in an effort to

silence the barbarian. "Why do you have to be mad about dying? If it happens, it happens!"

"You can say that," Neil retorted. "You came here *wanting* to die. And if you do, you won't have to face Arthur."

"Both of you stopper your mouths," Christopher ordered. "Neil, we have to know what we're going to do before we go out there, and we have to know what's out there. You've taken a peek. I haven't. I want to know." Christopher looked at Doyle. "Speak." Then at Neil. "And you don't interrupt him. That is, if you want to live."

"Are you threatening me?" Neil asked, his expression screwed into tight incredulity.

"Not at all," Christopher answered, "but I suspect the bowmen outside are." Then, to Doyle, "How many are there?"

"Two on the west wall with the sergeant, as I said. There are, I think, ten on the east wall and south walls, with another four in the southwest battlement, and another five or six in the southeast battlement."

"What about the battlement above us? And the northeast one?" Christopher asked.

Doyle shrugged. "If they have five or six in the southeast tower, it's safe to assume they have about the same in the northern one. As for the battlement above us, do you want to go up and find out?"

Doyle's question made Christopher realize he'd been foolish to ask about the battlement above them; one way to gain that information would be to ascend the staircase to the very top and greet the men there, not exactly a covert way of doing things. The other way would be to move into the open, turn, and look up. Once outside, they didn't plan on pausing for a second. It would be straight to the wall and into the air.

Christopher shook his head no. "It doesn't matter anyway. What about the north wall?"

Doyle smiled—and it was the most welcoming smile Christopher had seen in a long time. It was that smile Doyle made that reminded Christopher so much of Baines. It was Baines who had originated that playful, I-have-an-idea-that's-going-to-be-fun grin that was now, be it unconsciously, kept alive by Doyle. Besides the grin, Baines was usually at Christopher's side in the form of the broadsword he had given Christopher. Though lost now, Christopher was confident the blade would turn up; it was somewhere in the castle.

"All right," Christopher told Doyle, "I know that smile."

"Good news on the north wall. Not only is it the wall we're going to jump off of, but there isn't a single bowman on it! It seems the patron saint is with us this day in more ways than one." Doyle sneered at Neil. "Despite those who do not believe."

Neil twisted a clump of his beard between his thumb and index finger, then his hand darted for his belly, as if he'd been hit by a sudden pain. "It's not that I don't believe. You hear that? That's my belly grumbling! I need to eat! Soon! No, it's not that I don't believe, it's that as soon as we get onto the northern wall-walk, the archers in the battlement above us will look down, see us, and—"

"They'll order us to halt first," Christopher broke in.

Neil snickered over Christopher's assumption. "What if they don't?"

"Let's not give them time," Doyle said. "We run from here, slip in between a parapet, and launch ourselves into the air." The fire of the future, the very close future, flushed Doyle's face and widened his eyes.

"Lord, if we just had some shields to strap on our backs," Neil said wistfully. "Then at least if they fired at us we might stand a chance of living. Now we run from here as you say and launch ourselves into the air—all at *their* mercy."

Christopher sat down, stretched his legs out, shook them a little to work the kinks out, then realized that was a mistake since the bruises stung. "Neil, we can sit here and bicker for the rest of the day and eventually be caught and all of this discussion would have been for nothing. And the longer we sit here and talk, the more you're going to talk yourself out of this. Let's go. At least you'll know if you're right."

"About what?" the barbarian asked.

"If this is where I get you killed."

As Christopher pushed himself up to his feet, the pounding, chaotic beat of many footsteps rose in the stairwell behind them.

"Alert the herald, the cupbearer, and the chef," Doyle said. "We have guests for dinner."

"Don't jest now!" Neil whispered loudly to Doyle.

"All right," Christopher said, feeling his breath suddenly go short as he inspected his friends. "Doyle, you're loaded up and you have your blade. Good. Neil, you have your spatha and I have mine."

"All the good they're going to do," Neil said bleakly.

"Ready?" Doyle asked, a near-maniacal grin splitting his hairy face wide open. He loved this. Too much.

Neil looked about to cry. He would not nod in response to Doyle's question.

"Go," Christopher said with a shudder.

Doyle broke for the archway and jogged into the

sunlight of the north wall-walk, his crossbow up and
scanning from side to side.

Neil hesitated for a second, but Christopher shoved
his shoulders and forced the archer out of the alcove.
Once outside, Neil could do nothing else but follow
Doyle. He seemed too afraid to come back.

Christopher lingered a second in the doorway,
looking to see what the reactions of the archers
would be. He should be close on the heels of his
friends, but not knowing if an arrow was about to be
sent into his back was too much; it drove him mad.

Now he knew. It was perfect. No one noticed
Doyle and Neil as they charged toward the north
parapets. He adjusted his grip on his spatha and—

"Kimball!"

Christopher cocked his head, and his gaze at once
filled with the image of a young Saxon lunging at
him, a broadsword clutched in both of the demon's
hands. Over the Saxon's shoulder, at the entrance to
the landing, stood Seaver. Christopher had second-
guessed Seaver, and the short Saxon had done the
same—with a little help. At Seaver's side stood the
mat weaver, a blade held to his throat by a squat sentry.

"One of the boys said too much," the weaver
yelled. "He didn't mean it! An accident!"

Christopher heard the man's plea for forgiveness,
but had no time to consider it. His gaze flicked back
to the oncoming Saxon. In the last possible second,
his spatha came up to meet the Saxon's now familiar-
looking broadsword, and the fighter's blow was
increased substantially by his driving pace.
Christopher was slammed out past the archway and
onto the wall-walk. Metal ground on metal, and the
muscles in Christopher's forearms bulged with exer-

tion. It was hard to maintain balance. The Saxon did not drive steadily into him, but with unexpected bursts of force. His sandals scuffed over the stone, slipped, found purchase, then slipped again.

"Christopher!"

He heard Doyle's call behind him, but he could not chance a look at his friend. While holding his blade fast to the Saxon's, he yelled back, "Just go! Go!"

Seaver stepped onto the wall-walk and called up to the archers in the northwest battlement, "Hurry! Shoot them!" Grimacing, as though the movement pained him, Seaver pivoted and pointed to his left, toward the parapets behind Christopher where Neil and Doyle were about to leap off.

Up to that moment, it had been a good plan, a sound plan, a plan that was admittedly haphazardly conceived, but one which had served them well. Christopher was proud of his newfound capacity to think on his feet. Unfortunately, all of that meant nothing now, absolutely nothing. He stood, blade locked with a Saxon, and was more angry at himself than anyone in the world—including Seaver and Kenric. And the anger, he knew, weakened him. But he could not quell the feeling. He had to stop punishing himself and start punishing the swordsman.

Doyle let out a cry that drifted away. Christopher guessed that his blood brother had launched himself from the parapet. A moment later and—*Ka-thunk!*—he hit the moat.

The shouts of many of the Saxon archers echoed Doyle's fall into the water, and during them, another *Ka-thunk!* resounded. Christopher prayed that noise was made by Neil. It did sound a little louder than Doyle's splash.

The Saxon ripped his broadsword away from

Christopher's spatha, and the action sent Christopher stumbling forward. He'd been tricked by this maneuver before, and though he fell prey to it once again, he was quick to reclaim a fighting stance.

He was a polite fighter, this one, giving Christopher all the time he needed to regain his composure. The sword he used was—

No! It cannot be! He wields my sword!

Seaver, you lout. Though I don't subscribe to your ways, I will not let you dishonor me before your men. I will not die by my own sword. If I go, an arrow will take me.

"Don't fire at him! Don't fire!" Seaver ordered the archers in the west and east battlements.

Christopher pitched a look at those in the northwest tower; there were five men pressed along the east wall of the battlement, their longbows drawn and trained on him.

It was something that shouldn't have crossed his mind but did, since the fight was paused, though be it only for a second. This moment, this speck of time that would pass and be gone and long forgotten, could very well be his last memory. And what he would remember of it was the fact that never before had his life strayed down such a perilous path. The chaos of the battlefield was just that; one could be killed and never see one's killer. Fate seemed much more alive there. Here, if fate existed, it hid behind the long rafters of clouds that fettered the late afternoon sky. The elements of chance were gone. These men were close, very much armed, and very much wanting to kill him. He was their *only* target, as was the swordsman before him. And all of these opposing forces were not directed by fate, but by a little, wincing man in an ornate tunic with a flame in his heart and throat.

Seaver shouted to him, "Go on, fight Ware. Fight him well. But tell me one thing before you cross swords and lose your life. How is it that you escaped?"

Instead of addressing the little man gone awry, Christopher utilized the time to further deliberate his plight.

He eyed the Saxon known as Ware and hated the way he handled the broadsword Baines had given him, hated the fact that the Saxon's sweat was upon its intricately detailed hilt. He noted that the young man had trouble keeping the blade up, and swung it slower than he should. Ware was obviously unaccustomed to combat with a broadsword.

He glanced at Seaver, whose expression told of his demands; he waited impatiently for an answer. No, Christopher would not betray Owen. Though he and Neil had become pawns in the political strife of the Saxons, and Owen had used that as his only reason for freeing them, deep down Christopher suspected Owen was glad to release him. Christopher and Owen shared one thing in common: both were willing to risk their lives for their beliefs; in that they had found mutual admiration.

Once again, Christopher spied the archers in the northwest tower, then craned his head ever so slightly to the south and the east to see that many of the archers along those walls had turned from the parapets to level their bows on him. If Seaver ordered them to fire, Christopher would be struck by over a score of arrows. He could only imagine with a swallow what that would feel like.

There were a hundredscore better ways to die.

He looked to his immediate right, to the north wall, a mere two yards away. It was slightly higher

than his head, with the gaps in the battlements coming down to about his waist. He couldn't see much
through the gaps. He wouldn't even be able to estimate the distance between the berm and the moat
before leaping—if he got the chance. He would have
to draw Ware close to the wall, keep his back to it,
then leap backward, land on his rump inside the gap
and then tumble off the wall, all while trying to
ignore the soreness of his stone-beaten body. He
would have to remember to roll hard, in order to
launch himself far enough away to hit the water and
not the muddy bank just beyond the wall. He figured
he would be able to do that if he pushed off as hard
as he could; he doubted he had the strength to actually overshoot the moat. But that would be his luck,
wouldn't it? Well, not if St. Christopher had anything
to say in the matter. Hopefully the patron would
guide him toward the stagnant water.

"Tell me how you escaped, and maybe I'll let you
die quickly by poison, instead of being hacked apart,"
Seaver offered.

"And I *will* hack you apart," Ware added with a
resolute nod.

A salvo of epithets ignited in Christopher's mind.
Were he Lancelot, he would have, of course, voiced
them. But a verbal foray with Seaver would not get
him closer to the wall. He owed Seaver and Ware
nothing, would give them nothing, save for a fight to
preserve his own life. That was all that mattered.
Marigween and his son were all that mattered. The
universe narrowed to a single purpose: get off the
wall-walk and get back to his family. Empty words
were of no matter. The order of the day was freedom.

Seaver stepped toward him, coming up behind
Ware. Ware regarded his master with a quick look

over his shoulder, then resumed his gaze on Christopher.

"Tell me," Seaver said, a merchant's persuasive tone temporarily waxing his voice, "and maybe I won't even poison you. I'll let you live." He rounded Ware and moved just beyond the reach of Christopher's spatha. "You and I were once friends. I taught you to blend, to seek, to find, and slip to away unnoticed. What happened to you, Kimball? The Celts have doused your fire. Poor Arthur. What a fool. His land is about to be ripped away from him— because of his own stupidity. Is that the man you wish to serve? Squire to Arthur is it? Squire to a dolt, I say. You know we represent a new order in England. The Celts' days are numbered. You pledged your allegiance to us once, be it under a Celt. You *can* do it again. Kenric is as fair and noble as Garrett was. And he is much smarter—and a lover of Celtic culture. You and he would get along magnificently. And all you have to do is tell me how you escaped. I know you did not do it alone. Save my life and I'll save yours." His lips curled into a patently feigned grin. "Join me." Then the grin fell sharply. "Or die." With a flagrant wave of his arm, he added, "Look around you. There is no escape."

Without thinking about it, Christopher complied. He glimpsed once again at the archers facing him from three sides of the wall, and then shot a gaze to the men in the towers; none of them were going away.

He could take Seaver's offer or make an attempt to fight and jump off the wall. He hated having a choice. Taking the offer would put him in bed with the Saxons all over again. With his past service to them well-known, he would be indelibly marked a traitor by Arthur and the rest of the army. So, taking the offer meant taking it for life, possibly giving up his family—or at least not seeing them for a long time. And what if Arthur won the war? Then, Christopher would spend the rest of his life in exile, or perhaps lose it altogether.

What would Orvin think if he defected to the Saxons? His mentor, the old knight who had become not only his instructor but the only family he had had for a time, would be devastated. Christopher would betray everything Orvin had ever done for him. To willingly join the Saxons was to turn his back on the duties of a true servant; to turn his back on God.

Why am I even considering the offer?

Because you're scared. Because there are so many of them with their arrows on you. Because Ware did not fall down a flight of stairs and is fresh and wants to kill you with your sword. Because you're so afraid to die. So afraid of leaving Marigween and your baby son alone. It's the fear that's making you think this, Christopher.

I'm shaking. I can't catch my breath. I can't give in to how I feel right now. I can't! Blast fear! To the gallows tree with it!

"Don't you have anything at all to say?" Seaver asked.

Ware turned to his master. "I believe we've frightened him into silence." Cocky was one word to describe Ware; another was foolhardy.

Orvin, if you can hear me, I'm sorry. I'm sorry for being so rude to you, for being so hard, for thinking I'm all grown-up already. I have so much to learn, so much I want to learn. I wish there was some way you could help me now. I need you. The sky holds no answers for me, only for you. If it has revealed my fate, and I'm to die now, then know I love you. And thank you for making me who I am this day. If there is a small part of you in me, then I have to call upon it now. I can act and not think, but I cannot help feeling the pain all over my body, and in my heart. I don't think I can beat this swordsman. I don't think I can do it. I shouldn't have run away from the cave. I shouldn't have come here in the first place. Perhaps my job is done. I have saved my friend.

No! My duty as a father and husband has not even started. If there is anything that should inspire me, it is that task and those people who need me more than anything in the realm. I'm man enough to know what I must do, but not sure if I can do it.

A memory of Marigween cradling his son in her arms coalesced in his mind—and this time he was clearly aware of it, and welcomed it with a love that filled and warmed him. The image was far more detailed than any thus far. In one reality, he stared at Ware, but his gaze was possessed by another reality, the landscape of his mind, a panorama filled by soft, ivory skin and luxuriously long red hair; by a tender smile from full, thick lips; by eyes flecked with wonder and joy as they stared upon the gift of life so close; by the tiny, helpless form that looked back at those joyous eyes with wide eyes of its own, reaching up with tiny fingers and smiling as she played with those fingers, the fingers of her son. And then she looked up from her son to him, an aura of light encompassing her body. When she spoke, her words came softly, gently, but carried with them a meaning more powerful than anything Christopher had ever heard in his short life. "Come home, Christopher," she said. "Come home."

Squire, blood brother, father, and future husband.

He was all of those things and would remain true to each of them. If he died, he would die loyal. To himself.

He lifted his sword a little higher—closer to his fate.

"So it's to be a fight!" Ware said excitedly.

Christopher rocked back and forth, preparing to make his first thrust.

"I guess you are a fool after all," Seaver said disgustedly. "I let myself hope. That was wrong. You *do* belong with Arthur. You are birds of the same feather—a pale yellow." Seaver spun around and stepped back toward the alcove, calling back, "Take him down in pieces, Ware."

"Right!" Ware screamed back, then to Christopher: "Woden awaits you!" He stepped forward, put his back to the nearest gap in the battlement, lifted his broadsword high over his right shoulder, and then brought it down toward Christopher.

One-handing his spatha, Christopher whipped the blade right.

Wishhh! Klang!

He parried Ware's thrust, but not without feeling a dreadful lurch in his shoulder.

With timing honed to a thought's breadth, Ware slipped his blade from beneath Christopher's and, taking another step toward his prey, counterparried with a horizontal swipe toward Christopher's chest.

Christopher jumped back to avoid the sharp tip of the blade, but his reflexes were too slow. His linen shirt was sliced open across his chest, just below his nipples. He didn't feel any pain, and wondered if the blade had actually pierced his skin. Then his chest felt warm and wet. He averted his gaze. The wound was not deep, but as he flexed his torso, he felt the torn skin pop and fold, and the pain came and dizzied him for a second. He slammed his forearm onto his shirt so that it would soak up the blood and act as a meager bandage, then he readied to face Ware once more.

Despite his unfamiliarity with a blade as heavy as Christopher's, Ware had already done an exceedingly good job and, of course, needed to declare that to Christopher: "Your blade has good action for steel over copper; it's balanced well and keeps me light of foot— most unusual for a broadsword, wouldn't you say?"

Christopher had developed a tolerance for men like Ware. There were some, he knew, who loved to talk during combat. These swordsmen tried to draw their opponent's mind away from the action at hand and make him think angry thoughts that would impair his judgment and slow his reactions. Christopher ignored the words; he heard them, yes, but they had no effect; they only made him compare Ware to the many other unsuccessful combatants he'd seen employ the same trickery.

"What's the matter?" Ware asked. I cut your chest just now—not your tongue!"

Ware tilted his blade at a forty-five-degree angle toward Christopher, balancing the weapon evenly with both hands; he was quickly becoming more and more adept with the sword, bad news indeed.

There was no opening for Christopher to exploit, but he opted to strike offensively anyway. If nothing else, it might busy Ware so much that he would be unable to speak.

Christopher lifted his left hand to his spatha and gripped the balled hilt of the blade to add extra power to the blow. He swung the blade back to his left and brought it down sharply toward Ware, aiming for Ware's exposed forearm.

Klang!

The Saxon was too agile. Christopher's advance was met by a powerful parry that not only rendered it futile, but drove him back several steps and made him lose his balance.

Ware moved in, taking full advantage of Christopher's staggering frame. The Saxon's first riposte came out of nowhere, a strike from left to right that missed Christopher's chin by inches. Had he not been tripping backward, part of his face would already be lying on the ground.

The alcove of the northeast tower drew closer. He could not let Ware drive him back any further. He must remain on the wall-walk and make a break for a gap in the battlements.

But Ware knew that was his plan, for the Saxon blockaded the wall with his body, stepping deliberately in the way when Christopher got too close to it. Down below, to Christopher's left, was the pair of triangular roofs that made up the ceiling of the fourth floor sleeping quarters. If he got too close to the inner edge of the wall-walk, he would fall onto the wooden shingles and slide down the valley, only to be trapped there. There might as well be an endless void centering the square walkway. If he fell into the center he would be doomed. The fall would probably leave him badly hurt so that Ware could finish him at his leisure. Or, Seaver could simply give the order to the archers.

But I'm not going to fall in. I'm going to escape. I'm going to go home!

"Enough play!" Ware shouted. "We're fighting with *swords*—not quarterstaffs, squire!"

Christopher swallowed as Ware drew back once again with the broadsword. The flurry of blows that commenced from the Saxon were swifter and harder than any Christopher had parried thus far.

He reached up and met each of Ware's strokes with weakening arms, and by the fourth thrust, he felt the spatha slipping from his sweaty hands.

With his sword about to fall, Christopher withdrew and tried something he had never done before in hand-to-hand combat, a move of desperation that was as humiliating as it was risky.

Christopher threw his spatha between Ware's legs; it hit the giant wall stones and skittered across them behind Ware. He lunged toward Ware, seized both of Ware's sword-wielding hands in his own, brought his head down, and bit the tender flesh on the back of one of Ware's hands. He felt the warmth and salty tang of blood enter his mouth as the Saxon screamed and shoved Christopher away.

Christopher fell back toward the roofs centering the wall-walk, but whirled and let himself fall behind Ware. He scrambled toward his fallen spatha, the sweat on his palms drying as he used them to pull his body along the stone. His hand met the hilt of the blade and latched onto it. He rolled onto his back just as—

—the Saxon launched himself into the air and dropped toward him, a bloodcurdling war cry erupting from his lips.

It was a small gift of fate that their weapons crossed as their bodies collided; at least one sword should have pierced flesh, but neither did. On impact Christopher closed his eyes and then snapped them open as Ware, grappling on top of him, applied pressure to the broadsword.

The collision knocked Christopher onto his back, where new bruises would form alongside old ones.

With both swords coming closer to his face, the blade
end of his own in perfect slicing position, he reached
up and snapped his left hand onto his right to help
drive Ware back.

He tapped into the reserves of his energy, but knew
there was not enough strength there to liberate himself
from Ware. This is where it would end. Seaver coaxed
Ware on in the background, a mad coach with an
unwavering bloodlust. The little man was joined by the
occasional hoots and rising cheers of the archers.
Somewhere, very far down below, Christopher heard
the shouts of Celts, lone voices now, but very good
ones to hear. Simple reminders of home in a dire hour.

A summer gust whipped over the battlements and
chilled his limbs as a low grumble formed in his
throat. He pushed and pushed, drove up and up, trying to get Ware away, trying again, failing again.
There was always another move that came to him in
situations likes this, a trip, the use of a knee or foot,
or even a bit of spittle in an opponent's eyes. But
Ware's knees pinned his own. The blades blocked
his mouth. His hands were too busy to do anything
else but ward off Ware, bracing and driving up his
sword.

Christopher already knew the struggle would not
go on for much longer; he would be the first to concede—but this was no tournament. There was no
mercy here.

Bleeding, plagued by multiple bruises, muscles and
sinews torn and tired, he could only call on the mind
picture of his family for more energy. He closed his
eyes and concentrated on them, and try as he might,
he felt the swords slip another fingernail's length
toward him.

All I need is just one hearty shove. One hearty

*shove that catches him off guard. Marigween, tell me
how to do it. Tell me how to come home. . . .*

Ware growled, then sent more of his weight down
to the broadsword. "That's right, squire, close your
eyes. I, like Seaver, have a conscience. Maybe I'll slit
your throat and wait until enough blood has left you
to hack you apart. Or maybe I won't."

*Please, Marigween, what do I do? There is no
training of Orvin's that can help me now. I don't
want to leave you. I don't want to leave you and our
son as I did before. I want to come home! I want to!
But I'm so tired. I want so badly to go to sleep. But it
will be an eternal sleep, one without you. Is it time
for me to go? Tell me?*

She looked up from the child, her face radiating
with the brilliance of all the stars collected into one.
"Come home, Christopher," she said. "Come home."

Christopher felt his body quake. Tremors, as if he
were intensely cold, began and grew in intensity. His
sword, pressed onto Ware's blade, shook much more
than it had from the previous exertion. No thought
process had occurred that was responsible for this. It
was as if his body had taken over in its own fight to
preserve its life—or had it?

No. It was them. They were inside him, a much
deeper part of his being than they had ever been
before. Their presence made him realize he had made
a mistake. He had sought physical strength from
them, one hearty shove, when that was not what
would truly help him. He needed to harness the
strongest part of himself there was: his love.

It was love that rocked his being to the core, that
wanted more than ever to burst from him, aid him,
rekindle his tired limbs. He could not give up. He let
himself go to his love.

Finding new strength he fought back, fought back with everything he was, everything he believed in, and everything he cared for. Love blighted his pain, his fear, and his desperation, and it charged him with purpose and power. His mouth opened:

"AHHHHHHHHHH!"

He threw Ware right, and suddenly he was free, the pressure off his knees and blade.

He flipped onto his hands and knees, dropped his spatha, stood, then tottered toward the battlement.

"Don't let him get away!" Seaver cried.

The archers in the northwest tower screamed and argued amongst themselves over whether or not to fire. Had Seaver given the order—or was he speaking to Ware?

Having longed for this moment for too long, Christopher could not believe it was actually happening. He threw himself up into one of the stone gaps in the battlement, landed on his belly, then hoisted himself up onto the wall. At the shuffling of feet, he looked over his shoulder.

Ware dived forward, reaching with one hand to grab Christopher's foot, making use of his other to jab the broadsword forward.

Exhaling in surprise, Christopher recoiled quickly, but Ware kept on coming. He tossed a quick glance behind him to view the moat below:

At least a score of Celt mantlets were scattered along the shoreline, with probably twice as many archers behind the wooden shields. Perfect. He could exit the moat and dive for their cover, as he hoped Doyle and Neil already had. His gaze dipped the slightest bit lower to the moat itself, and that was a big mistake. Neil's trepidation had not been unwarranted; the distance from battlement to moat was enough to make his heart stand still. And for a second, he thought it had. Another sudden summer breeze raked the hair off his forehead and howled through the parapets, leaving him chilled inside and out.

Ware reached out in another attempt to grab him while trying to pull himself into the gap.

Christopher looked at Ware, then back over the side of the wall. A running leap with one's eyes closed was a neat and painless way to meet the challenge. That was the method Doyle and Neil had most likely used.

Christopher felt Ware's hand grab his shirt and tug him back toward the wall-walk. He wrenched back, but in doing so pulled Ware up and into the gap.

"Ware's going to lose him! Fire! Archers! Fire!" Seaver shrieked.

Ware let go of Christopher's shirt. He turned around, crying, "Noooooo!"

A whistling shower of arrows fell in a deafening chorus upon the man, cutting off his scream and impaling him far beyond the point of death.

Ware's body shielded Christopher from the deadly shafts, but once struck, it fell back toward him, a driving weight still nervelessly clutching the broadsword.

The last thing Christopher heard as he was knocked over the side of the wall was the pell-mell hollering of the longbowmen.

9

Ware's arrow-cushioned form drifted slightly to Christopher's right as he and the corpse plunged toward—what he could only pray was—the moat, and not the muddy, but hard-enough-to-kill berm between wall and water.

There was no odder sensation. The sky above tore away from him, the clouds seemingly shrinking. The gale that had howled above rose to new heights, only now it was a gale created by his fall. He wished he knew when he would hit the water, but was paralyzed in the moment and didn't even know if he could turn around. It was an awfully long fall. Awfully long. Any drop he had ever made had happened so quickly that he had never had time to contemplate the actual event until after it had happened. With this fall there were seconds to consider what was happening, to listen to the wind, his breathing, the shouting of the archers, the beating of his heart, loudest of all in his ears. For some reason, he didn't like the idea of having the extra time; it instilled a greater sense of helplessness.

Something flashed past his gaze, and as he realized it had been an arrow fired at him—

—he punched the water, head and shoulders first, with a tremendous, splashing *SA-MACK!*

He had experienced many sensations the world had to offer, but the moment defied description, and he immediately decided that he would never *ever* do it again.

Blasting down through the water, sinking like a heavy sword, he remembered nearly before it was too late to hold his breath.

The warmth of the moat surprised him, as it had

before. He assumed, as he had when he dived in behind Neil, that the waters would be cold. They were not. But they were fetid, and as he sank deeper and deeper, he snapped his eyes closed, not wanting them to be stung by whatever foul elements created the nasty odor that wafted as high as the battlements of the keep.

He was able to save his eyes from the pain, but not the wound on his chest; the momentum of his body forced water into the cut, stirring up the invisible needles contained within. He reacted to the piercing discomfort by blowing out air; the bubbles tingled his nose as they rose.

Christopher's descent subsided and he felt the need to turn himself around, head up, and swim toward what he guessed to be the surface. Breath gone, he kicked hard with his feet, lifted his arms, and paddled up.

The cut on his chest, his angrily protesting limbs, and the lack of fresh air provoked darkness to rim his mind. With three of his senses deadened, he could only feel the distress of his body and hear the bubbles around him. He wondered if he would black out. The movement of his limbs felt strangely distant, and the darkness he stared into fell into deepest obsidian. He would sleep forever. . . .

And then—

Water streamed down his face and ringed his neck. A sudden heat burst upon his cheek, and though his eyes were still closed, the darkness that had once deepened was torched away. He opened his mouth, discovered it was unencumbered by water, and drew in a loud, badly needed breath. Warm, moist air filled his lungs. A hand lifted above the water then came back down into it with a mild splash.

Thank you, dear Lord, and all the saints. Thank you.

He flickered his eyes open and found himself staring back at the north curtain wall of the castle.

"Christopher!" His name had been called from behind him. Was it Doyle?

He tilted his head up and saw an arrow soar down from the battlements of the keep—directly toward him.

Christopher took in a quick breath and ducked under the water, pushing upward with his hands to drive himself as deep as he could in the pair of seconds he had to avoid the shaft.

He heard the arrow *ka-thunk* into the water somewhere behind him, and then a trio of *ka-thunks* followed.

Then more arrows sank into the moat, a spate of iron-tipped heads probing for his tender flesh.

The fall had disoriented him so much that he had forgotten all about the archers.

Turn around and swim you fool! Toward the shore!

Where is it?

He cocked his head left, then right, not wanting to open his eyes but forcing them open. That didn't matter. The water was too murky to see where it tapered off, and as of now he could not touch bottom. He needed to surface for more air anyway. He headed up, thrusting once, twice with feet and hands, and then his head burst from the water.

He replenished his breath as his gaze blurred, then focused on the shoreline, a half turn of his body left.

"There he is!" a distant voice cried in Saxon.

Ka-thunk! Ka-thunk ka-thunk!

Christopher dived back under the water as the bowfire intensified. He swam forward, paddled with what energy was left in his exhausted, beaten, fallen, and bruised body. There wasn't much to draw on.

He heard the arrows continue and ignored their sounds as they hit the water, favoring the voice in his mind that repeated the simple word, simple action: *SWIM!*

His right hand plunged into the mire on bottom of the moat. He brought his leg down to discover the mud was not far below, maybe only a yard. But if he stood there would be no footing. He had to swim to the very edge of the channel in order to gain any kind of reasonable purchase. So he continued on, head low, hands and feet dredging through the warm ooze.

"That's him! It's him!"

He recognized that voice, thankfully Celt, thankfully close, definitely Doyle.

His chest ran aground on the harder edge of the shoreline. He lifted his head from the water and looked up toward the nearest mantlet, less than five yards away. A misfired arrow meant for him streaked high over his shoulder and struck the wooden shield, then from behind it, an archer ducked out, his bow drawn. The bowman let his arrow fly in answer. Behind the archer, another man ventured a peek. A very wet man with a bandage on his right hand.

"See him! There he is, right there!" Doyle pointed at Christopher while yelling to someone unseen behind the shield. "Help him!"

It was a relatively short distance from the moat to safety, but as it was, there wasn't enough of Christopher left to get him there. He legs felt like they weighed as much as boulders, and his arms were the lighter (for all the difference it made) weight of wall stones. Now he tasted the moat in his mouth, and it made his cheeks sink in nausea. He pulled himself a little farther out of the mud, his waist making it onto dry ground.

Fwit! Two-second delay. *Thump!* The arrow narrowly missed his head and landed just past him. Christopher gripped the sunken shaft and used it to hoist himself farther out of the moat.

I have to stand and run!

What about Doyle? Isn't he sending help?

The Saxon arrow fire was too heavy now for anyone to reveal himself from behind the mantlet. The shield was already impaled so many times that its oak surface was obscured by a multicolored hue of arrow fletching.

Saturated in muck, Christopher rose to his hands and knees. The horridly curious idea of looking over his shoulder at the enemy archers entered his mind, and he shut it out by putting his arms and legs into motion.

The shore ahead had been struck many times by fallen arrows, some having impaled the earth neatly, sticking up at varying degrees, others lying horizontal. If he could stand and run, he might be able to kick a straight path through the arrows, but crawling meant he'd have to thread through them—a much longer and arduous path home.

He couldn't stand. Remaining on hands and knees, he weaved his way onward, his pace steady but excruciatingly slow. He wiped his face free of more mud, blinked away the blurriness, and kept going. The bellows continued from behind him, and he swore he could hear Seaver screaming his name.

It would be ironic if you killed me now, little man. But I think I'm going to make it.

Christopher heard the arrow a breath before it hit him, catching him in the right calf, causing him to fall onto his side and extend the leg. White-hot pain shot chaotically up and down the limb. He looked back over his shoulder, down at the leg, almost not believing what he saw. His hand immediately found the arrow, locked around the base of it where it met his skin. He gave a little tug—*DEAR LORRRDDD!*—and howled like he never had before. The arrow would not budge.

"Finish him!" a voice echoed in Saxon.

"He's down. We've got to go out!"

"No. He's done! Leave him!"

"I won't!"

He listened to Doyle arguing with one of the archers, and could do nothing more than pray his blood brother would come. He tried to breathe steadily, but his pant was involuntary. A new world of pain shed all of its merciless misery onto him.

Fwit! Three . . . he looked up . . . two . . . the arrow fell perfectly, curving down toward him . . . one—he tucked his head into his chest . . . *thump!*

Christopher lifted his head and the back of it came to rest upon the arrow sunk in the ground, three or four inches away him. *Fwit! Fwit! Fwit! Fwit-Fwit-Fwit!*

Too many arrows. No more strength. Leg on fire. Sleep. Must go. Eyes heavy. Stomach turning.

No! I've come too far!

I'm going to die. I'm going to die alone, on the ground. My son will never know me.

He didn't hear the shuffle of Doyle's approach, only felt his friend's forearms go suddenly under his armpits and hoist him in one deft effort to his feet.

"Come on!" Doyle said, his voice hoarse from shouting. He slung one of Christopher's arms over his shoulder and drove him on toward the mantlet.

Christopher knew he was limping, but could not feel his wounded leg below the knee. In fact, he could not think of a single part of his body that *felt* normal. All of it was either bruised, covered in rank-smelling mud, wet, or strained to its very limits. Even his ears itched with water in them, and his nose was clogged with something other than mucus. He was an unknown kind of desperate animal, clinging to one of his kind for life.

They rounded the corner of the mantlet and Doyle lowered him quickly to the ground. He rolled to his side, keeping his arrow-impaled leg in the air. Out of the numbness came a short spasm of agony, like a breaker along the beach, and then it was gone.

There were a half dozen men behind the mantlet, unkempt but not weary. Two of them were peasant levy who wore the hapless faces of those forced into combat and the cheap, tattered tunics that betrayed their lot. The others, armored and well armed, went about their business of shooting arrows with quiet efficiency.

The oldest of the archers, his long, thin gray hair lashed back in the breeze, leaned over Christopher. "Shot in the calf, then, eh?" he asked rhetorically, inspecting Christopher's wound. He had a strong lisp, hard to ignore. "It's not all that bad. You'll live." He smiled, nearly every other tooth missing. "Might even keep the leg." The man straightened and then turned away.

For the first time in his life, Christopher wished he *would* black out. The archer's lispy nonchalance chilled him so much that he just wanted to sleep it all away. He rested his head on his arm, closed his eyes, then concentrated on the sun-spotted darkness.

"Neil's gone to fetch Hallam on the east side," Doyle said.

"Yes," Christopher whispered. "You both made it."

"Well that's a silly question!"

He was going. He felt it. Thank St. George, sleep at last. "Rest now. So tired. I'm sorry."

"Sleep well then, blood brother. You don't want to be awake when Hallam plucks this arrow out of your leg . . ."

Sound faded. He swam not in the moat, but in a black sea of naught. It was . . . bliss.

10

"I believe he's still sleeping."

"He can't be. The moon is up already."

"Why should that matter? You'd sleep longer if you were him."

"No I wouldn't. I'd sleep just as long—if I were him."

"He must be hungry."

"I'll bet he suffers his leg the way I do my hand. Thank the saints, Hallam says he'll be all right."

"Are you sure? Look at how pale he is."

"Hallam said he bled a lot."

"I wonder if he knows Brenna is here?"

"Shush, you fool. We don't want him to hear."

Christopher had been aware of the presence of Doyle and Neil for some time. He had stirred three or four times during his sleep in the tent, at first vaguely cognizant of the coming and going of Hallam, and then he had opened his eyes the last time the doctor had checked on him, probably a quarter hour ago. He feigned sleep to hear what his friends said when they thought he was in the distant land of dreams.

Doyle was right. His leg throbbed, a dull thud that

mimicked the beat of his heart. When he shifted the limb, the knives came and prodded him from all angles, and he imagined they were held by Saxon spirits under the direction of Seaver and Kenric; those two were not through with him yet. He lay on his back but could not get comfortable on the many layers of blankets beneath him. There was no trestle bed, but he doubted a mattress would have made a difference. The bruises kept him shifting, and when he moved, the leg kept him moving some more. It was, in actuality, very difficult to remain still. But the fact that he appeared to be asleep cursed him with a piece of information from the outside world: Brenna was in Shores.

Why? How? It left him puzzled. And it dawned on him that the confrontation was now at the fore. Perhaps she was just outside the tent, waiting to come in! How would he react to her? He knew she would fall to her knees and want to minister to him, run a soft steady hand over his forehead and kiss him slowly, gingerly, on the cheek. How would he respond? What did he really feel for her in the new, life-changing light of Marigween and his son? What should he do?

One of Seaver's disembodied demons struck his knee quite suddenly with his blade, and Christopher rolled onto his side and released a grunt.

"Christopher?" Neil called. "Can you hear me?"

His eyelids shuttered slowly open, and the semblance of his two friends sitting on the tent floor bedside him tightened into candlelit clarity. He lifted his head from his pillow, moved to sit up, could not, then opted to rest his weight on his forearm. "I think so . . . "

"What do you mean, you think so?" Doyle asked. "Of course you can."

He swallowed away the aftertaste of something bitter the doctor had made him swallow earlier, grimaced, then asked: "Brenna's here?"

Doyle looked at Neil, then shook his head in silent anger.

Neil caught Doyle's look, then shrugged. "What's the difference whether he finds out now or later?" He faced Christopher and nodded. "She's with Orvin. They sit before a cookfire near the eastern forest."

Christopher drew in a deep breath, sighed, then took the weight off his arm, let himself fall onto the blankets and pillow. He closed his eyes. "How did she get here? Why did she come?"

"We don't know," Doyle answered. "You'll find that out, though, won't you?" Christopher had never heard a more rhetorical question, nor one that conveyed such a powerfully heart-wrenching portent.

He opened his eyes, stared at the ceiling of the tent, then frowned. "I'm afraid so."

"You were going to have to tell her sometime," Doyle reminded. "It might as well be this eve."

"Do the words too much, too soon have any meaning for you?" he asked his friend.

"Not for me. I've already made my appointment to see King Arthur and I will be in his tent before the moon is overhead. I'm ready to get on with my life— or my death." Doyle spoke coldly, with enigmatic bravery.

"And you're not afraid?" Christopher asked, stealing a look at his blood brother.

"Of course he's not," Neil answered for Doyle. "He was ready to die when he first threw himself to the Saxons. He's had even *more* time to prepare."

"You don't like me, do you, Neil?" Doyle asked, incensed.

"Once I admired you. But now . . . I'd rather associate with someone who wants to live. Phelan loved life more than anything," Neil's voice cracked, "yet he had to die. You *want* to die, yet you're still here." Neil turned from Doyle, dropped his gaze to his lap. "Dear God, show me the justice here, for I fail to see it now."

A chill dropped from Christopher's head uninterrupted to his toes, sparing no part of his body from its rippling wrath. Death was attached to the wintry sensation; it was a feeling like no other.

No. Not Phelan. Not him.

Though he heard Neil correctly, he refused to believe it. "Phelan is dead?"

The bird had wanted very badly to go along on the rescue mission. He was the one who had convinced Neil to go after he had fallen ill. He had been so young, so courageous and determined—so similar to Christopher. There was so much of life he never experienced. No, he couldn't be dead.

"He's dead, Christopher. Dead and buried. There was a service for him, and about a score of others who died during the first assault on the castle. Phelan died not in battle, but of a damned problem with his stomach! It's not fair!" Neil turned his head away, rubbed his eyes.

Christopher lifted a palm to his own face and covered his eyes. He wanted to weep, and was amazed at how easily the tears spilled from his eyes. It was always that way when he was very tired or ill; the simplest things would make him cry—though he would admit the fact to no one. Now, the death of a friend brought on a torrent. He grieved silently, as did Neil. Doyle made not a sniffle. It seemed he was more imately connected to death than either Christopher or Neil, as if he were already dead and his body merely forgot to cease functioning.

Then again, Doyle dampered his pain, locked it up until it finally burst. His guilt over killing Innis and Leslie and subsequent suicide run to the Saxons was a crystalline example of that.

Christopher dried his cheeks, then, still facing the tent top, told Neil: "At least Phelan's last thoughts of us had to be fond ones—especially his thoughts of you, Neil."

"Who cares what his last thoughts were! He shouldn't have died. I'm sitting next to the man who should be dead!"

"I'll let that go, Neil, if you'll stop wishing me dead," Doyle said. "Besides, you may get your wish anyway."

"Neil, listen to me—"

"I have for too long, Christopher. I'm tired of hearing your voice."

"Phelan died knowing that he had inspired you to do something that he believed in very much. You were as true a friend to him as any I can think of. There is so much honor in you, so much respect I have for you. Don't you realize what a great service you paid Phelan? You championed his cause. You risked your life. You remained true. Those are the qualities of a knight, and if there is one man I should recommend to Arthur for knighthood, it is you. You'll never be a banner knight, but simple knighthood is something I'm sure has been a dream of yours." Christopher forced himself to a sitting position, not realizing that Hallam had stitched the cut on his chest. The wound tightened, the skin pulling and creasing, and he thought he could hear the cackle of a Saxon phantom. But the moment was too important to let it be overthrown by physical discomforts. "And if you have anyone to thank for bringing out the best in you, it is Doyle." Christopher's grin was wan and wanted badly to fall into a grimace because of the pain in his torso. He shivered into the pain and held his countenance.

"Why should I thank him?" Neil asked incredulously.

"Simple," Doyle said. "If I hadn't been captured, you would have never set foot in the castle. There would have been no test for you." He leveled his gaze on Christopher. "Clever word play, squire. And you're right. Neil was a true friend to Phelan. I, on the other hand, betrayed you, caused nothing but problems and pain for you. And so it is I am to do my penance." He held up his freshly bandaged hand. "And I will wear the scar of my sins for the rest of my life—however long that is. In a short while I will kneel before the mercy of Arthur. But it is strange. I am willing without contest to accept whatever he feels due me. I took the lives of two innocent men, boys really, like me. Perhaps an eye for an eye will be his judgment. I should run, but staying makes me feel better than I ever have since coming down from the Mendips. The burdens of my heart and mind will be lifted. At last I will atone for my sins."

"Let me talk to Arthur first," Christopher said.

"And what will you say?" Doyle snickered. "That I was a gentle murderer?"

"I'll tell him it was the ale. I'll tell him you didn't mean it. You didn't know what you were doing. I'll tell him everything about your past, your brother. I'll tell him about Weylin, the jewelry merchant who raised you, and the problem you have with your real parents. I can speak to him in a way that you cannot."

Doyle stood. "It's too late."

Christopher gritted his teeth and then trembled. "Don't go."

"If he does sentence me to the gallows tree, I'm sure there will be a moment for me to say good-bye, so we can spare ourselves that now." He spun on his heel, crossed to the tent flaps, ducked, and stepped outside.

The slightest bit of weight on Christopher's wounded leg prompted the sharp tips of the Saxon anlaces. There was no way he could rise and go after Doyle. He fixed Neil with an urgent look. "Stop him."

Neil folded his arms across his chest. "I won't. No one can stop him. No one."

Christopher wanted to say something more, but thoughts wouldn't connect to words during the rage that festered in him. He was angry at Doyle's dire need to rush off and be judged. Why couldn't he wait until the morrow? Yes, Christopher had urged him to confess his sins to Arthur, to release the burden of the secret from Christopher's heart and mind and his own, but a half-day's delay could mean the difference between life and death for Doyle. But Doyle didn't seem to care. Was Neil right? Did he really want to die? Was his impetuousness carefully planned? Christopher felt he would never know.

He sighed and sighed again, asking himself where the triumphant return was. They had escaped alive from the castle with Doyle. Christopher dreamed that that act would inspire every soldier in the army, that they would cheer for him as he extended his blade in victory. But here he was, wounded in bed, grieving over the loss of one friend, while another went off to his fate. And not far away was someone who had given him her heart, and now he would have to return it to her. At the moment, he did not feel bound by his duty. He felt choked by it.

Neil pushed himself up. "I've already eaten three times and I'm still not full. Would you like me to bring you back something?"

"Yes. Send it along with Orvin. I wish to speak to him—and then . . . to Brenna."

"I'll come back after you've spoken to both."

"Do that. I'll need you."

Neil was about to part the tent flaps when Christopher called out: "Hold."

The barbarian turned back; his brow rose in a query.

"So you were wrong about me."

Neil's grin curved slowly, but eventually came. "I guess I was. You didn't get me killed."

"And how was your drop from the keep?"

Neil closed his eyes and paused a long moment before answering. Then he burst out: "Never again, Christopher! Never again!"

As Neil left, Christopher lowered himself slowly onto his blankets. He let his eyelids fall shut and drew in a long, steady breath. The rise of his chest sent a spider trail of pain across his stitches.

I cannot even breathe without pain!

Forget that. You have much larger worries.

Christopher told himself Orvin would come. Orvin would tell him how to deal with Brenna. Everything would be all right very, very soon. He lay in fervent wait for the old man, thanking God Orvin was a part of his life and present to guide him once more.

11

He heard the soft, scuffling approach of someone, then lifted his head and opened his eyes as the tent flaps parted.

She moved inside and stood, poised, gaping, raven black hair framing her sun-browned face. "I . . . I can't believe I'm looking at you . . . "

Christopher felt the same, but for, of course, a very different reason.

What happened to Orvin? I cannot talk to her without his guidance!

Brenna rushed to his beside, fell to her knees, seized one of his hands in both of hers, then kissed the top of it long and hard. Her eyes were tightly closed, and a tiny, passionate moan reverberated in her throat.

He shivered, not knowing whether or not to pull the hand away. Before he could decide, she released it and looked up at him. "You don't know how far, how far I've come for this moment," she said. This was her heaven—in this dirty little tent, with him, a beaten and stitched-up squire.

Once her love, he would now be her Lucifer.

Won't you let go of my hand? Please?

"I-I-I know you wanted to, to speak to Orvin, but he, he urged me, he urged me on first. I hope it's . . . all right." She had trouble regulating her breath, and she tripped and backtracked over her words.

Her mood would soon change.

But wait a minute. Do I have to tell her now?

Why not now? What is Orvin really going to tell me?

He'll probably just tell me to tell her!

Perhaps he knows a clever way to do it.

There is no clever way to be honest. There is only

honesty and falsehood. Half-truths will not work now. She must know, for the longer she doesn't, the harder will be her suffering afterward.

I want so badly to hold her when I tell her, to make her somehow forgive me. But I cannot mislead her. Besides, she will not forgive me. I delude myself if I believe that.

"No, no, it's—" He lost his thought.

"Good," she finished. "I must tell you, everyone is talking about what you did. No one can believe you're alive—myself included!"

"To be honest, I don't *feel* completely alive yet," he said, smiling mildly over the quip.

"You look horribly wonderful to me!" she said, joy forming a reflective glaze in her eyes.

Tell her.

"That is *quite* a compliment," he said, then cowardly shifted paths. "Tell me then, why did you come? How did you manage it?"

No! Don't continue this slip-back-into-her-arms chat! Cut it off now! Where's your verbal sword?

"I love you so much, Christopher. And I could not wait for you any longer. Wynne and I borrowed a pair of horses and made it as far as Glastonbury, but I sent her home from there. She'd hurt herself."

"What did your parents say about your going?"

Coward! Tell her you have a son!

"I never told them beforehand."

Christopher formed his lips into an O and exhaled through them. The way he had risked everything for Doyle, so had Brenna for him. She had completely discarded her old life just to see him. Her love for him was that strong. She cared nothing about the punishment she would receive once she returned to Gore. This *was* the moment she had been waiting for.

Brenna was never more vulnerable.

Now I can't tell her! It'll crush her! She'll probably want to kill herself!

No she won't. If she finds out from someone else, she will. It is not your fault she came. It is your fault you courted her while you courted Marigween.

"You shouldn't have done that," Christopher said. "Now your parents are probably worried sick. And when you do return—you know what will happen."

"Perhaps I won't return. I believe I can stay here and serve the army. I'll send word to my parents by merchant or carrier pigeon and let them know I'm all right. But I'm not worried." Her next words came out in a tone Christopher had never heard from her before—the words of a woman, not a girl. "Christopher, coming here on my own has, for the first time in my life, made me feel strong. I thought of myself and what I wanted, instead of others. And it feels very, very good."

"I'm not worthy of the sacrifices you made."

"A squire as well as a knight is *modest* and true," she replied. "I am aware of the adages you live by."

"I have not been true," he said.

There. Now it's going to happen. St. Michael? St. George? St. Christopher? Lord?

The smile on her face did not fade, but it softened a tiny bit. "What do you mean?"

Ease her forthcoming pain.

There were so many places he could begin. He could tell her now, flat out, he had a son with Marigween. Or he could drift back to the days when Brenna had been at Gore while he had still been in Shores. He could tell her that while he had only seen her occasionally, he had seen Marigween daily and had let himself fall under her spell. He had not guarded his love carefully enough. He was wrong and willing to admit that to her, wanted to admit that to her, but how? How should he say any of it? Where to begin? Where to end?

"Come on," she urged. "Why the somber face? What have you done wrong? Oh, I know. You disobeyed King Arthur. I heard you had asked his permission to rescue Doyle and he denied you. But you went anyway. Your friend Neil told me about that. Is that what you're worried about?"

Slowly, Christopher shook his head in negation. "Disobeying a direct order from the king is certainly a punishable offense, but I doubt he will hang me."

"Then what?" she asked again, and the smile was completely gone. "What's wrong, Christopher? Aren't you glad to see me? You've hardly reacted. You barely smile. You quip, and now you tell me you have not been true. Have you not been true to me?"

She's making it easy for you. Let her.

Honesty and falsehood. No half-truths.

Christopher nodded.

She let out a shuddery sigh. "I know you've been away so long, and I hoped your gaze would not be caught by another. But the first time you left, I didn't remain true to you but you forgave me and understood. I think . . . I want . . . to do the same. Tell me, was it someone along the road? Perhaps even a Saxon woman? And is it over?"

"You and I," he began, then paused to gather thoughts, thoughts that demanded to be voiced, "what we once had, will never be again."

"No," she retorted, a quiver audible in her voice. "Don't tell me that. You don't have to shove me away. We can rekindle our love. It'll be better now. Stronger! I don't care about the past. I care about now!"

Her will drove him back against an internal wall, pinning him against abiding stone. Escape would only come through truth. And he would create a universe of suffering for her.

He would break her heart.

"Hear these words, then," he said, "and let me know if they change the present: Lady Marigween, daughter of the late Lord Devin, is the mother of my child. We have a son. I courted her at the same time I courted you—before I even left for the Mendip Hills. I returned from battle, only to discover that I was a father."

The news brought her to her feet. She opened and closed her mouth twice to speak, but only air came out. Her gaze panned around the room, as if she were searching for some signpost that would tell her how to react.

Muscles in his arms shaking under the strain, he pushed himself up, trying to keep his chest from bending. Trying was the operative word. The stitches sung a tune of agony so high it was beyond hearing. "I didn't mean for any of this to happen," he said, then wanted to retract the words. Too late.

"You didn't mean to court Marigween? And let me ask you something—what about Lord Woodward? Everyone knows she's betrothed to him!" A tear leaked from the corner of her left eye, slid in a single burst off her cheek, then dripped onto her shift.

"I meant to say, I didn't want to hurt you. I made a mistake."

"And now I have to pay for it." More tears fell, and she began furiously to wipe them off her cheeks. "Tell me, who do you love more?"

By answering the question, Christopher felt he would be murdering a part of himself, a slice of the past he wanted to maintain fondly in his heart but realized he never would. And it was his fault. He honestly didn't know who he loved more, but he did know he loved them differently:

His love for Marigween was alive and ever growing, founded on something they shared together—their son. The path ahead was steep and winding for them, but Christopher was determined to make them a family. His family. That was something he had lost with the death of his parents, but could have again. He was ready to face the challenge and the responsibility.

His love for Brenna was drawn from a deep well of the past, a time when life was as exciting as it was tragic. His parents had died, he'd become a squire in training and had met Brenna. She had been a breathtaking part of the new course that fate had handed him. She fitted perfectly into the empty half of his heart. Orvin had warned him not to look too deeply into her eyes—but he had. He had fallen in love with her, but the fact that her love had waned had triggered a gnawing darkness deep inside him. He did not trust her as he had. And that had made him raise his guard and had set him one step back from giving his heart completely to her again. Marigween did not know it, but she had exploited that tenuous link he had with Brenna, and it had been easy for him to shift from one set of arms to another, to kiss and hold and caress someone who had never wronged him.

Maybe that was why he'd courted Marigween.

But maybe not. Had it simply been lust? Lust that drives knights and beggars to ruin? Had it been the thrill of something so wrong, so against the church and the code of knight- and squirehood? Perhaps it had been his distrust of Brenna, lust, and the thrill? Perhaps it was something he hadn't even thought of yet.

He was lost and not certain about anything except

the facts. The whys would remain obscured until
years passed; then he would be able to look back on
the present with an objectivity and a reason unfettered by his roiling emotions. However, one realization was made known to him: there was nothing
more fragile in this realm than a relationship; it must
be nurtured and tended to constantly. A union must
be treated with the utmost respect, and with an
intrinsic kind of love—not a love of the body, but a
love of the soul. Absence had not made his heart
grow fonder; it had only caused him to find another
heart, and to abandon his loyalty. True, he and
Brenna were both victims of circumstances, but he
had made the choice to court Marigween.

A squire must own up to his responsibilities.

And his mistakes.

I know that!

Christopher knew what he was doing was right—as
much as Brenna didn't deserve it. As much as it murdered the past they shared, the present moment, and
the future plans they had made together. He was the
orchestrator of *their* death.

"I asked you a question," she said.

"Brenna, I don't want to hurt you, I . . . I don't
want to answer. If you really want to know the truth,
I love you both. But differently. I cannot explain it."

"I told myself a countless number of times I would
never find a person like you. Never. There is no one I
love more, no one I respect more and want to serve
more than you." Her gaze left him for the floor.
"Now you make me feel like a fool." She shifted away
from him and lowered her head.

And then she whirled around, dropped to her
knees, and grabbed him by his bare shoulders.
Shaking him, her face mere inches away from his, she

screamed, "How could you? How could you have done this to me? I came so far for you!"

"I'm sorry," he said, his face twisted in the suffering her shaking caused him. "Please, Brenna . . . "

She released his shoulders and collapsed on top of him, burying her face in his neck. As she sobbed, he felt the cool tinkle of her tears as they touched his skin. His thoughts charged back to the day he had met her outside March and Torrey's hut. She'd worn a headband of dark leather that had matched her hair, that raven black hair. She had told him that her name meant raven maid. She had spoken to him first. And she was so beautiful and smelled so wonderful and everything that was Christopher had leapt into the air and come back down, and then had leapt again. He thought of their midnight rendezvous in the dungeon, how they had nearly been caught by the guards. Then there had been the kiss, the long passionate kiss, their first true embrace. He remembered he had said good-bye to her and had told her to wait for him, that he would return from battle. He knew he had had to come back, if only to stop her tears.

But there was no way to stop Brenna's tears. Or his own. He wept, wept for the love lost, the memories, the simple looks she would toss his way, the tone in which she uttered his name, the softness of her hair and smoothness of her skin, the sweet honey of her lips, the way her body fitted so neatly against his when they stood embracing, as if they were truly two parts of a whole.

Her half of him was gone.

It had to be. It had to be.

She slid off of him, wiped her reddening cheeks clear of tears, sniffled, then stood. "Cry, Christopher. You should. I don't know what to say now. I guess farewell."

He swallowed, then rubbed knuckles over his own tearful eyes. "Wait."

"What more is there?"

He heard the question and realized there wasn't anything more. But he didn't want her to go. He felt too miserable. He wanted somehow to atone for what he'd done. What could he say? What could he do? He didn't just want her to leave, a sort of "sorry, I don't love you anymore . . . good-bye" ending to it all.

Was there an easy way, a gentle way to part?

He knew there would be nothing harder on his heart than to see her turn and leave, knowing he had just taken her love for him, thrown it on the ground, and stomped it into dust. The guilt of that was oppressive.

Who am I fooling? There's nothing more. There's no easy way. I am not gentle now. I am full of guilt and regret, but true to what I must do.

I will have to live with this. It is not unbearable, thought it seems so now. Let her go. From this tent. From your heart.

"There's, um—" he stammered, "I-I guess you are right."

Christopher closed his eyes, not wanting to watch her go. He thought sparing himself the very last image of her would make it a little easier. He listened to her feet over the smooth earth, heard her pull the tent flaps back and move past them.

He kept his eyes closed, and his mind wandered back to a frozen lake, to a cool winter's eve, to a mittened hand in his own, to a shivery voice full of promise and hope and love. "I'll wait for you, Christopher."

I'm sorry, Brenna.

"I'll never find anyone like you!"

I'm sorry!

"How could you do this to me?"

I'm sorry!
"You make me feel like a fool!"
I'm sorry!
"What else is there?"
"I guess . . . you are right."
She's gone. She's gone . . . I hurt her. God and all the saints above, forgive me.

He knew the suffering of the battlefield, had heard the last gasps of bloodied and mangled friends, touched the blood of his own fiery wounds, and dreaded the loss of his kinsman as much as he feared for his own life. But the pain he felt now was immeasurable, and the battlefield was a sanctuary compared to its black wrath.

It never felt worse to be home.

12

Soon after Brenna left, Neil returned to Christopher's tent. He questioned his friend about why Orvin had not come. Neil quoted the old knight: "'The young saint's eyes are clear, the vision of his future unobstructed now.'" And with that, Orvin had turned and left, bound for his tent somewhere in the eastern wood.

Orvin had deliberately left Christopher on his own to deal with Brenna. At first, Christopher was hurt and insulted that his master did not offer any guidance, but then he realized that by leaving him alone, Orvin had forced him to call upon his own inner strength to shape a small part of is own destiny. With that realization came peace, and though his sleep was troubled by his beaten body, his mind surrendered to the night.

The growing warmth of the tent advised him it was daybreak, and he lay there awake for some time listening to the pipits and larks proclaiming what must be a clear sky, a radiant sun, and a gentle, friendly breeze.

The rattle of armor drew near, and sunlight wedged into the tent. A bronze-armored figured lowered his head and stepped inside, and when he straightened, Christopher saw it was the king.

Immediately, Christopher rolled off his side and pushed himself up, about to stand. A night's rest had done little to alleviate the pain of his wounds, and the movement caused a flash of agony to darken his view. The ground tilted down a moment, then rose level. The dizziness passed.

"Do not get up, Christopher," Arthur said.

"My liege, I did not expect—"

"There is a battle going on outside, but there has also been a small one waging in my heart." Arthur tightened his lips and stroked his beard. "I have already passed judgment on your friends Doyle and Neil, and now I must do so on you." He stepped closer and leaned over, the armor constricting him from lowering himself too far. "It's a lonely life, Christopher, truly it is. There is no companionship in the decision-making of a king. One decides and hands down—and is judged by—one's decisions. Oftentimes I turn to others for guidance, only to hear what I already know: that the decision is mine and I know what I must do."

Christopher understood all too well what Arthur spoke of; his evening with Brenna involved just that kind of decision-making, the most painful sort of all: decisions that involve the ones you love.

He wanted to ask Arthur what the fate of his

friends was, but was too scared to do so. He found himself intent on his own punishment. Arthur's tone led him to believe the worst.

"What must you do with me, then, my lord?" he asked, feeling his heartbeat steadily increase and a shiver, sparked by a mind picture of a gallows tree, rip across his shoulders.

"You have won and failed all in the same day. And you have loved and lost, so I've heard. Not only that, but Sir Orvin tells me of a child—a child that is yours, a bastard son not unlike me. It seems you have a great many more responsibilities and problems than being in trouble with the king. But . . . I cannot ignore what you did. Yes, the information your friend Doyle told me you discovered is valuable. Had you not been inside to see the Saxons' supplies and estimate their numbers, I doubt very much we would have found them out on our own. And for that, I thank you. But for disobeying me, I break you. You are no longer squire of the body. I am going to give you to Woodward. You will serve him now."

"But lord, how am I to explain my—"

"Chamber doors have been opened and closed, new paths beaten while old ones were discarded. You will remain in Woodward's service. I have chosen another squire of the body to replace you—until you earn back my trust. Once worthy of the title, I believe you will be squire of the body again—in time."

Christopher lowered his gaze, dejected, stripped of honor. "Yes, lord." Then he added, "Who is to be the new squire?"

"Robert of Queen's Camel."

"Robert?" Christopher strained to remember who the boy was. Perhaps a newcomer. He must be. But what did he do to deserve such an honor? Christopher planned to find out.

Arthur nodded. "Yes. He shall become my squire of the body."

Christopher could not dampen his pout. "As you wish. May I ask, what of my friend Doyle?"

"He instructed me not to inform you of my judgment—he wanted to do so himself."

"Lord, if there is anything—"

"Before you beg for mercy for your friend, speak to him." He stretched a bit, flinching under the weight of the armor. "Heal yourself. Then go to your son. I only wish I could have known my own father. Make sure your son knows his." In a clatter, Arthur turned and exited the tent.

"But, lord! How am I to tell Woodward about Marigween . . . and my son?"

How am I to tell anyone about them?

13 Two days passed before word came to Christopher that Doyle wanted to speak to him. No one had seen or heard from the archer since. The message came from Neil, who rushed into the tent and spoke in a voice made ragged by his recent run.

"Where is he?" Christopher asked.

"He's down near the Cam. I've borrowed a supply cart and can take you there."

"Let's go."

Christopher limped out of the tent, smack into the brilliance of midmorning sun. He squinted as Neil helped him up onto the flatbed. A single rounsey was hitched to the cart, and by the looks of the animal, it had not been fed or groomed in several days.

"Are you sure this beast will get us down there?"

"He will," Neil called back. "Or I shall steal another!"

"I thought you said you borrowed this cart?" Christopher asked.

"That's right. That's what I said."

They took the long path around the ramparts of the castle, the one which gradually descended to the sun-browned grass of the tourney field. The dirt road was beset by potholes, many of them caused by the vast numbers of men who had recently moved through the area. Christopher had a far too intimate relationship with each and every one of those ditches, for the vibrations caused by them sent unseen awls through his injured leg and chest.

"Can you slow us a little?" Christopher asked, above the rustling and creaking of the cart and the thumping of the rounsey's hooves.

"Why?"

"The road is wreaking havoc with my wounds!"

"He won't wait long," Neil cried.

"What do you mean? Where's he going?"

"Blast! I've gone and done it again!"

"What?" Christopher asked, growing more anxious.

"Don't tell him I told you, please!" Neil said with more than a little fervor.

"He's going away, then?" But even as he voiced the question, Christopher had already guessed the answer. "Arthur banished him."

"And a lenient sentence it is," Neil replied.

Christopher sighed to himself. "Thank God."

"He'll live. But I doubt we'll ever see him again. This is your last chance. Does it justify me stealing this cart so you wouldn't have to hobble down to the river?"

Christopher sullenly nodded.

Neil forgot to slow the cart, but Christopher paid the fault no heed. He was focused so far away from his wounds that they could tear open and he might not notice.

Good-bye, Doyle.

Why? Why did you have to do it?

Don't tell me it's not your fault!

You could have risen to the challenge of your problems instead of drowning them in drink!

And why did you have to kill? Why, Doyle? Why?

Don't tell me you didn't know what you were doing! You did! You took out all of your anger on those two boys. Even though a dark side of me feels Innis deserved to die, it was not right. Leslie was an innocent. An innocent you killed. Your brother Baines was the one who gave me my first training, the first person to die in battle with me, the only person to gift me with a great sword. Doyle, you were the one who was supposed to carry on the tradition of Baines, but you failed your brother's memory. And you failed me.

You never gave me a chance to help you, Doyle. You kept everything inside. You should have let me try. But no, I turn and I find you with Innis's blood on your hands. You should have let me help.

But I love you, blood brother. And I forgive you. But my forgiveness will not keep you in Shores. There may be a day we run into each other again. But things will never, ever be the same.

Christopher heard the loud buzzing of several

dragonflies, looked up, then realized they were already approaching the shoreline of the Cam.

In the distance, beyond the river, the rolling hillocks were wrapped in the still-lingering morning mist, the color in the beech and oak trees washed away to silhouette. The water seemed unusually peaceful, and the tall grasses and reeds rooted in the banks were reflected perfectly, not a single ripple distorting their shafts. Except for the hum of insects and call of distant birds, the only other sounds were made by the hooves of the rounsey and the steady iron-and-timber rattle of the cart.

A figure rose from beneath a beech tree a few yards away from the Cam. Christopher squinted and saw a white bandage on one of the figure's hands.

Doyle met Christopher and Neil with a closed-lipped grin, striding toward the cart in a new pair of brown breeches, new riding boots, and a clean linen shirt, the drawstring untied. His hair and beard were slick from sweat or a recent bath.

Neil slowed the rounsey to a stop as Doyle circled around the cart and offered his good hand to help Christopher down. As he did, he said, "Thanks for coming."

There was mist in the air, yes, but the tension and awkwardness were far thicker. Christopher would try to put an end to that immediately. Saying good-bye was hard enough; the moment did not have to be stiff.

"Did you think I wouldn't come?" Christopher replied, setting his good foot upon the spongy ground, following ever-so-gingerly with his wounded one. "I'm your blood brother."

"This won't take long," Doyle said.

"If you want me to remain here—" Neil began.

"That's fine, Neil," Doyle said. "We're going over

by the tree." For a second, Doyle regarded the grazing rounsey hitched to the cart. "And by the way, where did you get that filthy beast?"

"A blind man does not question the succor he receives from the sighted," Neil said in the tone of an irked monk.

"Indeed," Christopher chipped in. "Nor does a thief the booty he takes from the innocent."

At that, Neil averted his gaze.

"I know I am missing something here," Doyle said, "but never mind." He gestured with his head for Christopher to follow him toward the tree.

Christopher was not used to limping, and found there was an art to it, though it was an art he would never master. For the first time in a long while he envied something about Doyle: his unimpeded stride.

Out of breath, he made it to the tree and threw a hand up to lean upon it. He looked down at the modest pile that was Doyle's gear: a filled and fastened riding bag; a woolen cap; an arrow-filled quiver; a longbow; and . . . a leather flagon.

"What are you drinking today?" he asked, trying to keep his tone casual, but there was no mistaking why he queried.

"Spiced cider," Doyle said curtly.

"So why did you want to talk here?"

"You already know. Neil, I assume, told you?"

Christopher could not help smiling. "You know the barbarian too well."

"We both do." Doyle sighed, gazing up into the gnarled tree limbs. "How to do this . . . I don't know." He closed his eyes. "Christopher, I'm sorry."

He thought of saying something that would let Doyle off the hook, but he felt if he interrupted his friend, Doyle might never open up, and he wanted so badly for his friend to do it now—possibly their very last time together.

Doyle opened his eyes, but did not continue. He bent down and picked up his longbow, stepped around the pile of gear, then pushed the bow toward Christopher. "I never gave you a birthday present back in the spring, when we were up on the Mendips."

Christopher accepted the weapon, his mouth suddenly as dry and rough as the wooden bow in his hands.

"Don't think I'm giving this to you because I don't need it anymore, although that's true. That's my best bow, and I spent many nights waxing its string. And remember, it did save your life. I know you'll always remember my brother by the sword he gave you. Remember me by my bow. It is . . . what I was. What we were. We're all brothers, and I guess we think alike. I fretted over something more original to give, but I don't have much."

There was no sheen in Doyle's eyes, no rift in his voice, no nervous twitch in any part of his body. All of the pain Christopher knew he must be feeling at the moment was surrounded and kept at bay by Doyle's uncompromising will. There was a struggle going on within the archer, for his calm demeanor was too calm, his words too steady, his body too still. He acted the part of Doyle, but was not living it. His emotions were frozen.

But that was all right. That was Doyle. To ask anything more would be asking too much. Christopher abandoned the idea of Doyle pouring out his emotions and would accept whatever his friend did.

Perhaps that was just as well. The departure of Brenna from his life still ravaged his system; to suffer through another scene like that with Doyle would be

too much. Yet he knew, even before coming to the
tree, that that would not be the case. As Doyle had
said, this would not take long.

A friendship. Blood brothers. Many moons to forge
the union. One moment to end it. There was something unjust about that; it was an unwritten law, a
law inherent, a law that stretched back to the day the
world was born. And there was no changing it.

*Relationships are more fragile than anything else
in the realm. . . .*

"Where will you go?" Christopher asked.

"The Saxons moved through Falls, but word has it
they're rebuilding with the help of Nolan's army.
There'll be a lot of traders passing through. I was
raised a jewelry merchant. Maybe I can form a partnership with one, go to the coast, perhaps Bristol or
Bath."

Christopher began to weep inside. Doyle had
described the miserable life of a drifter, scavenging
one meal to the next. And the chances he would be
able to form a partnership with a merchant were
slim. They brought their sons into the trade; they did
not need outsiders, and those who were loners were
alone for a reason—they preferred it that way.

"I know I'm not in the position to ask," Doyle
added, "but do me one last service."

"Anything."

"When your son is old enough to understand, tell
him about me. Tell him how we fought gloriously
together. Tell him we were blood brothers. And most
of all, tell him there is nothing more important in the
world than your mother and your father. No matter
what happens, they will always be there for you. Never
deny yourself their love, and your own for them."

"That is no favor, Doyle. My son will come to

know you . . . through me." Christopher hated the way
he sounded; he knew his voice revealed his sorrow.

His friend moved toward him. Christopher
dropped the bow. Their embrace came hard, and as
he felt Doyle squeeze his body, he returned the
squeeze, damning to hell the stitches on his chest.

Doyle broke the embrace and gathered his things
from the ground. He slung the riding bag over his
shoulder and, for a moment, Christopher thought he
saw a tear in the archer's eye, but couldn't be sure.
Doyle would not look at him.

The archer started off without another word.
Christopher hobbled toward the cart with the longbow and quiver, repeatedly repressing the desire to
glance back at his friend. To look back was to hang
on, and he had to let go. He closed his eyes and asked
Saints Michael, George—and especially Christopher—
to watch over his friend.

EPILOGUE

Injured, and relieved of his duty as squire of the
body, Christopher saw no point in staying in Shores
even a day longer. Immediately upon his return from
saying good-bye to Doyle he sought Orvin, wanting
to ask his master if he would like to accompany him
back to Merlin's cave. It was time to be reunited with
his family. In fact, he needed Orvin to escort him; he
could not remember the exact way back. The first
time he had traveled to the cave he had been forced

into black sleep by Orvin. And he had fled the cave so abruptly the details of the trek were vague, a forest here, a crag there; how the landmarks related to each other had been forgotten. Once on the canyon road, Christopher knew he would be all right. But he would never find that road without the old knight.

Orvin sat on a dusty, warped cider barrel outside his tent, nibbling on a handful of wild berries. His gaze was fixed on nothing in particular, as he was hard in thought—most likely contemplating the taste of the berries. He scarcely looked up as Christopher hitched near. "Oh, the saint. Splendid."

"Orvin, I'm upset with you."

"Are you ready to leave now?" he asked after swallowing a berry.

How do you know I want to leave? "Uh, yes. But—"

"I've managed a courser, believe it or not. Your courser, the one you rode into battle. And a mule for myself. Our riding bags are filled and strapped. Now, if you'll help me up."

"Wait a moment. Why didn't you come to see me? I've been here two, no three days. And I've been unable to find you."

"When I'm needed, I am to be found. Otherwise—"

"I did need you."

"No, you did not. But *now* you do. Would you like one of these?" He extended a cupped hand filled with berries.

"No, I've learned to hate those. Now, please answer my question."

"Back to making demands, are we?"

Christopher softened. "I'm sorry. I meant no disrespect. I just thought—"

"You still need me for guidance, young saint. But there *are* things you must do alone." He nodded over his own words, a self-agreement. "But I believe you already know that, don't you?" He smiled, his gapped, yellow teeth stained purple from the berries.

"Can you help me now? Can you make it easier for me to go back and face Marigween after I ran out on her and our son?" Christopher took another step toward Orvin, close enough so that he could put his hand on the old man's shoulder. In a tone that exposed his desperation, he added, "Tell me you can make it easier."

"I can make it easier."

Christopher sighed. "Good."

"Now, if you want an answer to your question—"

"I thought you just answered it!"

"I did not. I repeated what you wanted me to say."

Christopher huffed. "No games, Orvin. Can you help me?"

"No." He raised a bony index finger. "But I am marvelous company for the ride—and you do need me to navigate our way to the cave. So help me up." He lowered the finger and proffered the hand.

Brooding, Christopher helped his master to his feet, hearing the old knight's bones crack once, twice, a third time. "Was that you?"

Orvin pushed the rest of his berries into his mouth then wiped his callused palm on his breeches. Chewing, he replied, "With the passing of each winter, I find my body acquires another creak or crack. I feel in due time my bones will rattle even louder than my armor used to."

"I believe they already do."

"That makes me feel wonderful," Orvin chided with a smile, "you young snake."

"Where are our mounts?"

"I'll show you."

As Orvin led him around the tent, Christopher

asked once again, "Are you sure you cannot tell me
what to say to Marigween upon my return?"

"Oh, of course I could tell you," Orvin answered,
"but I'm going to have too much fun seeing you
sweat for three days over it!"

"Orvin, you are supposed to teach, not taunt!"

"I'll tell you this. Open your heart to her. You are
balanced now. Look very deeply into her eyes. The
words will come."

They had spoken often of women, and Orvin had
always warned him about not looking too deeply into
a woman's eyes; it was the undoing of a man. "Are
you sure?"

"I am certain of nothing, save for my faith in you."

"Then may your faith make things come to pass."

"Trust yourself, Christopher," Orvin said. "Trust
yourself, and God."

He surprised her when he stepped into the back of
the cave. She was in the process of donning her shift.
Their son slept soundly in the trestle bed, his tiny
face a little fuller, a little rounder than Christopher
remembered.

"I'm sorry I—"

"I don't—"

"I don't know what to say either," Christopher
blurted out.

Marigween tied the shift behind her back,
smoothed the garment out over her waist and hips,
then wrung her hands. "Merlin assured me you
would return, but I doubted him."

"There is so much I want to say, I don't know how
to do it."

"It can wait a moment." She stepped quickly toward him, her shift billowing behind her. She extended an arm, and he knew a long-awaited embrace was imminent.

Then she drew back the arm and smacked him so hard across the face that the blow wrenched his head right, causing a muscle in his neck to painfully stretch and tighten.

"Don't *ever* leave me like that again," she said. "This is our child. *Ours.* We are both responsible."

The image of a starry night was superimposed over Marigween's face. A hand went reflexively to his cheek, to where the fire was. For a moment he thought about protesting the blow, but then he realized he had it coming. Certainly he had much *more* coming for what he had done. Marigween, thus far, had been merciful.

These are truly the days when we must all atone for our sins. Doyle, you are not alone.

Something warm trickled onto Christopher's upper lip, and his finger went to the warmth. Blood.

Guilt swept over Marigween's face. "Oh, no, I didn't mean to—let me get a wet rag." She turned from him and circled around the bed.

Christopher pinched his unbleeding nostril with an index finger, tilted his head back, and inhaled deeply to keep the blood in. Then Marigween's hands were upon his face, ministering to his nose.

"Here, let me wipe it," she said softly.

Christopher removed his hand from his face. The rag Marigween used was cool and damp and felt very good. As she continued to wash him, he said, "I'm sorry."

"Don't talk. You'll bleed again."

"I deserve to bleed."

"You've bled enough already," she said. "I didn't mean to hit you that hard." She lowered her rag.

"I thought you were going to—"

He was cut off by her kiss, and he fell so easily into her embrace he forgot all about his nose and his stitched chest and leg, and all there was in the world was her smooth body against his. And then the liquid warmth of his blood touched his lip and cheek once again.

Marigween pulled away from him, a thin trickle of blood staining her cheek. She smiled, quickly wiped her own face, lifted Christopher's chin with a finger, then began to clean him all over again. "I still don't know if I forgive you yet," she said.

"Please do."

"I might . . . in time."

"I have time."

"*We* have time."

"I think it has stopped." Christopher lowered his head and stopped breathing, waiting for the blood to come again; it didn't. "There. I'm all right." He directed his gaze to his son in the bed; the infant's eyes were open and his fingers flexed slowly. "May I hold him?"

Marigween nodded, crossed to the bed, and lifted the child. She cradled the boy in her arms and brought him to Christopher. "Here. Keep his head up."

There *was* magic in the realm, and all of it was contained within Christopher at the moment he accepted his son. All of his black emotions were winked away. There was no fear in his heart, only a brimming love that poured forth with an intensity that could span lifetimes. The eyes of the boy, the face, were his. And he was so proud to be the father of this child. This was his blood, a part of him he could never, ever escape from—nor did he want to anymore. He thought of the future, how he would teach his son to be a man, even as he learned to become one himself. He would teach the boy to make saddles, in honor of Sanborn, and teach him to squire, in honor of Orvin, Hasdale, and even Garrett. And he would tell him about Baines and Doyle, and all of the other boys who served so proudly in the Celt armies with him. Beaming, he would tell his friends, "See there, that's my son!" And finally, he would teach the boy, as Orvin had taught him, how to become a true servant: to his heart, his mind, and to God.

"He hasn't a name," Marigween said, her gaze trained on the child. "I waited for you."

"You know," Christopher said, "I never asked my parents why they named me Christopher. I knew they named me after the patron saint of travelers, but I never asked where they got the idea."

"Would you like to name him after a saint?" she asked.

"I don't know. We could name him after your father, Devin."

"Or after Orvin," Marigween suggested. "I know how much he means to you—and I'm sure he would be more than flattered."

"There are two brothers who mean a lot to me as well," Christopher added. "Doyle and Baines. What do you think of those names?"

"They are strong, fine names. You know, we could name him after you . . . "

"Oh, no," Christopher said. "I don't want our son to have to suffer through Orvin's 'young patron saint' this, and 'young patron saint' that. That is my sentence, and my sentence alone," he said with a chuckle.

"Then what is his name?" Marigween threw up her hands in frustration.

"I still do not know. But hear this, I will not do to this boy what is done by the fathers of so many. I will teach him saddlemaking and squiring, but if he wishes to do something else, then so be it. It would be nice if his name could reflect the freedom I want him to have."

"Were we bards, we could think of such a name!" Marigween said.

Christopher furrowed his brow in thought. "There is another thing to consider. It will be known, no matter how hard we try to conceal it, that he was born a bastard. Arthur's influence over the church is not strong right now, and they will condemn us, whether we marry or not."

Marigween looked her question.

"I will ask you to marry me, Marigween. But I want the moment to be right. It will be soon."

She closed her eyes and nodded.

Christopher continued: "Our son will need a very, very strong name, if, for nothing else, to carry him through the scoffing and chides he will receive. He will grow up to become a gallant man, of that I am sure. A strong name will prove a vital shield."

A voice from the far end of the cave chimed in: "Strong deeds make a man strong, young saint. A name means nothing if not backed by valor, honor, courage, compassion, and faith."

Christopher craned his head and saw Orvin standing in the shadowed entrance. "Have you an idea what we should name this boy?"

"As I said, there are some things you must do alone. I think you can manage naming your own son!" With a laugh, Orvin turned and shuffled away toward the light outside.

"Are we making this too hard?" Christopher asked.

Marigween nodded. "Let's name him after one of your friends. Baines has passed, and you spoke so often about him. Let our son carry his name."

"Are you sure?"

She nodded.

Christopher gently rocked the bundle in his arms. "Do you like your name?" he asked his son. "Baines. It is a fine name, short and strong. You will wear it as well as my old friend did."

He handed his son back to Marigween and watched as she parted the neckline of her shift and exposed one of her breasts. Baines took to it immediately, a thirsty little fellow, Christopher thought. He dragged himself to the bed and sat down. Then collapsed onto his back and yawned contentedly.

Time spent in the cave would be a much-needed holiday to heal himself, and he would savor every moment of it, for he knew the day would come too soon when he would return to Shores and rejoin the siege on the castle. Not only would he face the Saxons again, but a new banner knight, Woodward. He and that lord would have much to talk about. . . .

Christopher drove the dire thought from his mind. He would fret over that meeting when the time came. He lifted his head as Marigween sat down on the bed beside him. He watched mother and child, absorbed by the beauty and warmth of them, his family.